PENGUIN 

WARD NO. 6 AND OTHER STORIES

ANTON PAVLOVICH CHEKHOV, the son of a former serf, was born in 1860 in Taganrog, a port on the Sea of Azov. He received a classical education at the Taganrog Gymnasium, then in 1879 he went to Moscow, where he entered the medical faculty of the university, graduating in 1884. During his university years he supported his family by contributing humorous stories and sketches to magazines. He published his first volume of stories, *Motley Tales*, in 1886 and a year later his second volume, *In the Twilight*, for which he was awarded the Pushkin Prize. His most famous stories were written after his return from the convict island of Sakhalin, which he visited in 1890. For five years he lived on his small country estate near Moscow, but when his health began to fail he moved to the Crimea. After 1900, the rest of his life was spent at Yalta, where he met Tolstoy and Gorky. He wrote very few stories during the last years of his life, devoting most of his time to a thorough revision of his stories, of which the first comprehensive edition was published in 1899–1901, and to the writing of his great plays. In 1901 Chekhov married Olga Knipper, an actress of the Moscow Art Theatre. He died of consumption in 1904.

RONALD WILKS studied Russian language and literature at Trinity College, Cambridge, after training as a Naval interpreter, and later Russian literature at London University, where he received his Ph.D. in 1972. Among his translations for Penguin Classics are *My Childhood*, *My Apprenticeship* and *My Universities* by Gorky, *Diary of a Madman* by Gogol, filmed for Irish Television, *The Golovlyov Family* by Saltykov-Shchedrin, *How Much Land Does a Man Need?* by Tolstoy, *Tales of Belkin and Other Prose Writings* by Pushkin, and five other volumes of stories by Chekhov: *The Party and Other Stories*, *The Kiss and Other Stories*, *The Fiancée and Other Stories*, *The Duel and Other Stories* and *The Steppe and Other Stories*. He has also translated *The Little Demon* by Sologub for Penguin.

J. DOUGLAS CLAYTON studied modern languages at Emmanuel College, Cambridge, and then completed a Ph.D. in Russian at the University of Illinois. He is Professor of Russian at the University of Ottawa, where he has been since 1971. Professor Clayton's publications on Russian literature include a study of Pushkin's *Eugene Onegin*, a volume on Russian modernist theatre and collections of essays on Pushkin and Chekhov. His current research focuses on the cultural dialogue between Russia and France.

ANTON CHEKHOV

Ward No. 6 and Other Stories, 1892–1895

Translated with Notes by RONALD WILKS
With an Introduction by J. DOUGLAS CLAYTON

PENGUIN BOOKS

PENGUIN BOOKS

Published by the Penguin Group
Penguin Books Ltd, 80 Strand, London WC2R 0RL, England
Penguin Putnam Inc., 375 Hudson Street, New York, New York 10014, USA
Penguin Books Australia Ltd, 250 Camberwell Road, Camberwell, Victoria 3124, Australia
Penguin Books Canada Ltd, 10 Alcorn Avenue, Toronto, Ontario, Canada M4V 3B2
Penguin Books India (P) Ltd, 11 Community Centre, Panchsheel Park, New Delhi – 110 017, India
Penguin Books (NZ) Ltd, Cnr Rosedale and Airborne Roads, Albany, Auckland, New Zealand
Penguin Books (South Africa) (Pty) Ltd, 24 Sturdee Avenue, Rosebank 2196, South Africa

Penguin Books Ltd, Registered Offices: 80 Strand, London WC2R 0RL, England

www.penguin.com

First published 2002

030

Set in 11/12.5 pt PostScript Monotype Fournier
Typeset by Rowland Phototypesetting Ltd, Bury St Edmunds, Suffolk
Printed and bound in Great Britain by Clays Ltd, Elcograf S.p.A.

CONTENTS

INTRODUCTION

The period 1892–5 was one of relative calm and considerable success in Chekhov's life; the journey to Sakhalin was now receding into the past, although it served as the inspiration for several stories, as well as his account of the journey, published in *Russian Thought* in 1893–5. It was in 1892 that Chekhov purchased a modest but charming country estate at Melikhovo, outside Moscow. There he settled into the life of a country doctor and writer, with his parents Pavel Yegorovich and Yevgeniya Yakovlevna and his sister Masha. The role of doctor proved to be a demanding one, as the country was ravaged by the scourges of famine and cholera, and Chekhov was called upon to help in the struggle with these social disasters. His personal life was marked by numerous flirtations and affairs, especially fed by his acquaintance with the world of Muscovite actresses, but it was his sister Masha who was to prove the most stable female element in his life. Finally, Chekhov the doctor could not help but be aware of the signs of his intensifying tubercular infection; the disease had already carried away his brother Nikolay in 1889, and its continually more insistent presence lent urgency to all Chekhov's plans, both literary and personal, however much he was to deny its importance in conversation. In Chekhov's literary activity the years 1892–5 represent a period of transition. It was during this time that he spread his wings and, in response to readers' demands, became sought after by different publishers. He ceased to publish in Suvorin's *New Times*, although his personal relationship with that right-wing publisher was to continue, especially in the correspondence. In addition to his activity as a short story writer, Chekhov began to look to the world of the theatre for new heights to conquer, and also, perhaps not insignificantly given his new commitments, an additional source of revenue.

'The Grasshopper' (1892) was the source of considerable scandal at the time of its publication, since numerous readers of Chekhov's acquaintance perceived in it a fictionalized account of the affair between S. P. Kuvshinnikova, a minor artist and doctor's wife, and the writer's friend, the painter Isaak Levitan. Chekhov himself was indignant that his readers should so trivialize the story, and, indeed, the point of it lies elsewhere. On the philosophical level the story is about the dichotomy between the aesthetic movement of *fin de siècle* culture and scientific positivism, symbolized respectively by the impressionist painter Ryabovsky and Olga Ivanovna's husband, the doctor Dymov. Ryabovsky defends the notion that all is appearance and all that counts is the moment; it is typical of Chekhov's ironic humour that Ryabovsky's speechifying on the subject should simply be a device to get Olga into bed. Dymov, on the other hand, is wedded to scientific progress; his self-absorption is different from that of Ryabovsky, but no less complete. Ironically, Ryabovsky is always declaring that he is tired, when it is Dymov who is working late into the night; Ryabovsky declares to Olga that it would be good to die, while Dymov does precisely that.

In the story Chekhov draws an understated but devastating portrait of the lack of communication between husband and wife; the tragedy receives additional emphasis through the missed opportunity for a renewal of the relationship when Dymov defends his dissertation successfully. If the title of the story – a reference to the Krylov fable of the grasshopper who sings all summer and makes no provision for the winter – would seem to point the finger of indictment at Olga, the carelessness to the point of suicide with which Dymov carries out postmortems suggests that he is just as responsible as she is for the breakdown of the marriage and the tragic outcome. Both Dymov and Olga suffer from an infantile inadequacy in dealing with life. This is subtly suggested by his calling her 'Mother' (something that is totally bizarre in her case), while she transfers to him her dependence on her deceased father. Typically for many of Chekhov's works, on the deepest level the story is about perception – the ironical gap between appearance and reality, the way we see things as we would like them to be, not as they are. This is expressed in the text by the frequent use of the verb 'to seem' and its synonyms, by the obsession with appearances common to Dymov, Ryabovsky and Olga Ivanovna, and by Olga Ivanovna's talentless and inappropriate comparisons of her husband to different artistic subjects – she paints him as a Bedouin, for example. Typically also, the self-deception is followed by a moment of recognition, an epiphany, when the hero (in this case Olga) sees him or herself as others do.

As a writer Chekhov was acutely aware that he was following in the footsteps of the 'greats' of the previous generation – Dostoyevsky and Tolstoy. In 'Ward No. 6' he is generally seen as overcoming Tolstoy's credo of non-resistance to evil; however, as Andrew Durkin has shown, the tale can also be read as an ironic pastiche of Dostoyevsky. This accounts for the abandonment of his usual style, with its understatement and oblique use of detail, in favour of an overtly satirical stance, and adoption of Dostoyevsky's practice of an intrusive narrator who addresses the reader directly. The depressing details of life in the mental ward of a provincial hospital – the guard Nikita and the grey fence topped with nails – can hardly be interpreted as anything other than a metaphor of the Russian state, to be read allegorically in the best 'Aesopian' tradition of Russian literature. Evidently, Chekhov's observation of the prisons and prison hospitals on Sakhalin had also left a deep impression, as well as his reading of a report on Russian mental hospitals. The carefully sketched inmates of the ward – the Jew who has lost his business, the totally insensate peasant, the minor functionary of the postal service who is obsessed with receiving a medal for good service – all serve as devastating, sarcastic indictments of the system, which is maintained by the indiscriminate beatings meted out by Nikita.

However, the principal target of Chekhov's satire is the Russian educated class, represented by the doctor Ragin and the paranoid inmate of noble origin, Ivan Dmitrich. A typical and telling detail in both their portraits is the passion for indiscriminate reading and their ability to indulge in endless and meaningless discussions about life. Ragin's vapid chatter ultimately serves one purpose – to justify inaction and complacency. His readings of Marcus Aurelius reflect the pessimism and indifferentism that was fashionable at the end of the nineteenth century (and which greatly interested Chekhov himself), and continue on a different plane Ryabovsky's self-serving arguments about the meaninglessness of reality. In Ivan Dmitrich's tauntings of the doctor who denies the reality of pain it is difficult not to hear Chekhov's exasperation with the inertia and complacency of many of his profession. The terrifying irony of the doctor's fate – to become himself an inmate of the ward that it was his function to supervise – serves as an unspoken expression of Chekhov's conclusion that if, despite everything, one does not do one's best to improve the lot of one's countrymen, one deserves to share their fate. It conveys too his anger and frustration at the self-serving attitudes of the Russian intellectual class.

Chekhov was acutely aware of the most fashionable preoccupations of the 1890s, for example, the notion of 'degeneration' or the excessive, morbid refinement of the nervous system, propagated by the appearance of Max Nordau's book on the subject, *Degeneration*; the Nietzschean idea of the genius who would advance humanity 'ten thousand years'; and the general interest in psychology, mysticism and subconscious states. All these are reflected in 'The Black Monk', written in Melikhovo in 1893. In it Kovrin wavers between two poles: extreme refinement and preoccupation with the mysteries of aesthetic pleasure – the path that defines him as a genius – or capitulation to the banality and meaninglessness of the 'herd' – the state to which he is reduced when he is being treated for his illness. The fantastic hallucinations that cause him to see the black monk may have one source in the stimulants – wine and tobacco – that Kovrin indulges in, and in the repeated motif of the violin music, but much more substantial is the fact, gradually conveyed to the reader, that he has tuberculosis. That is to say, the moments of intense bliss that he experiences are the result of the heightened nervous state caused by the disease, and may be seen as the precursors of death. Indeed it is in death that Kovrin attains the ultimate happiness, as suggested by the last words of the text – the 'smile' that appears on his face as he dies.

There is evidence from Chekhov's contemporaries that he himself experienced hallucinations (because of his illness), so that this aspect of Kovrin has certain roots in his own biography, but at the same time in the image of the old man Pesotsky we see another aspect of Chekhov's life at Melikhovo, namely his preoccupation with horticulture – planting trees and cultivating the garden. The descriptions of the orchards and garden have a carefully detailed poetry to them that affirms Chekhov's attachment to and interest in the scientifically perceived realia of the world, and his desire to improve that world. While evoking echoes of the myth of Eden, these descriptions also correspond to Chekhov's socially reformist vision of a regenerated landscape, to be expressed more fully in the image of Astrov in *Uncle Vanya*. Related to the descriptions of the estate is the issue of inheritance and preservation of a family enterprise. Pesotsky's only child is Tanya, who, despite her interest, will scarcely be able to maintain things after the death of the old man. Pesotsky's desire to see Kovrin as his son-in-law is therefore ironical, since it is motivated by respect for the 'magister' Kovrin and his scholarly career, and not by any common interest in horticulture. (Kovrin, despite his learning, has to have explained to him why the smoke protects the orchard from frost.) It is an unspoken element of the end of the story that the earthly Eden, on which Pesotsky has lavished so much care, is destined to be destroyed.

Chekhov had begun his career in the 1880s by writing short pieces, mostly humorous, for popular magazines and newspapers. 'The Two Volodyas' is a minor story that harks back to this earlier phase. As in 'The Grasshopper', the central figure is a young woman who has married foolishly and has a brief affair with another man. Here, too, the point of the story is the moment of recognition, when the young woman realizes her error and is left to face the truth – that she is empty-headed and mediocre, and now must face alone the truth of her own worthlessness. To intensify the effect, Chekhov introduces the figure of the young nun Olga. Olga too has undergone a change – a spiritual one that is signalled by the change in her appearance. Ironically, if in 'The Grasshopper' Olga is the name of the foolish heroine, here the latter is called 'Sophia' (meaning 'wisdom').

Another common motif of Chekhov's stories to be found here is the sound of the church bells, a reminder of the deep presence of at least the formal aspects of religion in Chekhov's life.

Chekhov was born in 1860, on the eve of the reforms that liberated the Russian serfs, and his life covered a period of intense social and economic transition in the country. These included the construction of the railways, a frequent motif in his stories, industrialization, with all the social ills and factory accidents that accompanied it, and the urbanization of the peasant population, which had begun to drift to the towns and cities in search of employment. Overcrowded tenements, prostitution and disease were among the undesirable byproducts of this process. The process of industrialization had created another new phenomenon – people from humble backgrounds who had become rich and moved up the social hierarchy. Himself from a family of liberated serfs, Chekhov had gone through the agonizing process of learning to be at ease socially, and knew at first hand the difficulties caused by social displacement. Such is the plight of the heroine in the tale 'A Woman's Kingdom'.

In the figure of Anna Akimovna in 'A Woman's Kingdom' Chekhov explores one of the undeveloped topics of 'The Black Monk', namely the situation of an only daughter who inherits the family enterprise. The father–daughter relationship, and the fate of the daughter of a deceased father, are key, related themes in Chekhov's *oeuvre*. Anna, unlike Tanya, is in a more complex situation in that she has to deal with the additional problem of social displacement, on top of the questions of financial management and social responsibility that being the owner of a factory or other enterprise entails. It would be wrong to see Chekhov's treatment of Anna's inadequacy as an indictment of women, even though the last word of the original story is *dury* – 'silly geese' – for the word comes from her lips, and expresses her own realization that women are foolish to seek happiness in men. In any case many of Chekhov's male characters are in their own way as inadequate and feckless. Chekhov's concern is simply to uncover the psychological quandary that lies at the root of her actions or lack of them. Anna has had the ownership of the factory thrust upon her by fate, and finds herself living in a strange double world. On the one hand there is the traditional Russian world of the merchant class, with its traditional food and beverages – the 'downstairs' world of her aunts and maids and cooks and hangers-on; and then there is the westernized world of the lawyer Lysevich, with his reading of western literature (Maupassant!), and his partiality to wine and French food.

Chekhov depicts Anna Akimovna's inner feelings with delicacy and understanding, especially the contradiction between her social displacement and her natural search for a mate. As often happens in Chekhov this, the central question of the text, is left unresolved. What kind of husband would be appropriate for her, considering the double world she lives in? Her attraction to Pimenov is natural, given her own background and the strong masculine qualities that he exudes; moreover, as a worker like her father, he would be able to provide the strength and direction the enterprise needs: stop the director from defrauding the company, send the blood-sucker Lysevich packing – in a word, save the factory. But then Anna tries to imagine Pimenov in her world, and immediately the attraction is lost. Moreover, the advice she gets from different quarters is contradictory: some recommend a husband from the nobility, others recommend a worker, while others recommend debauchery. Anna's problem is that she has too much – too much money, too much femininity to lavish on a potential partner, too many choices.

Philanthropy is an important secondary theme in the story. As Anna recalls, the Russian merchants prefer to give their money to the indigent rather than their own workers. While this idea is not explained directly, the perspicacious reader might suspect that it is because they relish the servile expressions of gratitude that such charity evokes. To salve her own conscience, Anna decides to give the fifteen hundred roubles that have fallen into her lap to an out-of-work bureaucrat, Chalikov, chosen at random. The picture of misery evoked by Chekhov in his depiction of the Chalikov household is subtly nuanced and unsentimental, and is realized from the perspective of Anna herself. Anna is too honest with herself to accept the insincere expressions of gratitude and self-abasement that her generosity evokes. Disgusted by Chalikov's self-abasement, she quickly renounces her idea of giving all the money to him: however much he receives, he will simply drink it. Chalikov wallows in self-pity and finds solace in vodka and in beating his wife and children. No charity will change that. Eventually the fifteen hundred roubles end up in the hands of the lawyer Lysevich, who will squander them. The Chalikov episode is suggestive of Chekhov's view of the hopelessness of out-and-out charity, its inability to change circumstances. At the same time, the portrait of Chalikov's shiftlessness and self-pity serves as a background for the contrasting image of Pimenov – the intelligent and industrious factory-worker, who has both her father's and her picture on his table and who, for his pains, will receive nothing. Chekhov's indictment of human attitudes is, as usual, understated and merciless.

Chekhov's art at its best constitutes an intense condensation of motifs and themes into a poetic whole. 'The Student' is perhaps the finest example of this, and indeed this was the opinion of the author himself. Among the typically Chekhovian images that we find in this work are the hunter, the sound of the birds (i.e. the hunter's prey . . .), the sudden springtime frost and the light of the fire. However, we find in it a new theme too, and one that was to light the way to certain key works of Russian literature in the century to come. It is the notion of the interconnectedness of history – the continuous chain of events that links the past to the present. The events from the Gospel that the theology student Ivan Velikopolsky recounts to the two widows acquire an unsuspected immediacy and relevance, to the point that the two widows, mother and daughter, react – the mother Vasilisa by smiling and bursting into tears, and the daughter by turning red. The English reader is tempted to compare the situation to Eliot's 'even now, in sordid particulars, / The eternal design may appear'. More relevant for Russian literature is the immediacy with which the retelling of the Gospel speaks to a suffering people; this was to become the leitmotif of two central works of twentieth-century Russian literature, Bulgakov's *The Master and Margarita* and Pasternak's *Doctor Zhivago*.

As in other works we have discussed, in this story too there is an epiphany. Velikopolsky has left his father, a parish priest, coughing at home (evidently suffering from tuberculosis); his barefoot mother is cleaning the samovar, while their twenty-two-year-old son goes shooting, hardly the most sacred Good Friday activity for a theology student from a religious family. Velikopolsky is hungry, since his family is observing the fast; his keenly felt hunger (*golod*) echoes the sudden drop in temperature (*kholod*). The student is reminded of two constants in the life of the Russian people. At the same time the two widows he encounters have just eaten and are warm because of the fire, yet there is a sense that their religious sentiments are more deeply and directly felt than his, even if they observe the outward trappings of religion less. It is through their reaction to his recounting the story from the Gospel that the student is suddenly overtaken by an intense feeling of joy: '. . . and an inexpressibly sweet anticipation of happiness, of a mysterious unfamiliar happiness, gradually took possession of him. And life seemed entrancing, wonderful and endowed with sublime meaning'. Much of Chekhov's search seems to be precisely for a definition of happiness; here, for a moment, it is captured – and indeed one gets the strong conviction from Chekhov's works that for him happiness can only be momentary. As a *fin de siècle* writer Chekhov echoes the impressionist notion that one can only capture the moment. To this, however, the story suggests two corollaries: first, that such joy is a chance occurrence, and second, that although it is momentary, it is linked to other such moments in a chain of recurrences. This is an important corrective to Ryabovsky's flashy 'impressionist' philosophy of the unrepeatable moment: for Velikopolsky the present joy holds within it the promise of joy to come.

There is, moreover, another, concealed message to be drawn from the story, namely the importance of literature. The student *recounts* the events from the Gospel: the widows are moved precisely by his words. That is to say, the role of Velikopolsky is analogous to that of a writer, and the story therefore has a metapoetic aspect to it. In other words, it constitutes among other things a reflection on the importance and meaning of art. One may compare Velikopolsky's function to that of the Russian icon-painter. The icon-painter's role is to reproduce through a miracle, an act of grace, the presence of the holy person in material form. It matters not that the end result resembles closely other icons – in fact, it is important that it *should* resemble them, should be the latest in a chain of miracles, a chain of moments of grace extending back in time. This is the realization that Velikopolsky has of the interconnectedness of history, of touching the two ends of a chain. Now more than ever, from the perspective of over a hundred years of bloodshed and tumult in Russia, we can see the justice of the idea that literature can provide consolation and catharsis to a suffering people through a retelling of age-old truths – the verbal equivalent of the consolation that the Russian people through history have derived from the icon.

Chekhov attempted several times to write a novel; the story 'Three Years' resulted from one of these attempts. The result is far from the novel form; rather it is an extended short story or 'tale'. Chekhov's art had moved far from the classical architecture of the Russian realist novel: its carefully developed beginning, evolution and lengthy epilogue contrasted radically with his brevity, truncated structures and open ending (for example, the astonishing last sentence of the tale). His notion of plot was different, since for him what was important was the internal evolution of feelings, not any overt set of events, and his elliptical form focused, not on detail, as the art of, say, Tolstoy had done, but on *the* detail – a crucial difference. That is to say, by a process of elimination, the details that remain acquire a force they do not have in the copious descriptions typical of the realist novel. As an example, one may point to the umbrella in this story that Julia leaves at Laptev's sister's and which serves as the crucial element that leads to his proposal of marriage. It is of deep significance that, at the end of the tale, Julia, dressed elegantly in fashionable clothes, is holding the old umbrella, which Laptev has recently produced from the chest of drawers where he had been keeping it, and given to her. Indeed, after the mention of this detail, the declaration of love that she makes to him is almost unnecessary.

The process of writing led to a concentration on fewer characters, rather than the development of multiple plot lines that would have been necessary for a novel. Nevertheless, in this case the extended form, and especially the longer chronological extent marked by the title of the work (the phrase 'three years' recurs several times in the text itself), enables Chekhov to develop his themes with greater effect. The central theme is, of course, Laptev and Julia's marriage; how it begins without love on her part, and how it is only after she has grown and changed that she begins to love him and makes her declaration. Chekhov very carefully nuances the effect by describing Laptev's inner feelings at this declaration (he is hungry and, we infer, unaffected), and Yartsev's apparent infatuation with Julia. The message is very Chekhovian – we should not rely on marriage as a source for happiness; Laptev recalls that the only time he had been happy was when he spent the night under Julia's umbrella. The marriage theme is developed in other parallel lines: Polina and Yartsev's relationship, for example, a relationship that, as Yartsev stresses, has nothing to do with love (an affirmation we might do well to question); and the outrageous behaviour of Panaurov towards women.

The growing maturity of Julia is reflected in her relationship with her father-in-law. In this figure we see the other profoundly Chekhovian theme, a theme that is related to that of marriage, namely that of fatherhood. Laptev recalls with bitterness his upbringing, especially the beatings he received from his dictatorial father (in a passage that surely has autobiographical overtones). Like Anna Akimovna in 'A Woman's Kingdom', Laptev and his brother Fyodor have made the wrenching social transition from being the grandchildren of a serf to inheriting a family business worth millions. Their father, although wealthy, had retained the patriarchal ways and the dictatorial manners of a peasant family head. The situation of Lida and Sasha, Laptev's nieces, and the loss of their father Panaurov to another woman also speak of the theme of fatherhood (and its concomitant, abandonment or orphanhood). It is predictable that Panaurov would eventually abandon his second wife, and also that he would even try to flirt with Julia and encourage her to acquire a lover. Panaurov's attitude to both marriage and fatherhood is totally cynical, and his shameless sponging off his brother-in-law Laptev simply confirms his spinelessness. At the end Laptev, although he and Julia have lost their own child, has become a father – to his sister's children, Lida and Sasha. This is part of his becoming a man, as is replacing his autocratic father at the head of the family business and taking over the reins.

As we have come to expect in Chekhov's work, the secondary characters are drawn with carefully chosen, often devastating detail that 'rubs the reader's nose' in reality. For example, there is the carefully noted fact that Panaurov's second wife has the beginnings of a moustache. We learn that Laptev's brother Fyodor is seriously ill, and that his flowery manner of speech and flippant manner hide a deep unhappiness; tellingly, it is Julia who consoles him when he breaks down. Yartsev is a typical member of the Russian intelligentsia; Chekhov first mocks his literary strivings – again the detail that he signs his articles with a single letter 'Ya' ('I') reads as ironical, a literary cliché – so that when we learn that his belief in science is matched by his optimism that 'we're on the threshold of some fantastic triumph' we know to take it with a huge pinch of salt. Yartsev's boosterism contrasts totally with Laptev's feelings of resignation: 'I feel as if our life's over and that some dull half-life is just beginning.' Such details might be multiplied many times over: what is important is that the reader becomes attuned to Chekhov's carefully modulated irony.

However understated, and however much the reader has to look between the lines to discover it, Chekhov's ultimate concern is spiritual. The crisis of faith that he documents may legitimately be seen as *the* theme of nineteenth-century Russian literature, as it grapples with the imported values of western culture and politics, and as the industrialization and westernization of the country led to a questioning and rejection of traditional religious values. It is precisely this crisis that is central to the story 'Murder'. Here we see the journey of the murderer Yakov from a stifling and stultifying preoccupation with the *form* of religion that leads to the murder of his cousin, to a new *faith* – religion's true spiritual content. Buried in the text are clues pointing back to two other key texts in Russian literature – Dostoyevsky's *The Devils* (in Russian *Besy*) and Pushkin's poem of the same name that Dostoyevsky used as an epigraph to his own work. Chekhov could rely on his readers' knowledge of the previous works to evoke certain echoes. Essentially, Pushkin's poem describes the situation of a young man who is lost in a snowstorm. Enough clues are built into the description of Matvey's return to the inn to create a resonance between the poem and the story; this is then maintained by the repeated use of the word *besy*. In using Pushkin's poem as an epigraph to his novel, Dostoyevsky had seized upon the latent potential of the poem to serve as a metaphor for the spiritual crisis of the young Russian lost in a world without faith, and document its consequences in terms of Stavrogin's sexual debauchery and Pyotr Verkhovensky's disdain for human life. The howling of the storm, that Pushkin had likened to the wailing of demons or devils, thus assumes an enormous symbolic significance.

At the same time, there are crucial differences between Chekhov's story and the two preceding texts. In part, they are class differences. Chekhov describes, not the milieu of a young Russian officer who has hired a coach, nor that of the provincial aristocracy we find in Dostoyevsky's story, but rather the world of the impoverished innkeeper who has been displaced by the advent of the railway, his cousin, the victim of an industrial accident, and the owner of a railway buffet who has fallen on hard times. There is a gritty reality to Chekhov's descriptions of a milieu he knew only too well. Moreover, the last part of the story takes place on Sakhalin Island and is the direct result of his observations of the life of the prisoners there. Chekhov simply describes this reality – unsentimentally, with an eye to the telling detail, without any attempt to sugar the pill and gloss over his characters' faults. Ironically, in the slight format of a short story, he achieves something that eluded Dostoyevsky in vastly organized novel after novel (e.g. Raskolnikov in *Crime and Punishment*) – namely a convincing description of the spiritual renewal of one man. One might call this the holy grail of nineteenth-century Russian literature.

The topography of Chekhov's work is largely located in two areas of Russia. The first of these is the south of Russia, initially the southern steppe around the town of Taganrog, where he was born and grew up; typical steppe landscapes with their two dominant features – the coal mine and the cherry orchard – are found in numerous works, not only of his early period. In the last years of his life the advanced state of his tuberculosis forced him to return south to seek a milder climate, this time in Yalta on the Crimean peninsula, but even before that Crimean landscapes began to occur in his work (e.g. in the final episode of 'The Black Monk'). The second region of Russia that figures largely in his work is Moscow, where he moved in 1879. His Muscovite experiences give rise to the many sketches of the country estates around that city and their denizens, the impoverished gentry, and also, of course, to the different areas in the city itself, as in 'Three Years'. Chekhov did not speak any foreign language fluently, and only went abroad to Western Europe (Italy and France) for the first time in early 1891, so that foreign scenes are almost totally absent from his work. The story 'Ariadna' is an exception; evidently the scenes that take place in Italy and the Adriatic coast were based on experiences gained during his 1891 trip. Shamokhin's comments on the Adriatic resorts no doubt reflect Chekhov's own sentiments. The Russian film director Nikita Mikhalkov used material from 'Ariadna' for his film *Dark Eyes* (*Ochi chornye*), starring Marcello Mastroianni.

The story that the hero Shamokhin tells seems very much to conform to the view of women and sex reflected in Chekhov's work in general. Chekhov once remarked of sex that it was either the vestige of something that was wonderful in the past, or else the beginning of something that might be wonderful one day. Shamokhin's idealistic view of love comes up against several snags. First, there is the fact that Ariadna, far from appreciating his idealistic love, instead falls for the sheer animal sexuality of Lubkov. Lubkov's technique might be described as 'full frontal attack', with no consideration of any abstraction such as love. His cynicism about women can be compared to that of Panaurov in 'Three Years' or Lysevich in 'A Woman's Kingdom'. Both Lubkov and Panaurov leave a trail of abandoned women and children behind them. It must be said, on the other hand, that the cold and narcissistic Ariadna, however beautiful she might be, hardly deserves the adulation that she harvests. Her seduction and abandonment is an appropriate response to her lack of redeeming qualities. She will presumably continue to drift from one dependent relationship to another. Shamokhin has chosen as an object for his infatuation a woman who conforms to and confirms his idea of women's worthlessness.

Lubkov's and Panaurov's parasitical relationships to their friends are totally of a piece with their cynical approach to women. The reader cannot help but be astonished by the way in which such individuals take advantage of their friends' unstinting and uncomplaining generosity with money (it being the Russian habit unashamedly to ask for a loan that clearly cannot be repaid). We read wide-eyed how Shamokhin again and again lends Lubkov money that he will clearly never see again. Shamokhin seems totally without willpower – to say no to either Ariadna or Lubkov, despite his critical attitude to both and disgust at their lifestyle, a lifestyle that he ends up sharing. His total disdain for money and willingness to incur endless debts to support first his wastrel friend and then Ariadna remind us that Russian attitudes to money and financial matters have historically been very different from those found in the West. The story that Shamokhin recounts of his relationship to Ariadna and Lubkov is subtly ironized by the device of the author/narrator to whom he tells his story and who finally is totally bored by it and falls asleep. We realize that Shamokhin's ultimate need is to tell in as much embarrassing detail as he can the story of his own abasement.

Chekhov's art is delicately poised between the achievements of nineteenth-century Russian realism and the abstraction and experimentation of the twentieth century. In his work we see a movement away from the large form, towards an increasingly poetic orientation towards the word and organization of the text. Such artistic movements as impressionism and the decorativeness of art nouveau find echoes in different stories. His world is not one in which there are easily discovered universal truths. Each grain of insight, each transcendental moment has to be earned at great cost, and the author unceasingly and mercilessly reminds us of its ephemeral nature. At the end of the day, there is a hard-hearted kindness in his work that refuses easy answers and comforting half-truths. To read his works with the insight they demand, and to learn to see the world with the courage with which he depicts it, is one of the most rewarding journeys literature has to offer.

FURTHER READING

Gordon McVay (tr.), *Anton Chekhov: A Life in Letters* (London: Folio Society, 1994), the best selection and translation of letters.

Brian Reeves (tr.), *The Island of Sakhalin* (Cambridge: Ian Faulkner, 1993).

SECONDARY LITERATURE: GENERAL BOOKS

Toby W. Clyman, *A Chekhov Companion* (Westport/London: Greenwood Press, 1985), a very valuable if expensive collection of essays, with extensive bibliography.

P. Debreczeny and T. Eekman (eds), *Chekhov's Art of Writing: A Collection of Critical Essays* (Columbus: Slavica, 1977).

Thomas Eekman (ed.), *Critical Essays on Anton Chekhov* (Boston: G. K. Hall, 1989), 208 pp.

W. Gerhardie, *Anton Chekhov: A Critical Study* (London: Macdonald, 1974), 'Bloomsbury' Chekhov, but well-informed.

R. L. Jackson, *Chekhov: A Collection of Essays: 20th-Century Views* (Englewood Cliffs, New Jersey: Prentice-Hall, 1967).

R. L. Jackson (ed.), *Reading Chekhov's Text* (Evanston, Ill.: Northwestern University Press, 1993).

S. Koteliansky (tr., ed.), *Anton Chekhov: Literary and Theatrical Reminiscences* (New York: Blom, 1968).

Virginia Llewellyn-Smith, *Chekhov and the Lady with the Little Dog* (London: Oxford University Press, 1973).

V. S. Pritchett, *Chekhov. A Spirit Set Free* (London: Hodder & Stoughton, 1988).

Donald Rayfield, *Anton Chekhov: A Life* (London: HarperCollins, 1997).

T. Winner, *Chekhov and his Prose* (New York: Holt, 1966).

WORKS ON INDIVIDUAL STORIES IN ALPHABETICAL ORDER

'The Black Monk'

Paul Debreczeny, '"The Black Monk": Chekhov's Version of Symbolism', in Robert Louis Jackson (ed.), *Reading Chekhov's Text* (Evanston, Ill.: Northwestern University Press, 1993), pp. 179–88.

'The Grasshopper'

George Pahomov, 'Čexov's "The Grasshopper": A Secular Saint's Life', *Slavic and East European Journal* 37:1 (Spring 1993), pp. 33–45.

'The Student'

Robert Louis Jackson, 'Chekhov's "The Student"', in Robert Louis Jackson (ed.), *Reading Chekhov's Text* (Evanston, Ill.: Northwestern University Press, 1993), pp. 127–33.

'Ward No. 6'

Andrew R. Durkin, 'Chekhov's Response to Dostoevskii: The Case of "Ward Six"', *Slavic Review* 40:1 (1981), pp. 49–59.

'A Woman's Kingdom'

Carol A. Flath, 'Delineating the Territory of Cechov's "A Woman's Kingdom"', *Russian Literature* 44:4 (1998), pp. 389–408.

Robert Louis Jackson, 'Chekhov's "A Woman's Kingdom": A Drama of Character and Fate', in Thomas A. Eekman (ed.), *Critical Essays on Anton Chekhov* (Boston: G. K. Hall, 1989), pp. 91–102.

CHRONOLOGY

1836 Gogol's *The Government Inspector*

1852 Turgenev's *Sketches from a Hunter's Album*

1860 Dostoyevsky's *Notes From the House of the Dead* (1860–61)
Anton Pavlovich Chekhov born on 17 January at Taganrog, a port on the Sea of Azov, the third son of Pavel Yegorovich Chekhov, a grocer, and Yevgeniya Yakovlevna, née Morozova

1861 Emancipation of the serfs by Alexander II. Formation of revolutionary Land and Liberty Movement

1862 Turgenev's *Fathers and Sons*

1863–4 Polish revolt. Commencement of intensive industrialization; spread of the railways; banks established; factories built. Elective District Councils (*zemstvos*) set up; judicial reform
Tolstoy's *The Cossacks* (1863)

1865 *Lady Macbeth of Mtsensk* (1864) by Leskov, a writer much admired by Chekhov

1866 Attempted assassination of Alexander II by Karakozov
Dostoyevsky's *Crime and Punishment*

1867 Emile Zola's *Thérèse Raquin*

1868 Dostoyevsky's *The Idiot*

1868 Chekhov begins to attend Taganrog Gymnasium after wasted year at a Greek school

1869 Tolstoy's *War and Peace*

1870 Municipal government reform

1870–71 Franco-Prussian War

1873 Tolstoy's *Anna Karenina* (1873–7)
Chekhov sees local productions of *Hamlet* and Gogol's *The Government Inspector*

1875 Chekhov writes and produces humorous magazine for his brothers in Moscow, *The Stammerer*, containing sketches of life in Taganrog

1876 Chekhov's father declared bankrupt and flees to Moscow, followed by family except Chekhov, who is left in Taganrog to complete schooling. Reads Buckle, Hugo and Schopenhauer

1877–8 War with Turkey

1877 Chekhov's first visit to Moscow; his family living in great hardship

1878 Chekhov writes dramatic juvenilia: full-length drama *Fatherlessness* (MS destroyed), comedy *Diamond Cut Diamond* and vaudeville *Why Hens Cluck* (none published)

1879 Dostoyevsky's *The Brothers Karamazov* (1879–80)
Tolstoy's *Confession* (1879–82)
Chekhov matriculates from Gymnasium with good grades. Wins scholarship to Moscow University to study medicine
Makes regular contributions to humorous magazine *Alarm Clock*

1880 General Loris-Melikov organizes struggle against terrorism
Guy de Maupassant's *Boule de Suif*
Chekhov introduced by artist brother Nikolay to landscape painter Levitan with whom has lifelong friendship
First short story, 'A Letter from the Don Landowner Vladimirovich N to His Learned Neighbour', published in humorous magazine *Dragonfly*. More stories published in *Dragonfly* under pseudonyms, chiefly Antosha Chekhonte.

1881 Assassination of Alexander II; reactionary, stifling regime of Alexander III begins
Sarah Bernhardt visits Moscow (Chekhov calls her acting 'superficial')
Chekhov continues to write very large numbers of humorous sketches for weekly magazines (until 1883). Becomes regular contributor to Nikolay Leykin's *Fragments*, a St Petersburg weekly humorous magazine. Writes (1881–2) play now usually known as *Platonov* (discovered 1923), rejected by Maly Theatre; tries to destroy manuscript

1882 Student riots at St Petersburg and Kazan universities. More discrimination against Jews
Chekhov is able to support the family with scholarship money and earnings from contributions to humorous weeklies

1883 Tolstoy's *What I Believe*
Chekhov gains practical experience at Chikino Rural Hospital

1884 Henrik Ibsen's *The Wild Duck*. J.-K. Huysmans' *À Rebours*
Chekhov graduates and becomes practising physician at Chikino. First signs of his tuberculosis in December
Six stories about the theatre published as *Fairy-Tales of Melpomene*. His crime novel, *The Shooting Party*, serialized in *Daily News*

1885–6 Tolstoy's *The Death of Ivan Ilich* (1886)
On first visit to St Petersburg, Chekhov begins friendship with very influential Aleksey Suvorin (1834–1912), editor of the highly regarded daily newspaper *New Times*. Chekhov has love affairs with Dunya Efros and Natalya Golden (later his sister-in-law). His TB is now unmistakable
Publishes more than 100 short stories. 'The Requiem' is the first story to appear under own name and his first in *New Times* (February 1886). First collection, *Motley Tales*

1887 Five students hanged for attempted assassination of Tsar; one is Lenin's brother
Tolstoy's drama *Power of Darkness* (first performed in Paris), for which he was called nihilist and blasphemer by Alexander III
Chekhov elected member of Literary Fund. Makes trip to Taganrog and Don steppes
Second book of collected short stories *In the Twilight*. *Ivanov* produced – a disaster

1888 Chekhov meets Stanislavsky. Attends many performances at Maly and Korsh theatres and becomes widely acquainted with actors, stage managers, etc. Meets Tchaikovsky
Completes 'The Steppe', which marks his 'entry' into serious literature. Wins Pushkin Prize for 'the best literary production distinguished by high artistic value' for *In the Twilight*, presented

by literary division of Academy of Sciences. His one-act farces *The Bear* (highly praised by Tolstoy) and *The Proposal* extremely successful. Begins work on *The Wood Demon* (later *Uncle Vanya*). Radically revises *Ivanov* for St Petersburg performance

1889 Tolstoy's *The Kreutzer Sonata* (at first highly praised by Chekhov)

Chekhov meets Lidiya Avilova, who later claims love affair with him. Tolstoy begins to take an interest in Chekhov, who is elected to Society of Lovers of Russian Literature

'A Dreary Story'. *The Wood Demon* a resounding failure

1890 World weary, Chekhov travels across Siberia by carriage and river boat to Sakhalin to investigate conditions at the penal colony (recorded in *The Island of Sakhalin*). After seven months returns to Moscow (via Hong Kong, Singapore and Ceylon (Sri Lanka))

Collection *Gloomy People* (dedicated to Tchaikovsky). Only two stories published – 'Gusev' and 'Thieves'. Immense amount of preparatory reading for *The Island of Sakhalin*

1891 Severe famine in Volga basin (Chekhov organizes relief)

Chekhov undertakes six-week tour of Western Europe with Suvorin. Intense affair with Lika Mizinova

Works on *The Island of Sakhalin*. 'The Duel' published serially. Works on 'The Grasshopper'

1892 Chekhov buys small estate at Melikhovo, near Moscow; parents and sister live there with him. Gives free medical aid to peasants. Re-reads Turgenev; regards him as inferior to Tolstoy and very critical of his heroines

'Ward No. 6' and 'An Anonymous Story'

1893 *The Island of Sakhalin* completed and published serially

1894 Death of Alexander III; accession of Nicholas II; 1,000 trampled to death at Khodynka Field during coronation celebrations. Strikes in St Petersburg

Chekhov makes another trip to Western Europe

'The Student', 'Teacher of Literature', 'At a Country House' and 'The Black Monk'

1895 'Three Years'. Writes 'Ariadna', 'Murder' and 'Anna Round the Neck'. First draft of *The Seagull*

1896 Chekhov agitates personally for projects in rural education and transport; helps in building of village school at Talezh; makes large donation of books to Taganrog Public Library
'My Life' published in instalments. *The Seagull* meets with hostile reception at Aleksandrinsky Theatre

1897 Chekhov works for national census; builds second rural school. Crisis in health with lung haemorrhage; convalesces in Nice
'Peasants' is strongly attacked by reactionary critics and mutilated by censors. Publishes *Uncle Vanya*, but refuses to allow performance (until 1899)

1898 Formation of Social Democrat Party. Dreyfus affair
Stanislavsky founds Moscow Art Theatre with Nemirovich-Danchenko
Chekhov very indignant over Dreyfus affair and supports Zola; conflict with anti-Semitic Suvorin over this. His father dies. Moves to Yalta, where he buys land. Friendly with Gorky and Bunin (both of whom left interesting memoirs of Chekhov). Attracted to Olga Knipper at Moscow Art Theatre rehearsal of *The Seagull*, but leaves almost immediately for Yalta. Correspondence with Gorky
Trilogy 'Man in a Case', 'Gooseberries' and 'About Love'. 'Ionych'. *The Seagull* has first performance at Moscow Art Theatre and Chekhov is established as a playwright

1899 Widespread student riots
Tolstoy's *Resurrection* serialized
Chekhov has rift with Suvorin over student riots. Olga Knipper visits Melikhovo. He sells Melikhovo in June and moves with mother and sister to Yalta. Awarded Order of St Stanislav for educational work
'Darling', 'New Country Villa' and 'On Official Duty'. Signs highly unfavourable contract with A. F. Marks for complete edition of his works. Taxing and time-consuming work of compiling first two volumes. Moderate success of *Uncle Vanya* at Moscow Art Theatre. Publishes one of finest

stories, 'The Lady with the Little Dog'. Completes 'In the Ravine'. Begins serious work on *Three Sisters*; goes to Nice to revise last two acts

1900 Chekhov settles in the house built by him in Yalta. Actors from the Moscow Art Theatre visit Sevastopol and Yalta at his request. Low opinion of Ibsen

Sees *Uncle Vanya* for first time

1901 Formation of Socialist Revolutionary Party. Tolstoy excommunicated by Russian Orthodox Church

Chekhov marries Olga Knipper

Première of *Three Sisters* at Moscow Art Theatre, with Olga Knipper as Masha. Works on 'The Bishop'

1902 Sipyagin, Minister of Interior, assassinated. Gorky excluded from Academy of Sciences by Nicholas II

Gorky's *The Lower Depths* produced at Moscow Art Theatre

Chekhov resigns from Academy of Sciences together with Korolenko in protest at exclusion of Gorky. Awarded Griboyedov Prize by Society of Dramatic Writers and Opera Composers for *Three Sisters*

Completes 'The Bishop'. Begins 'The Bride', his last story. Begins *The Cherry Orchard*

1903 Completion of Trans-Siberian Railway. Massacre of Jews at Kishinev pogrom

Chekhov elected provisional president of Society of Lovers of Russian Literature

Completes 'The Bride' and the first draft of *The Cherry Orchard*. Arrives in Moscow for Art Theatre rehearsal of *The Cherry Orchard*; strong disagreement with Stanislavsky over its interpretation

1904 Assassination of Pleve, Minister of Interior, by Socialist revolutionaries. War with Japan

Chekhov dies of TB on 15 July at Badenweiler in the Black Forest (Germany)

Première of *The Cherry Orchard* at Moscow Art Theatre

NOTE ON TEXT

Chekhov's stories (like most of the literature of the time) were not first published as separate books, but appeared in magazines or newspapers such as *New Times*, or in the thick journals, chiefly *Russian Thought*. Some of the stories were subsequently published in separate selections, such as *Tales and Stories* (1894).

In 1899 Chekhov made over the copyright of all his work (with the exception of the plays) to the publisher A. F. Marks in return for 75,000 roubles. Although the terms seemed favourable at the time, many of Chekhov's friends felt he had been highly imprudent in signing the contract (Gorky unsuccessfully tried to get him to break the contract) as they considered the terms grossly inadequate. In addition the need to collate all the stories that had so far appeared in magazines and newspapers, together with meticulous editing and improving the material, taxed Chekhov sorely and was very time-consuming. The Marks edition was published in 1899–1901, in ten volumes, and reprinted in 1903. However, the main drawback of this edition was that the stories were not printed chronologically. The first scholarly edition, with full notes and commentary, was published in Moscow, 1944–51.

Between 1973 and 1983, the definitive thirty-volume edition, *Polnoye Sobraniye Sochineniy i Pisem* (*Complete Collected Works and Letters*) was published in Moscow, with extensive commentaries by leading Soviet Chekhov scholars. It is on this edition that these translations are based.

PATRONYMICS

Russian names consist of first name, patronymic and surname, the patronymic or middle name being derived from the father's first name. For example, Chekhov's middle name, Pavlovich, derives from his father's first name, Pavel. In formal speech first name and patronymic are usual: a servant addressing his master would use both first name and patronymic. But a master would use only a first name when talking to a servant. In 'Murder' (p. 171), reference is made to the use of name and patronymic.

However, Chekhov does now and then use the direct equivalent of the English 'Mr' and 'Mrs', as in 'A Woman's Kingdom'.

Ward No. 6 and Other Stories

The Grasshopper

I

All Olga Ivanovna's friends and close acquaintances were at her wedding.

'Just look at him, don't you think there's something about him?' she was telling them, nodding towards her husband as if eager to explain why on earth she was marrying such a simple, very ordinary and thoroughly undistinguished man.

Her husband, Osip Stepanych Dymov, was a junior doctor who worked at two hospitals. In one of them he was a temporary registrar and in the other a pathologist. Every day, from nine in the morning until noon, he saw out-patients and visited his ward, and in the afternoon he would take a horse tram to the other hospital, where he performed postmortems on patients who had died there. His private practice was quite negligible, bringing in about five hundred roubles a year. That is all. What else can one say about him? On the other hand, Olga Ivanovna and her cronies were not altogether run-of-the-mill people. Every one of them was distinguished in some way, pretty well known, had forged a reputation and was considered a celebrity: and if they weren't actually famous yet, they showed brilliant promise. There was an actor with outstanding, long-recognized talent – an elegant, intelligent and modest man with a first-class delivery who gave Olga Ivanovna elocution lessons. There was the opera singer, a genial, fat man who would sigh and assure Olga Ivanovna that she was ruining herself and that if she would only stop being so lazy and apply herself she would develop into a remarkable singer. And there were several artists whose leading light was the genre, animal and landscape painter Ryabovsky, an extremely handsome man of about twenty-five, who had held successful exhibitions and whose latest picture had sold for five hundred roubles. He would put the finishing touches to Olga's sketches and say that perhaps she might make something of herself. Then there was the cellist who could make his instrument weep and who frankly admitted that of all the women he knew Olga Ivanovna alone could accompany him properly. Then there was the writer – young, but already well known – who wrote novellas, plays and short stories. And who else? Well, there was Vasily Vasilych, a gentleman landowner, amateur illustrator and vignettist with a profound feeling for the old Russian style, for folk ballads and epic poetry. This man could produce virtual miracles on paper, china and smoked plates. In this highly artistic, free and easy, spoilt company, sensitive and unpretentious though it was, but which acknowledged the existence of doctors only in times of illness and for which the name Dymov meant absolutely nothing – in this company Dymov was a stranger, a superfluous, diminutive figure, although he was actually tall and broad-shouldered. He seemed to be wearing someone else's frock coat and his beard was like a shop assistant's. Had he been a writer or artist, however, people would have said that he positively resembled Zola with that beard of his.

The actor told Olga Ivanovna that with her flaxen hair and in her wedding dress she bore a strong resemblance to a graceful cherry tree in spring when it is festooned with delicate white blossoms.

'Now, just you listen!' Olga Ivanovna told him, gripping his arm. 'How did all this happen so suddenly? Well, just listen, listen . . . You should know that Father worked in the same hospital as Dymov. When poor Father became ill Dymov sat at his bedside for days and nights. Such self-sacrifice! Now listen, Ryabovsky . . . And you too, Mr Writer – you'll find it most interesting. Come closer . . . Such self-sacrifice, such genuine concern! I too didn't sleep and stayed with Father. And then – what do you know! That fine young man had fallen for me! My Dymov was head over heels! It's true, fate can play such strange tricks. Well, after Father died he would come and visit me now and then. Or we'd meet in the street. Then, one fine evening – crash! bang! – he proposes, right out of the blue! I cried all night and I too fell madly in love. And now, as you see, I'm lawful wedded Mrs Dymov. Don't you think there's something brawny, something powerful and bear-like about him? Just now he's three-quarters turned towards us and the light's wrong, but when he turns round just look at that forehead! Ryabovsky, what do you say to that forehead? Dymov! We're talking about you!' she shouted to her husband. 'Come here. Hold out your honest hand to Ryabovsky . . . That's it. I want you two to be friends.' With a good-humoured, naïve smile Dymov offered his hand to Ryabovsky.

'Very pleased to meet you,' he said. 'There was a Ryabovsky in my last year at university. Could he be a relative of yours?'

II

Olga Ivanovna was twenty-two years old, Dymov thirty-one. After their marriage they settled down to a beautiful life. Olga Ivanovna covered the drawing-room walls with sketches – her own and other people's, framed and unframed – and she filled every inch of space around the grand piano with a picturesque array of Chinese parasols, easels, brightly coloured bits of material, daggers, small busts and photographs. She pasted cheap folksy prints on the dining-room walls, hung up bast sandals and sickles, and stood a rake and a scythe in one corner to create an effect truly *à la Russe*. To give their bedroom the appearance of a cave, she draped the ceiling and walls with dark cloth, hung a Venetian lantern over the beds and stationed a figure with a halberd by the door. Everyone thought that the newly-weds had created an awfully sweet nook for themselves.

Every day Olga Ivanovna rose at eleven o'clock and played the piano, but if it was sunny she painted in oils. After twelve she would drive to her dressmaker's. As both she and Dymov were very hard up, she and her dressmaker had to resort to all kinds of cunning devices so that she could always appear in new dresses to dazzling effect. Very often, from old dyed frocks or worthless scraps of tulle, lace, plush and silk there would emerge something miraculous and truly seductive – a dream of a dress. From the dressmaker Olga would usually drive to some actress friend to discover all the theatre news and at the same time try and get a ticket out of her for a first night or benefit performance. From the actress she would drive to some artist's studio or to an exhibition of paintings and then on to one of her celebrity friends to invite him home, to return a visit or simply for a chat. Everywhere she was given a joyful, friendly welcome, being assured that she was absolutely wonderful, charming, extra special. Those of her male friends whom she considered 'celebrated', great men, treated her as one of themselves, as an equal: with her talent, taste and brains, all unanimously predicted a brilliant future – as long as she didn't overstretch herself. She sang, played the piano, painted in oils, modelled, acted in amateur dramatics – not anyhow, but with real talent. Whether she made lanterns for illuminations, put on fancy dress or tied someone's tie, the final effect was always highly artistic, graceful and charming. But nowhere did her talent shine so bright as in her flair for striking up an acquaintance with celebrities and being on intimate terms with them in no time at all. Someone only needed to make some sort of name for himself, however insignificant, or get himself talked about, than she would make sure she was introduced to him right away and she invited him home that very same day.

Every time she made a new acquaintance was a red-letter day for her. She worshipped celebrities, revelled in them and dreamed of them every night. She craved them with a thirst nothing could assuage. Old ones departed the scene and were forgotten, new ones replaced them, but soon she grew used to these too, or was disappointed in them, and eagerly went in search of new and ever newer great men. And when she found them she continued the search. Why did she do this?

At about half past four she would dine at home with her husband. His lack of affectation, common sense and good nature sent her into raptures of delight. She would constantly jump up from the table, impulsively fling her arms around his head and shower it with kisses.

'You're such an intelligent man, Dymov, with such high principles, but you have one very serious shortcoming. You're not in the least bit interested in art. And you reject music and painting too.'

'I don't understand them,' he would say meekly. 'All my life I've been working in natural science and medicine and I've never had the time to take an interest in the arts.'

'But that's dreadful, Dymov!'

'How so? Your friends know nothing of the natural sciences and medicine, but you don't hold it against them, do you? Each to his own. I don't understand landscape or opera, but I do think that if clever people devote their whole lives to them and other clever people pay vast amounts for them, then they *must* be important. If I don't understand, it doesn't follow that I reject them.'

'Let me shake your honest hand!'

After dinner Olga would visit friends, then go to the theatre or a concert and return after midnight. And so it went on day after day.

On Wednesdays she was 'at home'. At these soirées hostess and guests did not play cards or dance, but entertained themselves with all kinds of artistic activity. The actor recited, the opera singer sang, the artists did sketches in albums – of which Olga had countless numbers – the cellist played and the hostess herself sketched, modelled, sang and played accompaniments. In the gaps between the recitation, music and singing they talked and argued about literature, the theatre, painting. Ladies were not invited, since Olga considered all women – actresses and her dressmaker excepted – as vulgar and boring. Not one soirée passed without the hostess giving a start every time the doorbell rang. 'It's *him*!' she would exclaim triumphantly – and by *him* she meant some newly invited celebrity. Dymov was never in the drawing-room and no one was even aware of his existence. But at precisely half past eleven the dining-room door would open and Dymov would appear.

'Supper is served, gentlemen,' he would say, rubbing his hands together.

Everyone would file into the dining-room and would invariably see the same display on the table: a plate of oysters, a joint of ham or veal, sardines, cheese, caviare, mushrooms, vodka and two carafes of wine.

'My dear *maître d'hôtel*!' Olga would say, throwing up her hands in rapture. 'You're so lovely! Just look at that face, gentlemen. Dymov! Turn your profile towards us. Just look, gentlemen – the face of a Bengal tiger, but the kindly, lovable expression of a deer. Oh, isn't he sweet!'

The guests would eat and as they looked at Dymov would think: 'Actually, a really nice chap!' But they soon forgot him and carried on talking about the theatre, music, painting.

The young couple were happy and all went swimmingly. However, the third week of their married life was not altogether happy – the reverse, in fact. Dymov caught erysipelas at the hospital, spent six days in bed and had to have his splendid black hair shaved to the roots. Olga sat at his bedside and wept bitterly, but the moment he felt better she draped a white handkerchief over his cropped head and started painting him as a Bedouin. Both found this immense fun. And then, a couple of days after he had recovered and had returned to the hospital, disaster struck again.

'I'm not having the best of luck, Mother!' he said one day over dinner. 'I did four postmortems today and right at the start I cut two fingers. I only noticed it when I got home.'

Olga was scared, but he smiled and said it was absolutely nothing and that he often cut his hands when doing autopsies.

'I get carried away, Mother, and then I become careless.'

Olga was worried that he might get blood poisoning and prayed every night, but all was well. Once again their quiet, happy life resumed its course without incident or alarm. The present was beautiful enough, but spring was coming to take its place, smiling from afar and bearing the promise of a thousand joys. There would be endless bliss! In April, May and June there would be the holiday cottage a long way from town, walks, sketching, fishing, nightingales and then, from July right up to autumn, a painting trip on the Volga in which Olga too would take part as an indispensable member of the *société*. She had already had two gingham travelling costumes made, purchased paints, brushes, canvases and a new palette for the trip. Ryabovsky called almost every day to see how she was getting on with her painting. When she showed him her work he would thrust his hands deep in his pockets, purse his lips, sniff loudly and say:

'Well now . . . that cloud over there is all wrong. And that's not evening light. The foreground is a bit chewed up . . . you know, something's not right . . . And that cottage seems to have choked on something, it's making a pitiful squeaking . . . And you should have used a darker shade for that corner. But on the whole quite a decent effort . . . well done!'

And the more unintelligibly he spoke the easier it was for Olga to understand him.

III

On Whit Monday afternoon Dymov bought food and chocolates and went to visit his wife at the cottage. Since he hadn't seen her for a fortnight he missed her terribly. When he was on the train and later, when he was looking for the cottage in a large wood, he felt hungry and exhausted the whole time and dreamed of a leisurely supper with his wife and then tumbling into bed. Just looking at the parcel, in which he had wrapped the caviare, cheese and white salmon, cheered him up.

By the time he had sought out and recognized the cottage the sun was setting. An ancient housemaid told him that the mistress was out, but that no doubt she'd soon be back. The cottage, which was really hideous to look at, had low ceilings pasted all over with sheets of writing paper and its uneven floorboards were full of gaps. There were only three rooms. In one of them was a bed, in another chairs and windowsills piled high with canvases, paintbrushes and scraps of greasy paper, men's overcoats and hats, whilst in the third Dymov found three men he had never set eyes on before. Two were dark and had small beards, while the third was fat and clean-shaven – an actor by all appearances. On the table a samovar was boiling away.

'What can I do for you?' asked the actor in a bass voice, giving

Dymov a chilly look. 'Looking for Olga Ivanovna? Wait here, she won't be long.'

Dymov sat down and waited. One of the dark men gave him a languid, sleepy look and poured himself some tea.

'Perhaps you'd care for a glass?' he asked.

Dymov was both thirsty and hungry, but he refused the tea, as he did not want to spoil his appetite. Soon he heard footsteps and a familiar laugh. The door slammed open and into the room ran Olga, in a wide-brimmed hat, carrying a box in her hands, followed by the jovial, rosy-cheeked Ryabovsky with a large parasol and a folding-chair.

'Dymov!' cried Olga, flushing for joy. 'Dymov!' she repeated, laying her head and hands on his chest. 'It's you! What took you so long? What?'

'When could I get away, Mother? I'm always so busy and when I *am* free the train times are no good.'

'But I'm so glad to see you. I dreamt of you all night long and I was afraid you might be ill. Oh, if only you knew how sweet you are – and you've come at just the right time! You'll be my salvation. Only *you* can save me! Tomorrow,' she continued, laughing and tying her husband's tie, 'there's going to be an amazing wedding here. The young telegraph clerk at the railway station, Chikildeyev, is getting married. A handsome young man and quite intelligent. And, do you know, there's something so powerful, so bear-like about his face . . . I could paint him as a young Viking. All of us holiday-makers here are taking an interest in him and we've given him our word that we'll be at his wedding . . . He doesn't have much money, he's got no family, he's shy and it would be shameful not to offer him moral support. Just picture it – the wedding ceremony will be after the church service and then everyone will leave for the bride's house . . . You see, there'll be the woods, birdsong, patches of sunlight on the grass, and all of us will look like variegated patches against a green background. Highly original, in French Expressionist style! But what am I going to wear in church, Dymov?' she added with a distressed look. 'I've nothing here – literally nothing! No dress, no flowers, no gloves . . . You *must* save me. The fact you've arrived means the fates themselves have ordered you to rescue me. Now, take the keys, dear, go home and fetch my pink dress from the wardrobe. You remember, it's hanging in front. And you'll find two cardboard boxes on the pantry floor, to the right. If you open the top one you'll find lots and lots of tulle and some bits and pieces . . . and underneath them some flowers. You must take the flowers out carefully – try not to crush them, darling! I'll choose the ones I need later. And buy me some gloves.'

'All right,' Dymov said. 'I'll go tomorrow and send them.'

'*Tomorrow?*' Olga said, looking at him in amazement. 'Tomorrow you won't have time – the first train leaves here at nine and the wedding's at eleven! No, my darling, you must go today – today without fail! And if you can't come yourself tomorrow, send the whole lot by special messenger. Hurry up, you must go now . . . the passenger train's due any minute! Don't miss it, darling!'

'All right.'

'Oh, I really don't like letting you go,' Olga said and tears came to her eyes. 'And why was I silly enough to promise that telegraph clerk?'

Dymov gulped his tea, grabbed a roll and went off to the station, gently smiling. The caviare, cheese and white salmon were eaten by the two dark men and the actor.

IV

On a tranquil moonlit night in July Olga was standing on the deck of a Volga steamboat, gazing now at the water, then at the beautiful banks. By her stood Ryabovsky: the black shadows on the water, he was telling her, were not shadows, but a fleeting vision. As one gazed at the magical water with its mysterious gleam, at the fathomless sky and those sad, brooding river banks that spoke of the vanity of our lives, of the existence of something loftier, of a world of everlasting bliss, one would be happy enough to swoon, to die, to become but a memory. The past was vulgar and drab, the future of no significance and that wonderful, unique night would soon come to an end and merge with eternity. Why live, then?

And now, as Olga listened to Ryabovsky's voice, now to the stillness of the night, she fancied she was immortal and could never die. The turquoise water which she had never seen before, the sky, the river banks, the black shadows and that unaccountable joy that filled her heart – all these things told her that she would become a great artist and that somewhere, far beyond the horizon, far beyond this moonlit night, in the boundlessness of space, success, fame, people's adulation awaited her . . . When she gazed long and unblinking into the distance she imagined she was seeing crowds, lights, hearing the sound of solemn music, cries of delight, herself in a white dress, and flowers being strewn on her from every side. She thought too that by her side, leaning his elbows on the rail, stood a truly great man, a genius, one of God's elect . . . All that he had created up to now was beautiful, new and unusual, but what he would create in time, when his rare talent grew to maturity, would be breathtaking, something incalculably sublime – all this was clear from his face, from the way he expressed himself and in his attitude to Nature. Of shadows, of evening tints and of moonlight he had his own very special way of talking, his own language, so that one could sense the irresistible fascination of his power over Nature. He was very handsome, unconventional and his life, so independent, so free, so remote from all that was mundane, resembled that of a bird.

'It's getting chilly,' Olga said, shivering.

Ryabovsky wrapped his cloak around her. 'I feel I'm in your power,' he said sadly. 'I'm your slave. Oh, why are you so bewitching tonight?'

He looked at her and he could not take his eyes off her – eyes that were so frightening she was scared to look at him.

'I love you madly . . .' he whispered, breathing on her cheek. 'Just say the word and I'll put an end to my life. I'll give up art . . .' he muttered with deep emotion. 'Love me, love me . . .'

'Don't say such things,' Olga said and closed her eyes. 'It frightens me. What about Dymov?'

'Dymov? Why bring Dymov up? What do I care about Dymov?

There's the Volga, the moon, beauty, my love for you, my ecstasy – but there's no Dymov . . . Oh, I know nothing. I care nothing for the past, grant me one instant, one fleeting moment . . .'

Olga's heart was pounding. She tried to think of her husband, but her entire past, with the wedding, Dymov and her soirées, seemed so small, trivial, dull, unnecessary, and so very, very far away. And in fact what did Dymov matter? Why Dymov? What did she care about Dymov? Did he really exist or was he only a dream?

'That simple, ordinary man has already had his fair share of happiness,' she thought, covering her face with her hands. 'Let them condemn me *there*, let them curse me – to spite the lot of them I'll follow the path of perdition, become a fallen woman . . . One must experience everything in life. Heavens, how terrifying – and how marvellous!'

'Well, what? What do you say?' muttered the artist, embracing her and greedily kissing her hands with which she feebly tried to push him away. 'Do you love me? Yes? Yes? Oh, what a night! A magical night!'

'Yes, what a night!' she whispered, looking into his eyes that were glistening with tears. Then she quickly looked round, embraced him and kissed him firmly on the mouth.

'We're approaching Kineshma!'[1] someone called out on the other side of the deck.

There was a sound of heavy footsteps – it was the bar waiter going past.

'Listen,' Olga called to him, laughing and crying with happiness. 'Please bring us some wine.'

Pale with emotion, the artist sat on a bench and looked at Olga with adoring, grateful eyes. As he closed them he said with a languid smile:

'I'm tired.'

And he leaned his head towards the rail.

V

September the second was warm and calm, but overcast. A light early morning mist was drifting over the Volga and after nine o'clock it began to drizzle. There was no hope of it clearing up. Over breakfast Ryabovsky told Olga that painting was the most thankless and boring art, that he was not an artist and that only fools thought that he had talent. Then, all of a sudden, for no apparent reason, he seized a knife and made scratches on his best sketch. After breakfast he sat gloomily at the window, gazing at the Volga. But the Volga no longer gleamed; it was dull and lustreless, with a cold look. Everything reminded them that dreary, miserable autumn was approaching. Nature seemed to have taken away everything that was showy and flamboyant from the Volga – those luxuriant green carpets on her banks, those diamond-like sunbeams, that crystal clear blue distance – and packed it away in boxes until spring; and the crows that were flying over the river were teasing it for being so bare. As Ryabovsky listened to their cawing he brooded over the fact that he was washed up, his talent had gone, that everything in this world was conditional, relative and stupid, and that he should never have got involved with that woman. In a word, he wasn't himself at all and he felt very depressed.

Olga sat on the bed behind a screen, running her fingers through her beautiful flaxen hair, picturing herself in her drawing-room, then in her bedroom, then in her husband's study. Her imagination transported her to the theatre, to the dressmaker, then to her celebrity friends. What would they all be doing now? Did they remember her? The season had already begun and it was time to think of soirées. What about Dymov? Dear Dymov! How gently – as plaintively as a child – he had implored her in his letters to hurry home! Every month he sent her seventy roubles and when she wrote that she owed the other artists one hundred roubles, he sent her that too. Such a kind, generous man! Olga was tired from the journey, bored and longing to get away as fast as she could from those peasants, that damp river smell, and to rid herself of that sensation of physical impurity she had felt all the time she had lived in those peasant huts and wandered from village to village. If Ryabovsky had not promised the artists that he would stay with them until 20 September she could have left that very same day. How lovely that would have been!

'God, when will the sun ever come out?' Ryabovsky groaned. 'How can I do a sunlit landscape without any sun?'

'But there's that sketch of yours with a cloudy sky,' Olga said, coming out from behind the screen. 'Remember? There's a wood in the right foreground and a herd of cows and some geese on the left. You could finish that one now.'

'Eh?' said Ryabovsky, frowning. 'Finish it!? Do you think I'm so stupid that I don't know what has to be done?'

'How you've changed towards me!' sighed Olga.

'And a jolly good thing too!'

Olga's face trembled; she went over to the stove and burst into tears.

'My God! Tears! That's all I need! Stop it! I've a thousand reasons for crying but you won't catch me at it.'

'A thousand reasons!' sobbed Olga. 'And the main one is that you're tired of me. Oh yes!' she said and began sobbing. 'The truth is, you're ashamed of our affair. You keep trying to hide it from the others even though it's impossible to hide – they've known about it for ages!'

'Olga, I ask only one thing of you,' the artist begged and laid his hand on his heart. 'One thing! Don't torment me! That's all I want from you!'

'But swear you still love me!'

'This is sheer hell!' Ryabovsky hissed between his teeth and leapt up. 'I'll end up by throwing myself into the Volga or going out of my mind! Leave me alone!'

'All right then, kill me!' cried Olga. 'Go on, kill me!'

Once again she burst out sobbing and went behind the screen. The rain rustled on the thatched roof of the hut. Ryabovsky clutched his head and paced up and down. Then, with a determined look, as if he wanted to prove something to someone, he put on his cap, threw his rifle over his shoulder and went out.

After he had gone Olga lay for a long time on the bed and wept. First she thought it would be a good idea to poison herself, so that

Ryabovsky would return to find her dead. But then her thoughts carried her off to her drawing-room, into her husband's study and she pictured herself sitting quite still at Dymov's side, enjoying the physical relaxation and cleanliness, and then in the theatre one evening, listening to Masini.[2] And a yearning for civilization, for the bustle of the city, for famous people, tugged at her heart-strings. A peasant woman entered the hut, and slowly started lighting the stove so that she could prepare dinner. There was a smell of burning and the air filled with blue smoke. The artists returned in their muddy topboots, their faces wet with rain. They inspected each other's sketches and consoled themselves with the thought that even in bad weather the Volga had a charm of its own. The cheap clock on the wall ticked away monotonously. Chilled flies crowded together and buzzed in the front corner by the icons – and the cockroaches could be heard scurrying about in the thick files underneath the benches.

Ryabovsky returned when the sun was setting. He threw his cap onto the table. With a pale, exhausted look, still wearing his muddy boots, he sank onto a bench and closed his eyes.

'I'm tired . . .' he said, twitching his eyebrows and trying to raise his eyelids.

In an effort to be nice to him and to show that she wasn't angry, Olga went over, kissed him and without saying a word ran her comb through his hair: she wanted to give it a really good tidy up.

'What's this?' he said, shuddering, as if something cold had touched him. He opened his eyes. 'What's this? Leave me in peace, I beg you.'

He pushed her aside and walked away – and his face seemed to show revulsion and irritation, she thought. Just then the peasant woman came in, carefully carrying a bowl of cabbage soup in both hands. Olga could see that the woman had dipped both thumbs in the soup. And that dirty old woman with her tightly belted stomach, the cabbage soup that Ryabovsky greedily started devouring, the hut and that whole life which she had loved so much at first for its simplicity and Bohemian chaos now struck her as downright appalling. Suddenly she felt insulted.

'We must separate for a while,' she said coldly, 'or we'll end up having a serious quarrel from the sheer boredom of it. I'm sick and tired of all this. I'm leaving today.'

'And how will you go? Ride on a broomstick?'

'Today's Thursday, there's a steamboat at half past nine.'

'Oh yes, so there is . . . well, take it then,' Ryabovsky said gently, wiping his mouth on a towel instead of a serviette. 'It's boring and there's nothing for you to do here. It would be terribly selfish of me if I tried to stop you. Go then, we'll meet after the twentieth.'

Olga gaily packed and her cheeks even glowed with pleasure. Could it be true, she wondered, that soon she would be painting in a drawing-room, sleeping in a bedroom and dining with a cloth on the table? She felt as if a weight had been lifted from her. And no longer did she feel angry with the artist.

'I'm leaving you my paints and brushes, my dear Ryabovsky,' she said. 'You can bring anything I've left behind . . . But mind you don't become lazy when I've gone, don't mope, and get on with your work. You're a very fine person, my dear old Ryabovsky.'

At nine o'clock Ryabovsky kissed her goodbye, so that he would not have to kiss her on the steamboat in front of the others (so she thought), and he saw her to the landing-stage. The steamboat soon arrived and carried her away.

Two and a half days later she arrived home. Without taking off her hat or raincoat and breathless with excitement she went into the drawing-room and from there into the dining-room. Dymov was sitting at the table without any jacket, his waistcoat unbuttoned, sharpening a knife on a fork. There was a grouse on the plate in front of him. When Olga entered she felt quite convinced that everything must be concealed from her husband and that she had the skill and strength to do this. But now, when she saw his broad, gentle, happy smile and his eyes bright with joy, she felt that to deceive that man would be as vile, detestable and just as inconceivable and beyond her as slandering, stealing or murdering. So in a flash she decided to tell all. After letting him kiss and embrace her she knelt before him and covered her face.

'What is it? What's wrong, Mother?' he asked tenderly. 'Did you miss me?'

She raised her face that was red with shame and gave him a guilty, imploring look. But fear and guilt prevented her from speaking the truth.

'It's nothing,' she said. 'I'm just . . .'

'Let's sit down,' he said, lifting her to her feet and sitting her at the table. 'That's it . . . Now, have some grouse. You must be starving, you poor thing.'

Eagerly she inhaled the air of home and ate some grouse, while he watched with loving tenderness and laughed for joy.

VI

By the middle of winter it was apparent that Dymov had begun to guess that he was being deceived. Just as if his own conscience was not clear, he could no longer look his wife in the eye, no longer smiled happily when they met, and in order to avoid being alone with her so much would often invite his colleague Korostelev home for a meal. This colleague was a short, close-cropped little man with a wrinkled face who, whenever he spoke to Olga, would keep buttoning and unbuttoning his jacket in embarrassment and then start tweaking the left side of his moustache with his right hand. At dinner both doctors would discuss elevation of the diaphragm being occasionally accompanied by irregular heartbeat, or how common neuritis was these days, or how Dymov had discovered cancer of the pancreas when performing a postmortem the day before on a patient diagnosed to have died of pernicious anaemia. Both seemed to be talking shop only so that Olga could remain silent – in other words, not tell any lies. After dinner Korostelev would sit at the piano.

'Ah well, my dear chap!' Dymov would sigh. 'Play us something sad!'

With his shoulders raised and his fingers spread wide apart, Korostelev would play a few chords and start to sing:

Show me that abode
Where the Russian peasant does not groan.[3]

Dymov would give another sigh, prop his head on his fist and ponder.

Of late Olga had been behaving with the greatest indiscretion. Every morning she would wake up in the foulest of moods, thinking that she no longer loved Ryabovsky and that it was all over, thank God. But by the time she had drunk her coffee she was inclined to believe that Ryabovsky had alienated her husband and that now she was left without husband or Ryabovsky. Then she would recall her friends saying that Ryabovsky was preparing something quite sensational for an exhibition, a combination of landscape and genre *à la* Polenov,[4] which sent every visitor to his studio into raptures. Surely it was thanks to her influence that he had produced such a painting? And in general it was thanks to her that he had improved so dramatically. Her influence was so beneficial, so vital, that if she were to desert him he would probably go right downhill. She also remembered that on his last visit he had worn a kind of grey patterned silk coat and a new tie. 'Do I look handsome!' he had languidly asked. And in fact (or so she thought) he was very handsome, so elegant with his long curls and blue eyes. And he had been very nice to her.

After much reminiscing and reflection, Olga would get dressed and – in a great tizzy – take a cab to Ryabovsky's studio. She would find him in a cheerful mood, in ecstasies over his painting, which was truly splendid. He would jump about, play the fool and reply to all serious questions by joking. Olga was jealous of Ryabovsky's picture: she hated it, but she would stand before it in silence for five minutes – for politeness' sake – and then sigh like someone viewing a sacred object.

'No, you've never done anything like it before,' she would softly say. 'You know, it's really awe-inspiring!'

Then she would start pleading with him to love her, not to desert her, to take pity on her, poor miserable wretch that she was. She would weep and kiss his hands and insist that he vowed his love for her, and she tried to prove to him that without her good influence he would lose his way and finally meet with disaster. And after dampening his spirits and feeling that she had been humiliated, she would take a cab to her dressmaker's or an actress friend to try to wangle a free theatre ticket.

Should she not find Ryabovsky in his studio she would leave a letter vowing to poison herself without fail if he didn't come and see her that very same day. He would panic, go and see her and stay for dinner. Uninhibited by her husband's presence, he would be impertinent to her – and she would reply in kind. Both found that they were cramping each other's style, that they were despots and deadly enemies. And they would become furious with one another – and in their fury they failed to notice how badly they were behaving and that even the close-cropped Korostelev knew everything that was going on. After the meal Ryabovsky would make a hasty farewell and leave.

'Where are you going?' Olga would ask him in the hall with a venomous look.

Frowning and screwing up his eyes, he would mention some woman they both knew – clearly he was gloating over her jealousy and all he wanted was to annoy her. She would go to her bedroom and lie down on the bed, biting the pillow and sobbing out loud from jealousy, vexation, humiliation and shame. Dymov would leave Korostelev in the drawing-room, go into the bedroom and softly say, embarrassed and dismayed:

'Don't cry so loud, Mother. What's the point? You must say nothing about it . . . You mustn't let people see . . . What's done cannot be undone – you know that.'

Not knowing how to deaden that nagging feeling of jealousy that even made her head ache and convinced that things could still be put right, she would wash, powder her tear-stained face and fly off to a woman friend. If she didn't find Ryabovsky there, she would go to another, then to a third. At first she was ashamed of running about like this, but then it became a habit and in a single evening she did the rounds of all the women she knew in her search for Ryabovsky, and all of them were well aware of this.

Once she told Ryabovsky about her husband:

'That man is crushing me with his magnanimity!'

So delighted was she with this phrase that whenever she met artists who knew of her affair with Ryabovsky she would say of her husband with a sweeping gesture:

'That man is crushing me with his magnanimity!'

Her routine was just the same as the previous year. On Wednesdays there were the soirées. The actor recited, the artists sketched, the cellist played, the opera singer sang and at half past eleven the dining-room door never failed to open and Dymov would say with a smile:

'Supper is served, gentlemen!'

And as before, Olga sought out great men, discovered them, found they were not up to scratch and continued searching. And as before she would come home late every night. But unlike the previous year Dymov would not be asleep, but would be sitting in his study working. He would go to bed at three and get up at eight.

One evening, when she was standing in front of her pier-glass before going to the theatre, Dymov entered the bedroom in tails and white tie. He smiled gently and joyfully looked his wife in the eye, just as he used to do. His face was radiant.

'I've just defended my thesis,' he said, sitting down and stroking his knee.

'Defended?' asked Olga.

'Oho!' he laughed and craned his neck to catch a glimpse of his wife's face in the mirror, as she was still doing her hair with her back to him. 'Oho!' he laughed again. 'Do you know, it's very much on the cards that I'm going to be offered a lectureship in general pathology. It certainly looks that way.'

It was plain from his blissful, radiant face that if Olga would only share in his joy and triumph he would forgive her everything, both present and future, and would forget the whole thing. But she had no idea what a lectureship or general pathology were – and besides, she was worried she might be late for the theatre. So she said nothing.

He sat there for another two minutes and then went out with a guilty smile on his face.

VII

It was a very disturbed day.

Dymov had a severe headache. He went without breakfast, did not go to the hospital and lay the whole time on the study sofa. As usual, after twelve, Olga set off for Ryabovsky's to show him her still-life and to ask why he had not come yesterday. She thought her sketch was rubbish – she had only painted it as an excuse to visit the artist.

She entered his flat without ringing and when she was removing her galoshes in the hall she thought she heard someone quietly running through the studio and the rustle of a woman's dress. When she hurried to take a look into the studio she caught a brief glimpse of a brown petticoat flashing past and vanishing behind the large painting that was draped – together with the easel – down to the ground with black calico. A woman was hiding there – no doubt about that! How often had Olga herself taken refuge behind that painting! Evidently embarrassed in the extreme and startled at her appearance, Ryabovsky stretched both hands towards her.

'A-a-a! How very nice to see you,' he said with a forced smile. 'And what's the latest news?'

Olga's eyes filled with tears. She felt ashamed and bitter – not for a million roubles would she have agreed to speak her mind in the presence of a strange woman, her rival, that liar who was now hiding behind the painting and probably enjoying a malicious giggle.

'I've brought you a sketch,' she said timidly, in a thin wispy voice, her lips trembling. 'A *nature morte*.'

'A-a-a! A sketch?'

The artist took the sketch and, still inspecting it, proceeded automaton-like into the next room.

Olga obediently followed him.

'*Nature morte* . . . the best sort,' he muttered, looking for rhymes. 'Resort, port, ought . . .'

The sound of footsteps and the rustle of a skirt came from the studio: that meant *she* had gone. Olga felt like shouting out loud, hitting the artist on the head with a heavy object and making her exit, but she was blinded by tears, overwhelmed with shame and no longer did she feel that she was Olga Ivanovna, no longer an artist, but a small insect.

'I'm tired,' the artist said languidly, examining the sketch and shaking his head to ward off sleepiness. 'It's very charming, of course, but today it's only a sketch, last year it was a sketch and in a month there'll be another sketch. How is it you don't get bored with it all? If I were you I'd give up painting and take up music seriously, or something. You see, you're not an artist, but a musician. But really, I'm so tired, you know! I'll order some tea right away . . . Eh?'

He left the room and Olga could hear him giving his manservant some orders. To avoid farewells and explanations, but mainly to stop herself sobbing, she rushed into the hall before Ryabovsky returned, put on her galoshes and went into the street. There she breathed easily and felt free once and for all from Ryabovsky, from painting, from that tiresome feeling of guilt that had so overwhelmed her in the studio. It was all over!

She drove to her dressmaker, then to Barnay,[5] who had arrived only yesterday, and from Barnay she went to a music shop, thinking the whole time of the cold, harsh letter, so full of injured pride, she would write to Ryabovsky – and of going with Dymov to the Crimea in the spring or summer, of finally breaking with the past and starting a new life.

When she returned home late that evening she sat down in the drawing-room without changing to write her letter. Ryabovsky had told her that she was no artist and to avenge herself she would tell him that year in year out he painted the same old picture, that every single day he repeated the same thing, that he was in a rut, that he would never be any better than he was now. She also wanted to tell him how much he owed her for her good influence and that if he was acting badly this was only because her influence was being undermined by various personages such as the one who had hidden herself behind the painting earlier that day.

'Mother!' Dymov called from his study without opening the door. 'Mother!'

'What's wrong?'

'Mother, don't come into the study, just come to the door ... Well, the day before yesterday I must have caught diphtheria at the hospital and now ... I'm feeling rotten. Send for Korostelev right away.'

Olga had always called her husband – like all the men she knew – by his surname instead of his Christian name. She did not like the name Osip, because it reminded her of Gogol's Osip[6] and that play upon words: 'Osip lost his voice from too much gossip.' But now she cried out:

'Osip! It's not possible!'

'Send for him! I'm not well ...' Dymov said from behind the door and she could hear him going back to the sofa and lying down. 'Send for him' – and his voice had a hollow sound.

'What's happening?' Olga thought, turning cold with fright. 'It's really dangerous, isn't it?'

Although she had no need for one, she took a candle and went to her bedroom and there, as she wondered what to do, she happened to catch a glimpse of herself in the pier-glass. Her pale, frightened face, her long-sleeved jacket with those yellow flounces at the breast, her skirt with those bizarrely sloping stripes – all this made her look ghastly and repulsive in her own eyes. Suddenly she felt a sharp twinge of pity for Dymov, for his boundless love for her, for his young life and even for that orphaned bed in which he had not slept for so long. And she remembered his customary smile, so meek and mild. She shed bitter tears and wrote Korostelev an imploring letter. It was two o'clock in the morning.

VIII

At about half past eight next morning, when Olga came out of her bedroom, her head heavy from lack of sleep, her hair uncombed, unappealing and with a guilty expression, a certain black-bearded gentleman – apparently a doctor – entered the hall.

There was a smell of medicine. Korostelev was standing by the study door, tweaking the left side of his moustache with his right hand.

'I'm sorry, but I can't let you go in,' he told Olga gloomily. 'It's infectious. In fact, there's no point at all in your going in, he's delirious.'

'Is it *really* diphtheria?' Olga whispered.

'Those who play with fire must face the consequences . . .' Korostelev muttered, ignoring the question. 'Do you know how he caught it? On Tuesday he sucked some diphtheria membrane from a little boy through a tube. What for? It was so stupid, he just didn't think . . .'

'Is it dangerous? Very?' asked Olga.

'Yes, it's the serious type. We really ought to send for Shrek.'

There arrived a little red-haired man with a long nose and Jewish accent, then a tall, stooping shaggy gentleman resembling an archdeacon, then a very stout, young, red-faced man with spectacles. These were the doctors who had come to sit at their colleague's bedside. When Korostelev had done his stint, he stayed on instead of going home, wandering wraith-like through every room. The maid served tea to the doctors at the bedside and was constantly running to the chemist's. As a result there was no one to tidy the rooms. It was quiet and depressing.

Olga sat in her bedroom and thought that God was punishing her for deceiving her husband. That silent, uncomplaining, mysterious being, deprived of any personality as a result of his own gentleness, so characterless and feeble because of his excessive kindness, was suffering acutely somewhere in his study, on his sofa, without a word of complaint. And were he to complain, even though delirious, the bedside doctors would know that diphtheria alone was not to blame. They only had to ask Korostelev: he knew everything about it – and it was not without reason that he looked at his friend's wife as if she were the real villain of the piece and as if the diphtheria were merely her accomplice. She had completely forgotten that moonlit night on the Volga, those declarations of love, that romantic life in the peasant's hut – all she remembered now was that because of some idle whim, from sheer self-gratification, she had soiled herself from head to foot with some sticky filth which she could never wash off . . .

'Oh, what two-faced lies I told!' she thought, recalling her stormy affair with Ryabovsky. 'Damn all of that!'

At four o'clock she sat at the dinner table with Korostelev. He ate nothing, drank only red wine and kept frowning. She too ate nothing. At times she would offer a silent prayer, vowing to God that if Dymov did recover she would love him again and be a faithful wife. Her thoughts momentarily wandered as she looked at Korostelev and reflected: 'How terribly boring to be such an ordinary, totally unremarkable, obscure nobody, with a wrinkled face too and such appalling manners!' And then she felt that God would strike her dead that very moment for never once having gone into her husband's study for fear of infection. And in general there was that dull feeling of dejection and the conviction that her life was already in ruins and that her situation was beyond redemption.

After dinner it grew dark. When Olga came into the dining-room Korostelev was sleeping on the sofa with a gold-embroidered silk cushion under his head. He was snoring regularly and hoarsely.

And the doctors who came to keep vigil at the bedside went away again without noticing the disorder everywhere. That snoring stranger asleep in the drawing-room, those sketches on the walls, the quaint décor, the uncombed, sloppily dressed mistress of the house – none of this aroused the slightest interest now. One of the doctors happened to laugh at something and his laughter had a strange, restrained ring to it – and this was frightening, even.

When Olga came into the drawing-room again Korostelev was not sleeping, but sitting up and smoking.

'He has diphtheria of the nasal cavity,' he said in an undertone. 'And his heart's not too good. It looks really grim.'

'You'd better send for Shrek,' Olga said.

'He's been. It was he who noticed that the diphtheria had spread to the nose. But what is Shrek, all said and done? He's an absolute nobody, really. He's Shrek and I'm Korostelev – that's all there is to say about it.'

Time dragged on painfully slowly. Olga lay fully dressed, dozing on her bed that had been unmade since early morning. She fancied that the whole flat was filled from floor to ceiling with an enormous lump of iron and that it only had to be removed for everyone to feel cheerful and relaxed. When she woke up she realized that it was not the iron that was weighing down on her but Dymov's illness.

'*Nature morte* ... port,' she thought, slipping into semi-consciousness again. 'Sport . . . resort . . . And what about Shrek? Shrek, peck, speck, deck. And where are my friends now? Do they know of our troubles? God help us . . . save us . . . Shrek, peck . . .'

And once again that lump of iron. Time dragged wearily and the ground-floor clock kept striking. The doorbell rang constantly as the doctors arrived. The maid entered with an empty glass on a tray.

'Shall I make the bed, madam?' she asked. Receiving no reply, she went out. The clock struck downstairs, Olga dreamt of that rain on the Volga and again someone entered the bedroom – a stranger, it seemed. Olga jumped up and recognized Korostelev.

'What's the time?' she asked.

'About three.'

'Well, how is it?'

'How is it!? I've come to tell you he's dying . . .'

He began to sob, sat down on the bed beside her and wiped the tears with his sleeve. At first she did not take it in, but then she went cold all over and started slowly crossing herself.

'He's dying,' he repeated in a thin little voice and sobbed once more. 'He's dying because he sacrificed himself . . . What a loss for science!' he said bitterly. 'Compared with all of us he was a great man, absolutely outstanding! What talent! What hopes all of us had for him!' Korostelev continued, wringing his hands. 'God in heaven . . . he was a true scientist – you won't find another like him in a month of Sundays! Dear Osip Dymov, Osip Dymov! What have you done? Oh, my God!'

Despairingly, Korostelev covered his face with both hands and shook his head. 'And what a moral force!' he continued, growing increasingly angry with someone. 'A kind, pure, loving soul – no ordinary mortal but a saint! He served science and he died for science. He worked like a horse, day in day out, no one spared him and a young scholar like him, a professor in the making, had to tout for private patients and spend his nights doing translations to pay for these . . . loathsome rags!'

Korostelev looked hatefully at Olga, seized the sheet in both hands and angrily ripped it, as if it were to blame.

'He didn't spare himself and no one spared him! Well, what's the use of talking?'

'Yes, he was one in a million!' someone said in the drawing-room, in a deep voice.

Olga recalled their whole life together, from beginning to end, in every single detail and suddenly she realized that he really had been a truly remarkable and unusual man – a *great* man compared with every single person she knew. And when she recalled what her late father and all his medical colleagues thought of him she realized that every one of them had seen in him a celebrity of the future. The walls, the ceiling, the lamp and the carpet winked at her mockingly, as if they wished to tell her: 'You're too late! You've missed your chance!' She rushed weeping from the bedroom and ran into her husband's study. He lay motionless on the sofa, covered with a blanket up to his waist. His face had become dreadfully thin and pinched, with that greyish, yellow colour you never find with the living. Only his forehead, his black eyebrows and familiar smile told her that it was Dymov. Olga quickly felt his chest, forehead and hands. His chest was still warm, but his forehead and hands were horribly cold. And his half-open eyes gazed at the blanket – not at Olga Ivanovna.

'Dymov!' she called out loud. 'Dymov!'

She wanted to explain that there had been a mistake, that all was not lost, that life could still be beautiful and happy, that he was a rare, a remarkable, a great man and that she would revere, idolize and go in awe of him all her life . . .

'Dymov!' she called, tugging at his shoulder, unable to believe that he would never wake again. 'Dymov! Say something!'

Meanwhile, in the drawing-room, Korostelev was telling the maid:

'Why do you have to ask? Just go to the church lodge and ask where the almswomen live. They'll wash the body and lay it out, they'll do all that has to be done.'

Ward No. 6

I

In the hospital yard there is a small outbuilding surrounded by a dense jungle of burdock, nettles and wild hemp. The roof is rusty, half of the chimney has collapsed, the steps to the door are rotten and overgrown with grass; only traces of plaster remain. The front faces the main hospital and the rear looks out on to open country, from which it is cut off by the grey hospital fence topped with nails. These nails, with their points sticking upwards, the fence and the outbuilding itself have that mournful, god-forsaken look that you find only in our hospitals and prisons.

If you are not afraid of being stung by the nettles let us go down the narrow path leading to this outbuilding and see what is going on inside. We open the first door and enter the lobby. Here, against the walls and by the stove, are piled great mountains of hospital rubbish. Mattresses, old tattered smocks, trousers, blue-striped shirts, useless, worn-out footwear – all this junk lies jumbled up in crumpled heaps, rotting and giving off a suffocating stench.

On top of all this rubbish, his pipe perpetually clenched between his teeth, lies Nikita the warder, an old soldier with faded reddish-brown chevrons. He has a red nose, a grim, haggard face and beetling eyebrows that give him the expression of a steppe sheepdog. Although short, thin and wiry, he has an intimidating air and powerful fists. He is one of those simple, efficient, thoroughly dependable, thick-headed men who worship discipline above all else in this world and who are therefore convinced that patients are there to be beaten. He showers blows on face, chest, back – on whatever comes first – in the firm belief that this is the only way to maintain discipline.

Next you enter a large and spacious room which occupies the rest of the building, apart from the lobby. Here the walls are painted dirty blue, the ceiling is black with soot, as in a chimneyless peasant hut – obviously the stoves smoke in winter and fill the place with fumes. On the inside the windows are disfigured with iron bars. The floor is grey and splintery; there is a stench of sour cabbage, burnt candlewicks, bed-bugs and ammonia – a stench that immediately makes you think you are entering a zoo.

Around the room there are beds screwed to the floor. On these beds men in dark blue hospital smocks and old-fashioned nightcaps are lying or sitting: these are the lunatics.

There are five in all. Only one is of the gentry, the others are all from the lower classes. Nearest the door is a tall, thin, working-class man with a sleek ginger moustache and tear-filled eyes. There he sits, head propped on hands, staring at one fixed point. Day and night he grieves, shakes his head, sighs and smiles bitterly. Rarely does he join in conversation and usually he doesn't reply to questions. When they bring him his food he eats and drinks like an automaton. Judging from his agonizing, hacking cough, his emaciated look and flushed cheeks, he is in the early stages of consumption.

Next is a small, lively, very active old man with a little pointed beard and the black fuzzy hair of a Negro. He spends all day sauntering from window to window, or squatting on his bed Turkish style; tirelessly, like a bullfinch, he chirrups, softly sings and titters. He shows his childish gaiety and liveliness of character at night as well, when he rises to pray – that is, to beat his breast with his fists and pick at the door. This is Moses the Jew, an imbecile who lost his reason about twenty years ago when his hat workshop burnt down.

He alone among the inmates of Ward No. 6 has permission to leave the outbuilding and he is even allowed to go out from the yard into the street. He has long enjoyed this privilege, probably because he is the hospital's oldest resident and a gentle, harmless idiot, the town buffoon, a long-familiar sight in the street with his retinue of urchins and dogs. In his smock, comical night-cap and slippers – sometimes barefoot and even trouserless – he walks the streets, stopping in doorways and going into shops to beg for money. At one place they give him kvass, at another some bread and somewhere else a copeck, so that he usually returns to the ward rich and well-fed. Everything he brings back is confiscated by Nikita for his own use. The old soldier does this roughly and angrily, turning out his pockets and calling upon God to witness that he will never let the Jew out into the street again and that for him the worst thing in this world is lack of discipline.

Moses loves doing everyone a good turn. He fetches water for his fellow inmates, tucks them up in bed, promises to bring each of them a copeck when he comes back from the streets, and to make them all new caps. He spoonfeeds his paralytic left-hand neighbour. This he does not out of compassion or for humanitarian reasons, but because he wants to imitate his right-hand neighbour Gromov and he involuntarily bows to his authority.

Ivan Dmitrich Gromov, about thirty-three years old, a gentleman by birth, former court usher and low-ranking civil servant, suffers from persecution mania. He tends to lie curled up on his bed or pace from corner to corner, as if taking a constitutional; only very rarely does he sit still. He is always in a state of great agitation and excitement, and some vague, indeterminate feeling of apprehension makes him perpetually tense. The slightest rustle in the lobby or shout from outside is enough to make him raise his head and listen intently. Are they coming for *him*? Is it *he* they are looking for? And then his face takes on an expression of extreme anxiety and revulsion.

I like his broad, high-cheekboned face, always pale and miserable, seemingly mirroring a soul tormented by inner turmoil and constant dread. His grimaces are weird and troubled, but the delicate lines etched on his face by profound, genuine suffering, express intelligence and reason, and his eyes have a healthy, warm glow. And I like the character of the man himself – so polite and obliging, so exceptionally sensitive in his attitude to everyone except Nikita. If someone happens to drop a button or spoon he immediately leaps from his bed to pick it up. Every morning he wishes his companions good morning and bids them good night every time he goes to bed.

But madness is apparent in other things besides his grimaces and persistent nervous tension. Some evenings he wraps himself tightly in his smock and dashes from corner to corner and in between the beds, trembling all over, his teeth chattering. It is as if he has a high fever. From his sudden stops to look at the other inmates he clearly has something very important to say. However, no doubt realizing that they won't listen to him or understand, he shakes his head impatiently and continues marching up and down. But soon the desire to speak outweighs all other considerations and he gives full vent to his feelings with a fervent, passionate tirade. His speech is disjointed, feverish, as if he is delirious, jerky and not always intelligible. But at the same time, in the way he talks, in his words and his voice, you can hear something that is extraordinarily fine. When he speaks you recognize both the lunatic and the human being in him. It is difficult to convey that mad gibberish on paper. He talks of human baseness, of violence trampling over truth, of the beautiful life that will eventually come to be on earth and of the barred windows – a constant reminder for him of the folly and cruelty of his oppressors. The result is a chaotic, incoherent medley of songs that are old but still fresh.

II

About twelve or fifteen years ago, in the town's main street, there lived in his own house a civil servant called Gromov, respectable and well-to-do. He had two sons, Sergey and Ivan. While in his fourth year at university Sergey contracted galloping consumption and died. This death was the first of a whole series of misfortunes that suddenly overtook the Gromovs. A week after Sergey's funeral the old man was prosecuted for forgery and embezzlement and died soon afterwards of typhus in the prison hospital. His house and all his property were sold off at auction and Ivan Dmitrich and his mother were left completely destitute.

When his father was alive Ivan Dmitrich had lived in St Petersburg, studied at the university, received an allowance of sixty to seventy roubles a month and had no idea of the meaning of poverty. But now he was forced to change his way of life drastically. From morning to night he had to do coaching for a mere pittance, copy out documents – yet still he went hungry, for all he earned went to support his mother. This kind of life was too much for him. He lost heart, became ill, abandoned his studies and went home. Here, in this little town, he obtained a teaching appointment in the district school through someone pulling strings for him, but he failed to get on with his colleagues, was disliked by the pupils and he soon gave it up. His mother died. For about six months he was unemployed, had to live on bread and water, and then he became a court usher. This post he held until he was discharged for reasons of ill health.

Never, even as a young student, had he looked like a healthy person. He was always pale and thin, and subject to colds, eating little and sleeping badly. One glass of wine went to his head and made him hysterical. He had always liked company, but thanks to his irritability and suspiciousness he was never able to make close friends with anyone. He always spoke with contempt about the townspeople, whose gross ignorance and torpid, brutish existence he found vile and disgusting. He talked in a high-pitched voice, loudly and excitedly, invariably indignant and exasperated, or with delight and surprise – and always sincerely.

Whatever you happened to be discussing with him he would always lead on to one and the same topic: life in that town was stifling and boring, society lacked any higher interests and led a lacklustre, aimless existence, varying it only with violence, crude debauchery and hypocrisy; the scoundrels were well-fed and well-dressed, while honest men ate crusts. There was a crying need for schools, an honest local newspaper, a theatre, public lectures, intellectual solidarity. It was time for society to wake up to its shortcomings and be duly shocked. When judging people he laid on the colours thickly, using only black and white and no intermediate shades. For him humanity was divided into the rogues and the honest: there was nothing in between. He always spoke passionately and rapturously of love and women, but he had never been in love.

Despite his harsh judgements and nervous character he was liked in the town and in his absence was affectionately called 'dear old Vanya'. His innate tact, helpfulness, decency, moral integrity, along with his shabby frock-coat, sickly appearance and family misfortunes, inspired sympathy, kindness – and sadness. Besides, he was an educated man and very well read – according to the townspeople he knew everything and was considered a kind of walking encyclopedia.

He read a great deal and would sit for hours in the club, nervously plucking his beard and leafing through magazines and books: from his expression he was obviously not simply reading, but devouring, barely giving himself time to digest the contents. Evidently, reading was a function of his illness, since he swooped on whatever came to hand with equal avidity, even old newspapers and almanacs. At home he always read lying down.

III

One autumn morning, his coat collar turned up, Ivan was tramping through the muddy side-streets and back alleys to collect a fine from some tradesman. As always in the mornings he was in a sombre mood. In a certain alley he passed two convicts in foot-irons, escorted by four guards armed with rifles. Gromov had often passed convicts before and they always made him feel awkward and compassionate, but this time the encounter produced a particularly odd impression. Suddenly it occurred to him that he too might be clapped in irons like them and taken through the mud to prison. When he had seen the tradesman and was on his way home he ran into a police inspector friend near the post office who greeted him and walked a few steps down the street with him. For some reason this struck him as suspicious. At home visions of convicts and armed guards haunted him all day and some inexplicable, deep feeling of unease prevented him from reading and concentrating. In the evenings he did not light his lamp and he lay awake all night in constant fear he might be arrested, clapped in irons and thrown into prison. He was not aware of having committed any crime and could solemnly guarantee that he would never commit murder, arson or robbery. But then, it was so easy to commit a crime accidentally or unintentionally. And how about false accusations and a miscarriage of justice? All that was highly possible, nothing odd about it at all. Indeed, hadn't the folk wisdom of old taught that one is never safe from poverty or prison? Given the present state of the law a miscarriage of justice was very much on the cards – and no wonder. People who adopt a professional, bureaucratic attitude to the suffering of others – judges, policemen and doctors, for example – become hardened to such a degree, from sheer force of habit, that even if they want to they cannot help treating their clients strictly by the book. In this respect they are no different from peasants who slaughter sheep and calves in their back yards without even noticing the blood. Having adopted this formal, soulless attitude to the individual, all a judge needs to deprive an innocent man of his civil rights and to sentence him to hard labour is *time*. Just give a judge time to observe the various formalities (for which he receives a salary) and then it's all over. Fat chance, then, of finding any justice and protection in this filthy little town a hundred and twenty-five miles from the nearest station! And how ludicrous even to think of justice when society considers every act of violence as rational, expedient and necessary, when every act of mercy – an acquittal, for instance – provokes a whole explosion of unsatisfied vindictiveness!

Next morning Gromov awoke in terror, with a cold sweat on his forehead. Now he was absolutely convinced that he might be arrested any moment. The very fact that yesterday's oppressive thoughts were still plaguing him meant that there must be a grain of truth in them. After all, those thoughts couldn't have entered his head for no reason, could they?

A policeman strolled leisurely past his window: there must be a reason for that! And now two men came and stood near the house and did not say one word. Why were they silent?

And for Gromov there began whole days and nights of agony. Every person who passed the window or entered the yard was a spy or detective. Every day at noon a police inspector usually drove down the street in his carriage and pair, on his way from his out-of-town estate to police headquarters, but on each occasion Gromov had the feeling that he was driving faster than was warranted and that there was a peculiar expression on his face: obviously he was in a hurry to report that a very dangerous criminal was at large in the town. With every ring of the doorbell or knock at the gate Gromov shuddered; he went through agonies every time a stranger visited his landlady. If he met a policeman or gendarme he would start smiling and whistling in an effort to appear unconcerned. He lay awake for nights on end expecting arrest, snoring and sighing loudly so that his landlady would think he was asleep. After all, if a man didn't sleep at night it could only mean that he was suffering pangs of conscience – and what evidence that would be! The actual facts of the matter and common sense convinced him that all these fears were absurd and neurotic, and that if one took a broader view there was nothing really so terrible in them as long as you had a clear conscience. But the more logically and consistently he reasoned, the more severe and excruciating his mental anguish became. He resembled the hermit who wanted to clear a plot for himself in virgin forest: the harder he wielded his axe the thicker and stronger grew the trees around him. Finally realizing how futile his efforts were, Gromov gave up the struggle and surrendered completely to despair and terror.

He became more solitary in his habits and avoided company. His job had always been disagreeable, now it was downright unbearable. He was afraid someone might trick him by slipping some money into his pocket and he would be accused of bribery. Or that he might accidentally make a mistake in an official document – that would be tantamount to forgery – or that he might lose money that had been entrusted to him. Strangely, never before had his mind been so supple and inventive as now, when every day he was busy thinking up a thousand different reasons for being seriously worried about his freedom and honour. On the other hand, his interest in the outside world had weakened significantly, particularly his interest in books – and his memory was failing badly.

In the spring, when the snow had melted, the semi-decomposed bodies of an old woman and a boy, showing signs of a violent death, were found in a gully near the cemetery. The townspeople talked of nothing but these corpses and the unidentified murderers. To make it quite clear to everyone that he wasn't the murderer, Gromov would walk down the street smiling and whenever he met a friend he would turn pale, blush, and then declare that there was no crime more detestable than killing the weak and defenceless. But he soon tired of this pretence and after reflection decided that the best thing he could do would be to hide in the landlady's cellar. He remained there for a whole day, then the next night and the day after that – and he was chilled to the bone. After that he waited until dark and sneaked back to his room like a thief. He stood in the middle of the room until daylight, stock-still, listening for every sound. Early in the morning, before sunrise, some stove-makers called on his landlady. Gromov knew very well that they had come to rebuild the kitchen stove, but his fear led him to believe that they were really policemen in disguise. He stole out of the flat and fled down the street in panic, hatless and coatless. Barking dogs ran after him, somewhere behind him a man shouted, the wind whistled in his ears and Gromov felt that all the violence in the world had joined forces behind his back and was pursuing him.

He was stopped and brought home. His landlady sent for the doctor. Dr Andrey Yefimych Ragin (of whom more later) prescribed cold compresses and laurel water drops. Then he shook his head sadly and left, telling the landlady that he wouldn't be calling any more since it was wrong to prevent people going out of their minds. As he could not afford to have treatment at home Gromov was soon sent to hospital and put in the ward for venereal patients. He did not sleep at night, made trouble and disturbed the other patients, so he was quickly transferred to Ward No. 6 on Dr Ragin's orders.

Within a year the townspeople had completely forgotten about Gromov and his books were dumped in a sledge in the landlady's shed, from which they were pilfered by boys from the street.

IV

As I have already pointed out, Gromov's left-hand neighbour is Moses the Jew, while his neighbour on the right is a bloated, almost globular peasant with a vacant, completely senseless expression. This torpid, gluttonous, filthy animal has long lost all capacity for thought or feeling. He constantly gives off an acrid, suffocating stench.

Nikita, who has to clear up after him, beats him mercilessly, taking huge swings and not pulling his punches. But it isn't the beatings that are so horrifying – one can get used to beatings – but the fact that this supine animal makes no response to them, either by sound, movement or the look in his eyes, but merely rocks slightly, like a heavy barrel.

The fifth and last inmate of Ward No. 6 is a working-class man from the town, once a post office sorter. He is small, thin and fair, with a kind but somewhat cunning face. Judging from his clever, calm eyes that view everything brightly and cheerfully, he seems to have his wits about him and possesses some important and pleasant secret. Under his pillow and mattress he keeps something hidden that he refuses to show to anyone – not for fear that it might be stolen or confiscated, but out of sheer modesty. Sometimes he goes to the window, turns his back to the others, pins something to his chest and inspects it with lowered head. But if anyone happens to approach him he becomes flustered and tears it off his chest: his secret is easily guessed.

'Congratulate me,' he often tells Gromov. 'I've been awarded the Order of St Stanislas,[1] second class with star. Normally the second class with star is only awarded to foreigners, but for some reason they want to make an exception in my case,' he says smiling and shrugging his shoulders in astonishment. 'Really, that's the last thing I expected, I must say!'

'I don't know anything about these things,' Gromov gloomily replies.

'Do you know what I shall get, sooner or later?' the ex-sorter continues, slyly winking. 'I'm going to be awarded the Swedish Polar

Star. An order like that is definitely worth trying hard for. A white cross and black ribbon. Very handsome!'

Probably nowhere else in the world is life so boring as in this building. Every morning the patients – with the exception of the paralytic and the fat peasant – go into the lobby, where they wash themselves from a large tub and dry themselves on the skirts of their smocks. Then they drink tea from tin mugs which Nikita brings from the main block. Each patient gets one mugful. At noon they have sour cabbage soup and porridge; in the evening they have the porridge left over from lunch. Between meals they lie down, sleep, look out of the window and pace from corner to corner. And so it goes on day after day. Even the ex-sorter can talk of nothing but those decorations.

Fresh faces are seldom seen in Ward No. 6. The doctor has long stopped admitting new patients and in this world there are few people who are fond of visiting lunatic asylums. Once every two months Semyon Lazarich, the barber, appears. I had better not describe how he shears the patients – with Nikita's assistance – and the panic on the patients' faces every time they see his drunken, grinning face.

Besides the barber no one ever looks into the ward. Day after day the patients are condemned to see only Nikita.

However, a rather strange rumour has recently been spreading through the hospital: that a doctor has started paying visits to Ward No. 6.

V

A strange rumour indeed!

Dr Andrey Yefimych Ragin is a remarkable person in his own way. As a young man he was said to be extremely pious and intended to go into the church. After leaving school in 1863 he prepared to enter a theological college, but his father – a surgeon and doctor of medicine – had apparently poured scorn over these plans and declared categorically that he would disown him if he became a priest. How much truth there was in this I do not know, but Andrey Yefimych admitted more than once that he had never felt any vocation for medicine or, come to that, for any specialized science.

Nevertheless, he took a degree in medicine and never became a priest: he showed no signs of godliness and at the start of his medical career bore as little resemblance to a priest as he does now.

He has a heavy, coarse, rough-hewn look. His face, flat hair and strong, clumsy build are reminiscent of some pot-bellied, intemperate, cantankerous highway innkeeper. His face is stern and a mass of blue veins, his eyes are small, his nose red. Tall and broad-shouldered, he has enormous hands and feet. With one grasp of a fist he could squeeze the life out of you. Yet his tread is slow and he walks cautiously, stealthily. If he meets someone in a narrow corridor he is always first to give way and say 'Sorry' – not in a bass voice as you might expect, but in a soft, reedy tenor. He has a small growth on his neck which prevents him from wearing starched collars and therefore he always wears soft linen or cotton shirts. In no way does he dress like a doctor. He'll wear the same shirt for ten years and when he does put on new clothes – usually from a cheap Jewish shop – they look just as worn and crumpled as the old ones. He sees patients, dines and goes visiting in one and the same frock-coat. But this isn't from meanness, but simply because he couldn't care less about his appearance.

When Dr Ragin first came to the town to take up his appointment, the so-called 'charitable institution' was in a dire state. In the wards, corridors and hospital yard one could hardly breathe for the stench. The male orderlies, the nurses and their children slept in the wards with the patients. They complained that the cockroaches, bed-bugs and mice made their lives a misery. Erysipelas was rampant in the surgical department. There were only two scalpels and not one thermometer in the whole hospital, and the baths were used for storing potatoes. The superintendent, matron, the assistant doctor robbed the patients, and the previous doctor, Ragin's predecessor, was said to have sold surgical spirits on the quiet and to have set up an entire harem recruited from nurses and female patients. These goings-on were all too well known in the town and even exaggerated, but the people were not concerned in the least. Some excused them on the ground that only lower-class people and peasants went into hospital – and *they* had no reason to complain since they were far worse off at home. Surely they didn't expect to be fed on roast pheasant, did they? Others argued that the town on its own could not be expected to maintain a good hospital without the help of the district council. They should thank God that they had a hospital at all, however bad it was. But the newly elected council refused to open a clinic either in town or in the neighbourhood, on the grounds that the town already had its own hospital.

After inspecting the hospital Ragin concluded that it was an immoral institution, highly injurious to the health of its patients. In his opinion it would be best to discharge the patients and close the hospital. But, he reasoned, will-power alone was not sufficient to achieve this – and it would have been useless anyway. Banish physical and moral filth from one place and it will turn up somewhere else. Therefore one should wait until it disappeared of its own accord. Besides, if people opened a hospital and tolerated it, that could only mean they needed it. All these prejudices, abominations and foul living conditions were necessary, since in the course of time they would be converted into something useful, like manure into fertile soil. There was nothing good in this world that did not contain some abomination in its earliest beginnings.

After taking up his appointment Ragin adopted a rather indifferent attitude to all these abuses, it seemed. All he did was ask the orderlies and nurses not to sleep in the wards and installed two instrument cupboards. But the superintendent, matron, the doctor's assistant and the surgical erysipelas stayed put.

Ragin has great admiration for intelligence and honesty but he has neither the character nor the confidence in his own authority to establish a decent and reasonable environment. To give orders, to prohibit or to insist is quite beyond him. It is as if he has solemnly vowed never to raise his voice or use the imperative mood. He even finds it difficult to say 'Give' or 'Bring'. When he is hungry he coughs irresolutely and tells his cook: 'I wouldn't say no to some tea . . .'; or: 'I rather fancy some lunch.' But he hasn't the gumption to tell the superintendent to stop pilfering, or to sack him, or to do away completely with his unnecessary, parasitical position there. When Ragin is tricked or flattered, when he is handed some patently falsified accounts for signature, he turns red as beetroot and feels guilty – but still he signs. When patients complain of hunger or about rude nurses he becomes flustered.

'All right, all right,' he mutters guiltily. 'I'll see to it later. Probably some sort of misunderstanding . . .'

At first Ragin worked very diligently. He received patients from morning to night, performed operations and even did midwifery. The ladies said that he was very attentive and an excellent diagnostician, especially of children's ailments. But as time passed he became visibly weary of the monotony and obvious futility of his work. One day he might see thirty patients, the next the number would rise to thirty-five, the day after that to forty, and so on, day in day out, year in year out. Yet the death-rate in the town didn't drop, nor did the number of patients who came for treatment. To provide forty patients with any real help in the few hours between breakfast and lunch was physically impossible and the result was deception, whether he liked it or not. In the current year he had seen twelve thousand patients – in plain language twelve thousand people had been duped. But to put seriously ill patients in wards and treat them according to the rules of medical science was impossible, since the rules they followed were in no way scientific. However, if one were to give up theorizing and follow the rules slavishly, like the other doctors, then the most urgent need was for proper hygiene and ventilation instead of filth, wholesome food instead of soup made from sour, stinking cabbage, and honest assistants, not thieves.

And why stop people dying if death was the normal, rightful end of everyone? What does it matter if some huckster or bureaucrat lives an extra five or ten years? If one views the aim of medicine as the mitigation of suffering, the question naturally arises: *why* mitigate it? In the first place, we are told that suffering leads mankind to perfection; in the second place, if man could teach himself how to alleviate suffering with pills and drops he would completely jettison religion and philosophy in which, up to now, he has found not only a defence against all kinds of ills, but even happiness. On his deathbed Pushkin[2] suffered terrible agonies. Heine,[3] poor man, lay paralysed for years. So why prevent the illness of a mere Andrey Yefimych Ragin or Matryona Savishna, whose lives are empty and would be utterly vacuous and amoeba-like were it not for suffering?

Deflated by such arguments, Ragin lost heart and ended his daily visits to the hospital.

VI

This is his daily routine. Usually he rises at eight, dresses and has breakfast. Then he either sits in his study and reads or goes to the hospital where, in the narrow, dark little corridor, sit the out-patients, waiting for surgery to begin. Orderlies and nurses rush past, their boots clattering on the brick floor, emaciated patients pass through in their smocks, corpses and bedpans are carried out, children cry; there's a terrible draught. Ragin knows what torment such an environment must be for the feverish and consumptive – and for all sensitive patients – but what can one do? In the surgery he is met by his assistant, Sergey Sergeich, a fat little man with a beardless, well-washed chubby face. With those gentle, relaxed manners and his new, loose-fitting suit he looks more like a senator than a doctor's assistant. He has a huge private practice in town, wears a white tie[4] and thinks he knows more than the doctor, who has no practice at all. In one corner of the surgery is a large icon in a case, with a large lamp, and next to it a candleholder in a white cover. On the walls are portraits of bishops, a view of Svyatogorsk Monastery[5] and garlands of dried cornflowers. Sergey Sergeich is religious and loves magnificence. The icon was put there at his expense. On Sundays, at his command, a patient reads the Psalms aloud in the surgery and after the reading Sergey Sergeich goes in person around all the wards with his censer and burns incense in them.

There are many patients and little time, so the examinations are limited to a few questions and the distribution of remedies such as ammoniated liniment or castor oil. Dr Ragin sits there, his cheek resting on his fist, lost in thought and mechanically asking questions. Sergey Sergeich sits there too, rubbing his hands and putting in a word now and then.

'We become ill and suffer hardship,' he says, 'because we don't pray enough to all-merciful God. Oh yes!'

During surgery hours Dr Ragin doesn't perform any operations. He has long been out of practice and the sight of blood has an unpleasant effect on him. When he has to open a child's mouth to examine its throat and the child cries and defends itself with its tiny hands, his head spins and his eyes fill with tears. He hastily writes out a prescription and gestures to the mother to take her child away as quickly as possible.

He soon tires of his patients' timidity, of their silly talk and stupidity, of the proximity of the grandiose Sergey Sergeich, of the portraits on the walls and of his own questions that he has been asking over and over for more than twenty years. And he leaves after having seen five or six patients. The rest are seen by his assistant.

Buoyed by the pleasant thought that he has given up private practice long ago – thank God! – and that there is no one to disturb him, the moment he is home he sits at his study table and begins to read. He reads voraciously and always with great pleasure. Half his salary is spent on books and of the six rooms in his flat three are crammed with books and old magazines. Most of all he likes history and philosophy. The only medical journal he subscribes to is *The Physician*,[6] which he always begins to read from the back. At each sitting he reads for several hours without break and this never tires him. He does not read as quickly and impulsively as Gromov used to do, but incisively, often pausing at passages that please him or which he does not understand. He always keeps a carafe of vodka on a table next to his books, with a gherkin or pickled apple lying on the table cloth, without a plate. Every half hour he pours himself a glass of vodka and drinks it without taking his eyes off his book. Then, again without looking up, he feels for the gherkin and takes a small bite.

At three o'clock he gingerly approaches the kitchen door and coughs. 'Daryushka,' he says, 'I wouldn't mind some dinner.' After a poor, badly served meal Dr Ragin wanders around his rooms, his arms crossed on his chest: he is thinking. Four o'clock strikes, then five, and still he is pacing and thinking. The kitchen door occasionally creaks and Daryushka's sleepy red face appears.

'Andrey Yefimych, isn't it time for your beer?'[7] she asks solicitously.

'No, not yet,' he replies. 'I'll wait a bit . . .'

Towards evening Mikhail Averyanych, the postmaster, usually arrives. He is the one person in the entire town whose company doesn't weary Ragin. Once Mikhail Averyanych had been a very wealthy landowner and cavalry officer, but he lost everything and straitened circumstances obliged him to take a job in late middle age at the post office. He has a lively, healthy look, magnificent grey sideburns, refined manners and a loud but pleasant voice. He is kind and sensitive, but hot-tempered. When a post office customer complains, voices dissent or simply starts arguing, Mikhail Averyanych turns purple, shakes all over and shouts thunderously: 'Silence!' Consequently the post office has long acquired the reputation of a fearsome place to be. Mikhail Averyanych likes and respects Ragin for his erudition and lofty principles, but he treats the other townspeople condescendingly, as if they were his subordinates.

'Well, here I am!' he says as he comes in. 'How are you, my dear chap? I suppose you're bored with me by now, eh?'

'On the contrary, I'm delighted,' the doctor replies. 'I'm always glad to see you!'

The friends sit on the study sofa and smoke for a while in silence.

'Daryushka! I wonder if we might have a little beer?' Ragin asks.

The first bottle is drunk – also in silence: the doctor is deep in thought and Mikhail Averyanych has the gay, animated expression of someone with fascinating things to relate. It is always the doctor who begins the conversation.

'What a pity,' he slowly says, quietly shaking his head without looking at his friend (he never looks people in the eye). 'What a great pity, my dear Mikhail Averyanych, there's simply no one in this town who can or who would like to conduct an intelligent conversation. That's a great drawback as far as we're concerned. Even the educated classes don't rise above mediocrity – the level of their development, I assure you, is in no way higher than that of the lower classes.'

'Perfectly true! I do agree.'

'And as you yourself know very well,' the doctor softly continues, with quiet deliberation, 'in this world everything is insignificant and boring except the higher spiritual manifestations of the human intellect. The intellect draws a sharp distinction between animals and men, it indicates the divinity of man and to some extent even compensates him for the fact that he's not immortal. Consequently, the mind is our only possible source of pleasure. But we don't see or hear any evidence of intellect around us – that means we are deprived of genuine pleasure. True, we do have our books, but all that's poles apart from living conversation and personal contact. If I may use a rather infelicitous simile, books are the accompaniment whilst conversation is the singing.'

'Perfectly true!'

Silence follows. Daryushka emerges from the kitchen and with an expression of mute anguish and with her head propped on her fist she stops in the doorway to listen.

'Oh dear!' sighs Mikhail Averyanych. 'It's no good looking for intellect among the people of today!'

And he starts telling how healthy, cheerful and interesting life was in the old days, how enlightened the Russian intelligentsia was, how highly concepts of honour and friendship were valued. They would lend money without IOUs and to refuse a friend in need a helping hand was considered shameful. And what crusades there were, what adventures, skirmishes, what comrades-in-arms, what women! As for the Caucasus – such an amazing part of the world! There was that battalion commander's wife, a really odd woman, who would dress as an officer and ride out at night into the mountains, alone, without any escort. She was said to be having an affair in a village up there with some petty prince.

'Mother of God!' sighs Daryushka.

'And how we drank! And what fanatical liberals we were!'

Ragin listens but hears nothing: he is pondering something else as he sips his beer.

'I often dream of clever people and having conversations with them,' he says unexpectedly, interrupting Mikhail Averyanych. 'My father gave me an excellent education, but he was influenced by the ideas of the sixties and forced me to become a doctor. I think that had I disobeyed him I might now be at the very hub of current intellectual activity. Probably I'd be a member of some faculty. Of course, the intellect isn't eternal either, it's transitory, but you know very well the great liking I have for it. Life is a vicious trap. When a thinking person reaches manhood and his consciousness has matured, he cannot help thinking that he's caught in a snare, as it were, from which there's no escape. In fact he's been called into life from non-existence against his will, by some sort of accident . . . Why? If he wants to know the meaning and purpose of his existence, either he meets with silence or is palmed off with some nonsense. He knocks, but the door isn't opened. Death creeps up on him – also against his will. It's the same with people in prison: united in common misfortune they find things easier if they all join together. And similarly in life – you don't notice these pitfalls when men inclined towards analysis and generalization come together and spend their time exchanging proud, unfettered ideas. In this sense the intellect is an indispensable source of enjoyment.'

'Perfectly true!'

With his eyes still averted from his friend, in a quiet voice and constantly pausing, Ragin continues to discuss clever people and conversations with them, while Mikhail Averyanych is all ears.

'Perfectly true!' he agrees.

'So you don't believe in the immortality of the soul?' the postmaster suddenly asks.

'No, my dear Mikhail Averyanych, I do not. Nor do I have any reason to believe.'

'I must say, I have my doubts too. Even so, I still have the feeling that I shall never die. "Heavens!" I think to myself, "you old fogey! It's time for you to die!" But deep down some little voice keeps telling me: "Don't you believe it, you'll never die!"'

Soon after nine o'clock Mikhail Averyanych leaves. As he puts on his fur coat in the hall he says with a sigh:

'What a godforsaken hole fate has landed us in! And what's most annoying – this is where we'll have to die. Oh dear!'

VII

After seeing his friend out Ragin sits at his table and starts reading again. The evening hush, and then the stillness of night, are not broken by a single sound. Time seems to be standing still, becomes transfixed, like the doctor over his book, so that nothing seems to exist except the book and the lamp with its green shade. The doctor's coarse, rough face gradually lights up with a smile of deep emotion and delight at the achievements of the mind of man. 'Oh, why isn't man immortal?' he asks himself. 'Why these cerebral cortices and convolutions, why vision, speech, sensation, genius, if all are doomed to pass into the soil and finally grow cold with the earth's crust and then to be borne for millions of years with the earth around the sun, without rhyme or reason? Merely for him to grow cold and be whirled around there was absolutely no need to draw man – with his sublime, almost divine intellect – out of nothingness and then to turn him into clay, as if in mockery.

'Transmutation of matter! But how cowardly to console oneself with this substitute for immortality! The unconscious processes at work in nature are even lower than human folly, for in folly there is at least consciousness and volition, but in these processes there is nothing! Only a coward who displays more fear than dignity in the face of death can comfort himself with the thought that in the course of time his body will be reborn, to exist as grass, as a stone, as a toad. It is just as strange to seek immortality in the transmutation of matter as predicting a brilliant future for the case after a valuable violin has been smashed and rendered useless.'

When the clock strikes Ragin leans back in his chair and closes his eyes to reflect for a while. Moved by the fine thoughts he has gleaned from his book, he happens to review his past and present. The past is loathsome and best forgotten. And his present is no different from the past. He knows that at the very moment his thoughts are whirling around the sun with the frozen earth, men are lying tormented by illness and physical filth in the huge block next to his lodgings. Perhaps one of them cannot sleep for the insects, is contracting erysipelas and groaning because his bandages are too tight.

Perhaps patients are playing cards with the nurses and drinking vodka. In the current year twelve thousand people had been duped; the whole hospital regime was based on pilfering, squabbles, slander, favouritism and gross quackery, just as it had been twenty years before – and it still was an immoral institution, extremely damaging to the patients' health. He knows that behind the barred windows in Ward No. 6 Nikita beats the patients with his fists and that every day Moses goes begging in the streets.

For all that he is well aware that over the past twenty-five years a fantastic change had taken place in medicine. In his university days he used to think that medicine would soon suffer the fate of alchemy or metaphysics but now, when he reads at night, the advances in medicine move him deeply, fill him with astonishment and even with delight. And in fact, what unexpected brilliance! What a revolution! Thanks to antiseptics, operations are being performed that the great Pirogov[8] did not think possible, even in his wildest dreams. Ordinary district doctors do not think twice about operating on the knee joint, out of one hundred stomach operations there had been only one fatality, whilst gallstones are so trivial they are not even written about. Syphilis is being treated with radically new methods. And what about the theory of heredity, hypnotism, the discoveries of Pasteur[9] and Koch,[10] hygiene and statistics and our own Russian rural medicine? Compared with the past, psychiatry with its current classification[11] of diseases, its diagnostic procedures and methods of treatment, had taken an enormous leap forward. No longer are the insane doused with cold water. Nor are they put in straitjackets: they are treated as human beings and according to newspaper reports they even have their own dramatic entertainments and dances. Ragin knows very well that with modern views and tastes as they are such abominations as Ward No. 6 are possible only in a small town a hundred and twenty-five miles from the nearest railway, where the mayor and councillors are semi-literate barbarians who look upon doctors as high priests who must be trusted blindly, even if they pour molten lead down patients' throats. Anywhere else the public and the press would have smashed this little Bastille to pieces long ago.

'Well, what's the upshot of all this?' Ragin asks himself, opening his eyes. 'What does it prove? Antiseptics, Koch, Pasteur are all very well, but nothing has basically changed. Sickness and mortality still exist. They put on shows and organize dances for the lunatics, but still they don't let them go out when they want to. Therefore it's all nonsense and vanity, and there's really no difference between the best clinic in Vienna and my hospital.'

But vexation and a feeling akin to envy do not allow him to remain indifferent. Exhaustion is probably to blame. His weary head nods towards his book, he cushions his face on his hands to make himself more comfortable.

'I'm serving a harmful cause,' he thinks, 'and I receive a salary from those I deceive. So I'm dishonest. But then I'm nothing by myself, just a mere particle in a necessary social evil. All the district officials are crooks and they get paid for doing nothing . . . That means it's not myself who is guilty of dishonesty, but the times we live in . . . If I were to be born two hundred years from now I'd be a different person.'

When the clock strikes three he puts the lamp out and goes to his bedroom. But he doesn't feel sleepy.

VIII

Two years before, in a fit of generosity, the Rural District Council decided to allocate three hundred roubles annually to reinforce the personnel at the town hospital until the district hospital was opened. So they invited a local doctor, Yevgeny Fyodorych Khobotov to help out. This Khobotov is a very young man, not yet thirty, tall and dark, with broad cheekbones and tiny eyes: most likely his ancestors were of Asiatic descent. He arrived without a copeck to his name, with only a small suitcase and accompanied by a young, most unattractive woman whom he called his cook. This woman had a young baby. Yevgeny Fyodorych wears a peaked cap, top boots and a sheepskin jacket in winter. He soon became great friends with Ragin's assistant Sergey Sergeich and also with the hospital bursar, but for some reason he refers to the rest of the officials as aristocrats and avoids them. In his entire flat there is only one book – *Latest Prescriptions of the Vienna Clinic 1881*. This little book he invariably takes with him when visiting patients. In the evenings he plays billiards at the club, but he doesn't care for cards. In conversations he simply loves using such expressions as: 'What a palaver!', 'Hocus-pocus with icing on top', 'Don't confuse the issue', and so on.

He visits the hospital about twice a week, inspects the wards and sees out-patients. The total lack of antiseptics and cupping-glasses worries him, but he doesn't introduce any changes for fear of upsetting Ragin, whom he considers an old rogue, suspects of being a man of means and secretly envies. He would love to have Ragin's job.

IX

One spring-like evening at the end of March, when the snow had melted and starlings sang in the hospital garden, the doctor came out to see his friend the postmaster to the gate. At that moment the Jew Moses happened to come into the yard, bearing booty from the town. He was hatless, wore thin galoshes over his sockless feet and held a small bag of coins he had collected.

'Give us a copeck!' he asked the doctor, shivering from the cold and grinning.

Ragin, who could never refuse, gave him a ten copeck piece.

'That's very bad,' he thought as he glanced at the Jew's bare legs and thin red ankles. 'It's wet outside.'

Prompted by a feeling close to both compassion and squeamishness, he followed the Jew into the building, glancing in turn at his bald head and then at his ankles. When the doctor entered Nikita leapt up from his rubbish heap and stood to attention.

'Good evening, Nikita,' Ragin said softly. 'Perhaps you could let this Jew have a pair of boots, he might catch cold.'

'Yes, sir, I'll tell the superintendent.'

'Please do that. Ask him in my name. Tell him I requested it.'

The door from the lobby into the ward was open. Gromov, who was lying on his bed, leaning on one elbow and listening anxiously to the strange voice, suddenly ran into the middle of the ward with a flushed, malicious face and his eyes bulging.

'The doctor's arrived!' he shouted and burst out laughing. 'He's finally made it! Gentlemen, I offer my congratulations, the doctor's honouring us with his presence. Bloody vermin!' he screeched and stamped his foot in a fit of rage never before seen in the ward. 'Exterminate the vermin! No, killing's not good enough! Drown him in the latrines!'

Hearing this Ragin peeped into the ward.

'For what?' he softly asked.

'For *what*!?' shouted Gromov, approaching him menacingly and frenetically wrapping his smock around himself. 'For *what*? Thief!' he said disgustedly and twisted his lips as if about to spit. 'Charlatan! Hangman!'

'Calm yourself,' Ragin said, smiling guiltily. 'I assure you I've never stolen anything and you're probably greatly exaggerating the other things. I see you're angry with me. Calm yourself if you can, I beg you, and tell me why you're so angry.'

'Why are you keeping me here?'

'Because you're ill.'

'Yes, I'm ill. But tens, hundreds of madmen roam around at will, because you in your ignorance cannot distinguish them from the sane. Why do I and all these other poor devils have to be cooped up here like scapegoats? You, your assistant, the superintendent and all you hospital scum are, as far as morals go, infinitely lower than each one of us, so why are we cooped up and you aren't? Where's the logic?'

'Morals and logic have nothing to do with it. It all depends on chance. Those who are put here stay here, and those who aren't are free. That's all there is to it. There's no morality or logic in the fact that I'm a doctor and you're mentally ill – it's pure chance.'

'I don't understand this rubbish,' Gromov said in a hollow voice and sat on his bed.

Moses, whom Nikita did not dare search in the doctor's presence, spread out his booty on the bed – bits of bread, paper and small bones. Still shivering from the cold he rapidly muttered something in Yiddish, in a singsong voice. Probably he imagined he had opened a shop.

'Set me free!' Gromov said – and his voice trembled.

'I cannot.'

'Why not? Why ever not?'

'Because it's not in my power. Just think for yourself: what good would it do you if I released you? All right, go. The townspeople or the police will only arrest you and send you back here.'

'Yes, yes, that's true,' Gromov murmured, rubbing his forehead. 'It's terrible! But what can I do? *What?*'

Ragin took a liking to Gromov's voice and his youthful, clever, grimacing face. He wanted to be kind to the young man and calm him down, so he sat beside him on the bed and thought for a moment.

'You asked me what you can do,' he said. 'The best thing in your position would be to run away from here. But unfortunately that's useless. You would be arrested. When society decides to protect itself from criminals, the mentally ill and undesirables in general, it is invincible. There's only one thing left: console yourself with the thought that your stay here is necessary.'

'It's not necessary to anyone.'

'Once prisons and lunatic asylums exist someone has to live in them. If it isn't you it will be me; if not me, then someone else. But you wait. In the distant future, when prisons and asylums are no longer, there will be neither barred windows nor hospital smocks. Such a time is bound to come – sooner or later, of course.'

Gromov smiled sarcastically.

'You're joking,' he said, screwing up his eyes. 'People like yourself and your assistant Nikita couldn't care less about the future, but you can rest assured, my dear sir, better times will come! What if I do express myself tritely – yes, you may laugh! – but one day the dawn of a new life will begin to glow, truth will triumph and our day will come! I shan't live to see it – I'll have pegged out by then – but someone's great grandchildren will. I salute them with all my heart and soul. I rejoice for them! Forward! May God help you, my friends!'

Gromov's eyes gleamed. He stood up and stretched his arms towards the window.

'I bless you from behind these bars!' he continued, his voice quivering with emotion. 'Long live truth! I rejoice!'

'I can see no particular reason for rejoicing,' Ragin said, finding Gromov's gesticulations rather theatrical, but at the same time very pleasing. 'There will be no more prisons or asylums and truth, as you chose to put it, will triumph. But the *essence* of things will not change, the law of nature will remain the same. People will fall ill, grow old and die, just as now. However magnificent the dawn that will illumine your life, in the end you'll still be nailed down in your coffin and thrown into a pit.'

'What about immortality?'

'Don't talk nonsense!'

'*You* may not believe, but *I* do. Someone in Voltaire or Dostoyevsky[12] says that if there were no God man would have invented Him. But I strongly believe that, if there's no immortality, man's powerful intellect will invent it sooner or later.'

'Well said,' replied Ragin, smiling with pleasure. 'It's good that you believe. With faith such as yours you would be living in clover even if you were bricked up in a wall. Did you have a good education?'

'Yes, I went to university, but I never graduated.'

'You're a thoughtful, serious-minded man. You're the kind who would find peace of mind in any surroundings. Unfettered, profound reflection that aspires to unravel the meaning of life, utter contempt for the vain bustle of this world – these are two blessings higher than which man has known nothing. And these you can possess, even if you lived behind three rows of bars. Diogenes[13] lived in a tub, yet he was happier than all the monarchs of this world.'

'Your Diogenes was a blockhead,' Gromov gloomily intoned. 'Why do you keep telling me about Diogenes and some sort of comprehension of life?' he said, suddenly flaring up and leaping to his feet. 'I love life! I love it passionately! I suffer from persecution mania, from a constant, agonizing dread, but there are moments when I'm seized by a lust for life and then I'm afraid I might go out of my mind. I long to live. Oh, so much!'

In great excitement he walked up and down the ward.

'When I daydream I have visions!' he said, lowering his voice. 'Certain people come and visit me, I hear voices and music and it seems as if I'm walking through some woods, or along the seashore and I have a terrible yearning for all the hustle and bustle. Tell me, what's the latest news?' Gromov asked. 'What's going on?'

'Do you mean in town or in general?'

'First tell me about the town, then things in general.'

'Well, what shall I tell you? It's excruciatingly boring in the town . . . No one to talk to, no one to listen. There are no new faces. But not so long ago a young doctor by the name of Khobotov arrived.'

'He arrived when I was still around. What's he like – a complete oaf?'

'Yes, a bit of a philistine. Do you know, it's a strange thing . . . by all accounts, in Moscow and St Petersburg there's no intellectual stagnation, things are buzzing, so there must be real people there. But for some reason they persist in sending us people who are pretty useless. It's an unlucky town!'

'Yes, an unlucky town,' Gromov sighed and then burst out laughing. 'But how are things in general? What do the papers and magazines say?'

In the ward it was already dark. The doctor rose and, still standing, began to describe what was being written abroad and in Russia, and what the latest intellectual trends were. Gromov listened attentively and asked questions. But suddenly, as if he had remembered something awful, he clutched his head and threw himself on his bed with his back to the doctor.

'What's wrong?' Ragin asked.

'That's all you're going to hear from me today!' Gromov snapped. 'Leave me alone!'

'But why?'

'I'm telling you to leave me alone. To hell with it!'

Ragin shrugged his shoulders, sighed and went out. As he passed through the lobby he said:

'I wonder if you wouldn't mind cleaning up a bit here, Nikita. There's a terrible smell!'

'Yes, sir.'

'What a pleasant young man!' thought Ragin as he returned to his lodgings. 'All the time I've been here he's the first person I can really talk to. He can argue and he takes an interest in what really matters.'

After reading and going to bed, he couldn't stop thinking about Gromov and when he awoke next morning he remembered that he had got to know an intelligent, interesting man – and so he decided to pay him another visit at the first opportunity.

X

Gromov was lying in the same position as on the day before, clutching his head and with his legs tucked underneath him. His face was hidden.

'Good morning, my friend,' said Ragin. 'You're not sleeping?'

'Firstly, I'm not your friend,' Gromov replied into his pillow, 'and secondly you're wasting your time. You won't get one word out of me.'

'That's odd,' Ragin muttered. 'Yesterday we were having such a nice friendly chat, but suddenly you got the needle and broke off. Probably it's because I expressed myself awkwardly, or perhaps because I expressed an opinion that conflicted with your own convictions.'

'You won't catch me out!' Gromov said, raising himself a little and looking at the doctor ironically and anxiously. His eyes were bloodshot. 'You can go and do your spying and interrogating somewhere else, you're wasting your time here. I saw very well what you were up to yesterday.'

'What a crazy idea!' laughed the doctor. 'So you suppose I'm a spy?'

'Yes, I do suppose! Whether you're a spy or a doctor sent to test me . . . it makes no difference . . .'

'Well, I'm sorry to say this, but you really are a strange person!'

The doctor sat on a stool beside the bed and shook his head reproachfully.

'Let's suppose you're right,' he said. 'Let's suppose I'm acting treacherously and trying to catch you out, so that I can hand you over to the police. They'd arrest you and put you on trial. But will you be any worse off in court or in prison than here? And would deportation or hard labour in Siberia be any worse than staying cooped up here in this building? I don't think so . . . So what are you afraid of?'

These words visibly affected Gromov . . . he calmly sat down.

It was about half past four, the time when Ragin usually paced his rooms and Daryushka asked if it was time for his beer. The weather was calm and bright.

'I went for a stroll after dinner and I thought I'd drop in, as you can see,' said the doctor. 'Spring is here.'

'What month is it? March?' Gromov asked.

'Yes, the end of March.'

'Is it very muddy outside?'

'Not very. The garden paths are clear.'

'It would be nice to go for a carriage drive somewhere out of town now,' Gromov said, rubbing his bloodshot eyes as if he were sleepy. 'And then come back to a warm, cosy study . . . and let a decent doctor cure my headache . . . For years now I haven't lived like a human being. It's so foul here! Unbearably disgusting!'

After yesterday evening's excitement he was tired and sluggish, and he spoke reluctantly. His fingers twitched and clearly he was suffering from a severe headache.

'Between a warm comfortable study and this ward there's absolutely no difference,' Ragin said. 'Man finds peace and contentment within himself, not outside.'

'What do you mean?'

'The ordinary man finds good or evil outside himself, that is, in carriage rides or in warm studies. But the thinking man finds them within himself.'

'Go and preach that philosophy in Greece, where it's warm and where it smells of orange blossom. But it doesn't suit our climate. To whom was I talking about Diogenes yesterday? Was it you?'

'Yes, it was yesterday, to me.'

'Diogenes didn't need a study or a warm house. He was warm enough without them. It's all very well, lying in his little tub and eating oranges and olives! But just let him come and live in Russia – he'll be longing for a warm room in May, let alone December! He'd be doubled up with the cold.'

'No. Cold, like any other kind of pain, can be ignored. Marcus Aurelius[14] said: "Pain is the living concept of pain. Will yourself to change this concept, shrug it off, stop complaining and the pain will go." It's true. Sages or any thinking, reflective men are distinguished by this very contempt for suffering. They are always contented and they are surprised by nothing.'

'So, I'm an idiot, because I suffer, because I'm discontented and because I marvel at man's baseness.'

'You are wrong. If you stopped to think you'd begin to understand how trifling these external things that disturb us really are. You must strive to find the meaning of life, for there lies true bliss.'

'*Understand?*' Gromov said, frowning. 'External? Internal? I'm sorry, but I don't follow. I know only one thing,' he added, rising and glaring at the doctor. 'I do know that God created me from warm blood and nerves. Oh yes, sir! And organic tissue, if it bears the spark of life, reacts to all sorts of stimuli. And I do react! I react to pain by weeping or shouting, to baseness with indignation, to vileness with revulsion. In my opinion that's a fact, that's what's called *life*. The lower the organism the less sensitive it is and the more feebly it reacts to stimuli. The higher it is, the more sensitively and energetically it responds to the external world. How is it you don't know that? Fancy a doctor not knowing such plain facts! To despise suffering, to be ever contented and never marvel at anything you must sink to *his* level!' – and Gromov pointed to the fat, bloated peasant – 'or you must so harden yourself by suffering that you lose all sensitivity. In other words, you must stop living. I'm sorry, I'm no sage or philosopher,' Gromov continued irritably, 'and that kind of stuff is beyond me. I'm not much good at arguing.'

'But you argue very well.'

'The Stoics, whom you are travestying, were remarkable men, but their teaching came to a dead end two thousand years ago and hasn't advanced one inch since. Nor will it ever advance, since it's not practical or applicable to real life. It has only succeeded with the minority, which spends its time studying and sampling all sorts of creeds, but the majority never understood it. A doctrine that preaches indifference to wealth and creature comforts, contempt for suffering and death, is beyond the comprehension of the vast majority, since this majority never had any knowledge of wealth or creature comforts. And for that majority contempt for suffering would amount to contempt for life itself, since man's whole being consists of the sensations of cold, hunger, insults, loss and a Hamlet-like fear of death. These sensations are the quintessence of life, which might strike you as tiresome or hateful, but is never to be despised. And so I repeat, the teaching of the Stoics can never have a future. On the other hand, as you can see, from the beginning of the century to the present day, the struggle for survival, sensitivity to pain, responsiveness to stimuli, are all moving forward . . .'

Gromov suddenly lost the thread, paused and rubbed his forehead in annoyance.

'I had something important to say, but I'm all muddled up . . .' he said. 'What was I saying? Oh yes! What I wanted to say is this: one of the Stoics sold himself into slavery as a ransom for a friend. So, as you can see for yourself, the Stoic reacted to a stimulus, since so magnanimous a deed as self-annihilation on behalf of one's neighbour calls for an outraged, feeling heart. Here in prison I've forgotten all I ever learned, otherwise I would have remembered something else to illustrate my point. Now, shall we consider Christ? He reacted to reality with weeping, smiling, grieving, being angry, with yearning even. He didn't go forth to meet suffering with a smile, nor did He despise death, but prayed in the Garden of Gethsemane that He might not drain the cup of woe.'[15]

Gromov laughed and sat down.

'Let's suppose peace and contentment are not outside a man, but within him,' he said. 'Let's suppose we should despise suffering and marvel at nothing. But what grounds do *you* have for preaching this? Are you a sage? A philosopher?'

'No, I'm not a philosopher, but everyone should preach this creed because it's rational.'

'But I'd like to know why you consider yourself competent to pass judgement on the meaning of life, on contempt for suffering and the rest of it? Have you ever suffered? Do you have any conception of suffering? Tell me, were you beaten as a child?'

'No, my parents were averse to corporal punishment.'

'But I was cruelly beaten by my father. He was a harsh, haemorrhoidal bureaucrat with a long nose and yellow neck. But let's talk about you. In your whole life no one so much as laid a finger on you, no one frightened you, no one beat you. You're as strong as an ox. You grew up under your father's wing and studied at his expense. You immediately found yourself a nice cushy job. For more than twenty years you lived rent-free, with heating, lighting, servants. At the same time you had the right to work how and as much as you pleased – even to do nothing. By nature you're idle and feeble, you've tried to arrange your life so that nothing disturbs you or forces you to budge from where you are. You delegated your work to your assistant and other scum, while you yourself basked in the warmth and quiet. You piled up money, read the occasional book, sweetened your life with reflections on all kinds of elevated rubbish and became a hard drinker.' (Gromov glanced at the doctor's red nose.) 'In other words, you've never seen life, you know nothing about it and are acquainted with reality only in theory. But you despise suffering and are surprised at nothing for one very simple reason: your philosophy of vanity of vanities, the external and internal, contempt for life, suffering and death, understanding the meaning of life, the True Good – that kind of philosophy's best suited to a Russian layabout. For instance, you see a peasant beating his wife. Why interfere? Let him beat her! They'll both die sooner or later anyway. Besides, it's the person who does the beating who injures himself, not his victim. Getting drunk is stupid and indecent, but you'll die whether you drink or not. A peasant woman comes to you with toothache. What of it? Pain is only our idea of pain and besides, in this world you can't expect to get away without illness, all of us must die. So, away with you woman and don't interfere with my thoughts or my vodka! A young man comes for advice: what should he do, how should he live? Someone else would have stopped to think before replying, but you're always ready with an answer: aspire to discover the meaning of life or the True Good. But what is this fantastic "True Good"? There's no answer, of course. Here we are imprisoned behind bars, left to rot, tortured, but all that's beautiful and rational, because there's absolutely no difference between this ward and a warm comfortable study! A very convenient philosophy – just do nothing, your conscience is clear and you can consider yourself a very wise man . . . No, my dear sir, that's not philosophy or reflection or breadth of vision, but idleness, mortification of the flesh and stupefaction . . .

'Yes!' Gromov declared, losing his temper again. 'You despise suffering, but just catch your finger in the door and you'll bawl your head off!'

'But perhaps I wouldn't bawl my head off,' Ragin said with a gentle smile.

'Oh yes you would! Suppose you were suddenly paralysed or some bumptious moron used his position and rank to insult you in public and you knew he'd get away with it – then you'd know what it means to tell others to aspire to understanding and the True Good!'

'Highly original!' Ragin exclaimed, beaming with pleasure and rubbing his hands. 'I'm agreeably impressed by your love of generalization and the character sketch you've just been good enough to draw of me is simply brilliant. Talking to you gives me immense pleasure, I must confess. Well now, you've had your say so please be good enough to listen to what I have to say . . .'

XI

This conversation lasted about another hour and clearly made a deep impression on Ragin. He took to visiting the ward every day. He went there in the morning and afternoon, and often darkness would find him in discussion with Gromov. At first Gromov was wary of him, suspected him of evil motives and openly voiced his hostility. But then he grew used to him and his brusque manner became one of indulgent irony.

A rumour soon spread through the hospital that Dr Ragin was paying daily visits to Ward No. 6. No one – neither the medical assistant, nor Nikita, nor the nurses – could understand why he went there. Why did he sit there for hours on end? What did he talk about? Why didn't he write any prescriptions? His behaviour struck everyone as most odd. Mikhail Averyanych often failed to find him at home – something that had never happened before – and Daryushka was most anxious, since the doctor did not drink his beer at the usual time and sometimes was even late for dinner.

One day – it was the end of June – Dr Khobotov went to see Dr Ragin on business. Not finding him at home he went to look for him in the yard, where he was told that the old doctor had gone to see the mental patients. When he entered the building and paused in the lobby, he heard the following conversation:

'We'll never see eye to eye and you'll never succeed in converting me to your faith,' Gromov was saying irritably. 'You know nothing of reality, you've never suffered, you've only fed on the sufferings of others, like a leech. But I've suffered constantly from the day I was born. Therefore I'm telling you bluntly that I consider myself superior to you, more competent in every way. It's not for *you* to teach *me*!'

'I certainly would not presume to convert you to my faith,' Ragin said softly, regretting the other's reluctance to understand him. 'But that's not the point, my friend. The point isn't that you have suffered, whereas I haven't. Suffering and joy are transitory; let's forget them – and good luck to them! The point is, you and I are thinking men;

we see ourselves as people who are capable of thinking and arguing, and this creates a bond between us, however much our views may differ. If you only knew, my friend, how weary I am of this universal idiocy, this mediocrity, this obtuseness. If you only knew the joy it gives me every time I have a talk with you! You're an intelligent man and I thoroughly enjoy your company.'

Khobotov opened the door an inch or so and peered into the ward: Gromov in his night-cap and Dr Ragin were sitting side by side on the bed. The lunatic was pulling faces, shuddering and convulsively clutching his smock. The doctor sat quite still, his head bowed, and his face was flushed, helpless and sad. Khobotov shrugged his shoulders, grinned and exchanged glances with Nikita, who also shrugged his shoulders.

Next day Khobotov and the medical assistant went to the building. Both of them stood in the lobby and listened.

'Seems like the old boy's gone off his rocker!' Khobotov remarked as he left.

'Lord have mercy on us sinners!' sighed the grandiose Sergey Sergeich, carefully skirting the puddles to avoid soiling his brightly polished boots. 'I must confess, my dear Khobotov, I've been expecting this for some time!'

XII

From now on Ragin began to notice a strange atmosphere of mystery around him. Whenever he met orderlies, nurses and patients they would give him quizzical looks and whisper among themselves. Whenever he smilingly went up to Masha, the superintendent's little daughter (whom he loved meeting in the hospital garden), to stroke her head, she would run away from him. Instead of his usual 'perfectly true!' when listening to him, Mikhail Averyanych the postmaster would become strangely embarrassed, mutter 'Oh, yes . . . yes' and look sadly and pensively at him. For some reason he now advised his friend to give up vodka and beer, but he never told him this straight out, but by dropping gentle hints – he was a tactful man – and by telling him stories, of the battalion commander (an excellent fellow), or of the regimental chaplain (a first-class chap), who drank too much and became ill. But once they stopped they became quite well again. Once or twice Ragin's colleague Khobotov called. He too advised him to give up alcohol and without giving any reason recommended that he take potassium bromide.

In August Ragin received a letter from the mayor, asking him to come and see him on a very important matter. Arriving at the town hall at the appointed time, Ragin found there the district military commander, the superintendent of the county high school, a member of the town council, Khobotov, and a corpulent, fair-haired gentleman who was introduced as a doctor. This doctor, who had an unpronounceable Polish name, lived on a stud farm about twenty miles away and just happened to be passing through.

'Here's a little memo that's your cup of tea,' the town councillor said, turning to Ragin after all the others had greeted each other and sat down at the table. 'You see, Dr Khobotov says there ain't much room for a dispensary in the main block and that it ought to be moved to one of the outbuildings. Of course, it ain't no problem moving it, but the main reason is that the place needs repairing.'

'Yes, it certainly will have to be repaired,' Ragin said, after a pause for thought. 'Now, if the corner building is fitted out as a dispensary, then at least five hundred roubles will have to be spent, I suppose. Now, that's unproductive expenditure.'

There was a brief silence.

'Ten years ago,' Ragin said quietly, 'I had the honour to report that this hospital, in its present state, was a luxury the town could ill afford. It was built in the forties, but then more funds were available. This town spends too much on unnecessary buildings and superfluous staff. I think that two model hospitals could be maintained on the same money – if the system were different.'

'Oh, so let's have a new system then,' the councillor said briskly.

'I have already had the honour of submitting my report that the medical department should be under the supervision of the Rural District Council.'

'Yes, transfer the money to the RDC and they'll put it in their pockets!' laughed the fair-haired doctor.

'That's the way things are,' agreed the councillor and he too laughed.

'We must be fair,' Ragin said, giving the fair doctor a feeble, vacant look.

Again a silence. Tea was served. The military commander, highly embarrassed for some reason, touched Ragin's hand across the table and said:

'You've completely forgotten us, doctor! Then you always were like a monk. You don't play cards and you don't care for women. I'm afraid we must bore you here.'

Everyone began to speak of how boring it was for any decent, self-respecting man to live in that town. No theatre, no concerts and at the last club dance there were about twenty ladies and only two men. The young men never danced, but crowded around the bar the whole time or played cards. Without directly looking at anyone, slowly and quietly, Ragin told them what a dreadful pity it was that the townspeople wasted their vital energy, their hearts and minds on cards and idle gossip, that they neither cared nor knew how to pass the time in interesting conversation, in reading, or in enjoying the pleasures that only the mind provides. Intellect alone was interesting and worthy of note, all the rest was petty and squalid. Khobotov listened to his colleague attentively and suddenly asked:

'What's today's date?'

Receiving no reply, he and the fair doctor then began to ask Ragin – in the tone of examiners aware of their own incompetence – what day of the week it was, how many days in a year and was it true that there was a remarkable prophet in Ward No. 6.

In reply to the last question Ragin flushed and said:

'Yes, he's a mental patient, but he's an interesting young man.'

He was asked no further questions.

As he was putting on his coat in the lobby, the military commander put his hand on his shoulder and sighed.

'It's time for us oldies to call it a day!' he said.

When he left the town hall Ragin realized that he had been before a committee appointed to test his mental faculties. Remembering the questions they had asked he went red in the face and for the first time in his life he felt bitterly sorry for medicine.

'My God!' he thought, remembering how those doctors had just examined him. 'Surely it wasn't so long ago that they were going to their psychiatry lectures and sitting their exams? So how come such abysmal ignorance? They don't have a clue about psychiatry!' And for the first time in his life he felt outraged and infuriated.

That evening Mikhail Averyanych called. Without a word of greeting the postmaster went up to him and took him by both hands.

'My dear, dear friend,' he said in a highly emotional voice. 'Please show me that you trust in my sincere affection for you and consider me your friend.' Without allowing Ragin to say one word he continued excitedly:

'My dear friend! I admire you for your education and nobility of soul. Now, listen to me, my dear chap. I know medical etiquette obliged those doctors to hide the truth from you, but I'm going to give it you straight from the shoulder, like an old trooper! You're not well. I'm very sorry, old chap, but it's the truth. It's been noticed by everyone around here for some time now. Dr Khobotov has just told me that you need rest and recreation for the sake of your health. Perfectly true! A splendid idea! In a few days' time I'm taking some leave and going off somewhere for a whiff of fresh air. Now then, prove that you're my friend and come with me! Let's go – it will be like old times again!'

'I feel perfectly well,' Ragin said after a moment's thought. 'But I cannot go. Allow me to prove my friendship in some other way.'

The idea of travelling to some unknown destination, for no good reason, without his books, without Daryushka, rudely breaking a twenty-year-old routine, at first struck him as wild and preposterous. But when he recalled that conversation in the town hall and how terribly depressed he had felt on the way home, the idea of a short break away from that town where stupid people thought him insane appeared most attractive.

'And where precisely are you thinking of going?' he asked.

'To Moscow, St Petersburg, Warsaw. I spent the five happiest years of my life in Warsaw. An amazing city! Let's go, my dear chap!'

XIII

A week later Dr Ragin received a formal request to take a rest – in other words, to resign. He was quite unconcerned at this and a week later he and Mikhail Averyanych were sitting in a mail coach on their way to the nearest station. The weather was cool and bright, the sky blue and the distant prospect crystal clear. They travelled the hundred and twenty-five miles to the station in forty-eight hours, with two overnight stops. Whenever they were given tea in dirty glasses at coaching inns or had to wait ages while they harnessed the horses, Mikhail Averyanych would shake all over and roar: 'Shut up! Don't you argue with me!' As they sat in the coach he told of his travels in the Caucasus and Poland without relenting for one minute. So many adventures, so many encounters! He spoke so loudly and there was such astonishment in his eyes that one could only assume he was lying. Worse still, he breathed right into Ragin's face as he told his tales and laughed into his ear. This irritated the doctor so much that he was unable to think or concentrate.

To economize they travelled third class on the train, in a non-smoker. Half the passengers were respectable people. Mikhail Averyanych soon got to know everyone, going from seat to seat and loudly asserting that it was a big mistake to travel on these disgraceful railways. It was all a huge swindle! What a difference if you travelled on horseback! In one day you could clock up seventy miles and at the end of it feel thoroughly in the pink and fresh as a daisy. And yes, we had crop failures because they went and drained the Pripet marshes.[16] There was the most dreadful shambles *everywhere*. He grew excited, spoke very loudly and did not let anyone else get a word in edgeways. His endless chatter was broken by loud guffaws and his dramatic gesticulations wearied Ragin to the point of exhaustion.

'Which one of us is insane?' he thought in vexation. 'Is it I, who am trying my best not to disturb my fellow-passengers in any way, or that egoist who thinks that he's more clever and interesting than everyone else and consequently doesn't give anyone a moment's peace?'

In Moscow Mikhail Averyanych donned his military tunic without epaulettes and his trousers with red piping. He walked down the street in an officer's peaked cap and greatcoat – and soldiers saluted him. Ragin felt that here was a man who had dissipated all the fine, gentlemanly qualities he had ever possessed and retained only the bad ones. He loved people dancing attendance on him, even when it was quite unnecessary. If a box of matches was lying on the table before him and he saw them, he would still roar to a waiter to bring him a light. He had no qualms about appearing in his underclothes in front of the chambermaid. He did not stand on ceremony with any servants, whoever they were, even elderly ones, and when he was angry called the lot of them blockheads and idiots. All this struck Ragin as behaving like a lord – but it was so cheap and nasty.

Mikhail Averyanych first took his friend to see the Iverian Madonna.[17] He prayed fervently, bowing to the ground and weeping, and when he had finished he sighed deeply. 'Even if you're not a believer you somehow feel more at peace with yourself after praying. Kiss the icon, old chap.'

Ragin was embarrassed as he kissed the icon, but Mikhail Averyanych puffed his lips out, shook his head and whispered some prayers – and once again the tears came to his eyes. Then they visited the Kremlin and saw the Tsar-Cannon and the Tsar-Bell[18] – and they even touched them with their fingers. They admired the view across the Moscow River and spent some time in St Saviour's Temple and the Rumyantsev Museum.[19]

They dined at Testov's.[20] Mikhail Averyanych gazed long at the menu, stroking his side-whiskers and then pronouncing in the voice of a gourmet, of one completely at home in restaurants:

'Well now, what are you going to feed us on today, old chum?'

XIV

The doctor walked, looked, ate and drank, but his feelings were still the same: of annoyance with Mikhail Averyanych. He longed for some respite from his friend, to escape from him, to go somewhere and hide, but his friend felt duty bound not to let him out of his sight and to ensure he enjoyed every possible form of diversion. When they had run out of sights he entertained him with conversation. For two days Ragin endured it, but on the third he declared that he wasn't feeling well and wanted to stay all day in the hotel. 'In that case,' his friend replied, 'I won't go out either.' And in fact they needed to rest as their feet couldn't have taken any more punishment. Ragin lay on the sofa facing the back and with clenched teeth listened to his friend eagerly assuring him that sooner or later France was bound to destroy Germany, that Moscow was swarming with crooks, that one shouldn't judge a horse from its appearance. The doctor had ringing in the ears and palpitations, but he was too polite to ask his friend to leave him alone or be quiet. Fortunately though, Mikhail Averyanych grew bored with staying in the room and after dinner went out for a stroll.

Left to himself Ragin was able to relax. How pleasant to lie quite still on a sofa in the knowledge there's only yourself in the room! True happiness is impossible without solitude. The fallen angel most probably betrayed God because he longed for solitude, of which angels have no inkling. Ragin wanted to ponder all he had seen and heard in the past few days, but he could not get Mikhail Averyanych out of his mind.

'But then he did go on leave and come on this trip out of friendship and goodness of heart,' the doctor thought with vexation. 'But there's nothing worse than being under a friend's wing. He's kind enough, it seems, a good-hearted, jolly companion, yet he's a bore. A crashing bore. He's one of those people who say only fine and clever things but all the same you feel that they're stupid.'

During the days that followed Ragin pretended that he was not feeling well and stayed in the room. He lay facing the back of the sofa and fretted when his friend tried to distract him with conversation, but when he went out he was able to relax. He was annoyed with himself for having made the trip, he was annoyed with his friend who was becoming more talkative and perky every day. He failed dismally to pitch his thoughts on a serious, elevated plane.

'That reality of which Gromov spoke is really putting me to the test,' he thought, furious at his own pettiness. 'Anyway, it's all so stupid . . . Once I'm home everything will be as it was before.'

But things were no different in St Petersburg. For days on end he didn't leave his room, but lay on the sofa and got up only for a glass of beer.

Mikhail Averyanych was constantly pressing him to go to Warsaw.

'Why should I go there, my friend?' pleaded Ragin. 'Go on your own, but please let me go home! I beg you!'

'Not under any circumstances!' Mikhail Averyanych protested. 'It's an amazing city! I spent the five happiest years of my life there!'

Ragin lacked the strength of character to persist. Reluctantly he went to Warsaw. After arriving there he never left the room, but lay on the sofa, incensed with his friend and with the waiters, who stubbornly refused to understand Russian. Healthy, sprightly, jolly as ever, Mikhail Averyanych roamed around the city from dawn to dusk, seeking out old friends. Several times he stayed out all night. After one of these nights, spent God knows where, he returned in the early hours in an extremely agitated state, red-faced and dishevelled. He paced up and down for a long time, muttering to himself and then stopped.

'Honour above all else!' he exclaimed.

After a little more pacing he clutched his head and declaimed in tragic accents:

'Yes, honour above all else! Cursed be the moment when first I thought of coming to this Babylon! My dear friend,' he added, turning to the doctor, 'despise me! I've lost everything at cards. Lend me five hundred roubles!'

Ragin counted out five hundred roubles and silently handed them to his friend who, still purple with shame and anger, uttered some incoherent and quite uncalled-for imprecation, donned his cap and left. Two hours later he returned, slumped into an armchair and gave a loud sigh.

'My honour's saved! Let's go, my friend! I don't want to stay in this city a moment longer. They're all crooks . . . Austrian spies!'

When the friends returned home it was already November and snow lay deep in the streets. Ragin's job had now been taken by Dr Khobotov – he was still living in his old rooms, waiting for Ragin to return and move out of his hospital lodgings. The ugly woman he called his cook was already living in one of the hospital outbuildings.

Fresh rumours about the hospital were circulating in town. It was said that the ugly woman had quarrelled with the superintendent, who had apparently gone crawling on his knees and begged forgiveness.

The first day after his return Ragin had to find new lodgings.

'My dear chap,' the postmaster asked timorously, 'please forgive this indelicate question, but how much money have you got?'

Ragin silently counted his money.

'Eighty-six roubles,' he replied.

'I didn't mean that,' Mikhail Averyanych said, misunderstanding the doctor and feeling embarrassed. 'I'm asking how much money you have altogether.'

'I've already told you: eighty-six roubles . . . that's all I have.'

Mikhail Averyanych knew that the doctor was honest and decent, but had suspected that he was worth at least twenty thousand. But now that he discovered that Ragin was destitute, with nothing at all to live on, for some reason he suddenly started to cry and he embraced his friend.

XV

Ragin was now living in a small, three-windowed house belonging to a Mrs Belov, a townswoman from the lower classes. In this house there were only three rooms, plus a kitchen. Two of them, whose windows overlooked the street, were occupied by the doctor, whilst Daryushka, the landlady and her three children lived in the third.

Now and then the landlady's lover – a drunken workman who went berserk at night and terrified the children and Daryushka – came to spend the night. As soon as he arrived he settled himself in the kitchen and demanded vodka – and everyone felt crowded out. Feeling sorry for the weeping children, the doctor would take them to his room and put them to sleep on the floor, which gave him great satisfaction.

He still rose at eight and after breakfast would sit down and read his old books and magazines. He had no money for new books. Whether it was because the books were old or perhaps because his surroundings were different, reading had lost its hold on him and made him feel tired. In order not to spend the time unprofitably, he compiled a detailed catalogue of his books, gluing little labels on the spines, and this mechanical, laborious work struck him as more interesting than reading. For some mysterious reason that monotonous painstaking labour relaxed him, his mind would go blank and time passed swiftly. Even sitting in the kitchen and peeling potatoes with Daryushka, or picking dirt out of buckwheat meal was interesting. On Saturdays and Sundays he went to church. He would stand by the wall, screw up his eyes and listen to the choir, thinking of his father, his mother, the university, religion. He would feel calm and sad, and when he left the church he regretted that the service had not lasted longer.

Twice he went to the hospital to talk to Gromov, but on both occasions Gromov was unusually agitated and angry: he asked to be left in peace, since he had long become sick and tired of idle chatter and maintained that the only compensation he wanted from those damned bastards for all his sufferings was to be kept in solitary confinement. Surely they wouldn't deny him that? On the two occasions Ragin took leave of him and wished him good night he snapped: 'Go to hell!'

And now Ragin was unable to decide whether to go a third time or not. But he wanted to go.

Ragin had previously been in the habit of wandering around his room between lunch and tea and thinking. But now he would lie on the sofa, face the back and abandon himself to trivial thoughts that he was unable to suppress. He felt insulted that he had been awarded neither pension nor golden handshake after twenty years of service. True, he hadn't worked honestly, but then, weren't all old employees given pensions irrespective of whether they were honest or otherwise? That just about summed up modern justice – it wasn't moral integrity and ability that were rewarded by promotions, medals, pensions, but simply getting on with the job, whatever it was. So why should he be an exception? He had no money whatsoever. He was ashamed of passing the shop he used in town and seeing the lady proprietor: he already owed her thirty-two roubles for beer. He also owed Mrs Belov money. Daryushka secretly sold his old clothes and books, lying to the landlady that soon he would be coming into a lot of money.

He was angry with himself for wasting on that trip the one thousand roubles he had saved. How handy that thousand would come in now! He was annoyed that people would not leave him in peace. Khobotov felt obliged to visit his sick colleague from time to time. Everything about that man repelled Ragin: his sated face, his nasty, condescending manner, the way he called him 'colleague', and his topboots. But most repellent of all was that he considered it his duty to cure Ragin – and he was convinced that he was doing just that. With every visit he brought a phial of potassium bromide and rhubarb pills.

Mikhail Averyanych also considered it his duty to visit his friend and amuse him. On each occasion he entered his lodgings with an air of feigned abandon, laughed unnaturally, assured him that today he looked marvellous and that things were on the mend, thank God. From which it was easy to conclude that he considered his friend's position hopeless. He still had not repaid the Warsaw debt and was weighed down by a strong feeling of guilt; he felt tense and this made him try to laugh louder and tell funnier stories. Now his anecdotes and tales seemed endless and were sheer agony, both for Ragin and himself.

When his friend was there Ragin would usually lie on the sofa, facing the wall and listening with clenched teeth. Layers of sediment seemed to be forming around his heart and after every visit he felt that the sediment was reaching ever higher, towards his throat.

To suppress these petty feelings he quickly turned his thoughts to the fact that sooner or later he, Khobotov and Mikhail Averyanych would perish, without leaving even a trace of their existence in this world behind. He imagined that in a million years' time a spirit, flying through space past the earth, would see only clay and bare rocks. Everything – including culture and the moral law – would have vanished and would not even have become overgrown with burdock. As for his guilty feelings towards the shopkeeper, that insignificant Khobotov, Mikhail Averyanych's oppressive friendship – what did they matter? It was all trivial nonsense.

But such reflections were no longer of any help. No sooner had he visualized the earth's globe a million years hence than Khobotov appeared from behind a rock in his topboots, or Mikhail Averyanych with his forced laughter – and he could even hear his guilty whisper: 'Now, about that Warsaw debt, old man. I'll pay you back any day now . . . Without fail!'

XVI

One day Mikhail Averyanych arrived after dinner, when Ragin was lying on the sofa. At the same time Dr Khobotov happened to turn up with his potassium bromide. Ragin rose wearily and sat down again, supporting himself with his hands on the sofa.

'You're a much better colour today, old man,' Mikhail Averyanych began. 'You look really great. Oh yes, fantastic!'

'It's high time you were on the mend, colleague,' yawned Khobotov. 'You must be tired of all this palaver.'

'Oh yes, we'll get better!' Mikhail Averyranych gaily declared. 'We'll live another hundred years – you bet we will!'

'I'm not sure about a hundred, but I think we're good for another twenty,' Khobotov said comfortingly. 'It's all right, colleague. Don't despair . . . Now, don't confuse the issue . . .'

'We'll show them what we're made of!' Mikhail Averyanych

chortled, slapping his friend on the knee. 'We'll show them all right. Next summer, God willing, we'll dash off to the Caucasus and gallop all over it on horseback – clip-clop, clip-clop! And when we get back – you'll see – we'll probably dance at your wedding!' Here Mikhail Averyanych winked slyly. 'Yes, we'll marry you off, old man, we'll marry you off . . . !'

Ragin suddenly felt that the sediment was rising to his throat. His heart beat violently.

'That's so cheap,' he said, quickly standing up and going over to the window. 'Don't you realize what cheap nonsense you're talking!'

He wanted to speak gently and politely, but in spite of himself he suddenly clenched his fists and raised them above his head.

'Leave me alone!' he shouted in a voice that sounded most peculiar, turning purple and shaking all over. 'Clear out! Both of you! Clear out!'

Mikhail Averyanych and Khobotov rose to their feet and stared at him – first in bewilderment and then in terror.

'Clear off – both of you!' he shouted again. 'You stupid people! Morons! I don't need your friendship or your medicines. It's so cheap! It's disgusting!'

Khobotov and Mikhail Averyanych looked at each other in dismay, backed towards the door and went out into the lobby. Ragin seized the phial of potassium bromide and hurled it after them. It made a ringing noise as it smashed to smithereens on the threshold.

'Go to hell!' he shouted in a tearful voice as he ran out into the lobby. 'Go to hell!'

When his visitors had left Ragin lay down on the sofa, feverishly trembling. For some time he kept repeating: 'Morons! Stupid people!'

After he had calmed down his first thought was how dreadfully ashamed and wretched that poor Mikhail Averyanych must be feeling now, how terrible the whole thing had been. Nothing like it had ever happened before. What had become of his intelligence and tact? Where were his understanding of life and his philosophic detachment?

Feelings of shame and annoyance with himself kept the doctor awake all night. Towards ten o'clock next morning he went to the post office and apologized to the postmaster.

'Let's forget all about it,' sighed Mikhail Averyanych, deeply moved and warmly shaking his hand. 'Let bygones be bygones! Lyubavkin!' he suddenly roared, so loudly that all the clerks and customers shook in their shoes. 'Bring us a chair! And *you* can wait!' he yelled at a peasant woman who was handing him a registered letter through the grille. 'Can't you see I'm busy? Let's forget it ever happened,' he said gently, turning to Ragin. 'Now, please sit down old man, I beg you.'

For a minute he stroked his knees in silence.

'It never occurred to me to take offence,' he continued. 'One must make allowances for illness – that I do realize. That attack of yours yesterday scared the wits out of the doctor and myself, and afterwards we had a long talk about you. My dear chap, why don't you take your illness more seriously? You can't go on like this. Excuse the frankness of a friend,' (he began to whisper) 'but you're living in the worst possible surroundings. You're cooped up, it's filthy, there's no one to look after you, no money for treatment . . . My dear friend, the doctor and I beg you, from the bottom of our hearts – listen to our advice! Go into hospital! You'll get good wholesome food there and proper care and treatment. Between ourselves, Khobotov may be a bit of a boor, but he's an experienced doctor and you can rely on him completely. He gave me his word that he'd take care of you.'

Ragin was touched by this genuine concern and by the tears that suddenly glistened on the postmaster's cheeks.

'Don't you believe them, my friend!' he whispered, putting his hand to his heart. 'Don't you believe them! It's all a nasty trick. All that's wrong with me is that in twenty years I've managed to find only one intelligent man in the whole town – and he's a lunatic. I'm not ill at all. I've simply been caught in a vicious circle from which there's no escape. But it doesn't matter, I'm ready for anything.'

'Go into hospital, my dear chap.'

'I couldn't care less if it's a hole in the ground.'

'Give me your word, old man, that you'll do everything Khobotov says.'

'All right, I give you my word. But I repeat, my dear sir, that I've fallen into a vicious circle. Everything – even the genuine concern of my friend – points the same way – to my eventual destruction. I'm done for and I have the courage to admit it.'

'You'll get better, old man!'

'Why do you say that?' Ragin said irritably. 'There are very few men in their twilight years who don't go through what I'm going through now. When people tell you that you have diseased kidneys or an enlarged heart and you go and have treatment, or if you're told you're insane or a criminal – in a word, when people start taking notice of you – then you can be certain you've fallen into a vicious circle from which there's no escape. And the more you try to escape, the more you get caught up in it. One might as well give in, since no human effort can save you. That's how it strikes me!'

Meanwhile a crowd had gathered at the grille. Ragin did not want to be in the way, so he got up to say goodbye. Mikhail Averyanych once again made him promise and escorted him to the outer door.

That same day, towards evening, Dr Khobotov unexpectedly turned up in his sheepskin jacket and topboots.

'I've come to see you about something, colleague. I have an invitation for you: would you care to come to a consultation with me, eh?'

Thinking that Khobotov wanted to distract him by having him go for a walk or by actually giving him the chance to earn some money, Ragin put on his coat and went out into the street with him. He was glad of the opportunity to make amends for yesterday's lapse, to make peace, and in his heart of hearts he was grateful to Khobotov for not even so much as hinting at the incident – clearly he wanted to spare his feelings. One would hardly have expected such delicacy from that uncultured boor.

'And where's your patient?' asked Ragin.

'At the hospital. I've been meaning to show you him for ages . . . A most interesting case.'

They entered the hospital yard and after rounding the main block headed for the outbuilding where the insane were housed. For some reason all this took place in silence. When they entered the outbuilding Nikita leapt up as usual and stood to attention.

'One of them has lung complications,' Khobotov said in an undertone as he entered the ward with Ragin. 'Now, you wait here and I'll be back immediately. I must get my stethoscope.'

And he left.

XVII

Twilight was falling. Gromov was lying on his bed, his face buried in the pillow. The paralytic sat motionless, softly weeping and twitching his lips. The fat peasant and the ex-sorter were asleep. All was quiet.

Ragin sat on Gromov's bed and waited. Half an hour passed and instead of Khobotov in came Nikita clasping a smock, some kind of underclothes and a pair of slippers.

'Please put these on, sir,' he said softly. 'That's your bed – this way, please,' he added, pointing to a vacant bed that obviously had only just been set up. 'Now don't you worry, you'll soon get better, God willing.'

And now Ragin understood everything. Without a word he went over to the bed indicated by Nikita and sat down. When he saw that Nikita was standing there waiting he stripped naked – and he felt ashamed. Then he put on the hospital clothing. The pants were terribly short, the shirt too long and the smock reeked of smoked fish.

'You'll soon be all right, God willing,' Nikita repeated. He gathered Ragin's clothes in an armful and went out, closing the door behind him.

'I couldn't care less,' thought Ragin, bashfully wrapping himself in the smock and feeling like a convict in his new garments. 'I just don't care . . . Whether it's a dress coat, uniform, or this smock . . . it's all the same . . .'

But what about his watch? And the notebook in his side pocket?

And his cigarettes? And what had Nikita done with his clothes? From now on, perhaps, until his dying day, he would have no need of trousers, waistcoat or shoes. All this seemed rather strange, even incomprehensible at first. Now Ragin was firmly convinced that there was absolutely no difference between Mrs Belov's house and Ward No. 6, and that everything in this world is vanity and folly. But his hands were trembling, his legs were cold and he was terrified at the thought that Gromov might soon get up and see that he was wearing a smock. He rose, walked up and down and sat down again.

And so he sat for another half hour, then an hour – and he suffered agonies of boredom. Could he live here a day, a week, years even, like these people? Well, he might sit down, walk up and down and sit down again; he might go and look out of the window and then pace from corner to corner again. And then what? Just sit there all day like a dummy and brood? No, that was hardly possible.

Ragin lay on his bed, but he immediately rose to his feet and wiped the cold sweat from his forehead with his sleeve. And he felt that his whole face was reeking of smoked fish. Again he paced up and down.

'It must be some sort of misunderstanding,' he muttered, spreading out his arms in bewilderment. 'I must have it out with them . . . there's some misunderstanding.'

Just then Gromov awoke. He sat up, rested his cheeks on his fists and spat. Then he idly glanced at the doctor and clearly did not realize at first what was going on. But soon his sleepy face grew evil and mocking.

'Aha! So they've dumped you here too, old chap!' he said in a voice hoarse from sleep and narrowing one eye. 'I'm absolutely delighted. Once you used to drink people's blood, now they'll be drinking yours. Splendid!'

'It's some kind of misunderstanding . . . ,' Ragin murmured, alarmed at what Gromov had said. 'Some sort of misunderstanding . . .'

Gromov spat again and lay down.

'What a wretched life!' he growled. 'But the most galling, insulting thing is that this life doesn't end with you being rewarded for suffering or with an operatic apotheosis, but in death. The male nurses will come and carry the corpse by its hands and feet into a cellar. Ugh! But never mind . . . we'll have a ball in the next world . . . I'll keep returning from the other world as a ghost to haunt this vermin – I'll frighten the daylights out of them, turn their hair white!'

Moses came in and held his hand out when he saw the doctor. 'Give us a copeck!' he said.

XVIII

Ragin went to the window and looked out on to the open country. It was getting dark now and on the horizon a cold crimson moon was rising. Near the hospital fence, no more than eight yards away, stood a tall white building surrounded by a stone wall. This was the prison.

'So this is reality!' Ragin thought – and he felt terrified.

Everything was terrifying – the moon, the prison, the nails on the fence and the distant flames in the glue factory. A sigh came from behind. Ragin turned around and saw a man with glittering stars and medals on his chest, smiling and slyly winking. And this too was terrifying.

Ragin tried to reassure himself that there was nothing strange about the moon and the prison, that even sane men wore medals and that in time all this would turn to clay. But suddenly he was gripped by despair, seized the bars with both hands and shook them with all his might. The strong bars stood firm. And then, to ease his fears, he went over to Gromov's bed and sat down.

'I feel really low, dear chap,' he muttered, trembling and wiping away the cold sweat. 'Really low . . .'

'Then go and do some philosophizing,' scoffed Gromov.

'Good God! Yes . . . yes . . . you once said that there's no philosophy in Russia, but in fact everyone philosophizes, even perfect nobodies. But then, the philosophizing of nobodies does no one any harm,' Ragin said, as if he wanted to cry and gain sympathy. 'But why, my dear chap, this malicious laughter? And why shouldn't these nobodies philosophize if they're dissatisfied? For any intelligent, educated, proud, freedom-loving man, made in God's image, the only course is to become a doctor in a filthy, stupid little town, where one's whole life is nothing but cupping-glasses, leeches, mustard poultices! My God, such charlatanry, parochialism, vulgarity! Oh God!'

'Absolute nonsense. If you hated becoming a doctor so much you should have been a government minister.'

'But *nothing*'s any good, nothing. We're weak, my friend. I used to be indifferent, I argued forcefully and sensibly, but it only needed some hard knocks from life for me to lose heart . . . and I buckled. We're a feeble load of trash. And you included, my dear chap. You're clever, high-minded, you imbibed lofty principles with your mother's milk, but hardly had you stepped out in life than you grew weary and ill . . . Feeble! Oh, so feeble!'

Besides fear and indignation, some other craving had been gnawing away at Ragin ever since nightfall. Finally he concluded that he wanted some beer and a smoke.

'I'm going out, my friend,' he said. 'I'll tell them to give me a light . . . I can't take this . . . I'm in no state . . .'

Ragin went to the door and opened it, but Nikita leapt up like a shot and barred his way.

'Where d'yer think you're going, eh? It ain't allowed,' he said. 'It's time for bed!'

'But I only want to go for a little walk in the yard,' Ragin replied, dumbfounded.

'You can't. It ain't allowed. You know that!'

Nikita slammed the door and set his back against it.

'What harm will it do if I just go out?' Ragin asked, shrugging his shoulders. 'I don't understand. Nikita! I *must* go out,' he said in a trembling voice. 'I've got to!'

'Now don't you start causing trouble, can't 'ave that,' Nikita said in an edifying tone.

'What the hell is this!' Gromov suddenly shouted and leapt up. 'What right does he have to refuse to let us go out? How dare they keep us here! The law clearly states that no man can be deprived of his freedom without a trial! It's an outrage! Tyranny!'

'Of course it's tyranny!' said Ragin, encouraged by Gromov's shouting. 'I must go out, I *have* to! Let me out, I'm telling you!'

'Do you hear, you stupid bastard?' shouted Gromov and banged his fist on the door. 'Open up or I'll break the door down. You filthy brute!'

'Open up!' shouted Ragin, trembling all over. 'I demand it!'

'One more squeak out of you!' Nikita replied from behind the door. 'Just one more squeak!'

'At least go and fetch Dr Khobotov. Tell him I want him to come . . . just for a moment.'

'The doctor's coming tomorrow anyway.'

'They'll never let us out,' Gromov continued meanwhile. 'They'll leave us here to rot. Oh God, can there be no hell in the next world and will these bastards be forgiven? Where's the justice? Open up, you swine, I'm choking!' he shouted hoarsely and threw himself against the door. 'I'll beat my brains out! Murderers!'

Nikita flung open the door and roughly shoved Ragin back with both hands and a knee. Then he took a mighty swing and smashed his fist into his face. Ragin felt that a huge salt wave had suddenly washed over his head and dragged him back towards his bed. And in fact his mouth did taste salty – probably it was from the blood pouring from his gums. Just as if he were trying to swim away he made a wild flourish with his arms and grabbed hold of someone's bed. At that moment he felt Nikita hitting him twice on the back.

Gromov gave a loud scream: they must be beating him too.

Then all was silent. The thin moonlight filtered through the bars and a network of shadows lay on the floor. It was terrifying. Ragin lay down and held his breath in terror, waiting for the next blow. It was as if someone had thrust a sickle into him and twisted it several times in his chest and guts. The pain made him bite the pillow and grind his teeth. Suddenly, amidst all the chaos, a terrifying, unbearable thought flashed through his mind: it must be precisely this kind of pain that was suffered every day, year in year out, by those people who now appeared like black shadows in the moonlight. How could it be that for more than twenty years he had not known and had not wanted to know this? He had never known pain, he had no conception of it, so he was not to blame. But his conscience, as intractable and crude as Nikita, sent a bitter chill through him from head to foot. He leapt up and felt like shouting at the top of his voice, rushing to kill Nikita, then Khobotov, then the superintendent and the doctor's assistant and then himself, but no sound came from his throat and his legs would not obey him. Gasping for breath he tugged at his smock and shirt on his chest, ripped them and fell unconscious onto the bed.

XIX

Next morning his head ached, his ears hummed and he felt weak all over. He did not feel ashamed when he recalled his weakness of the day before. Then he had been faint-hearted, had even feared the moon, had given frank expression to thoughts and feelings he never suspected he possessed. For example, those thoughts about the discontents of philosophizing nobodies. But now he could not care less.

He neither ate nor drank, but lay motionless and silent.

'I really don't care,' he thought when they questioned him. 'I'm not going to answer . . . It's all the same . . .'

Towards evening Mikhail Averyanych brought him a quarter pound of tea and a pound of marmalade. Daryushka came too, and for a whole hour she stood by the bed with a vacant expression of uncomprehending sorrow. And Dr Khobotov came to visit him too. He brought a phial of potassium bromide and instructed Nikita to fumigate the ward.

Towards evening Ragin died of a stroke. At first he felt an overwhelming chill and nausea. Something repulsive seemed to be permeating his whole body, even his fingers, spreading from stomach to head and flooding his eyes and ears. Green lights flashed in his eyes. Ragin realized that his hour had come and he remembered that Gromov, Mikhail Averyanych and millions of others believed in immortality. And what if it really did exist? But he had no desire for immortality and he thought about it for only one fleeting moment. A herd of exceptionally beautiful and graceful deer, of which he had been reading the day before, darted past him; then a peasant woman held out a registered letter to him. Mikhail Averyanych said something. Then everything disappeared and Ragin sank into everlasting oblivion.

The male nurses came in, grabbed his feet and hands and carried him to the chapel. There he lay on the table with his eyes open, and at night the moon shone on him. In the morning Sergey Sergeich came, prayed devoutly before the crucifix and closed the eyes of his former superior.

Next day they buried Ragin. Only Mikhail Averyanych and Daryushka attended the funeral.

Ariadna

On the deck of a steamer sailing from Odessa to Sevastopol[1] a rather good-looking gentleman with a small round beard came up to ask me for a light.

'Take a look at those Germans sitting by the deck-house,' he said. 'When the Germans or English meet they discuss the price of wool, crops, their private affairs. But for some reason, when we Russians meet, we can talk only of women and elevated matters. But mainly of women.'

This man's face was already familiar. The previous day we had returned from abroad in the same train and I'd seen him standing with his female travelling companion at the Customs at Volochisk[2] before a veritable mountain of trunks and baskets crammed with women's dresses. How irritated and downhearted he had been when he had to pay duty on some bits of silk, while his companion protested and threatened to make a complaint. Later, on our way to Odessa, I saw him carrying pies and oranges to the ladies' compartment.

It was rather damp, the sea was a little rough and the ladies had returned to their cabins. The gentleman with the round beard sat down beside me.

'Yes,' he continued, 'when we Russians get together we can only talk of higher matters and women. We're so intellectual, so self-important, that we can only utter eternal verities and decide problems of the highest order. Russian actors can never play the fool – they even act seriously in light comedies. Even when we happen to talk about trifles, we can only discuss them from the most exalted viewpoint. We lack boldness, sincerity and simplicity. The reason why we talk about women so often is because – so it seems to me –

we're discontented. We idolize women too much and make demands out of all proportion to what we should expect in reality. What we get is poles apart from what we want and the result is dissatisfaction, shattered hopes, spiritual anguish. And if someone has a pain he likes to talk about it . . . I'm not boring you, am I?'

'No – not at all.'

'In that case allow me to introduce myself,' said the gentleman, rising slightly from his seat. 'Ivan Ilich Shamokhin, a Moscow landowner – after a fashion. But I know you very well.'

He sat down and continued, giving me a warm, open look.

'Any second-rate philosopher, like Max Nordau,[3] would explain this perpetual talk of women as a form of sexual mania or by the fact that we're advocates of serfdom and so on. But I take a different view. I repeat: we're dissatisfied because we're idealists. We want the creatures who give birth to us and our children to be superior to us, superior to anything else in this world. When we are young we romanticize, we worship those with whom we fall in love; for us, love and happiness are synonymous. We Russians despise people who don't marry for love, we find sensuality ludicrous and repulsive – and the most successful novels and short stories are those where women are beautiful, romantic and exalted. And if from time immemorial Russians have rhapsodized over Raphael's Madonna or preoccupied themselves with women's emancipation, I can assure you that there's nothing artificial about it. But here is the root of the trouble: the moment we marry or have an affair it takes only two or three years for us to feel disappointed and let down. We have affairs with others – and there's that terrible disappointment and horror again – until we're finally convinced that women are perfidious, frivolous, unfair, naïve, undeveloped and cruel. In effect, far from being superior we consider them lower than men – by a long chalk! And all that's left for us dissatisfied, disillusioned men is to grumble and to talk out of hand about how cruelly we've been deceived.'

As Shamokhin spoke I noticed that his native language and surroundings gave him infinite pleasure. Probably this was because he had been terribly homesick abroad. While he praised Russians and considered them highly idealistic, he had nothing to say about foreigners, which was in his favour. I could see he was experiencing some inner turmoil, that he wanted to talk about himself rather than about women and that I wasn't going to escape without having to listen to some interminable story, a confession of sorts.

And in fact, when we had ordered a bottle of wine and had each drunk a glass, he began:

'I seem to remember – in a story by Veltman[4] – someone says: "What a story!" and someone else replies: "No, it's not the story but just the introduction to one." In the same way, what I've just told you is only the introduction, but what I really want to tell you about is my latest affair. You don't mind if I ask again – I'm not boring you, am I?'

I told him that he was not, so he continued:

'The action takes place in the province of Moscow, in one of the northern districts. The countryside there, I must tell you, is simply amazing. Our estate lies on the high bank of a fast-flowing river, near some rapids, where the water thunders past day and night. Just picture a large old garden, nice little flowerbeds, beehives, a kitchen garden, the river below with leafy willows which seem to lose their lustre after a heavy dew and turn grey. On the other side of the river is a meadow and beyond it, on a hill, is a dark, forbidding pine forest. In this forest there are masses and masses of saffron milk cap mushrooms, while in its very depths elk live. When I'm dead and lying in my coffin I think I'll still be dreaming of those early mornings when the sun hurts your eyes, or of those wonderful spring evenings when nightingales and corncrakes call out in the garden and beyond, when the sounds of an accordion come drifting from the village, when someone in the house is playing the piano, when the river thunders – in brief, the kind of music that makes you want to cry and sing out loud. We don't have much plough land, but the pastures help us out and together with the forest bring in about two thousand roubles a year.

I'm an only son – we're both unpretentious people – and this money, together with Father's pension, is quite enough for us to live on. I spent the first three years in the country after graduating, managing the farm and waiting for some settled job to turn up. But the main thing is that I was deeply in love with a stunningly beautiful, charming girl. She was the sister of my neighbour, a bankrupt landowner by the name of Kotlovich. On his estate there were pineapples, amazing peaches, lightning conductors, a fountain in the middle of the courtyard – but at the same time he didn't have a copeck to his name. He was a lazy, ignorant, limp character, seemingly fashioned from boiled turnip. He treated his sick peasants by homoeopathy and dabbled in spiritualism. For all that, he was a gentle, sensitive kind of person and no fool. But I cannot stomach people who converse with spirits and treat peasant women with magnetism. Firstly, you always find these muddled ideas in people of limited intellectual horizons, and having a conversation with them is really hard going. In the second place, they don't normally fall in love, they don't live with women and this air of mystery tends to be disconcerting for impressionable people. And I didn't like his appearance. He was tall, plump, white, with a small head, tiny sparkling eyes and chubby white fingers. He didn't actually shake your hand – he kneaded it. And he was constantly apologizing. Whenever he asked for something he'd say: "Sorry!"; if he gave you something – again, "Sorry!" As for his sister, she was quite another matter. I must point out that in my younger days I hadn't known the Kotloviches, since my father was a professor in N— and for a long time we lived in the provinces. But when I did get to know them the girl was already twenty-two, she had long left boarding-school and had been living two or three years in Moscow with a rich aunt, who brought her out. When I met her and had my first talk with her, what struck me most of all was her unusual and beautiful name – Ariadna. It suited her so well! She was a brunette, very slim, lissom, shapely, extraordinarily graceful, with elegant, extremely refined features. She too had sparkling eyes, but whereas her brother's had a cold, sickly glint, like boiled sweets, hers were radiant with youth, beauty and pride. I fell in love the very day we met – and it was inevitable. My first impressions were so powerful that to this day I still cannot rid myself of my illusions. I would still like to think that Nature had some majestic, grandiose design in mind when she created that girl. Ariadna's voice, her walk, her hat – even the imprint of her feet on the sandy bank where she used to fish for gudgeon – filled me with joy and a passionate lust for life. From Ariadna's beautiful face and figure I was able to judge her inner self, and her every word, her every smile enchanted, captivated me and led me to suppose that hers was a noble soul. She was affectionate, talkative, cheerful, unaffected. Her belief in God was truly poetic, as were her thoughts on death, and her cast of mind was so rich with delicate nuances that she could make even her faults appear unique and endearing. Let's suppose she wanted a new horse but couldn't afford one – well, so what! One could always sell or pawn something, and if the estate steward swore blindly that there was simply nothing to be pawned, then the iron roofs could be stripped off the outbuildings and sent to the factory. Or carthorses could be taken to market at the busiest season and sold for a song. These wild impulses often reduced the whole estate to despair, but she expressed them with such refinement that in the end all was forgiven, all was allowed, as if she were a goddess or Caesar's wife. My love was truly touching and before long everyone – my father, the neighbours, the peasants – was aware of it. And all of them sympathized with me. When ever I treated the farm labourers to vodka they would bow and say: "God grant that you marry Miss Kotlovich, master."

And Ariadna herself knew that I loved her. She would often ride over to see us, or come by cabriolet, and sometimes she would spend whole days with myself and my father. She became firm friends with the old man and he even taught her to ride a bicycle – that was his favourite pastime. I remember, when she was about to go for a ride one evening, helping her on to her bicycle – and then she struck me as so wonderful that I felt my fingers were on fire when I touched her. I trembled with delight, and when that handsome, graceful pair rode off down the road together a black horse ridden by the steward bolted to one side as they passed by. This, I thought, was because it too was staggered by her beauty. My love, my adulation, deeply moved Ariadna and she too yearned to be similarly enchanted and to reciprocate my love. Oh yes, it was so romantic!

But she was as incapable of true love as I was capable of it, since she was frigid and already pretty well corrupted. A demon was lurking inside her, whispering day and night that she was enchanting, simply divine. And she had no idea why she had come into this world, why she had been created: she could only visualize herself in the future as rich and famous. She had visions of balls, horse races, livery, luxurious drawing-rooms, her own salon with a swarm of counts, princes, ambassadors, famous painters and actors who would worship at her feet and go into ecstasies over her beauty and her fine dresses. Craving for power and constantly one-track ideas tend to make people cold. And Ariadna was cold: towards me, towards nature and towards music. Meanwhile time was passing and still no ambassadors turned up, still Ariadna continued to live with her spiritualist brother. Things went from bad to worse, until she couldn't afford any more dresses or hats and had to resort to all sorts of evasion and cunning to conceal her poverty.

And sure enough, while she was still living at her aunt's, a Prince Maktuyev – rich, but a complete nonentity – proposed to her. She refused him point-blank. But now she felt the occasional twinge of regret. Why had she turned him down? Just as your peasant blows in disgust on his kvass with cockroaches floating in it but still drinks it, so she frowned squeamishly on remembering the prince. Yet she would tell me: "Say what you like, but there's something mysterious and fascinating about a title!"

She dreamt of titles, of the glamorous life, but at the same time she didn't want to let me go. However much one may dream of ambassadors, all the same one's heart isn't a stone and you're only young once. Ariadna tried to fall in love, pretended to be in love and even swore solemnly that she loved me. But I'm a highly-strung, sensitive man: I can tell at a distance when someone loves me – I don't need assurances or vows. But this was like a draught of cold air and when she spoke to me of love I imagined I heard a mechanical nightingale singing. Ariadna herself felt that she lacked that vital spark – and this upset her. More than once I saw her in tears. Well, you can imagine what I was thinking when once, on a sudden impulse, she suddenly kissed and embraced me (it happened one evening, on the river bank), and I could see from her eyes that she didn't love me but had only embraced me because she was curious and this was a kind of test to see what would happen. And I was shocked. I took her hands. "These loveless endearments make me feel terrible!" I said in desperation.

"What a strange person you are!" she replied irritably and went away.

I would most probably have married her after two or three years and that would have been the end of my story. But fate decided otherwise. It happened that a new personality made his appearance on our horizon. A university friend of Ariadna's brother, Mikhail Ivanych Lubkov, a charming man of whom the coachmen and footmen would say: "A most amusing gent!" came to stay with Ariadna's brother. He was of medium height, rather skinny, and bald. He had the face of a good bourgeois – rather uninspiring but attractive, pale, with a bristly well-tended moustache. He had goose pimples on his neck and an oversize Adam's apple. He wore pince-nez on a wide black ribbon, couldn't pronounce his r's or l's, so that "really" turned out "weawy", for instance. He was always in high spirits and everything for him was one big joke. He had made a particularly stupid marriage, at the age of twenty, received two houses in Moscow near the Novodevichy Convent,[5] carried out repairs on them, built a bath-house and utterly ruined himself. Now his wife and children were living in abject poverty at the Oriental Rooms and he had to support them: this he found funny. He was thirty-six and his wife forty-two – that was funny too. His mother, a smug, arrogant, terribly snooty woman, despised his wife and lived on her own with a whole horde of cats and dogs, and he had to pay her seventy-five roubles a month – in addition to his wife's allowance. He himself was a man of taste, loved lunching at the Slav Fair Hotel[6] and dining at the Hermitage.[7] For this he needed a great deal of money, but his uncle allowed him only two thousand a year, which wasn't enough, and for days on end he'd go running around Moscow – with his tongue hanging out, as the saying goes – trying to scrounge money from someone – that was great fun too. He had come to stay with Kotlovich, so he said, to relax in "nature's bosom", away from his family. At lunch and supper, during walks, he would tell us all about his wife, his mother, his creditors, bailiffs – and he would laugh at them. He would laugh at himself and claim that thanks to his flair for borrowing he had made a lot of nice new friends. In fact, he never stopped laughing – and we laughed too. While he was around we spent our time differently too. I was given to quiet, idyllic pleasures, so to speak. I loved fishing, evening strolls, picking mushrooms. But Lubkov preferred picnics, fireworks, hunting with the hounds. About three times a week he organized picnics, and Ariadna, with a serious, inspired expression would write out a list, with oysters, champagne, chocolates, and send me off to Moscow – naturally without first asking whether I had any money. And at our picnics toasts were drunk, there was laughter – and once again those stories, so full of *joie de vivre*, about how old his wife was, how fat his mother's dogs were, what charming people creditors were . . .

Lubkov loved nature, but considered it something infinitely beneath him, created for his pleasure alone. Stopping before some magnificent view he would say: "Nice spot for a cup of tea!" Once, seeing Ariadna walking some way off with her parasol, he nodded towards her and said: "She's thin, but I like that. I don't care for plump ones."

That really jarred on me. I asked him not to talk that way about women in my presence. He looked at me in amazement.

"What's wrong if I prefer thin ones to fat ones?" he replied.

I made no answer. Then on another occasion when he was in an excellent mood and slightly tipsy he said:

"I've noticed that Ariadna likes you. I can't understand why you're letting the chance slip."

These words made me feel awkward and in my embarrassment I told him rather bashfully my views on love and women.

"I don't know," he sighed. "As I see it, women are women. Ariadna may well be the romantic, exalted type you say she is, but that doesn't mean the laws of nature don't apply to her. You can see for yourself that she's at an age when she needs a husband or a lover. I respect women no less than you, but I do think that certain relationships don't rule out romance. Romance is one thing, a lover is another. It's the same with farming! The beauty of nature's one thing and income from forests and fields another."

When Ariadna and I were fishing for gudgeon, Lubkov would lie nearby on the sand, make fun of me and instruct me in the art of living.

"I'm amazed, my dear sir, how you can possibly exist without having an affair," he said. "You're young, handsome, interesting – in short, a terrific chap, yet you live like a monk. Oh, I've no time for these old fogeys at twenty-eight! I'm almost ten years older than you, but who's the younger? Ariadna Grigoryevna – who?"

"Well, you are of course," Ariadna replied.

And when he grew bored with our silence and the close attention we were giving our fishing floats he returned to the house.

"In actual fact you're not a man at all," she told me with a furious look, "but a real ditherer, God forgive me! A man should get carried away, do mad things, make mistakes, suffer! Women will forgive you if you're rude and insolent, but they'll never forgive you for being so stodgy!"

She was really very angry.

"To be successful you must be decisive and bold," she continued. "Lubkov's not as good-looking as you, but he's more interesting and he'll always be more successful with women because – unlike you – he's a *man*."

And there was even a note of bitterness in her voice. Once over supper – ignoring me – she declared that if she were a man she wouldn't be vegetating in the country but would have gone travelling, spending the winter somewhere abroad – Italy, for example. Oh, Italy! Here my father unwittingly added fuel to the fire. He gave us a long lecture on the wonders of Italy, how marvellous the weather, how remarkable the museums. Suddenly Ariadna was simply dying to go to Italy. She even struck the table with her fist and her eyes sparkled as if they were saying: "Let's go!"

And this started everyone talking about how nice it would be in Italy – oooh, *Italy!* – and so it went on every day, and when Ariadna glanced over her shoulder at me I could tell from her cold, stubborn expression that in her dreams she already had Italy at her feet, with all its salons, famous foreigners, tourists, and that there was no stopping her now. I advised her to wait a little, to postpone the trip for a year or two, but she frowned disdainfully.

"You're such a stick-in-the-mud – just like an old woman!" she said.

But Lubkov was in favour of the trip. He said that it would work out very cheaply and that he would be delighted to go to Italy as well and have a rest from family life. I must admit I behaved with the naïvety of a schoolboy. Whenever possible I tried not to leave the two of them alone – not from jealousy, but because I had the feeling that something awful would happen. And they would play jokes on me. For instance, when I came into the room they would pretend they'd just been kissing, and so on.

But then, one fine morning, her plump white spiritualist brother appeared and said he wished to have a few words in private with me. That man was completely lacking in all willpower. For all his education and sense of tact he couldn't resist reading other people's letters if they happened to be lying on a table. And now, as we were talking, he admitted that he had "accidentally" read Lubkov's letter to Ariadna.

"I found out from this letter that she's going abroad very soon. My dear chap, I'm terribly upset. For God's sake explain it to me! I can't make head or tail of it."

As he spoke he was breathing heavily, right into my face – and his breath smelt of boiled beef.

"I do apologize for initiating you into the secrets of that letter," he continued, "but you're a friend of Ariadna, she has great respect for you. Perhaps you know something. She wants to go – but with whom? *Lubkov* intends going with her. I'm sorry to have to say this, but it's most peculiar behaviour on his part. He's a married man, with children, yet he declares his love to Ariadna and calls her sweetheart in his letter. It's really most odd, I must say!"

I went cold all over, my arms and legs grew numb and I felt an extremely sharp pain in my chest. Kotlovich slumped into the armchair, utterly exhausted, his arms dangling limply at his sides.

"But what can *I* do?" I asked.

"Bring her to her senses, talk her round . . . Just judge for yourself: what does she want with Lubkov? Is he any sort of match for her? God, it's terrible, simply terrible!" he continued, clutching his head. "She has such wonderful prospects – Prince Maktuyev and . . . all the others. The prince adores her and only last Wednesday his late grandfather Ilarion categorically affirmed – as plain as could be – that Ariadna would be his wife. Categorically! Grandfather Ilarion may be dead, but he's an exceptionally brilliant man. We summon his spirit every day."

After this conversation I didn't sleep all night and I wanted to shoot myself. In the morning I wrote five letters and tore them all to shreds. Then I went to have a cry in the threshing barn, after which I borrowed some money from my father and left for the Caucasus without saying goodbye.

Of course, women are women and men are men, but can it really be as simple these days as it was before the Flood? Must I, a man of culture, with a complex spiritual make-up, explain my overwhelming attraction towards a woman by the sole fact that her body is a different shape from mine? Oh, what a dreadful thought! I would like to think that the genius of man, in his struggle against nature, has also done battle with physical love as if it were an enemy, and that if he hasn't succeeded in defeating it he has at least managed to enmesh it in illusions of brotherhood and love. And for me at least all this wasn't merely a function of my animal organism, as if I were a dog or a frog, but true love. And every embrace is inspired by a pure impulse of the heart and by respect for women. In fact, revulsion for the animal instinct has been nurtured for hundreds of centuries in hundreds of generations. It has been inherited by me, it is in my blood and is a part of my very being. And if I happen to be romanticizing love now, isn't that as natural and necessary as the fact that I can't wiggle my ears or that I'm not covered with fur? I think that most educated people think this way, since the absence of anything moral and romantic about love is nowadays considered an atavistic phenomenon. It's said to be a symptom of degeneracy, of many forms of insanity. True, in romanticizing love we ascribe virtues to those whom we love that very often they don't possess at all, and this is a source of repeated mistakes and constant suffering. But if you ask me, it's better like this – I mean, it's better to suffer than to try and console yourself with the thought that women are women and men are men.

In Tiflis[8] I received a letter from my father. He wrote that on such-and-such date Ariadna had gone abroad with the intention of staying away all winter. A month later I went home. It was autumn. Every week Ariadna sent my father some very interesting letters written in excellent literary style, on scented paper. I really do think that every woman is a potential author. Ariadna described in great detail how difficult it was for her to make peace with her aunt and to borrow a thousand roubles for the journey, how long she'd spent in Moscow trying to track down a distant relative, an old lady, to persuade her to make the trip with her. This excessive detail struck me as pure invention and of course I realized that no such chaperone existed. Soon afterwards I too received a letter from her, also scented and most elegantly written. She wrote that she missed me and my clever, lovelorn eyes, and in friendly terms she reproached me for ruining my youth, for vegetating in the country when I could be living like her, under the palm trees, inhaling the fragrance of orange trees. And she signed herself "Your forsaken Ariadna". Two days later another letter in the same style arrived, with the signature: "Your forgotten one." My head went round. I loved her passionately, dreamt of her every night and now there were all these "forsakens", "forgottens". Why? What for? But then there was the boredom of living in the country, interminable evenings, nagging thoughts about Lubkov . . . The uncertainty tormented me, poisoned my days and nights, became insufferable. So I gave in and went abroad.

Ariadna asked me to come to Abbazia.[9] I arrived there one fine warm day after a shower, when raindrops were still hanging on the trees, and I took a room in the same huge barrack-like hotel annexe where Ariadna and Lubkov were staying. They happened to be out, so I went to the local park, wandered along the paths for a while and then sat down. An Austrian general came by with his hands behind his back and with those same red stripes on his trousers as our generals wore. A baby was pushed past in a pram and the wheels squeaked on the damp sand. A decrepit old man with jaundice went by, followed by a group of Englishwomen, a Polish priest, then the same general again. Some military bandsmen who had just arrived from Fiume[10] marched to the bandstand, their brass instruments gleaming in the sun, and struck up a tune. Were you ever in Abbazia? It's a filthy little Slav town with only one street that stinks and which you can only get down in galoshes after it's been raining. I'd read so much about this earthly paradise – and always with deep emotion – that later, when I was gingerly crossing the street with my trousers hitched up and out of sheer boredom bought some hard pears from an old woman who, seeing I was Russian, deliberately garbled her words; when I was at a loss where to go or what to do; when I was bound to meet other Russians as disenchanted as myself, I felt amazed and ashamed.

There's a calm bay crossed by steamers and small boats with sails of every colour. From here you can see Fiume and some distant islands veiled in a lilac haze. All this would have been highly picturesque if the view hadn't been obscured by hotels and their annexes, all constructed in that absurd suburban style used by greedy speculators developing the whole of this verdant coast, so that for the most part all you can see of the paradise is windows, terraces and little squares with small white tables and waiters' black tailcoats. Here there's a park, the kind you'll find in any foreign resort. The dark, motionless, silent foliage of the palm trees, the bright yellow sand on the paths, the bright green benches, the gleam of the soldiers' blaring trumpets and the general's red stripes – all this bores you stiff within ten minutes. Meanwhile you're stuck here for ten days, ten weeks! Having reluctantly dragged myself from one resort to another, I became even more convinced of the uncomfortable, mean lives led by the rich and overfed, of how dull and sluggish their imagination was, how narrow their tastes and desires. How infinitely happier are those tourists, young and old, who are unable to afford a hotel and live where they can, who admire the sea view as they lie on the green grass up in the hills, go everywhere on foot, see forests, villages close up, observe a country's customs, listen to its songs, fall in love with its women . . .

While I was sitting in the park darkness began to fall and then my Ariadna appeared in the dusk – elegant and chic, as beautifully dressed as a princess. She was followed by Lubkov, wearing a loose-fitting suit, most likely bought in Vienna.

"Why are you so angwy?" he was saying. "What have I done?"

When she saw me she gave a joyful cry and if we hadn't been in a park she would certainly have thrown her arms around my neck. She firmly squeezed my hands and laughed. I laughed too and almost wept from emotion. The cross-examination began: How were things in the country? How was my father? Had I seen her brother? And so on. She insisted that I look her in the eye and asked if I remembered the gudgeon, our little quarrels, the picnics . . . "Oh yes! How wonderful it all was," she sighed. "But we're not bored here either – we've loads of friends. My darling! My sweet! Tomorrow I'm going to introduce you to a Russian family. Only for heaven's sake buy yourself another hat." She looked me up and down and frowned. "Abbazia's not a little village," she said. "Here you must be *comme il faut*."

Later we went to a restaurant. Ariadna laughed the whole time, was full of fun and kept calling me "darling", "dear", "clever", as if she just couldn't believe I was there. We stayed until eleven o'clock and departed highly satisfied with the supper and each other. Next day Ariadna introduced me to the Russian family as the "son of a distinguished professor who lives on the neighbouring estate". All she could talk about with these people was estates and harvests, with constant reference to me. She wanted to create the impression that she came from a rich landowning family – and to be honest she succeeded. She bore herself superbly, like a true-born aristocrat – which in fact she was.

"Isn't Auntie a scream!" she said suddenly, smiling at me. "We had a little tiff and she's gone off to Merano.[11] What do you think of that?"

Later, when I was strolling in the park with her I asked:

"Whose aunt were you talking about yesterday? I didn't know anything about an aunt."

"That was a lie, for the sake of my reputation," Ariadna laughed.

"They mustn't know I'm here without a chaperone." After a minute's silence she snuggled up to me and said:

"Darling, please be friends with Lubkov! He's so unhappy. His mother and wife are simply awful."

She was rather offhand towards Lubkov and when she went to bed she wished him goodnight with a "see you in the morning" – just as she did me. And their rooms were on different floors – this led me to hope that it was all nonsense about them having an affair – so I felt very relaxed with him. And once, when he asked for a loan of three hundred roubles, I was delighted to give him the money.

Every day we did nothing but enjoy ourselves. We'd wander around the park, eat and drink. Every day we had a conversation with the Russian family. Gradually I became used to the fact that if I went to the park I'd be bound to meet the old man with jaundice, the Polish priest and the Austrian general, who always carried a small pack of cards – wherever possible he would sit down and lay out patience, nervously twitching his shoulders. And the bandsmen would play the same tunes over and over. Back home in the country I would normally feel ashamed in front of the peasants whenever I drove out with friends for a picnic on a weekday, or went fishing. Similarly I felt ashamed here with all the servants, coachmen or workmen I happened to meet. I had the impression that they were looking at me and wondering why I did nothing. And I had this feeling of shame from morning to night, every single day. It was a strange, unpleasant, tedious time, relieved only when Lubkov borrowed one hundred, then fifty, francs – and like morphine for an addict the money would suddenly cheer him up and he would roar with laughter – at his wife, himself or his creditors.

But then the rains and cold weather set in. We travelled to Italy and I telegraphed my father, begging him – for God's sake – to cable me a money order for eight hundred roubles, in Rome. We stopped in Venice, Bologna, Florence, and in each city we invariably stayed at an expensive hotel, where they fleeced us, charging extra for lighting, service and heating, for bread with lunch and for the privilege of dining in a private room. We ate a tremendous amount.

In the morning we had a full breakfast. At one o'clock we lunched on meat, fish, some kind of omelette, cheese, fruit and wine. At six we had an eight-course dinner, with long pauses, when we drank beer and wine. After eight o'clock we had some tea. Towards midnight Ariadna would announce that she was starving and ordered ham and boiled eggs. We would eat too, to keep her company. In the intervals between meals we would dash around museums and exhibitions with the thought that we mustn't be late for dinner or lunch uppermost in our minds. Pictures bored me, I just wanted to go back to the hotel and lie down. I would become exhausted, look for a chair with my eyes and hypocritically repeat with the others: "How magnificent! What a feeling for space!" Like bloated boa constrictors we took notice only of objects that glittered. Shop windows mesmerized us and we went into raptures over cheap brooches – and we bought a great deal of worthless, useless junk.

It was the same in Rome. There a cold wind blew and it rained. After a greasy breakfast we went off to look at St Peter's and because we had been gorging ourselves – or perhaps because of the bad weather – it did not impress us at all and we almost started quarrelling, accusing one another of indifference to art.

The money arrived from Father. I remember going off in the morning to collect it. Lubkov came with me.

"When one has a past one can't have a full and happy life in the present," he said. "My past is like a millstone around my neck. However, it wouldn't be so bad if I had some money . . . but I'm broke . . . Believe me, I've only eight francs left," he continued, lowering his voice, "and yet I have to send my wife a hundred and my mother the same amount. And then I have to live here. Ariadna's just like a child, she turns a blind eye to everything and throws money around like a duchess. Why did she have to go and buy a watch yesterday? And why do we have to go around acting as if we were little children? You tell me! With me staying in a separate room it's costing me an extra ten to fifteen francs a day to hide our relationship from servants and friends. What's the point?"

I felt that same sharp pain in my chest. The uncertainty was gone, everything was quite clear to me now. I felt cold all over and I decided immediately not to see either of them, to escape and return home without delay . . .

"Having sex is easy," he continued. "All you need do is undress the woman. But it's what comes afterwards that's such a drag, such a load of nonsense!"

As I was counting the money he said:

"I'm finished if you don't lend me a thousand francs. That money's my very last hope."

I gave him the money and he immediately cheered up and started laughing at his uncle, that silly old fool who hadn't managed to keep his address a secret from his wife. Back in the hotel I packed and paid the bill. It only remained to say goodbye to Ariadna. I knocked at her door.

"*Entrez!*"

Her room was in the usual morning chaos – tea things on the table, a half-eaten roll, an eggshell. There was a strong, stifling smell of scent. The bed hadn't been made and it was obvious that two people had slept in it. Ariadna had only just got up and she was wearing a flannel bed jacket; her hair was uncombed.

I said good morning, then I sat for a minute in silence while she tried to tidy her hair. Then, trembling all over, I asked:

"Why . . . why did you have to make me come out here?"

Clearly she guessed what I was thinking. She took my hand.

"I just want you to be here," she said. "You're so decent!"

I was ashamed of my distress and trembling. Next thing I'd be bursting into tears! I went out without another word and an hour later I was on the train. The whole day I kept visualizing Ariadna as pregnant – and she repelled me: for some reason all the women I saw in railway compartments and at stations seemed pregnant and I found them similarly repellent and pathetic. I was like a fanatical miser who suddenly discovers that all his gold coins are counterfeit. Those pure, gracious images which my imagination, inflamed by love, had cherished for so long, my plans, my hopes, my memories, my views of love and women – all this was mocking and taunting me. "How could Ariadna," I asked myself in horror, "that exceptionally beautiful, intelligent girl, a senator's daughter, be having an affair with that vulgar, dreary philistine? But then, why shouldn't she love Lubkov? In what way was he worse than me? She could love anyone she liked – but why lie about it? And why on earth should she be honest with me?" And so on, all in the same vein, until I felt stupefied.

It was cold in the train. I was travelling first class, but there were three to a side, no double windows and no corridor. I felt that I was in the stocks – cramped, abandoned, pathetic; my feet were absolutely freezing. Meanwhile I kept remembering how seductive she had looked earlier that day in her jacket, with her hair down. And suddenly I was gripped by such violent pangs of jealousy that I leapt from my seat from the agony of it all, so that the passengers next to me looked at me in amazement – in terror, even.

Back home I was confronted by snowdrifts and twenty degrees of frost. I love the winter because then the house is particularly warm, even during severe frosts. On fine frosty days it's so pleasant to put on a sheepskin jacket and felt boots, to do jobs in the garden or yard, or read in my well-heated room, or sit by the fire in my father's study, or have a rustic-style steam-bath . . . Only, if there's no mother, sister or children around, winter evenings can be somehow eerie, and they seem dreadfully long and quiet. The warmer and more comfortable it is the more keenly you feel their absence. After I returned from abroad that winter the evenings seemed endless. I was deeply depressed, so much so that I couldn't even read. During the day this didn't matter – I could always clear the snow in the garden, feed the hens and calves – but the evenings were sheer hell.

Before, I used to dislike having visitors, but now I was only too glad of them, since I knew that there was bound to be talk of Ariadna. Our spiritualist Kotlovich would often drive over for a chat about his sister and sometimes he brought along his friend Prince Maktuyev, who was no less in love with Ariadna than myself. To sit in Ariadna's room, to run his fingers over the piano keys, to look at her music books was simply a necessity for the prince – life was impossible for him without it. Grandfather Ilarion's ghost still predicted that she would be his wife sooner or later. The prince would usually stay with us for ages – roughly, from lunch to midnight – and he hardly opened his mouth. He would drink two or three bottles of beer without saying one word and only now and then, just to show he was still with us, would produce a staccato, inane laugh. Before going home he would always take me to one side.

"When did you last see Ariadna?" he would ask in an undertone. "Is she well? She's not getting bored there, is she?"

Spring arrived, with woodcock shooting, and after that the spring wheat and clover had to be sown. I felt sad, but it was now a springtime sadness. As I worked in the fields and listened to the skylarks I wondered whether I should settle that question of personal happiness once and for all by marrying, unpretentiously, a simple country girl? But suddenly, when work was in full swing, I received a letter with an Italian stamp. Clover, beehives, calves, peasant girls all vanished into thin air. This time Ariadna wrote that she was profoundly, frightfully unhappy. She reproached me for not lending her a helping hand, for looking down on her from the dizzy heights of my virtue and for abandoning her in her hour of peril. All this was written in large, shaky handwriting, with smudges and blots – her letter was obviously dashed off in a great hurry and in great distress. She concluded by begging me to come and save her.

So once again I was torn from my moorings and swept away. Ariadna was living in Rome. I arrived at her place late one evening and when she saw me she burst into tears and threw herself around my neck. During the winter she hadn't changed at all and she looked just as young and enchanting as ever. We had supper together and then drove around Rome until dawn. The whole time she kept telling me about what she had been doing. I asked her where Lubkov was.

"Don't mention that fellow to me!" she cried. "He's disgusting, loathsome!"

"But surely you loved him, didn't you?" I said.

"Never! At first he seemed rather different and I felt sorry for him – but that was all! He's insolent, he takes women by storm, which is attractive. But let's not talk about him. It's a sad chapter in my life. He's gone to Russia to get some money – and good riddance! I told him not to dare come back."

She wasn't staying in a hotel any more, but in a two-roomed private apartment which she had furnished to her own taste in cold luxury. After Lubkov left she borrowed about five thousand francs from her friends and my arrival really was her salvation. I was counting on taking her back to the country, but I didn't succeed. She was terribly homesick, but memories of the hardships she had suffered, of past shortcomings, of the rusty roof on her brother's house, made her shake with revulsion, and when I suggested going home she grabbed my hands convulsively.

"Oh no, no! I'd die of boredom there!" she exclaimed.

And then my love entered its final stage, its last quarter.

"Be a darling again, love me a teeny bit," Ariadna said, leaning towards me. "You're so gloomy, so strait-laced, you're scared of letting yourself go. All you think of is the consequences – and that's a real bore. Well, I'm asking you, begging you, to be nice to me! Oh, my honest, saintly darling. I love you so much!"

I became her lover. For at least a month I was like a madman, crazy with delight. To hold that young, beautiful body in my arms, to enjoy it, feel her warmth every time I woke up and to realize that she was there – she, my Ariadna! Oh, that took some getting used to! But get used to it I did and gradually I began to take a more sober view of my new position. Most important, I understood that Ariadna didn't love me any more than before, she yearned for serious love and she was afraid of being lonely. Most of all, I was young, healthy and strong, whilst she was sensual, like all unemotional people, and we both pretended that our affair was based on mutual, grand passion. Later a few other things came to light.

We stayed in Rome, Naples and Florence. We went to Paris, but found it cold there, so we returned to Italy. Everywhere we introduced ourselves as husband and wife and made ourselves out to be rich landowners, so people were eager to make friends with us. Ariadna was a great success. As she was taking painting lessons she was called an artist and as you can imagine this suited her down to the ground, although she didn't have a scrap of talent. Every day she slept until two or three in the afternoon; she had coffee and lunch in bed. For dinner she had soup, lobsters, fish, meat, asparagus, game. And then, when she went to bed I would bring her something, such as roast beef for instance, which she would eat with a sad, worried expression. If she woke up at night she would eat apples and oranges.

The chief, so to speak basic, characteristic of this woman was her astonishing cunning. Constantly, every minute of the day, she was up to some trick, apparently without any need – instinctively, as it were, from the same urge which makes a sparrow chirp or a cockroach twitch its feelers. She played tricks on me, on the servants, on the porter, on shopkeepers, on friends. Not a single conversation or meeting took place without affectation and pretence on her part. A man only had to come into our room – it made no difference whether waiter or baron – for the look in her eyes, her expression, her voice and even the outline of her figure to change. If you'd seen her then – if only once – you would have said that there were no more fashionable and wealthier people than us in the whole of Italy. Not one artist or musician escaped without her telling him a whole load of stupid lies about his remarkable talent.

"You're a real genius!" she would chant in a sugary voice. "It's quite frightening! I should think you can see straight through people."

All this merely to please, to enjoy success.

Every morning she woke up with but one thought in mind: to please! And this was the sole purpose and object of her life. If I'd told her that in such-and-such a street, in such-and-such a house there lived someone to whom she didn't appeal, she would have been terribly upset. Every day she needed to enchant, to captivate, to drive men out of their minds. To have me in her power, reduced to a complete nonentity by her witchlike charms, gave her the same pleasure once enjoyed by victors at knightly tournaments. It was as if my humiliation wasn't enough and at night she would sprawl about like a tigress – naked, as she always felt too hot – and she would read Lubkov's letters. He begged her to return to Russia: if she didn't he vowed to rob or murder someone just to get the money to come and see her. Although she hated him, she was excited by his passionate, crawling letters. She had an extremely high opinion of her own charms: she felt that if people could see her superb figure at a large gathering somewhere, her complexion, she would have all Italy, the whole world at her feet. This talk of her figure, her complexion, appalled me and whenever she noticed this and was in a bad mood she would taunt me with all sorts of cheap remarks, just to annoy me. Things became so bad that once, at some lady's country villa, she lost her temper and told me: "If you don't stop boring me with your sermons I'll take my clothes off here and now and lie naked on these flowers!"

Often, when I watched her sleeping, or eating, or trying to look innocent, I would ask myself why God had given her such remarkable beauty, grace, intelligence. Surely not just to sprawl around in bed, to eat, to tell lies – nothing but lies the whole time? But *was* she in fact intelligent? She thought that three candles in a row and the number thirteen were unlucky; she was terrified of the evil eye and of nightmares; she talked of free love and freedom in general like some pious old crone; she claimed that Boleslav Markevich[12] was a better writer than Turgenev. But she was diabolically cunning and astute and knew how to pass herself off as a very educated, progressive woman in society.

When she was in a cheerful mood she thought nothing of insulting servants or killing insects. She loved bullfights and reading about murders, and she was angry when defendants were acquitted.

To live the kind of life Ariadna and I were leading a great deal of money was needed. My poor father sent me his pension, all his various scraps of income and borrowed on my behalf wherever he could. Once, when he replied *non habeo*,[13] I sent him a desperate telegram, begging him to mortgage the estate. Shortly afterwards I asked him to take out a second mortgage somewhere. He did both without murmur and sent me the money down to the last copeck. But Ariadna felt contempt for the practical side of life – that kind of thing wasn't her concern and while I was throwing around thousands of francs to satisfy her mad cravings, groaning like an ancient oak tree, she would light-heartedly hum *Addio, bella Napoli*.[14] I gradually cooled towards her and began to feel ashamed of our affair. I don't care for pregnancies and labour pains, but now I was sometimes dreaming of a child which would have been at least a formal justification of our life. To avoid becoming completely loathsome to myself I took to visiting museums and galleries and reading books. I ate little and I gave up drinking. If you keep on the go from dawn to dusk you somehow feel all the better for it.

And I bored Ariadna as well. Incidentally, it was only among mediocrities that she enjoyed success: those earlier visions of ambassadors and salons had evaporated. Money was short, which distressed her and reduced her to tears. In the end she announced that she would have no objection to returning to Russia after all. So, here we are on our way back. During the last months before our departure she had been furiously corresponding with her brother. Obviously she has some secret plans in mind – what they are, God only knows. I'm long sick and tired of trying to find out what cunning tricks she's up to. We're not going to the country, though, but to Yalta[15] and then to the Caucasus. Now she can live only in holiday resorts – if you only knew how I detest all these places, how suffocated I feel in them, how ashamed. Now I want to go to the country! I want to work, earn my living by the sweat of my brow, atone for my sins. Now I feel brimful of energy and I think that if I buckled down I could clear the estate of debt within five years. But as you can see, there are complications. Here we're not abroad but back in dear old Mother Russia and we need to think of lawful wedlock. Of course, the infatuation's passed, not a trace of love any more. But come what may, I'm duty bound to marry her."'

Shamokhin (who was agitated after telling his story) and myself went below, still talking about women. It was late. As it happened we were sharing the same cabin.

'These days,' said Shamokhin, 'it's only in villages that women don't lag behind men. There they think and feel like them, fight just as hard against nature in the name of culture as men do. But the educated, middle-class urban woman fell behind long ago and is reverting to her primitive state. She is half animal now and it's thanks to her that a great deal of what human genius has achieved has been lost. Women are gradually disappearing and their place is being taken by the primitive female. The backwardness of educated women is a serious threat to civilization. As women regress, they try to drag men after them and they're retarding their progress. There's no doubt about it.'

I asked him: why generalize? Why judge all women by Ariadna alone? Surely women's striving for education and sexual equality – which I take as a striving towards justice – in itself rules out any idea of regression. But Shamokhin was hardly listening and smiled sceptically. Here was an impassioned, confirmed misogynist and it was impossible to make him change his mind.

'Hey! Enough of that!' he interrupted. 'Once a woman doesn't see me as a man or as an equal, but as the male of the species and spends her whole life worrying about how to please me – taking possession of me that is – then how can there be any talk of equal rights? Oh, don't trust them, they are very, very crafty! We men go to enormous trouble about their freedom, but they don't want freedom at all and are only pretending that they want it. Oh, they're so very crafty! Dreadfully crafty!'

I was tired of arguing and wanted to sleep, so I turned my face to the wall.

'Yes,' I heard as I was falling asleep. 'Oh yes, sir! And our upbringing's entirely to blame, old man! In the long run all that your urban woman's upbringing and education essentially boils down to is that she's turned into a human animal – that is, she can attract the male and knows how to conquer him. Yes, sir,' sighed Shamokhin. 'Girls should be brought up and educated together with boys so that they're always together. Women must be brought up so that, like men, they're able to admit they're in the wrong, otherwise they'll always think that they're in the right. We must instil into girls from the cradle that men are first and foremost not mere escorts or suitors, but their friends and neighbours, equal to them in every respect. Teach them to think logically, to make inferences, and don't go telling them[16] that their brain weighs less than a man's and that therefore they don't have to trouble themselves about science, art and cultural matters. A boy who is an apprentice cobbler or house-painter also has a brain that's smaller than a grown man's, but he plays a part in the general struggle for survival, working and suffering. And we must also abandon this habit of explaining everything away by physiology, pregnancy and childbirth. In the first place, a woman doesn't give birth every month. Secondly, not all women have children. Thirdly, a normal peasant woman will be working in the fields the day before she gives birth and she's none the worse for it. There should be absolute equality in daily life. If a man offers his seat or picks up a woman's handkerchief – then let her do the same for him! I don't mind if a girl of good family helps me on with my coat or gives me a glass of water . . .'

That was all I heard, as I fell asleep. When we were approaching Sevastopol next morning the weather was wet and unpleasant. The sea was rather rough. Shamokhin sat with me in the deck-house silently brooding. When the tea bell rang gentlemen with turned-up collars and ladies with pale, sleepy faces started going below. One young and very beautiful lady – the same lady who had been furious with the Customs officials at Volochisk – stopped in front of Shamokhin and told him in the voice of a capricious, spoilt child:

'Jean, your little birdie's been sick!'

Later, when I was living in Yalta, I saw that beautiful lady on horseback, galloping so fast that two officers could barely keep up with her. And one morning I saw her in a Phrygian cap, wearing a small apron, sitting on the front sketching in oils, while a large crowd stood admiringly at a distance. And I was introduced to her. She shook my hand very firmly, looked at me with delight and thanked me in that sugary, singsong voice for the pleasure my writings gave her.

'Don't you believe her,' Shamokhin whispered. 'She hasn't read a word of yours.'

Towards evening, when I was strolling along the front, I bumped into Shamokhin. His arms were filled with large parcels of savouries and fruit.

'Prince Maktuyev is here!' he exclaimed delightedly. 'He arrived yesterday with that spiritualist brother of hers. Now I understand what she was writing to him about! Heavens!' he continued, gazing at the sky and pressing the parcels to his chest. 'If she manages to hit it off with the prince that means I'm free and can go back to my father in the country!'

And he ran on further.

'I'm beginning to believe in ghosts!' he shouted to me as he looked back. 'Grandfather Ilarion's ghost seems to have predicted the truth! Oh, if only!'

The day after this encounter I left Yalta and I really don't know how Shamokhin's affair ended.

The Black Monk

I

Andrey Vasilich Kovrin, MA, was exhausted, his nerves were shattered. He did not take any medical treatment but mentioned his condition in passing to a doctor friend over a bottle of wine, and was advised to spend the spring and summer in the country. And as it happened he received just then a long letter from Tanya Pesotskaya, inviting him to come and stay at Borisovka. So he decided he really must get away.

At first – this was in April – he went to his own estate, Kovrinka, where he lived on his own for three weeks. Then after waiting until the roads were passable, he drove off in a carriage to see his former guardian and mentor Pesotsky the horticulturalist, who was famous throughout Russia. It was no more than about fifty miles from Kovrinka to Pesotsky's place at Borisovka and it was pure joy travelling along the soft road in spring, in a comfortable sprung carriage.

Pesotsky's house was huge, with columns, peeling plaster lions, and a footman in coat and tails at the entrance. The gloomy, severe, old-fashioned park was strictly laid out in the landscaped English style, stretched almost half a mile from the house to the river, and ended in a precipitous clayey bank where pines grew, their exposed roots resembling shaggy paws. Down below, the water glinted uninvitingly, sandpipers flew past squeaking plaintively, and it was generally the kind of place to make you want to sit down and write a ballad. But near the house itself, in the courtyard and the orchard, which took up about eighty acres, including the nursery beds, it was cheerful and lively, even in bad weather. Nowhere, except at Pesotsky's, had Kovrin seen such wonderful roses, lilies, camellias, so many different tulips, with colours ranging from white to soot-black, such a profusion of flowers. It was only the beginning of spring and the real splendours of the flowerbeds were still hidden in the hothouses. But the flowers in bloom along the paths – and here and there in the beds – were enough to make you feel that you were in the very kingdom of tender hues as you strolled in the garden, especially early in the morning, when dew sparkled on every petal.

The ornamental section of the garden, which Pesotsky disparagingly called 'sheer nonsense', had seemed like a fairyland to Kovrin as a child. The oddities, elaborate monstrosities and travesties of nature that were to be seen here! There were trellised fruit trees, a pear tree shaped like a Lombardy poplar, globe-shaped oaks and limes, an apple tree umbrella, arches, initials, candelabra, and even an '1862' made from plums – this was the year Pesotsky first took up horticulture. Here also were fine, graceful saplings with straight, firm stems like palm trees, and only after a very close look could you tell that they were gooseberries or blackcurrants. But what most of all made the garden a cheerful, lively place was the constant activity. From dawn to dusk gardeners with wheelbarrows, hoes and watering-cans swarmed like ants near the trees and bushes, on the paths and flowerbeds.

Kovrin arrived at the Pesotskys' after nine in the evening. He found Tanya and her father Yegor Semyonych in a terribly worried state. The clear, starry sky and the thermometer foretold frost towards morning, but the head gardener Ivan Karlych had gone off to town and there was no one left they could rely on.

During supper, they talked only of this morning frost and decided that Tanya would not go to bed, but would go round the orchard after midnight to check if everything was all right, while Yegor Semyonych would get up at three, even earlier perhaps. Kovrin sat with Tanya the whole evening and after midnight went with her into the garden. It was cold and there was a strong smell of burning. In the big orchard, called 'commercial' as it brought Yegor Semyonych several thousand roubles profit every year, a dense, black, acrid smoke was spreading over the ground and enveloping the trees, saving all those thousands from the frost. Here the trees were planted like draughts pieces, in straight, even rows, like columns of soldiers. This strict, pedantic regularity, plus the fact that all the trees were exactly the same height, all of them having absolutely identical crowns and trunks, made a monotonous, even boring picture. Kovrin and Tanya walked between the rows, where bonfires of manure, straw and all kind of refuse were smouldering, and every now and then they met workers drifting through the smoke like shadows. Only cherries, plums and certain varieties of apple were in bloom, but the whole orchard was drowning in smoke. Kovrin breathed a deep breath only when they reached the nurseries.

'When I was a child the smoke used to make me sneeze,' he said, shrugging his shoulders, 'but I still don't understand why this smoke saves the plants from frost.'

'Smoke is a substitute for clouds when the sky is clear . . .' Tanya said.

'But what use are *they*?'

'You don't normally get a frost when it's dull and overcast.'

'That's right!'

He laughed and took her arm. Her broad, very serious face, chill from the cold, with its fine black eyebrows, the raised coat collar which cramped her movements, her whole slim, graceful body, her dress tucked up from the dew – all this moved him deeply.

'Heavens, how you've grown up!' he said. 'Last time I left here, five years ago, you were still a child. You were so thin, long-legged, bareheaded, with that short little dress you used to wear. And I teased you and called you a heron . . . How time changes everything!'

'Yes, five years!' Tanya sighed. 'A lot of water has flowed under the bridge since then. Tell me, Andrey, in all honesty,' she said in an animated voice, peering into his face, 'have you grown tired of us? But why am I asking you this? You're a man, you live your own interesting life, you're an eminent person . . . Becoming like strangers to each other is really so natural! Anyway, Andrey, I want you to treat us as your family, we have a right to that.'

'But I do, Tanya.'

'Word of honour?'

'Yes, word of honour.'

'You were surprised before that we had so many of your photos. You must know Father idolizes you. At times I think he loves you more than me. He's proud of you. You are a scholar, a remarkable person, you've made a dazzling career for yourself and he's convinced this is because he brought you up. I let him think this, I don't see why I should stop him.'

Dawn was breaking – this was particularly evident from the clarity with which puffs of smoke and the tree tops were outlined now in the air. Nightingales were singing and the cries of quails came from the fields.

'But it's time for bed,' Tanya said. 'Besides that, it's cold.' She took his arm. 'Thanks for coming, Andrey. Our friends aren't very interesting, not that we have many. All we have is the garden, garden, garden, nothing else.' She laughed. 'First-class, second-class, Oporto,[1] rennets and winter apples, budding, grafting. Our whole life has gone into this garden, I dream of nothing but apple and pear trees. Of course, it's all very nice and useful, but sometimes I want something else, to break the monotony. I remember the times you came for the holidays, or just for a short visit, how the house became somehow fresher and brighter then, as though the covers had been taken off the chandeliers and furniture. I was a little girl then, but I did understand.'

She spoke for a long time and with great feeling. Suddenly Kovrin was struck by the idea that he might even conceive an affection for this small, fragile, loquacious creature during the course of the summer, become attracted to her and fall in love. In their situation that would be so natural and possible! He was both touched and amused by the thought. He leant down towards that dear, worried face and softly sang:

> Onegin, I will not hide it,
> I love Tatyana madly . . .[2]

Yegor Semyonych was up already when they returned to the house. Kovrin did not feel like sleeping, got into conversation with the old man and went back to the garden with him. Yegor Semyonych was a tall, broad-shouldered man, with a large paunch. Although he suffered from short breath, he always walked so fast it was hard keeping up with him. He had an extremely worried look and was always hurrying off somewhere as if all would be lost should he be just one minute late.

'It's a peculiar thing, my dear boy,' he began, then paused for breath. 'As you see, it's freezing down on the ground, but just you hold a thermometer on a stick about twelve feet above it and you'll find it's warm there . . . Why is it?'

'I honestly don't know,' Kovrin said, laughing.

'Hm . . . one can't know everything of course . . . However capacious your brain is, it won't accommodate everything. Philosophy's more your line, isn't it?'

'I give lectures on psychology, but my main interest is philosophy.'

'And you're not bored?'

'On the contrary, it's my life.'

'Well, God bless you . . .' Yegor Semyonych murmured, thoughtfully stroking his grey side-whiskers. 'God bless you . . . I'm very pleased for you . . . very pleased, dear boy.'

But suddenly he pricked up his ears, pulled a horrified face, ran to one side and soon disappeared in the clouds of smoke behind the trees.

'Who tied a horse to that apple tree?' the despairing, heart-rending cry rang out. 'What swine, what scum dared to tie a horse to an apple tree? Good Lord! They've ruined, frozen, polluted, mucked everything up! The garden's ruined! Ruined! Oh, God!'

He went back to Kovrin, looking exhausted, outraged. 'What can you do with this confounded riff-raff?' he said tearfully, flinging his arms out helplessly. 'Last night Stepka was carting manure and tied his horse to the apple tree. He twisted the reins so hellishly tight, damn him, that the bark's rubbed off. How could he do it? I had words with him, but the idiot just stood gaping. Hanging's too good for him!'

After he had calmed down he put his arms round Kovrin and kissed him on the check. 'Well, God bless, God bless . . .' he muttered.

'I'm very pleased you came. I can't say how glad I am . . . Thanks.'

Then, at the same rapid pace and with that same worried look, he toured the whole garden, showing his former ward all the conservatories, greenhouses, cold frames, and the two apiaries he called the 'wonder of the century'.

As they walked along, the sun rose, filling the garden with a bright light. It grew warm. Anticipating a fine, cheerful, long day, Kovrin recalled that in fact it was only the beginning of May and that the whole summer lay ahead – just as bright, cheerful and long, and suddenly there welled up within him that feeling of radiant, joyous youth he had known in his childhood, when he had run around this garden. And he embraced the old man in turn and kissed him tenderly. Both of them, deeply moved, went into the house and drank tea from old-fashioned porcelain cups, with cream and rich pastries. These little things again reminded Kovrin of his childhood and youth. The beautiful present, the freshly awakened impressions of the past, blended together: they had a somewhat inhibiting effect, but none the less gave him a feeling of well-being.

He waited for Tanya to wake up, drank coffee with her, went for a stroll, and then returned to his room and sat down to work. He read attentively, took notes, now and again looking up at the open window or the fresh flowers that stood, still moist with dew, in vases on the table, then lowering his eyes on his book again; it seemed every vein in his body was pulsating and throbbing with pleasure.

II

In the country he continued to lead the same nervous, restless life as in town. He read and wrote a great deal, studied Italian, and on his strolls took pleasure in the thought that he would soon be back at work again. Everyone was amazed he slept so little. If he chanced to doze off during the day for half an hour, he could not sleep at all later and would emerge from a night of insomnia vigorous and cheerful, as if nothing was wrong.

He talked a lot, drank wine and smoked expensive cigars. Young ladies who lived nearby called on the Pesotskys almost every day and played the piano and sang with Tanya. Sometimes a young gentleman from the neighbourhood, an excellent violinist, would call. Kovrin would listen so hungrily to the playing and singing it tired him out, and the exhaustion was plainly visible from the way his eyelids seemed to stick together and his head dropped to one side.

One evening, after tea, he was sitting on the balcony reading. At the same time Tanya, who sang soprano, together with one of the young ladies – a contralto – and the young violinist, were practising Braga's famous *Serenade*.[3] Kovrin listened hard to the words (they were Russian) but could not understand them at all. Finally, after putting his book aside and listening very closely, he did understand: a young girl, with a morbid imagination, was in her garden one night and heard some mysterious sounds, so beautiful and strange, she had to admit that their harmony was something divine, incomprehensible to mere mortals as it soared up again into the heavens whence it came. Kovrin began to feel sleepy. He rose to his feet, wearily walked up and down the drawing-room, then the ballroom. When the singing stopped, he took Tanya by the arm and went out onto the balcony with her.

'Since early this morning I haven't been able to get a certain legend out of my mind,' he said. 'I can't remember if I read it somewhere or if I heard it, but it's really quite strange – doesn't appear to make any sense at all. I should say from the start that it's not distinguished for its clarity. A thousand years ago a certain monk, dressed in black, was walking across a desert – somewhere in Syria or Arabia . . . A few miles from where he was walking a fisherman saw another black monk slowly moving across the surface of a lake. This second monk was a mirage. Now forget the laws of optics, which the legend apparently doesn't acknowledge, and listen to what happened next. The mirage produced another one. This second mirage produced a third, so that the image of the black monk began to be transmitted endlessly from one layer of the atmosphere to the other. He was sighted in Africa, then Spain, India, the far north . . .

He finally left the earth's atmosphere and now wanders through the whole universe, never meeting the conditions which would make it possible for him to fade away. Perhaps he'll be seen somewhere on Mars now, or on some star in the Southern Cross. But, my dear, the essence, the real crux of the legend is this: precisely one thousand years after that monk first walked across the desert, the mirage will return to the earth's atmosphere and appear to people. And it seems these thousand years are almost up. According to the legend, we can expect the black monk any day now.'

'A strange mirage,' said Tanya, who did not care for the legend.

'But the most amazing thing is,' Kovrin said, laughing, 'I just can't remember what prompted me to think of it. Did I read it somewhere? Did I hear about it? Perhaps the black monk was only a dream? I swear to God, I can't remember. But I'm intrigued by this legend. I've been thinking about it all day.'

Leaving Tanya to her guests, he went out of the house and strolled by the flowerbeds, deep in thought. The sun was setting. The freshly watered flowers gave off a moist, irritating scent. In the house the singing had started again; from the distance the violin sounded like a human voice. Kovrin racked his brains trying to remember where he had read or heard about that legend as he walked unhurriedly towards the park, reaching the river before he knew where he was.

He descended the path that ran down a steep bank, past bare roots, to the water, where he disturbed some sandpipers and frightened two ducks away. Here and there on the gloomy pines gleamed the last rays of the setting sun, but evening had already come over the surface of the river. Kovrin crossed the footbridge to the other side. Before him lay a broad field full of young rye not yet in ear. There was no human habitation, not a living soul out there, and it seemed the path would lead him to that same unknown, mysterious spot where the sun had just set and where the evening glow spread its flames so magnificently over all that wide expanse.

'So much space, freedom, peace here!' Kovrin thought as he walked along the path. 'The whole world seems to be looking at me, has gone silent, and is waiting for me to understand it.'

But just then some ripples spread across the rye and a gentle evening breeze lightly caressed his bare head. A moment later there was another gust, stronger this time, and the rye rustled and he could hear the dull murmur of the pines behind him. Kovrin stood motionless in astonishment. On the horizon a tall black column was rising up into the sky, like a whirlwind or tornado. Its outlines were blurred, but he could see at once that it was not standing still, but moving at terrifying speed straight towards him – and the nearer it came, the smaller and clearer it grew. Kovrin leapt aside into the rye to make way – and he was only just in time . . . A monk in black vestments, grey-haired and with black eyebrows, his arms across his chest, flashed past; his bare feet did not touch the ground. After he had raced on another six yards he looked round at Kovrin, nodded and gave him a friendly, but artful, smile. What a pale, terribly pale, thin face though! Growing larger again, he flew across the river, struck the clayey bank and the pines without making a sound, passed straight through and disappeared into thin air.

'So, there it is . . .' murmured Kovrin. 'That shows there's truth in the legend.'

Without trying to find an explanation for this strange apparition and satisfied that he had managed to get such a close look, not only at the black vestments, but even at the monk's face and eyes, he went back to the house feeling pleasantly excited.

People were strolling peacefully in the park and garden, the musicians were playing in the house, so only he had seen the monk. He had a strong urge to tell Tanya and Yegor Semyonych about everything, but he realized they would surely think the story crazy and be scared stiff. Better keep quiet about it. He laughed out loud, sang, danced a mazurka; he was in high spirits and everyone – Tanya, her guests – found that he really had a radiant, inspired look about him that evening, that he was most interesting.

III

After supper, when the guests had left, he went to his room and lay on the couch. He wanted to think about the monk, but a moment later in came Tanya.

'Here, Andrey, read Father's articles,' she said, handing him a bundle of pamphlets and offprints. 'They're wonderful, he's an excellent writer.'

'I wouldn't say that!' Yegor Semyonych said, forcing a laugh as he followed her into the room; he felt embarrassed. 'Don't listen to her, please! Don't read them! But if you need something to make you sleep, then go ahead. They're an excellent soporific!'

'In my opinion they're magnificent,' Tanya said with great conviction. 'Read them, Andrey, and persuade Father to write more often. He could write a whole course in horticulture.'

Yegor Semyonych gave a forced laugh, blushed and started speaking in the way shy authors usually do. In the end he gave in. 'In that case, read Gaucher's article[4] first, then these short ones in Russian,' he muttered, turning over the pamphlets with trembling hands. 'Otherwise you won't understand a thing. Before you read my objections, you must know what it is I'm objecting to. However, it's rubbish . . . boring. What's more, I think it's time for bed.'

Tanya went out. Yegor Semyonych sat beside Kovrin on the couch and sighed deeply. 'Yes, my dear boy,' he began after a short silence. 'Yes, my dear Master of Arts. Here I am writing articles and exhibiting at shows and winning medals . . . They say Pesotsky has "apples as big as your head" and that he made his fortune with his orchard. Pesotsky is monarch of all he surveys,[5] in short. But, you may ask, what's the point of it all? The garden is really beautiful, a show-garden in fact. It's not so much a garden as a complete institution, of the greatest importance to the state, a step, so to speak, towards a new era in Russian economics and industry. But what's the point of it? What's the use?'

'It speaks for itself.'

'That's not what I mean. I'd like to know, what will happen to the garden when I die? It won't be kept up to its present standard for more than one month. The secret of my success isn't that it's a big garden, with lots of gardeners, but because I love the work – do you follow? Perhaps I love it better than myself. I work from dawn till dusk. The grafting, pruning, planting – I do them all myself. When people start helping me, I get jealous and irritated until I'm downright rude to them. The whole secret is *love*, and by that I mean the keen eye and head of the master looking after his own place, the feeling that comes over you when you've gone visiting for an hour and you just sit still. But your heart's not there, you're miles away – afraid something might be going wrong in the garden. And when I die who'll look after it? Who'll do the work? The head gardener? The ordinary gardeners? What do you think? So let me tell you, dear boy, the principal enemy in our work isn't hares, cockchafers or frost, but the man who doesn't care.'

'And Tanya?' laughed Kovrin. 'She couldn't possibly do more harm than a hare. She loves the work, she understands it.'

'Yes, she loves and understands it. If the garden passes into *her* hands after my death and she takes charge, I could hope for nothing better. But supposing she marries, God forbid?' Yegor Semyonych whispered and gave Kovrin a frightened look. 'This is my point! She'll marry, have children and then she'll have no time to think about the garden. But my main worry is her marrying some young whipper-snapper who'll grow greedy, rent the garden out to some market-woman and it'll all go to rack and ruin within a year! In this kind of business women are like the plague!'

Yegor Semyonych sighed and was silent for a few minutes. 'Perhaps it's just egotism, but I'm telling you quite frankly: I don't want Tanya to marry. I'm afraid! There's that young fop who comes here scraping his fiddle. I know Tanya won't marry him, I know that very well, but I just can't stand the sight of him. On the whole I'm quite a crank, dear boy. I admit it.' Yegor Semyonych got up and paced the room excitedly; it was plain he wanted to say something very important, but he couldn't bring himself to.

'I'm extremely fond of you and I'll be open with you,' he said at last, stuffing his hands into his pockets. 'I'm usually quite straightforward when it comes to certain ticklish questions and I'm telling you exactly what I think – I can't stand these so-called "innermost thoughts". I'm telling you straight: you're the only man I wouldn't mind marrying my daughter. You're clever, you have feelings and you wouldn't let my beloved work perish. But the main reason is – I love you like a son . . . and I'm proud of you. If Tanya and yourself became fond of each other, well then, I'd be very glad, happy even. I'm telling you straight, without frills, as an honest man.'

Kovrin burst out laughing. Yegor Semyonych opened the door to go out and stopped on the threshold. 'If Tanya gave you a son I'd make a gardener out of him,' he said thoughtfully. 'However, that's an idle dream . . . Good night.'

Left alone, Kovrin settled himself more comfortably on the couch and started on the articles. One bore the title *Intermedial Cultivation*, another *A few Observations on Mr Z's Remarks on Double-Trenching in New Gardens*, and another *More about Grafting Dormant Buds*; and there were other titles like that. But what a restless, uneven tone, what highly charged, almost pathological fervour! Here was an article with apparently the most inoffensive title and unexceptionable subject – the winter dessert apple. But Yegor Semyonych first weighed in with an *audiatur altera pars*[6] and ended with *sapienti sat*,[7] interpolating these dicta with a whole torrent of venomous animadversions apropos the 'learned ignorance of our self-appointed gentlemen-horticulturalists who look down on nature from their Olympian heights': or Gaucher, 'whose reputation was made by ignoramuses and dilettantes'. These remarks were followed by the totally irrelevant, forced, sham regret for the fact that it was no longer legal to birch peasants who stole fruit and damaged trees in the process.

'It's a fine, pleasant, healthy occupation, but even here it's passion and warfare,' Kovrin thought. 'Probably, it's because intellectuals are neurotic and over-sensitive everywhere, in all walks of life. Perhaps it can't be avoided.'

He thought of Tanya who liked Yegor Semyonych's articles so much. She was not tall, was pale and thin, with protruding collarbones; her dark, clever, staring eyes were always peering, seeking something. She walked just like her father, taking short, quick steps.

Very talkative, she loved to argue and would accompany the most trivial phrase with highly expressive mimicry and gesticulations. She was probably highly strung.

Kovrin read on, but he understood nothing and gave up. That same, agreeable feeling of excitement he had had when dancing his mazurka and listening to the music made him weary now and stirred a multitude of thoughts. He stood up and started walking round the room, thinking about the black monk. It occurred to him that if he alone had seen that strange, supernatural apparition, then he must be ill and a prey to hallucinations. This thought frightened him, but not for long.

'In fact I feel fine. I'm not harming anyone. So that means there's nothing bad in these hallucinations,' he thought and felt fine again.

He sat on the couch and clasped his head to hold in check that incomprehensible feeling of joy which filled his whole being; then he paced up and down again and started to work. But the ideas he found in the book left him unsatisfied. He wanted something gigantic, immense, staggering. Towards dawn he undressed and reluctantly got into bed. After all, he had to sleep!

When he heard Yegor Semyonych's footsteps receding into the garden, Kovrin rang the bell and told the servant to bring him some wine. After enjoying a few glasses of claret his senses grew dim and he fell asleep.

IV

Yegor Semyonych and Tanya had frequent quarrels and said nasty things to each other. One morning, after a squabble about something, Tanya burst into tears and went to her room. She didn't appear for lunch, or tea. At first Yegor Semyonych walked around solemnly and pompously, as if he wanted to make it known that he considered justice and order more important than anything else in the world. But he could not keep up the pose for long and lost heart. Sadly he wandered through the park, sighing the whole time, 'Ah, Good Lord,

Good Lord!' and he did not eat a thing for dinner. Finally, full of guilt and remorse, he knocked on the locked door and called out timidly, 'Tanya! Tanya?'

A weak voice, drained by tears, but still determined, replied from behind the door, 'Leave me alone, I beg you.'

The anguish of the master and mistress was reflected all over the house, even in the gardeners. Kovrin was immersed in his interesting work, but in the end he too felt bored and embarrassed. Trying to dispel the prevailing unpleasant atmosphere, he decided to intervene and towards evening knocked at Tanya's door. She let him in.

'Come now, you should be ashamed!' he joked, looking in amazement at Tanya's tear-stained, mournful face that was covered in red blotches. 'Surely it's not as bad as all that? Now, now!'

'If you only knew how he torments me!' she said and copious, bitter tears welled from her large eyes. 'He's tormented the life out of me,' she went on, wringing her hands. 'I didn't say *anything* to him . . . nothing at all. I only said we don't need to keep on extra workers when . . . when we can engage day-labourers if we want to. You know, our gardeners have been standing idle for a whole week. That's all I said, but he shouted and said many insulting, deeply offensive things. Why?'

'Now, that's enough, enough,' Kovrin said, smoothing her hair. 'You've had your quarrel and a good cry, and that's enough. You must stop being angry now, it's not good . . . especially as he loves you so very much.'

'He's ruined my whole life,' Tanya continued, sobbing. 'All I hear is insults and abuse . . . He thinks there's no place for me in this house. Agreed. He's right. I'll leave this place tomorrow, get a job as a telegraphist . . . That's what I'll do.'

'Come now, there's no need to cry, Tanya. Please don't, my dear . . . You're both quick-tempered, easily upset, and you're both to blame. Come on, I'll make peace between you.'

Kovrin spoke with feeling, convincingly, but she kept on crying, her shoulders twitching and her hands clenched as if something really terrible had happened to her. He felt all the more sorry for her because, although her grief was nothing serious, she was suffering deeply. How little it took to make this creature unhappy all day long, for her whole life perhaps! As he comforted Tanya, Kovrin thought that he wouldn't find two people who loved him so much as Tanya and her father in a month of Sundays. Having lost his father and mother as a small child, but for these two, probably, he would never have known true affection until his dying day. He would never have known that simple, disinterested love that is felt only for those who are very close, for blood relations. And he felt that this weeping, trembling girl's nerves were reacting to his own half-sick, overwrought nerves like iron to a magnet. He could never have loved a healthy, strong, rosy-cheeked woman, but that pale, weak, unhappy Tanya attracted him.

And he gladly stroked her hair and shoulders, pressed her hands and wiped away the tears . . . Finally she stopped crying. For a long time she complained about her father and her hard, intolerable life in that house, imploring Kovrin to see things as she did. Then gradually, she began to smile and said sighing that God had given her *such* a bad character. In the end she laughed out loud, called herself a fool and ran out of the room.

Shortly afterwards, when Kovrin went into the garden, Yegor Semyonych and Tanya were strolling side by side along the path as if nothing had happened. They were both eating rye bread with salt, as they were hungry.

V

Pleased with his success as peacemaker, Kovrin went into the park. As he sat pondering on a bench he heard the clatter of carriages and a woman's laughter – guests had arrived. As the shadows of evening fell across the garden he heard the vague sounds of a violin, voices singing, which reminded him of the black monk. Where, in what country or on what planet was that optical absurdity wandering now?

Hardly had he recalled that legend, conjuring up the dark spectre he had seen in the rye field, when quite silently, without the slightest rustling, a man of medium height, his grey head uncovered, all in black, barefoot like a beggar, his black eyebrows sharply defined on his deathly white face, slipped out from behind the pine trees just opposite. Nodding his head welcomingly, this beggar or pilgrim silently came over to the bench and Kovrin could see it was the black monk. For a minute they both eyed each other – Kovrin in amazement, the monk in a friendly way, with that same rather crafty look.

'You're just a mirage,' Kovrin murmured. 'Why are you here, sitting still like that? It doesn't tally with the legend.'

'Never mind,' the monk answered softly after a brief pause, turning his face towards him. 'The legend, myself, the mirage are all products of your overheated imagination. I'm an apparition . . .'

'That means you don't exist?' Kovrin asked.

'Think what you like,' the monk said with a weak smile. 'I exist in your imagination, and your imagination is part of nature, so I exist in nature too.'

'You have a very aged, clever and extremely expressive face, as if you really have lived more than a thousand years,' Kovrin said. 'I didn't know my imagination could create such phenomena. But why are you looking at me so rapturously? Do you like me?'

'Yes. You're one of the few who are rightly called God's Chosen. You serve Eternal Truth. Your ideas, intentions, your amazing erudition, your whole life – all bear the divine, heavenly stamp, since they are devoted to the Rational and the Beautiful, that is, to the Eternal.'

'You mentioned "Eternal Truth" . . . But is that within men's reach, do they need it if there's no such thing as eternal life?'

'There *is* eternal life,' the monk said.

'Do you believe in immortality?'

'Yes, of course. A great, bright future awaits you human beings. And the more men there are like you on earth, the quicker will this future come about. Without men like you serving the highest principles, living intelligently and freely, humanity would be worthless. In the normal course of events it would have to wait a long time for its life upon earth to come to an end. But you will lead it into the Kingdom of Eternal Truth a few thousand years ahead of time – this is your noble service. You are the embodiment of God's blessing which has come to dwell among men.'

'But what is the purpose of eternal life?' asked Kovrin.

'Like any other kind of life – pleasure. True pleasure is knowledge, and eternal life will afford innumerable and inexhaustible sources of knowledge: this is the meaning of the saying, "In my Father's house are many mansions." '[8]

'If you only knew how enjoyable it is listening to you!' Kovrin said, rubbing his hands with pleasure.

'I'm very pleased.'

'But I know one thing: when you've gone I'll start worrying whether you really do exist. You're a phantom, a hallucination. Does that mean I'm mentally ill, insane?'

'Even if that were so, why let it bother you? You're ill from overworking, you've worn yourself out. I'm trying to say that you've sacrificed your health for an idea and it won't be long before you sacrifice your very life to it. What could be better? All noble spirits blessed with gifts from on high have this as their aim.'

'If I *know* that I'm mentally ill, how can I have any faith in myself?'

'But how do you know that men of genius, in whom the whole world puts its faith, haven't seen ghosts too? Nowadays scientists say genius is akin to madness. My friend, only the mediocre, the common herd are healthy and normal. Thoughts about an age of neurosis, overwork, degeneracy and so on can seriously worry only those for whom the purpose of life lies in the present – that is, the common herd.'

'The Romans used to speak of *mens sana in corpore sano*.'[9]

'Not all that the Greeks and Romans said is true. Heightened awareness, excitement, ecstasy – everything that distinguishes prophets, poets, martyrs to an idea, from ordinary people is hostile to man's animal side – I mean, his physical health. I repeat: if you want to be healthy and normal, go and join the herd.'

'It's strange the way you repeat things I think of myself very often,' Kovrin said. 'It's as though you spied out and eavesdropped on my most secret thoughts. But let's not talk about me. What do you mean by Eternal Truth?'

The monk did not answer. Kovrin looked at him and could not make out his face – its features had become hazy and indistinct. Then the monk's head and arms began to disappear. His torso merged with the bench and the twilight shadows, and he vanished completely.

'The hallucination's over!' Kovrin said laughing. 'A pity!'

He went back to the house happy and cheerful. The monk's few words had flattered not his pride, but his very soul, his whole being. To be one of the Chosen, to serve Eternal Truth, to stand in the ranks of those who, a thousand years ahead of time, would make men worthy of the Kingdom of God, thereby saving them from several thousand years of needless struggle, sin and suffering, to surrender, to surrender everything – youth, strength, health – to an idea, to be ready to die for the common weal – what a noble, blissful destiny! The memory of his pure, chaste, hardworking past flashed through his mind; he remembered what he had learned, what he had taught others, and he decided that the monk had not been exaggerating.

As he went through the park he met Tanya. She was wearing a different dress now.

'So you're here,' she said. 'We've all been looking for you, looking everywhere . . . But what's the matter?' she asked in surprise, studying his radiant, glowing face. 'How strange you are, Andrey.'

'I'm contented, Tanya,' Kovrin said as he put his hands on her shoulders. 'I'm more than contented, I'm happy! Tanya, dear Tanya, you're such a likeable person! Dear Tanya, I'm so glad, so glad!'

He kissed both her hands passionately and went on, 'I've just experienced some bright, wonderful, divine moments. But I can't tell you everything, because you'd call me mad or disbelieve me. Let's talk about you. Dear, wonderful Tanya! I love you. I'm *used* to loving you now. Having you near me, meeting you ten times a day has become a spiritual necessity. I don't know how I will cope when I go home.'

'Well!' Tanya laughed. 'You'll forget about us in a couple of days. We're small fry and you're a great man.'

'No, let's be serious!' he said. 'I shall take you with me, Tanya. Will you say yes? Will you come with me? Will you be mine?'

'Well!' Tanya said and felt like laughing again. But she could not and her face came out in red blotches. Her breath came faster and she quickly went away, not towards the house, but further into the park. 'I hadn't given it any thought . . . I hadn't thought . . .' she said, wringing her hands despairingly.

But Kovrin kept following her, still speaking with that same radiant, rapturous expression on his face, 'I want a love which will completely transport me, and only *you* can give me that love, Tanya! I'm happy, so happy!'

Quite stunned, she stooped, shrank and suddenly seemed to have aged ten years. But he found her beautiful and shouted out in delight, 'How beautiful she is!'

VI

When he heard from Kovrin that not only were they enamoured of each other, but that there was even going to be a wedding, Yegor Semyonych paced up and down for a long time, trying to conceal his excitement. His hands started shaking, his neck swelled up and turned crimson. He ordered his racing droshky to be harnessed and drove off somewhere. When Tanya saw him whipping the horses and pulling his cap almost onto his ears, she realized the kind of mood he was in, locked herself in her room and cried all day long.

The peaches and plums in the hothouses were already ripe. The packing and despatch of this delicate, temperamental cargo required a great deal of care, labour and trouble. Because of the very hot, dry summer, each tree needed watering, which involved a great deal of the gardeners' time. Swarms of caterpillars appeared, which the gardeners – even Yegor Semyonych and Tanya – squashed with their bare fingers, much to Kovrin's disgust. Besides this, they had to take orders for fruit and trees for the autumn and conduct an extensive correspondence. And at the most critical time, when no one seemed to have a moment to spare, the harvesting started and this took half the workforce away from the garden. Extremely sunburnt, worn-out and in a dreadful mood, Yegor Semyonych would tear off into the garden, then out into the fields, shouting that they were tearing him to pieces and that he was going to put a bullet in his head.

And now there were rows about the trousseau, to which the Pesotskys attached no little importance. The snipping of scissors, the rattle of sewing-machines, the fumes from the hot-irons, the tantrums of the dressmaker – a nervous, touchy woman – had everyone's head in a whirl in that household. And as ill luck would have it, guests turned up every day and had to be amused, fed, even put up for the night. But all this toil passed by unnoticed, as though in a mist. Tanya felt as if she had been caught quite unawares by love and happiness, although, from the age of fourteen, she had been somehow sure that Kovrin would marry her, and no one else. She was amazed, bewildered and could not believe what had happened. One moment she would feel such joy that she wanted to fly up into the clouds and offer prayers to God; another time she would suddenly remember that she would have to leave her little nest and part from her father in August; on another occasion the thought would come to her, God knows from where, that she was an insignificant, trivial sort of woman, unworthy of a great man like Kovrin, and she would go to her room, lock the door and cry bitterly for several hours. When they had visitors she would suddenly find Kovrin extremely handsome and think that all the women were in love with him and jealous of her. And her heart would fill with rapturous pride, as if she had conquered the whole world. But he only had to give some young woman a welcoming smile and she would tremble with jealousy, go to her room – and there would be tears again. These new feelings took complete hold of her, she helped her father as though she were a machine and was blind to peaches, caterpillars, workers, oblivious of how swiftly the time was passing.

Almost exactly the same thing was happening to Yegor Semyonych. He worked from morning till night, was always hurrying off somewhere, would boil over and lose his temper, but all this in some kind of magical half-sleep. He seemed to be two different persons at once: one was the real Yegor Semyonych, listening to the head gardener Ivan Karlych's reports of things going wrong, flaring up and clutching his head in despair; the other was not the real Yegor Semyonych, a half-intoxicated person who would suddenly break off a conversation about business in the middle of a sentence, tap the head gardener on the shoulder and mutter, 'Whatever you say, good stock matters. His mother was an amazing, noble, brilliant woman. It was a pleasure looking at her kind, bright, pure face, the face of an angel. She was excellent at drawing, wrote poetry, spoke five languages, sang . . . The poor woman, God rest her soul, died of consumption.'

The unreal Yegor Semyonych would continue after a brief silence, 'When he was a boy, growing up in my house, he had the same angelic, bright, kind face. And his look, his movements and his conversation were like his mother's – gentle and refined. And as for his intellect, he always staggered us with his intellect. By the way, he didn't become an MA for nothing, oh no! But you wait and see, Ivan Karlych, what he'll be like in ten years' time! There'll be no touching him!'

But at this point the real Yegor Semyonych would suddenly take charge, pull a terrifying face, clutch his head and shout, 'The swines! They've polluted, fouled, frozen everything solid! The garden's ruined! It's finished!'

But Kovrin kept on working with his former enthusiasm and did not notice all the commotion around him. Love only added fuel to the flames. After every meeting with Tanya he would return to his room feeling happy, exultant and would pick up a book or manuscript with the same passion with which he had just kissed Tanya and declared his love. What the black monk had told him about God's Chosen, Eternal Truth, humanity's glittering future and so on lent his work a special, remarkable significance and filled his heart with pride and awareness of his own outstanding qualities. Once or twice a week he met the black monk in the park or in the house, had a talk with him, but it did not frighten him. On the contrary, it delighted him, as he was now firmly convinced that these kinds of visions visited only the select few, only outstanding men who had dedicated themselves to an idea.

One day the monk appeared at dinner time and sat by the window in the dining-room. Kovrin was overjoyed and deftly started a conversation with Yegor Semyonych on a topic that the monk would very likely find interesting. The black visitor listened and nodded his head amiably. Yegor Semyonych and Tanya listened too, cheerfully smiling and without suspecting that Kovrin was speaking not to them, but to his hallucination.

The Fast of the Assumption[10] came unnoticed and soon afterwards the wedding day, which, as Yegor Semyonych insisted, was celebrated with 'a great splash', that is to say, with senseless festivities that went on for two whole days. They got through three thousand roubles' worth of food and drink, but with that miserable hired band, the riotous toasts and scurrying servants, the noise and the crush, they did not appreciate the expensive wines, nor the startling delicacies that had been ordered from Moscow.

VII

One long winter's night Kovrin was reading a French novel in bed. Poor Tanya, who suffered from headaches in the evening as she wasn't used to town life, had long been asleep and was muttering something incoherent.

Three o'clock struck. Kovrin snuffed the candle and lay down. He remained with eyes closed for a long time, but he could not sleep, possibly because the bedroom was very hot and Tanya was talking in her sleep. At half past four he lit the candle again and this time he saw the black monk sitting in the armchair near the bed.

'Good evening,' the monk said. After a brief pause he asked, 'What are you thinking about now?'

'Fame,' Kovrin answered. 'I've just been reading a French novel about a young scholar who does stupid things and who's wasting away because of his longing for fame. This longing is something I can't understand.'

'That's because you're intelligent. You're indifferent to fame, it's a toy that doesn't interest you.'

'Yes, that's true.'

'Fame doesn't tempt you. What is flattering, or amusing, or edifying in having your name carved on a tombstone only for it to be rubbed off by time, gilding as well? Fortunately there are too many of you for humanity's weak memory to retain your names.'

'I understand that,' Kovrin agreed. 'And why should they be remembered? But let's talk about something else. Happiness, for example. What is happiness?'

When the clock struck five he was sitting on the bed, his feet dangling over the carpet. He turned to the monk and said, 'In antiquity, a certain happy man grew scared of his own good fortune in the end, it was so immense. So, to propitiate the Gods, he sacrificed his favourite ring. Do you know that I myself, like Polycrates,[11] am getting rather uneasy about my own good fortune? It seems strange that from morning to night I feel only joy, it fills my whole being and stifles all other feelings. As for sorrow, sadness or boredom, I just don't know what they are. Here I am, unable to sleep, suffering from insomnia, but I'm not bored. Seriously, I'm beginning to wonder what it all means.'

'But why?' the monk said in astonishment. 'Is joy something supernatural? Shouldn't it be looked on as man's normal state? The higher man's intellectual and moral development, the freer he is and the more pleasure life gives him. Socrates,[12] Diogenes[13] and Marcus Aurelius[14] experienced joy, not sadness. And the Apostle says, "Rejoice evermore."[15] So rejoice and be happy.'

'But supposing the Gods suddenly became angry?' Kovrin said jokingly and burst out laughing. 'If they were to take my comforts away and make me freeze and starve I don't think I would like that.'

Meanwhile Tanya had woken up and she looked at her husband in horror and bewilderment. He was talking to the armchair, laughing and gesticulating. His eyes shone and there was something peculiar in his laughter.

'Andrey, who are you talking to?' she asked, clutching the hand he had held out to the monk. 'Andrey, who is it?'

'What? Who?' Kovrin said, taken aback. 'Well, to *him* . . . He's sitting over there,' he said, pointing at the black monk.

'There's no one here . . . no one! Andrey, you're ill!' Tanya embraced her husband and pressed herself against him, as if to protect him from ghosts, and covered his eyes with her hand. 'You're ill!' she sobbed, shaking all over. 'Forgive me, my dearest, but for some time now I've noticed something's wrong with you. You're sick in your mind, Andrey . . .'

Her trembling infected him as well. He looked once more at the armchair, which was empty now and felt a sudden weakness in his arms and legs. This frightened him and he started to dress.

'It's nothing, Tanya, nothing,' he muttered, trembling. 'But to tell the truth, I am a little unwell . . . it's time I admitted it.'

'I noticed it some time ago . . . and Papa did too,' she said, trying to hold back her sobs. 'You talk to yourself, you smile so strangely . . . you're not sleeping. Oh, good God, good God, save us!' she said in horror. 'But don't be afraid, Andrey dear, don't be afraid. For God's sake don't be afraid . . .'

She began to dress too. Only now, as he looked at her, did Kovrin fully realize how dangerous his position was, only now did he understand the meaning of the black monk and his talks with him. He was quite convinced now that he was insane.

Both of them got dressed, without understanding why, and went into the ballroom, she first and he following. And there stood Yegor Semyonych (he was staying with them and had been awakened by the sobbing) in his dressing-gown, with a candle in his hand.

'Don't be afraid, Andrey,' Tanya said, shaking as though in a fever.'Don't be afraid . . . Papa, it will pass . . . it will pass . . .'

Kovrin could not speak, he was so upset. He wanted to tell his father-in-law, just for a joke, 'Please congratulate me, I think I've gone mad . . .', but all he could do was move his lips and smile bitterly.

At nine in the morning they put his greatcoat and furs on, wrapped a shawl round him and took him in a carriage to the doctor's. He began a course of treatment.

VIII

Summer had come and the doctor ordered him into the country. Kovrin was better now, had stopped seeing the black monk and it only remained for him to get his strength back. Living with his father-in-law in the country, he drank a lot of milk, worked only two hours a day, and did not drink or smoke.

On the eve of Elijah's Day[16] evening service was held in the house. When the lay reader handed the priest the censer, the enormous old ballroom smelt like a graveyard. Kovrin grew bored. He went out into the garden, wandered about without noticing the gorgeous flowers, sat down on a bench, and then strolled through the park. When he reached the river he went down the slope and stood looking thoughtfully at the water. The gloomy pines with their shaggy roots which had seen him here the previous year looking so young, joyful and lively, no longer talked in whispers, but stood motionless and dumb, as though they did not recognize him. And in fact his hair had been cut short, it was no longer beautiful, he walked sluggishly and his face had grown fuller and paler since the previous summer.

He crossed the footbridge to the other side. Where rye had been growing last year were rows of reaped oats. The sun had already set and a broad red glow burned on the horizon, a sign that it would be windy next day. It was quiet. Looking hard in the direction where the black monk had first appeared last year, Kovrin stood for about twenty minutes until the evening glow began to fade.

When he returned to the house, feeling listless and dissatisfied, the service was over. Yegor Semyonych and Tanya were sitting on the terrace steps drinking tea. They were discussing something, but suddenly became silent when they saw Kovrin, and he guessed from their expressions that they had been talking about him.

'Well, I think it's time for your milk,' Tanya told her husband.

'No, it's not,' he answered, sitting on the lowest step. 'Drink it yourself, I don't want any.'

Tanya anxiously exchanged glances with her father and said quietly, 'But you yourself said the milk does you a lot of good!'

'Yes, a lot of good!' Kovrin replied, grinning. 'I congratulate you – since Friday I've put on another pound.' He firmly clasped his head and said in an anguished voice, 'Why, why did you try to cure me? All those bromides, idleness, warm baths, supervision, the cowardly fear with every mouthful, every step. All this will finally turn me into a complete idiot. I was going out of my mind, I had megalomania, but I was bright and cheerful, even happy. I was interesting and original. Now I've grown more rational and stable, but I'm just like everyone else, a nobody. Life bores me . . . Oh, how cruelly you've treated me! I did have hallucinations, but did they harm anyone? Whom did they harm, that's what I'd like to know?'

'God knows what you're talking about!' Yegor Semyonych sighed. 'It's downright boring listening to you.'

'Then don't listen.'

Kovrin found other people's presence, especially Yegor Semyonych's, irritating and he would answer him drily, coldly, rudely even; and he could not look at him without a feeling of hatred and mockery, which embarrassed Yegor Semyonych, who would cough guiltily, although he didn't feel he was in the least to blame. Unable to understand why their friendly, loving relationship had changed so suddenly, Tanya pressed close to her father and looked him anxiously in the eye. She wanted to understand, but she could not, and she could only see that with every day relations were getting worse, that her father had aged considerably recently, while her husband had become irritable, moody, quarrelsome and uninteresting. No longer could she laugh and sing, she ate nothing at mealtimes, and lay awake whole nights expecting something terrible. She went through such torture that once she lay in a faint from lunch until the evening. During the service she thought that her father was crying and now, when the three of them sat on the terrace, she endeavoured not to think about it.

'How fortunate Buddha, Muhammad or Shakespeare were in not being treated by kind-hearted relatives for ecstasy and inspiration!' Kovrin said. 'If Muhammad had taken potassium bromide for his nerves, had worked only two hours a day and drunk milk, then that remarkable man would have left as much to posterity as his dog. In the long run doctors and kind relatives will turn humanity into a lot of morons. Mediocrity will pass for genius and civilization will perish. If only you knew,' Kovrin added with annoyance, 'how grateful I am to you!'

He was absolutely infuriated and quickly got up and went into the house, in case he said too much. It was quiet and the smell of tobacco flowers and jalap[17] drifted in from the garden through the open windows. Green patches of moonlight lay on the floor in the huge dark ballroom and on the grand piano. Kovrin recalled the joys of the previous summer, when there was that same smell of jalap, and the moon had shone through the windows. Trying to recapture that mood he hurried to his study, lit a strong cigar and told a servant to bring him some wine. But the cigar left a bitter, disgusting taste and the wine tasted differently from last year: these were the effects of having given up the habit. The cigar and two mouthfuls of wine made his head go round, he had palpitations, for which he had to take potassium bromide.

Before she went to bed Tanya told him, 'Father adores you. You're cross with him about something and this is killing him. Just look, he's ageing by the hour, not by the day. I beg you, Andrey, for God's sake, for the sake of your late father, for the sake of my peace of mind, *please* be nice to him!'

'I can't and I won't!'

'But why not?' Tanya asked, trembling all over. 'Tell me, why not?'

'Because I don't like him, that's all,' Kovrin said nonchalantly, with a shrug of the shoulders. 'But let's not talk about him, he's *your* father.'

'I just can't understand, I really can't!' Tanya said, clutching her temples and staring fixedly at something. 'Something incomprehensible and horrible is going on in this house. You've changed, you're not your normal self. A clever, remarkable man like you losing your temper over trifles, getting mixed up in petty squabbles . . . These little things worry you and sometimes I'm simply amazed, I just can't believe it's really you.' Then she continued, frightened of her own words and kissing his hands, 'Now, now, don't be angry, don't be angry. You are a clever man, and a good man. You will be fair to Father, he's so kind.'

'He's not kind, only smug. Music-hall clowns like your father, bounteous old cranks, with their well-fed, smug faces, used to touch and amuse me once in stories, farces and in real life. But now I find them repugnant. They're egotists to the marrow. What I find most disgusting is their being so well fed, with that optimism that comes from a full belly. They're just like oxen or wild pigs.'

Tanya sat on the bed and lay her head on the pillow. 'This is sheer torture,' she said and from her voice it was plain that she was utterly exhausted and that she found it hard to speak. 'Not a single moment's peace since winter . . . It's so terrible. Oh God, I feel shocking!'

'Yes, of course I'm the monster and you and your Papa are the sweet innocents. Of course!'

His face seemed ugly and unpleasant to Tanya. Hatred and that mocking expression did not suit him. And she had in fact noticed before that there was something lacking in his face, as if that had changed too since his hair was cut short. She wanted to say something to hurt him, but immediately she became aware of this hostile feeling she grew frightened and left the bedroom.

IX

Kovrin was awarded a professorship. His inaugural lecture was fixed for 2 December and a notice announcing it was put up in the university corridor. But on the appointed day he cabled the dean, informing him he was not well enough to lecture.

He had a haemorrhage in the throat. He would spit blood, but twice a month there was considerable loss of blood, which left him extremely weak and drowsy. The illness did not frighten him particularly, since he knew his late mother had lived with exactly the same disease for ten years or more. And the doctors assured him it was not dangerous, and merely advised him not to get excited, to lead a regular life and to talk as little as possible.

In January the lecture was again cancelled for the same reason and in February it was too late to start the course, which had to be postponed until the following year.

He no longer lived with Tanya, but with another woman two years older than he was and who cared for him as though he were a child. His state of mind was calm, submissive. He eagerly gave in to her and when Barbara (his mistress's name) decided to take him to the Crimea he agreed, although he expected no good to come from the trip.

They reached Sevastopol one evening and rested at a hotel before going on to Yalta the next day. They were both exhausted from the journey. Barbara drank some tea, went to bed and soon fell asleep. But Kovrin did not go to bed. Before he had left home – an hour before setting off for the station – he had received a letter from Tanya and had decided not to open it. It was now in one of his coat pockets and the thought of it had a disagreeable, unsettling effect on him. In the very depths of his heart he now considered his marriage to Tanya had been a mistake, and was pleased he had finally broken with her. The memory of that woman who had ended up as a walking skeleton and in whom everything seemed to have died – except for those large, clever, staring eyes – this memory aroused only pity in him and annoyance with himself. The writing on the envelope reminded him how unjust and cruel he had been two years ago, how he had taken revenge on others for his spiritual emptiness, his boredom, his loneliness, his dissatisfaction with life.

In this respect he remembered how he had once torn his dissertation and all the articles written during his illness into shreds and thrown them out of the window, the scraps of paper fluttering in the breeze, catching on trees and flowers. In every line he saw strange, utterly unfounded claims, enthusiasm run riot, audacity and megalomania, which had made him feel as if he were reading a description of his own vices. But when the last notebook had been torn up and had flown through the window, he felt for some reason bitterly annoyed: he had gone to his wife and told her many unpleasant things. God, how he had tormented her! Once, when he wanted to hurt his wife, he told her that her father had played a most distasteful role in their romance, having asked him if he would marry her. Yegor Semyonych happened to hear this and rushed into the room speechless with despair; all he could do was stamp his feet and make a strange bellowing noise, as if he had lost the power of speech, while Tanya looked at her father, gave a heart-rending shriek and fainted. It was an ugly scene.

All this came to mind at the sight of the familiar handwriting. Kovrin went out onto the balcony. The weather was warm and calm, and he could smell the sea. The magnificent bay reflected the moon and the lights, and its colour was hard to describe. It was a delicate, soft blending of dark blue and green; in places the water was like blue vitriol, in others the moonlight seemed to have taken on material substance and filled the bay instead of water. But what a harmony of colour, what a peaceful, calm and ennobling mood reigned over all!

The windows were most probably open in the room below, beneath the balcony, as he could hear women's voices and laughter quite distinctly. Someone was having a party, it seemed.

Kovrin forced himself to open the letter, returned to his room and read: 'Father has just died. I owe that to you, as you killed him. Our garden is going to rack and ruin – strangers are running it – that's to say, what poor father feared so much has come about. I owe this to you as well. I hate you with all my heart and hope you'll soon be dead. Oh, how I'm suffering! An unbearable pain is burning inside me. May you be damned! I took you for an outstanding man, for a genius, I loved you, but you turned out a madman . . .'

Kovrin could not read any more, tore the letter up and threw it away. He was seized by a feeling of anxiety that was very close to terror. Barbara was sleeping behind a screen and he could hear her breathing. From the ground floor came women's voices and laughter, but he felt that besides himself there wasn't a living soul in the whole hotel. He was terrified because the unhappy, broken-hearted Tanya had cursed him in her letter and had wished for his death. He glanced at the door, as if fearing that the unknown force which had wrought such havoc in his life and in the lives of those near and dear over the last two years might come into the room and take possession of him again.

He knew from experience that the best cure for shattered nerves is work. One should sit down at a table and force oneself at all costs to concentrate on one idea, no matter what. From his red briefcase he took out a notebook in which he had sketched out a plan for a short work he had considered compiling in case he was bored doing nothing in the Crimea. He sat at the table and busied himself with the plan, and it seemed his calm, resigned, detached state of mind was returning. The notebook and plan even stimulated him to meditate on the world's vanity. He thought how much life demands in return for those insignificant or very ordinary blessings that it can bestow. For example, to receive a university chair in one's late thirties, to be a run-of-the-mill professor, expounding in turgid, boring, ponderous language commonplace ideas that were not even original, in brief, to achieve the status of a third-rate scholar he, Kovrin, had had to study fifteen years – working day and night – suffer severe mental illness, experience a broken marriage and do any number of stupid, unjust things that were best forgotten. Kovrin realized quite clearly now that he was a nobody and eagerly accepted the fact since, in his opinion, every man should be content with what he is.

The plan would have calmed his nerves, but the sight of the shiny white pieces of letter on the floor stopped him concentrating. He got up from the table, picked up the pieces and threw them out of the window, but a light breeze blew in from the sea and scattered them over the windowsill. Once again he was gripped by that restless feeling, akin to panic, and he began to think that there was no one else besides him in the whole hotel . . . He went out onto the balcony. The bay, which seemed to be alive, looked at him with its many sky-blue, dark-blue, turquoise and flame-coloured eyes and beckoned him. It was truly hot and humid, and a bathe would not have come amiss. A violin began to play on the ground floor, under his balcony, and two female voices softly sang a song he knew. It was about some young girl, sick in her mind, who heard mysterious sounds one night in her garden and thought it must be a truly divine harmony, incomprehensible to us mortals . . . Kovrin caught his breath, he felt twinges of sadness in his heart and a wonderful, sweet, long-forgotten gladness quivered in his heart.

A tall black column like a whirlwind or tornado appeared on the far side of the bay. With terrifying speed it moved over the water towards the hotel, growing smaller and darker as it approached, and Kovrin barely had time to move out of its path . . . Barefoot, arms folded over chest, with a bare grey head and black eyebrows, the monk floated past and stopped in the middle of the room.

'Why didn't you trust me?' he asked reproachfully, looking affectionately at Kovrin. 'If you had trusted me then, when I told you that you were a genius, you wouldn't have spent these two years so miserably, so unprofitably.'

Kovrin believed now that he was one of God's Chosen, and a genius, and he vividly recollected all his previous conversations with the black monk; he wanted to speak, but the blood welled out of his throat onto his chest. Not knowing what to do, he drew his hands over his chest and his shirt cuffs became soaked with blood. He wanted to call Barbara, who was sleeping behind the screen, and with a great effort murmured, 'Tanya!'

He fell on the floor, lifted himself on his arms and called again, 'Tanya!'

He called on Tanya, on the great garden with its gorgeous flowers sprinkled with dew, he called on the park, the pines with their shaggy roots, the rye field, his wonderful learning, his youth, his daring, his joy; he called on life, which had been so beautiful. On the floor near his face, he saw a large pool of blood and was too weak now to say one word, but an ineffable, boundless happiness flooded his whole being. Beneath the balcony they were playing a serenade, and at the same time the black monk whispered to him that he was a genius and that he was dying only because his weak human body had lost its balance and could no longer serve to house a genius. When Barbara woke and came out from behind the screen Kovrin was dead and a blissful smile was frozen on his face.

Murder

I

They were celebrating vespers at Progonnaya Station. A crowd of railwaymen, their wives and children, with some woodcutters and sawyers working nearby along the line, were standing before the great icon brightly painted on a gold background. All of them stood in silence, spellbound by the glittering light and the howling blizzard which had blown up all of a sudden, although it was the eve of Annunciation Day. The old priest from Vedenyapino was officiating and the singers were the precentor, and Matvey Terekhov.

Matvey's face glowed with joy; and as he sang he craned his neck, as though he wanted to fly up into the sky. He sang tenor and read the canon in the same sweet, persuasive tenor voice. While they were singing 'Song of Archangels'[1] he waved his hand like a choirmaster and produced some extremely complicated sounds in his effort to harmonize with the old lay reader's hollow bass. One could see from his face that he was thoroughly enjoying himself. But then the service ended, the congregation quietly left, the place became dark and empty again, and that silence descended which is found only at lonely stations in the open country or in forests when nothing can be heard except the moaning of the wind; all one feels is emptiness all around and the wretchedness of life slowly slipping by.

Matvey lived near the station, at his cousin's inn. But he did not feel like going home and sat at the counter in the refreshment room talking in a low voice. 'We had our own choir at the tile-works. And I must say, although we were just simple workmen, we were great singers. It was marvellous. We were often invited into town and when Ivan the suffragan bishop took the service at Trinity Church the cathedral choir sang in the right-hand stalls, while we were on the left. But people in the town complained we sang too long and said that lot from the tile-works were dragging things out. They were right, St Andrew's Vigil and the Te Deum[2] began before seven and didn't finish till after ten, so very often it was gone midnight before we were back at the works.'

Matvey sighed. 'Really marvellous it was, Sergey Nikanorych, really marvellous. But I don't get much joy living here in the old house. The nearest church is three miles away, I can't manage that in my state of health and there's no choir. And you can't get a moment's peace with our family, just one long racket all day, with swearing, filth, everyone eating from the same bowl like peasants, and cockroaches in the soup. If God had blessed me with good health I'd have cleared off ages ago, Sergey Nikanorych.'

Matvey Terekhov was not old – about forty-five – but he had an unhealthy look. His face was covered in wrinkles and his thin, weedy beard was already completely white, which made him seem a lot older. He spoke cautiously, in a feeble voice, clasped his chest when he coughed – then he had the uneasy, worried look of a true hypochondriac. He would never say what exactly was wrong, but he loved telling a long story about straining himself lifting a heavy box once at the tile-works, giving himself a 'rumpture', as he put it, which forced him to leave his job there and go back home. But what a 'rumpture' was, he could not explain.

'I must say, I don't like that cousin of mine,' he continued, pouring himself some tea. 'He's older than me, it's wrong to say things against him, and I'm a God-fearing man. But I just can't stand him. He's a proud, stern man, always swearing and tormenting the life out of his relatives and workmen, and he doesn't go to confession. Last Sunday I asked him, all nice and friendly, "Let's go to the service at Pakhomo, Cousin," and he replies: "Not me, the priest there plays cards." And he didn't come here today either, he says the priest at Vedenyapino smokes and drinks vodka. He just hates the clergy! He says his own offices, and matins, and vespers, and his sister's his lay reader. While he's saying his "We beseech Thee, oh Lord", she's screeching away like a turkey-hen with her "Lord have mercy". Right sinful, that's what it is. Every day I tell him, "Come to your senses, Cousin Yakov! Repent, Cousin!", but he just ignores me.'

Sergey Nikanorych the buffet attendant poured out five glasses of tea and carried them to the ladies' waiting-room on a tray. A moment later they could hear someone shouting, 'Is that the way to serve tea, you pig? You don't know your job!' It was the stationmaster. A timid muttering followed, then more shouting, angry and brusque: 'Clear off!'

The buffet attendant returned looking very put out. 'Time was when I waited on counts and princes,' he said softly, 'but now I don't know how to serve tea, do you see? Swearing at me in front of a priest and ladies!'

Sergey Nikanorych the buffet attendant once had money and managed the refreshment room at a main-line junction in a county town. In those days he used to wear coat and tails, and a gold watch. But then he fell on bad times, all his money wasted on fancy equipment and his staff robbing him. Gradually sinking deeper and deeper into debt, he moved to a station that was not so busy. There his wife ran off with all the silver. He moved to a third station, which was even worse – they did not serve hot meals there. Then he went to a fourth. After numerous moves, sinking lower and lower the whole time, he finally ended up at Progonnaya, where all he sold was tea and cheap vodka, and where the only food he served was hard-boiled eggs and tough sausage that smelt of tar: he himself thought it was a joke, calling it 'bandsmen's food'. He was completely bald on top, had bulging blue eyes and thick, fluffy whiskers which he was always combing, peering at himself in a small hand-mirror. He was perpetually tormented by memories and just could not get used to 'bandsmen's sausage', to the stationmaster's insults and the haggling peasants – in his opinion haggling was just as improper in a station refreshment room as in a chemist's. He was ashamed of being so poverty-stricken and degraded, and this feeling of shame was his chief worry in life.

'Spring's late this year,' Matvey said, listening hard. 'And it's a good thing. I don't like the spring, it's very muddy, Sergey Nikanorych. In books they write about the spring, birds singing and the sun setting, but what's so nice about it? A bird's a bird, that's all. I like good company, so I can hear what people have to say, I like chatting about religion or singing something nice in the choir. But I've no time for all them nightingales and nice little flowers!'

He went on again about the tile-works and the choir, but Sergey Nikanorych was deeply offended, would not calm down and kept shrugging his shoulders and muttering. Matvey said good night and went home.

It was not freezing – it was thawing on the roofs – yet it was snowing hard. The snow swiftly whirled through the air and white clouds chased each other along the railway track. Dimly lit by a moon that lay hidden high up in the clouds, the oak grove lining both sides of the track kept up a constant roar. How terrifying trees can be when they are shaken by a violent storm! Matvey walked along the road by the track, covering his face and hands. The wind shoved him in the back. Suddenly he caught sight of a small, wretched-looking horse, plastered with snow; a sledge scraped the bare cobbles of the road and a peasant, his muffled head as white as his horse, cracked a whip. Matvey looked round, but the sledge and peasant had already vanished as if in a dream, and he quickened his pace, suddenly feeling scared – of what, he did not know.

He reached the level crossing and the dark hut where the keeper lived. The barrier was raised and all around were massive snowdrifts and clouds of snow whirling like witches at a sabbath. The track was crossed here by an old road, once a main trunk route and still called the highway. On the right, just by the level crossing and on the road, was Terekhov's inn, an old coaching-house. A small light always glimmered there at night.

When Matvey arrived home the whole house, even the hall, smelled strongly of incense. Cousin Yakov Ivanych was still celebrating vespers. In the corner of the 'chapel' where the service was being held, facing the door, stood an icon-case filled with old-fashioned family icons, all in gilt, and both walls to right and left were covered with icons in the old and new style, some in cases, some without. On the table, draped with a cloth that touched the floor, was an icon of the Annunciation, as well as a cross made from cypress wood, and a censer. Candles were burning. Near the table stood a lectern. As he passed the chapel, Matvey stopped to look through the door. Yakov Ivanych was reading at the lectern and worshipping with him was his sister Aglaya, a tall, skinny old woman in a dark-blue dress and white kerchief. Yakov Ivanych's daughter Dashutka was there as well – she was an ugly girl of about eighteen, covered in freckles. As usual, she was barefoot and wearing the dress in which she watered the cattle in the evenings.

'Glory to Thee who has shown us the light!' chanted Yakov Ivanych as he bowed low.

Aglaya propped her chin on her hand and, without hurrying, sang in a thin, shrill voice. From the room above came vague voices: they sounded sinister and seemed to be issuing threats. After the fire of long ago no one had lived on the upper storey; the windows were boarded up and empty bottles were scattered about on the floor between the wooden beams. The wind banged and howled up there and it sounded as though someone was running around and stumbling over the beams.

Half of the ground floor was taken up by the inn and the Terekhovs lived in the other, so when drunken visitors called at the inn they could hear every word from their living-room. Matvey lived next to the kitchen in a room with a large stove, where they had baked the bread every day when the coaching-inn had been there. Dashutka, without her own room, had her little space here, behind the stove. At night a cricket was always chirping and mice scurried about.

Matvey lit a candle and started reading a book he had borrowed from the railway policeman. While he sat reading, the prayers finished and everyone went to bed, Dashutka included. She immediately started snoring but soon woke up and said, yawning, 'Uncle Matvey, you shouldn't waste candles.'

'It's my own,' Matvey replied. 'I bought it myself.'

Dashutka tossed and turned for a while, then fell asleep again. Matvey stayed up for a long time, as he did not feel sleepy, and when he had finished the last page he took a pencil from a trunk and wrote in the book: 'I, Matvey Terekhov, have read this book and I find it the best of all those read by me, in which I hereby impress me grettitude to Kuzma Nikolayev Zhukov, senior officer of the railway police, owner of the aforesaid priceless book.'

He considered it only polite to make inscriptions in other people's books.

II

When Annunciation Day arrived, after they had seen the mail train off, Matvey sat in the refreshment room drinking tea with lemon, and talking. The buffet attendant and Constable Zhukov were listening.

'Let me tell you,' Matvey was saying, 'even when I was a nipper I was all for relidgun. When I was only twelve I was already reading the Acts and the Epistles[3] in church and this was a great comfort to my parents. And every summer I used to go on a pilgrimage with Mother, God rest her soul. Other boys used to sing songs or go after crayfish, but I stayed with Mother. The older folk thought well of me and I was pleased, because I was such a well-behaved boy. And after I'd gone off to the tile-works with Mother's blessing I'd sing tenor in our choir, in my spare time, never enjoyed anything so much. Of course, I didn't touch vodka, or smoke, and I kept myself clean. As you know, the Devil don't like that way of life and took it into his head to ruin me and he began to cloud my mind, just as he's doing to Cousin Yakov. The first thing I did was vow to fast on Mondays and not to eat meat on any day, and it wasn't long before I went a bit soft in the head. The Holy Fathers say you must have cold dry food in the first week in Lent, up to the Saturday, but it's no sin for the weak or them that toil to have a cup of tea even. Not a crumb passed my lips until the Sunday. And the whole of Lent I didn't take a scrap of butter, and on Wednesdays and Fridays I didn't eat anything at all. It was the same during the minor fasts. At St Peter's Fast my mates at the works had their fish soup, but I would just suck a dry biscuit. Some folk are stronger than others, of course, but I didn't find it too hard on fast days, and in fact the harder you try, the easier it is. You only get hungry during the first few days, but then you take it in your stride, it gets easier and easier and by the end of the week it's not hard at all and all you have is that numb feeling in your legs, as though you were walking on clouds. And what's more, I imposed all sorts of penances on myself – I'd get up at night and prostrate myself, drag heavy stones around and walk barefoot in the snow. And I'd wear irons.

'But a little later, when I was at confession, the idea suddenly dawned on me: that priest's married, he doesn't keep the fasts and he smokes. Then why should he hear me confess, what authority did he have to pardon my sins, with him more of a sinner than me? I even kept away from vegetable oil, but he'd have his sturgeon all right, I dare say. I went to another priest, but as luck would have it I landed myself with a real fatty in a silk cassock that rustled like a lady's dress – and he smelt of tobacco too. I went to a monastery to prepare for communion, but I was ill at ease there too, it struck me the monks didn't keep to their rules. After that I couldn't find any kind of church service to my liking. In one place they rushed it or sang the wrong hymns, in another the lay reader spoke through his nose. And there was once a time – God forgive me, sinner that I am – when I'd stand in the church seething with rage, and that's no way to pray. And it seemed to me that the congregation weren't crossing themselves properly or listening right. Whoever I looked at seemed to be a drunkard, fast-breaker, smoker, fornicator, card-sharper. Only *I* kept the Commandments. The Devil didn't sleep and things got even worse. I didn't sing in the choir any more and didn't go to church. I didn't think the church was good enough for a godly man like me. I was a fallen angel, swollen-headed beyond belief. Then I tried to start my own church. I rented a poky little room from a deaf woman a long way out of town, by the cemetery, and I set up a chapel – like my cousin's, but I had proper candlesticks and a real censer. In this chapel I abided by the rules of Mount Athos,[4] that's to say, matins always began at midnight, and on the eve of the twelve great festivals vespers went on for ten, sometimes twelve hours even. According to their rules monks could sit while the Psalms and Parables were read, but I wanted to go one better, so I stood up the whole time. I wept and sighed as I read and sang, dragging everything out and lifting my arms up. And I went straight from prayers to work, without any sleep, and I'd still be praying while I worked.

'Well now, people in town started saying, "Matvey's a saint, Matvey heals the sick and insane." Of course, I never healed anyone, but everyone knows when you have any kind of schism or heresy you just can't keep the women away, they're like flies round a jam-pot. Some women and old maids started calling on me, threw themselves at my feet, kissed my hand and shouted that I was a saint and so on. One of them even saw a halo round my head. It grew cramped in my chapel, so I took a larger room and it was absolute bedlam! The Devil really had his claws into me and his accursed hooves blotted the true light from my eyes. And we all seemed possessed by the Devil. I'd read, and the old girls and maids would sing. After going without food or drink for long periods, after being on their feet for twenty-four hours or more they'd suddenly get the shakes, as if they'd caught a fever. Then one would cry out, then another – it was terrifying! And I was shaking all over too, like a cat on hot bricks and I didn't know why. There we were, all jumping about! It's very odd, I must say, when you are jumping away and swinging your arms, and you can't stop yourself. After this there was shouting and screaming, and we all danced and kept chasing each other till we dropped. This was how, in one of these frenzied fits, I became a fornicator.'

The policeman burst out laughing, but became serious when he saw no one else was.

'It's like the Molokans,'[5] he said. 'I've read they're all that way inclined in the Caucasus.'

'But I was not struck by lightning,' Matvey went on, crossing himself before the icon and moving his lips. 'My mother must have prayed in heaven for me. When everyone in town thought me a saint and even fine ladies and gents started visiting me on the sly for comfort, I chanced to go and see the boss, Osip Varlamych, to ask him to forgive me, as it was Forgiveness Day.[6] Well, he put the latch on the door and there we were, the two of us face to face. He gave me a real ticking-off. I should mention that Osip Varlamych's got no education, but he's no fool and everyone feared and respected him, because he led a strict and holy life and was a real hard worker. He'd been mayor and churchwarden for twenty years, I think, and he did a lot of good. He laid gravel on the New Moscow Road and had the church painted – the pillars were done up to look like malkalite.

'So he shuts the door. "I've been after you for a long time, you damned so-and-so," he says. "Think you're a saint, do you? No, you're no saint, but an apostate, a heretic and a scoundrel!" On and on he went, can't say it the way he did, all smooth and clever like in books, enough to make you weep, it was. He carried on for two hours. His words struck home and my eyes were opened. I listened and listened – and I just sobbed my heart out! And he said, "Be like normal men, eat, drink, dress and pray like everyone else. Doing more than you ought is the work of the Devil. Those irons of yours are the Devil's, your fasts are from the Devil and your chapel's a Devil's chapel. It's all pride."

'Next day – the first Monday in Lent – God willed me to fall ill. I'd strained myself and was taken to hospital. I suffered something cruel I did, wept bitter tears and trembled. I thought I'd go straight from hospital to hell, and it nearly finished me off. About six months I lay suffering in bed and when they let me out the first thing I did was take proper communion and I became a human being again.

'Osip Varlamych let me go home. "Now don't forget, Matvey," he ordered, "doing more than you should is the Devil's work." So now I eat and drink and pray like everyone else. If I meet an old priest who smells of tobacco or spirits I daren't condemn him, as priests are normal human beings too. But the moment I hear some holy man's set himself up in the town or country and doesn't eat for weeks, keeping to his own rules, then I know for sure who's at the bottom of it all. Well, my dear sirs, all that happened to me once. And now I'm just like Osip Varlamych, I order my cousin and his sister around, I reproach them, but mine is a voice of one crying in the wilderness.[7] God didn't grant me the gift.'

Matvey's story evidently made no impression at all. Sergey Nikanorych said nothing and began clearing food from the counter, while the police constable observed how rich Matvey's cousin Yakov Ivanych was: 'He's worth at least thirty thousand.'

Constable Zhukov was red-haired, full-faced (his cheeks quivered as he walked), healthy and well-fed. When his superiors weren't around he usually sprawled in his chair, his legs crossed. He would rock to and fro as he spoke, nonchalantly whistling, with a smug, sated expression as if he had just had dinner. He had plenty of money and always spoke of it as if he were an expert on the subject. He was a commission agent and whenever people had an estate, a horse or a second-hand carriage to sell they would come to him.

'Yes, he could be worth thirty thousand,' Sergey Nikanorych agreed. 'Your grandpa had a large fortune,' he added, turning to Matvey. 'Really enormous! Then everything went to your father and uncle. Your father died young and your uncle got the lot, and then Yakov Ivanych of course. While you were going round churches and monasteries with your mother and singing in the factory choir, there were some here who weren't standing idle.'

'Your share's about fifteen thousand,' the policeman said, rocking in his chair. 'The inn's jointly owned by you, so's the capital. Yes. If I'd been in your shoes I'd have sued them long ago. Of course, I'd have taken him to court, but while it was being sorted out I'd have got him to one side and given him a right good bash in the mug.'

Yakov Ivanych was not liked, because people with queer beliefs tend to upset others, even those who are indifferent to religion. And in any case the policeman did not like him, as he too dealt in horses and second-hand carriages.

'You won't sue your cousin because you've plenty of money of your own,' the buffet attendant told Matvey, giving him an envious look. 'It's all right for those what has means, but I'll probably be stuck here in this job until I die.'

Matvey tried to assure them that he had no money at all, but Sergey Nikanorych was not listening any more. Memories of his past life, of the daily insults he had suffered, came flooding over him. His bald head sweated, he went red in the face and blinked.

'Oh, this damned life!' he exclaimed, deeply annoyed, and threw a piece of sausage on the floor.

III

The coaching-inn was said to have been built back in Alexander I's reign by a widow, Avdotya Terekhov, who had settled there with her son. Travellers passing in mail coaches, especially on moonlit nights, would feel depressed and strangely uneasy at the sight of that dark yard with its lean-to shed and perpetually locked gates. It was as if the place were the haunt of sorcerers or robbers. Drivers would look back and urge on their horses every time they went past. People never liked staying overnight there, as the innkeepers were always unfriendly and charged exorbitant prices. The yard was muddy even in summer and huge fat pigs wallowed in the muck; horses – the Terekhovs were dealers – wandered around loose, often becoming restive; then they would race out of the yard and tear like mad down the road, frightening women pilgrims. In those days there was a lot of traffic. Long trains of loaded wagons would pass through and there were incidents, like the one about thirty years ago for example, when some angry wagoners had lost their tempers, started a fight and murdered a passing merchant. A crooked cross still stands about a quarter of a mile from the inn. Mail troikas with bells and landowners' heavy *dormeuses*[8] would drive by, and herds of bellowing cattle passed in clouds of dust.

When they first built the railway, there had been only a halt here, simply called a passing-point. Then about ten years later the present Progonnaya Station was built. The traffic along the old post road almost vanished; now it was used only by local landowners and peasants, and in spring and autumn gangs of workmen crowded along it on foot. The coaching-inn became just an ordinary tavern. The top floor was damaged by fire, the roof went yellow with rust, the lean-to shed gradually collapsed, but enormous fat pigs – pink and revolting – still wallowed in the mud in the yard. As before, horses would sometimes tear out of the yard and race furiously down the road with tails streaming. At the inn they sold tea, hay, oats, flour, as well as vodka or beer for consumption on or off the premises.

They were a little tight-lipped about the alcohol they sold, however, since they had never been licensed.

The Terekhovs had always been renowned for their piety and had even earned the nickname 'Pillars of the Faith'. But perhaps because they lived like bears, keeping to themselves, avoiding company and thinking out things for themselves, they were prone to wild dreaming, religious wavering, and almost every generation had its own approach to religion and matters of faith.

Grandma Avdotya, who had built the coaching-inn, was an Old Believer, but her son and two grandsons (Matvey and Yakov's fathers) worshipped at the Orthodox Church, entertained the clergy and prayed to the new icons just as reverently as to the old. In his old age her son gave up meat and took a vow of silence, considering any kind of talk at all a sin, while the grandsons were odd in not taking the Scriptures at their face value – they were always seeking some hidden meaning, maintaining that every holy word must hold some secret. Avdotya's great-grandson Matvey had struggled against lack of faith since he was a young boy and this was very nearly his undoing. Yakov, the other great-grandson, was Orthodox, but he suddenly stopped going to church when his wife died, and worshipped at home. Aglaya followed his bad example, stayed away from church and did not let Dashutka go either. It was said that when Aglaya was a young girl she used to go to Flagellant meetings at Vedenyapino and that she was still a secret member of the sect, which was why she went around in a white kerchief.[9]

Yakov Ivanych was ten years older than Matvey. He was a handsome old man, tall, with a broad grey beard that nearly reached his waist and bushy eyebrows that lent his face a grim, even malevolent expression. He wore a long coat of good cloth, or a black sheepskin jacket, and always tried to dress neatly and decently. Even in fine weather he wore galoshes. He stayed away from church because, in his opinion, they did not observe the rites properly and because the priests drank wine at the wrong times and smoked. Every day he read and sang the service at home with Aglaya. During matins at Vedenyapino they did not read the canon, omitted vespers – even on high holidays – whereas he read through the prescribed portion at home, not hurrying or leaving out one line. In his spare time he would read aloud from the lives of the saints. And in his everyday life he stuck close to the rules. For example, if wine was permitted on a certain day during Lent 'because of the long vigil', he would invariably have a drink, even if he did not feel like one.

He did not read, sing or burn incense in the hope that God might shower his blessings down on him, but for form's sake. Man cannot live without faith, and faith must be correctly expressed, from year to year and from day to day according to established formulae which laid down that man should address God each morning and evening with the exact words and thoughts appropriate to that particular day or hour. His life, and therefore his method of prayer, must be pleasing to God and so he should read and sing each day only what pleased God, that is, what was laid down by Church law. Therefore the first chapter of St John should be read only on Easter Sunday, and from Easter Sunday till Ascension Day certain hymns must not be sung. Awareness of this procedure and its importance gave Yakov Ivanych great pleasure during hours of prayer. When he was forced to depart from his routine – having to fetch goods from town or go to the bank – then his conscience tormented him and this made him feel wretched.

When Cousin Matvey unexpectedly arrived from the tile-works, making the inn his home, he started breaking the rules right from the start. He did not wish to pray with the others, had his meals and tea at the wrong times, got up late and drank milk on Wednesdays and Fridays because of his poor health. Almost every day, at prayer-time, he would go into the chapel and shout: 'Listen to reason, Cousin! Repent, Cousin!' This would make Yakov Ivanych see red and Aglaya lose her temper and start swearing. Or Matvey would sneak into the chapel at night and softly say: 'Cousin, your prayer is not pleasing to the Lord, as it is said, "First be reconciled to thy brother, and then come and offer thy gift."[10] But you're nothing but a money-lender and a vodka trader. Repent!'

In Matvey's words Yakov could see only the usual lame excuse made by empty, sloppy people who always talk about 'love thy neighbour', 'be reconciled with thy brother' and the rest of it just to avoid fasting, praying and reading sacred books, and who turn their noses up at profit and interest because they don't like hard work. Indeed, it's far easier being poor, not to save up – much easier than being rich.

For all this, he felt worried and could not worship as he used to. No sooner did he enter the chapel and open his book than he began to feel apprehensive – any moment his cousin might come in and interrupt him. And in fact Matvey would soon appear and shout in a trembling voice, 'Come to your senses, Cousin! Repent, Cousin!' His sister would start cursing and Yakov would lose his temper and shout, 'Clear out of my house!'

Matvey told him, 'This house belongs to all of us.'

Yakov would return to his reading and singing but was never able to calm himself and he would suddenly start daydreaming over his book without even noticing it. Although he thought his cousin's words were nonsense, why had *he* recently taken to thinking that it was hard for the rich to enter the Kingdom of Heaven, that he had done very nicely out of that stolen horse he had bought two years ago, that a drunk had died at the inn from too much vodka, in his wife's lifetime? . . .

Now he slept very badly, lightly at night and he heard Matvey, who could not sleep either, sighing as he pined for his tile-works. And as he tossed and turned Yakov recalled that stolen horse, the drunkard, what the Gospels said about camels.

He was beginning to have doubts again, it seemed. And although it was already the end of March, it snowed every day, as if on purpose; the forest roared as though it were winter and it seemed impossible that spring would ever come. This kind of weather made everyone bored, quarrelsome and hateful, and when the wind howled above the ceiling at night it seemed someone was living up there in the empty storey. And then doubts gradually flooded his mind, his head burnt and he did not want to sleep.

IV

On the morning of the Monday in Passion Week, Matvey was in his room and could hear Dashutka saying to Aglaya, 'A few days ago Uncle Matvey was telling me I don't need to fast.'

Matvey remembered the whole conversation he'd had with Dashutka the previous day and suddenly felt insulted.

'That's a sinful way to speak, girl,' he said in the moaning voice of a sick man. 'There has to be fasting. Our Lord Himself fasted forty days. I was just trying to tell you even fasting won't help the wicked.'

'Just hark at him with his tile-work sermons, trying to teach us to be good,' scoffed Aglaya as she washed the floor (she normally washed the floors on weekdays and lost her temper with everyone in the process). 'We know how they fast at the tile-works! Just ask that old uncle of yours about his little darling, how him and that filthy bitch guzzled milk in Lent. Likes preaching to others all right but forgets that slut quick enough. Ask him who he left the money with. Who?'

Matvey took pains to hide the fact, as though it were a festering sore, that when he'd been frisking about and making merry with those old women and young girls at prayer meetings he had had an affair with a woman from the town, who bore him a child. Before he went home he gave her everything he had saved up at the tile-works and borrowed the money for his fare from the boss. And now he had only a few roubles for tea and candles. Later on his 'darling' informed him that the baby had died, and wrote to ask what she should do with the money. The workman brought the letter from the station but Aglaya intercepted it and read it, and every day after that kept reproaching Matvey about his 'darling'.

'Mere chicken-feed, only nine hundred roubles!' Aglaya continued. 'Gave nine hundred to a stranger, that bitch, that factory tart! Damn you!' She flew off the handle and shrieked, 'Nothing to say for yourself then? I could tear you to pieces, you spineless wretch! Nine hundred roubles, like chicken-feed! You should have left it to

Dashutka, she's your own flesh and blood. Or sent it to the poor orphans' home in Belyov. Why couldn't she choke, that cow of yours, blast her! Bloody bitch, damn her eyes! May she rot in hell!'

Yakov Ivanych called her, as it was time to begin lauds. She washed, put on a white kerchief and now went quietly and meekly to her beloved brother in the chapel. When she spoke to Matvey or served tea to peasants at the inn she was a skinny, sharp-eyed old hag, but in chapel she looked pure and radiant. Making elaborate curtsies, coyly pursing her lips even, she looked so much younger.

As always during Lent, Yakov Ivanych began to read the offices in a soft, mournful voice. After a little while he stopped to savour the calm that reigned over the whole house. Then he started reading again, deriving great pleasure from it. He clasped his hands as if to pray, turned his eyes up, shook his head and sighed.

Suddenly he heard some voices. Sergey Nikanorych and the policeman had come to visit Matvey. Yakov Ivanych felt awkward reading out loud and singing with strangers in the house and now the sound of voices made him read slowly, in a whisper. In the chapel they could hear what the buffet attendant was saying:

'The Tartar at Shchepovo is selling his business for fifteen hundred. He'll accept five hundred now and we can draw up a bill of exchange for the rest. So please, Matvey Vasilich, help me out and lend me the five hundred. I'll pay you two per cent a month interest.'

Matvey was staggered and said, 'But what money? What money have *I* got?'

'Two per cent a month would be a godsend for you,' the policeman explained. 'But if the money's left lying around here, it'll only be food for moths and that'll do you no good at all.'

The visitors left and silence fell. But Yakov had hardly returned to his reading and singing than a voice came through the door: 'Cousin, give me a horse, I want to go to Vedenyapino.'

It was Matvey. Yakov felt uneasy again. 'But which one?' he asked after a moment's thought. 'The workman's taking the bay to cart a pig and I'm off to Shuteykino on the stallion as soon as I'm finished here.'

'My dear cousin, why are you allowed to do what you want with the horses while I'm not?' Matvey asked angrily.

'Because I'm not going on a joyride, they're needed for a job.'

'The property belongs to all of us, that means horses as well. You must understand that, Cousin.'

Silence fell. Yakov did not go back to his devotions, but waited for Matvey to go away from the door.

'Cousin,' Matvey said, 'I'm a sick man, I don't want any part of the estate. You can keep it, I don't care, but just let me have enough to live on seeing as I'm so poorly. Give it to me and I'll go away.'

Yakov did not reply. He dearly wanted to be rid of Matvey, but he could not let him have any money, since it was all tied up in the business. Among the whole Terekhov clan there had never been a single case of cousins sharing – that meant going broke.

Yakov still said nothing, waiting for Matvey to leave and he kept looking at his sister, frightened she might interfere and start another quarrel like they'd had that morning. When Matvey had gone at last he went back to his reading, but he took no enjoyment in it. His head was heavy from all those prostrations, his eyes were dim and he found the sound of his own soft, mournful voice most monotonous. When he was depressed like this at night he ascribed it to lack of sleep, but during the day it scared him and he began to think devils were sitting on his head and shoulders.

After he somehow finished reading the offices he left for Shuteykino, feeling disgruntled and irritable. In the autumn, navvies had dug a boundary ditch near Progonnaya and run up a bill for eighteen roubles at the inn: now he had to catch their foreman in Shuteykino and get his money. The thaw and snowstorms had ruined the road. It was dark, full of potholes and already breaking up in places. The snow was lying lower than the road level, along the verges, so that it was like driving along a narrow embankment. Giving way to oncoming traffic was quite a job. The sky had been overcast since morning and a moist wind was blowing . . .

A long train of sledges was coming towards him – some women were carting bricks – so Yakov had to turn off the road. His horse sank up to its belly in the snow, his one-man sledge tilted to the right. He bent over to the left to stop himself falling off and sat that way while the sledges slowly moved past. Through the wind he could hear the sledges creaking, the skinny horses panting, and the women saying: 'There goes His Grace.' One of them looked pityingly at his horse and said quickly, 'Looks like the snow'll last until St George's Day. We're fair worn out!'

Yakov sat uncomfortably hunched, screwing up his eyes in the wind as horses and red bricks went by. Perhaps it was because he felt cramped and had a pain in his side that he suddenly began to feel annoyed; the purpose of his journey struck him as unimportant and he concluded that he could send his man to Shuteykino tomorrow. Once again, as on the last sleepless night, he recalled the words about the camel and then all sorts of memories came to mind – the peasant who sold him the stolen horse, the drunkard, the women who pawned their samovars with him. Of course, every trader was out for all he could get, but he was tired of it and wanted to go as far away as he could from that mode of life. The thought that he would have to read vespers that evening depressed him. The wind that lashed him right in the face and rustled in his collar seemed to be whispering all these thoughts to him, carrying them from the wide white fields . . . As he looked at these fields he had known from childhood, Yakov remembered having had just the same feelings of apprehension, just the same worries as a young man, when he was assailed by serious doubts and his faith began to waver.

It was frightening being all alone in the open fields and he turned back and slowly followed the sledge train. The women laughed and said, 'His Grace's turned back.'

As it was Lent, no cooking was done at home and they did not use the samovar, which made the day seem very long. Yakov Ivanych had long ago stabled the horse and sent flour to the station. Once or twice he had started reading the Psalms, but it was a long time till evening. Aglaya had already washed down the floors and for something to do was tidying her trunk. The inside of its lid had bottle labels stuck all over it. Hungry and depressed, Matvey sat reading or went over to the tiled stove, where he stood a long time inspecting the tiles, which made him think of the works. Dashutka slept, but soon woke up again and went off to water the cattle. As she was drawing water from the well, the rope broke and the bucket fell into the water. The workman hunted around for a hook to haul it out with, and Dashutka followed him over the muddy snow, her bare feet as red as a goose's. She kept repeating, 'It's *dippy* there!' – she wanted to say the water in the well was too deep for the hook, but the man did not understand. Evidently she had got on his nerves, as he suddenly turned round and swore at her. Yakov happened to come out into the yard just then and heard Dashutka quickly reply with a stream of choice obscenities she could only have picked up from drunken peasants at the inn. He shouted at her and even became quite frightened: 'What's that, you shameless bitch? What kind of language is that?'

She gave her father a stupid, puzzled look, not understanding why such words were forbidden. He wanted to give her a good telling-off, but she seemed so barbarous, so ignorant. For the very first time since she had been with him he realized that she believed in nothing. His whole way of life – the forests, snow, drunken peasants, swearing – struck him as just as wild and barbarous as the girl, so instead of telling her off he merely waved his arm and went back to his room.

Just then the policeman and Sergey Nikanorych came back to see Matvey again. Yakov Ivanych recalled that these people had no faith either – this didn't worry them in the least and his life seemed strange, mad and hopeless, a real dog's life in fact. He paced up and down the yard bareheaded, then he went out into the road and walked up and down with fists clenched (at that moment the snow began to fall in large flakes) and his beard streamed in the wind. He kept shaking his head, as something seemed to be weighing down on his head and shoulders – it was just as though devils were sitting on them. It was not he who was wandering about, so he thought, but some huge and terrifying wild beast, and it seemed he only had to shout for his voice to roar through the fields and woods, terrifying everyone . . .

V

When he returned to the house, the policeman had gone and the buffet attendant was sitting in Matvey's room working with his abacus. Earlier he had been in the habit of calling at the inn almost every day. Then he would go and see Yakov Ivanych, but now it was Matvey. He was always busy with his abacus, and then his face would be tense and sweaty; or he would ask for money, or stroke his whiskers and tell how he had once made punch for some officers at a main-line station and had personally served the sturgeon soup at regimental dinners. His sole interest in life was catering, his sole topic of conversation food, cutlery and wines. Once, wanting to say something pleasant, he had told a young mother feeding her baby, 'A mother's breast is milk-bar for baby!'

As he worked away at the abacus in Matvey's room he asked for money, saying he could not live at Progonnaya any more and as if about to burst into tears he asked, 'Oh, where can I go now? Please tell me where I can go?'

Then Matvey came into the kitchen and started peeling some boiled potatoes he had probably put by the day before. It was quiet and Yakov Ivanych thought that the buffet attendant had gone. It was high time for vespers. He called Aglaya and, thinking no one was at home, began singing in a loud, uninhibited voice. He sang and read, but in his mind he recited something quite different, 'Lord forgive me! Lord save me!'

And without stopping he performed a series of low bows, as though he wanted to tire himself out, shaking his head the whole time so that Aglaya looked at him in astonishment. He was scared Matvey might come in – he was convinced he would and neither his prayers nor his many prostrations were enough to suppress his feeling of anger towards him.

Matvey opened the door extremely quietly and entered the chapel. 'What a sin, what a sin!' he sighed reproachfully. 'Repent! Come to your senses, Cousin!'

Yakov dashed out of the chapel, fists clenched, without looking at him, in case he was tempted to hit him. He felt he was a huge terrible beast again – the same feeling he'd had a little while before on the road – and he crossed the hall into the grey, dirty part of the inn, thick with haze and smoke, where peasants usually drank their tea. For some time he paced up and down, treading so heavily that the china on the shelves rattled and the tables shook. Now he realized quite clearly that he was no longer satisfied with the way he believed and he could no longer carry on praying as before. He must repent, come to his senses, see reason, live and worship somehow differently. But how was he to worship? Perhaps all this was only the Devil trying to confuse him and he really needed to do none of these things? . . . What would happen? What should he do? Who could teach him? How helpless he felt! He stopped, clutched his head and started to think, but could not take stock of everything in peace, since Matvey was so near. And he quickly returned to the living-quarters.

Matvey was sitting in the kitchen eating from a bowl of potatoes which he had in front of him. Aglaya and Dashutka were sitting in the kitchen too, by the stove, facing each other and winding yarn. An ironing-board had been set up between the stove and the table where Matvey was sitting; on it was a cold flat-iron.

'Cousin Aglaya,' asked Matvey, 'give me some oil, please!'

'But no one has oil in Lent!' Aglaya said.

'I'm not a monk, Cousin Aglaya, I'm an ordinary man. Being so poorly I'm even allowed milk, let alone oil.'

'You factory lot think you can do just what you like!'

Aglaya reached for a bottle of vegetable oil from the shelf and banged it angrily in front of Matvey with a spiteful grin, obviously delighted to see he was such a sinner.

'I'm telling you, you're not allowed any oil!' Yakov shouted.

Aglaya and Dashutka shuddered, but Matvey poured some oil into his bowl and went on eating as though he had not heard.

'I'm telling you that you mustn't have oil!' Yakov shouted even louder. He went red, suddenly seized the bowl, held it above his head and dashed it on the floor as hard as he could; the pieces went flying.

'Don't you dare say anything!' he shouted furiously, although

Matvey did not say one word. 'Don't you dare!' he repeated and thumped his fist on the table.

Matvey went pale and got up. 'Cousin!' he said, still chewing. 'Come to your senses, Cousin!'

'Get out of my house this minute!' Yakov shouted. Matvey's wrinkled face, his voice, the crumbs in his moustache revolted him. 'I'm telling you to get out!'

'Cousin, calm down! Your pride is the Devil's work!'

'Shut up!' Yakov said, stamping his feet. 'Clear off, you devil!'

'If you really want to know,' Matvey kept on shouting, beginning to lose his temper now, 'you're an apostate and heretic. Accursed demons have blotted out the true light from your eyes, your prayers don't satisfy God. Repent, before it's too late! A sinner's death is terrible! Repent, Cousin!'

Yakov grabbed him by the shoulders and dragged him away from the table. Matvey turned even paler. Terrified out of his wits he muttered, 'What's all this? What's going on?'

As he struggled and fought to free himself from Yakov's grip, Matvey accidentally caught hold of his shirt near the neck and tore the collar. But Aglaya thought he wanted to hit Yakov, screamed, seized the bottle of oil and brought it down with all her strength on the crown of this hateful cousin's head. Matvey staggered and in an instant his face became calm, indifferent. Yakov breathed heavily. He was very excited and took great pleasure in hearing the bottle grunt like a living thing as it made contact with Matvey's head. He held him up and several times (this he remembered very clearly later) directed Aglaya's attention to the iron. Only when the blood was streaming through his hands, when he heard Dashutka's loud sobbing, when the ironing-board had crashed to the ground with Matvey slumped over it did his anger subside and he realized what had happened.

'Let him die, that factory ram!' Aglaya said with loathing, still holding on to the iron. Her white, blood-spattered kerchief had slipped down to her shoulders and her grey hair fell loose. 'Serves him right!'

It was a terrible sight. Dashutka was sitting on the floor by the stove with yarn in her hands, sobbing and prostrating herself, making a kind of munching sound each time she bowed. But nothing terrified Yakov so much as the bloodstained boiled potatoes, and he was afraid of treading on them. And there was something even more terrifying, which oppressed him like a dreadful nightmare and which seemed to pose the greatest threat and did not register at first. Sergey Nikanorych the buffet attendant was standing in the doorway holding his abacus. He was very pale and looked in horror at the scene in the kitchen. Only after he had turned, dashed through the hall and then outside did Yakov realize who it was, and he went after him.

He pondered everything as he walked along, rubbing snow on his hands. The thought flashed through his mind that the workman had asked if he could spend the night at home and had long since left for his village. The day before they had killed a pig and large patches of blood lay on the snow and the sledge. Even one side of the well-head was spattered with blood. Consequently, even if all Yakov's family were up to their eyes in blood, no one would have suspected a thing. The thought of concealing the murder was torment enough, but the idea of a policeman turning up whistling and sneering from the station, that peasants would come and bind Yakov and Aglaya's hands tightly together and haul them off triumphantly to the largest village in the district, then to the town – this was the most agonizing thing of all. Everyone would point at them on the way and scoff: 'Their Graces've been nabbed!'

Yakov wanted to put off the evil day somehow so that he could suffer the disgrace some time later, not now.

'I can lend you a thousand roubles . . .' he said, catching up with Sergey Nikanorych. 'Won't do any good telling anyone, no good at all . . . We can't bring him back from the dead anyway.'

He could hardly keep up with the buffet attendant, who never looked round and was quickening his pace.

'I could lend you fifteen hundred,' he added.

He stopped for breath, but Sergey Nikanorych kept going at the same pace, possibly scared *he* might be next. Only when he had passed the level crossing and was half way along the road to the station did he take a brief look back and slow down. Red and green lamps were already shining at the station and along the line; the wind had slackened, but it was still snowing hard and the road had turned white again. Then, almost at the station, Sergey Nikanorych stopped, thought for a moment, and then determinedly retraced his steps. It was growing dark.

'I'll take the whole fifteen hundred then, Yakov Ivanych,' he said softly, trembling all over. 'Yes, I'll take 'em!'

VI

Yakov Ivanych's money was held at the town bank or lent out on mortgage. He kept a little petty cash in the house for immediate business expenses. He went into the kitchen and groped around for the tin of matches, and from the blue, sulphurous flame was able to take a close look at Matvey, still lying in the same place by the table, but draped in a white sheet now, so that only his boots showed. A cricket was chirping. Aglaya and Dashutka weren't in any of the living-rooms, but sat behind the counter in the tea-room silently winding yarn. Yakov Ivanych went to his room with a lamp and pulled out the small chest in which he kept the petty cash from under the bed. There happened to be four hundred and twenty roubles in small notes and thirty-five in silver. The notes had an unpleasant, oppressive smell. Stuffing the money into his cap he went into the yard and out through the gate. He looked to each side as he went, but there was no sign of the buffet attendant.

'Hullo!' Yakov shouted.

Right by the level crossing a dark figure detached itself from the swing barrier and approached him hesitantly. Yakov recognized the buffet attendant.

'Why can't you stay put?' he asked irritably. 'Here you are, just short of five hundred . . . there's no more in the house.'

'Fine . . . much obliged,' Sergey Nikanorych muttered as he greedily snatched the money and stuffed it in his pockets. Even though it was dark he was clearly shaking all over.

'But don't worry yourself, Yakov Ivanych . . . Why should *I* let on? All I did was come here and then go away. As they say, hear no evil . . .' Then he sighed and added, 'It's a lousy, rotten life!'

They stood in silence for a moment, without looking at each other.

'All for nothing, God knows how . . .' the buffet attendant said trembling. 'There I was doing me adding when suddenly I hear a noise . . . I look through the door and see you all having a row over some oil . . . Where is he now?'

'Lying in the kitchen.'

'You should ditch the body somewhere . . . Don't hang about!'

Without saying a word Yakov went with him as far as the station, then went back home and harnessed the horse to take Matvey to Limarovo – he had decided to take him to the forest there and leave him on the road. Afterwards he would tell everyone that Matvey had gone off to Vedenyapino and had not returned. They would all think he had been murdered by some people on the way. He knew that no one would be fooled by that story, but he felt that being on the move, doing things and keeping himself busy was less of an ordeal than just sitting around waiting. He called Dashutka and the two of them took Matvey away, while Aglaya stayed behind to clean up the kitchen.

When Yakov and Dashutka were on the way back they had to stop at the level crossing, as the barrier was down. A long goods train passed through, drawn by two panting engines which threw sheaves of crimson fire from their funnels. The engine in front gave a piercing whistle at the crossing when it was in view of the station.

'What a noise, goes right through you . . .' Dashutka said.

The train at last passed through and the keeper slowly raised the barrier. 'Is that you, Yakov Ivanych?' he asked. 'They say it's lucky not recognizing someone.'

When they were back in the house they had to get some sleep. Aglaya and Dashutka made up a bed on the tea-room floor and lay side by side, while Yakov settled down on the counter. They did not pray before going to sleep, nor did they light the icon-lamps. All three of them lay awake till morning, but they did not say one word and all night long felt someone was moving around in the empty storey above.

Two days later the district police officer and an examining magistrate came from town, searched Matvey's room and then the whole place. Yakov was questioned first and he testified that Matvey had left that Monday evening for Vedenyapino to prepare for communion in the church there, so he must have been murdered on the way by some sawyers working along the track. But when the magistrate asked why it was that Matvey had been found on the road, while his cap turned up at home – would he really have gone to Vedenyapino without it? – and why hadn't they found a single drop of blood near him in the snow on the road considering his head was smashed in and his face and chest were black with blood, Yakov became confused, lost his head and replied, 'Don't know sir.'

Yakov's worst fears were realized: the railway policeman arrived, a local constable smoked in the chapel, and Aglaya attacked him with a torrent of abuse and was rude to the inspector. And later, when Yakov and Aglaya were being taken away, peasants thronged the gate and called out, 'They've nabbed His Grace!' Everyone seemed glad.

The railway policeman said outright, under cross-examination, that Yakov and Aglaya had murdered Matvey to avoid having to share the property with him and if none of it had turned up when they were searching the place, then obviously Yakov and Aglaya had used it. Dashutka was questioned as well. She said Uncle Matvey quarrelled with Aunt Aglaya every day, that they almost came to blows over the money. Uncle must have been rich, she said, to have given a 'lady friend' a present of nine hundred roubles.

Dashutka was left on her own at the inn. No one came for tea or vodka and she would either tidy up or drink mead and eat buns. But a few days later the level crossing keeper was questioned and he testified that he had seen Yakov and Dashutka driving back late on Monday evening from Limarovo. Dashutka was arrested as well, taken to town and put in prison. It soon transpired, from what Aglaya said, that Sergey Nikanorych had been there at the time of the murder. They searched his room and found the money in a strange place – a felt boot under the stove, all in small change. There was three hundred in one-rouble notes alone. He swore he had earned it from the business and that he hadn't been to the inn for over a year; but witnesses testified that he was poor and that recently he had been particularly short of cash. They said he had been coming to the inn every day to borrow from Matvey. The railway policeman told how, on the day of the murder, he himself had gone twice to the inn with the buffet attendant to help him raise a loan. Incidentally, people remembered that on the Monday evening Sergey Nikanorych had not been there to meet the combined goods and passenger train, but had wandered off somewhere. So he was arrested too and sent to town.

The trial took place eleven months later. Yakov Ivanych had aged terribly, grown thinner and spoke in the subdued voice of a sick man. He felt weak and pathetic and that he was shorter than anyone else, and pangs of conscience and religious doubts that constantly preyed on him in prison too seemed to have aged and emaciated his spirit as much as his body. When his absence from church was brought up the judge asked, 'Are you a dissenter?'; to which he replied, 'Don't know, sir.'

By now his faith had completely deserted him. He knew nothing, understood nothing and his former religion repelled him and struck him as irrational and barbarous. Aglaya was still on the warpath and still swore at poor departed Matvey, blaming him for all her misfortunes. Instead of whiskers, Sergey Nikanorych grew a beard now. In the courtroom he sweated and blushed and was plainly ashamed of his grey prison coat and of having to sit in the dock with common peasants. Clumsily, he tried to defend himself, and in his efforts to prove that he had not visited the inn for a whole year, argued with all the witnesses, which made him a general laughing-stock. Dashutka had put on weight while she was in prison. She did not understand any of the questions she was asked in court and only managed to reply that while Uncle Matvey was being killed she had been scared stiff, but that she had felt all right afterwards.

All four were found guilty of murder for gain. Yakov Ivanych was sentenced to twenty years' hard labour, Aglaya to thirteen, Sergey Nikanorych to ten and Dashutka to six.

VII

Late one evening a foreign steamer anchored in the Dué Roads[11] and asked for coal. The captain was requested to wait until morning, but he wasn't disposed to wait one hour even, and said that should the weather break during the night he risked having to leave without any coal at all. In the Tartary Straits the weather can deteriorate very sharply – in a matter of half an hour – and then the Sakhalin coast becomes extremely dangerous. The wind was freshening already and quite a swell was running.

A convict gang was ordered out to the coalpits from the Voyevoda prison[12] – the gloomiest and most forbidding prison on the island. The convicts were to load coal onto barges which a steam launch would tow to the steamer anchored about half a mile out. There they would have to transfer the load (backbreaking work), with the launch smashing against the ship and the men hardly able to stand for seasickness. Turned out of bed only a short time before, the convicts went along the shore half asleep, stumbling in the dark and clanking their chains. To the left they could barely make out a high, incredibly gloomy cliff, while to the right was pitch-black, unrelieved darkness and the long, drawn-out, monotonous groaning of the sea. Only when a warder lit his pipe, casting a brief light on a guard with a rifle and two or three rough-looking convicts standing nearby, or when he went close to the water with his lantern, could the white crests of the nearest waves be seen.

In this party was Yakov Ivanych, who had been nicknamed 'Old Shaggy' on account of his long beard. No one ever called him by his name and patronymic now, he was simply plain Yakov. Now his stock stood very low, for three months after reaching the penal settlement he had become terribly, unbearably homesick, yielded to temptation and ran away. But he was soon caught, given a life sentence and forty lashes. Subsequently he was flogged twice more for losing prison clothing, although in both cases the clothing had been stolen from him. He had begun to feel homesick the moment he was on the way to Odessa. The convict train had stopped during the night at Progonnaya and Yakov had pressed against the window, trying to make out the old place, but it was too dark to see anything.

There was no one he could talk to about home. His sister Aglaya had been sent to a prison on the other side of Siberia and he did not know where she was now. Dashutka was on Sakhalin but had been given to some ex-convict, to live with him in some remote settlement. There was no news of her at all; but once a settler who came to the Voyevoda prison told Yakov that Dashutka had three children. Sergey Nikanorych was not far away, working in some official's house in Dué, but one could not be sure of meeting him, since he was too stuck-up to associate with rank-and-file convicts.

The gang reached the pithead and the convicts took their positions on the quayside. The news went round that the weather was getting too bad for loading and the steamer appeared to be about to weigh anchor.

Three lights were visible. One was moving – this was the steam launch that had gone out to the ship and which was apparently returning now to report if there would be any work or not. Shivering from the autumn cold and the damp sea air, and wrapped tight in his short, torn sheepskin coat, Yakov Ivanych stared unblinking in the direction of his native land. Ever since his life had begun in prison with others who had been brought there – Russians, Ukrainians, Tatars, Georgians, Chinese, Finns, gypsies and Jews – ever since he had listened to what they had to say and seen them suffer, he had once again begun to pray to God. He felt that at last he had discovered the true faith that his entire family had thirsted for from the time of Grandma Avdotya, had sought for so long without ever finding it. Now he knew all this and he understood where God was and how he could serve Him. But one thing he did not understand – why one man's destiny should differ so much from another's. Why had that simple faith, God's gift to other men, cost him so dear? What was the reason for all those horrible sufferings which made his arms and legs twitch like a drunkard's and which would clearly give him no respite until his dying day? He peered hard into the gloom and thought he could make out, over thousands of miles of pitch darkness, his homeland, his native province, his district, Progonnaya; he thought he could see the ignorance, savagery, heartlessness, the blind, harsh, bestial indifference of those he had left behind. His eyes were blurred with tears, but still he peered into the distance where the steamer's pale lights faintly glimmered. And his heart ached with longing for his native land, and he felt an urge to *live*, to go back home and tell them all about his new-found faith. If only he could save just one man from ruin – and be free of suffering for just one day!

The launch arrived and the warder announced in a loud voice that the job was off. 'Back!' he ordered. 'Stand to attention!'

He could hear the anchor chain being stowed on board the ship. A strong biting wind was blowing now and somewhere, high up on the steep cliffs, the trees were creaking. Most probably a storm was getting up.

A Woman's Kingdom

I

ON THE EVE

Here was a thick wad of banknotes from her forest manager: he had enclosed fifteen hundred roubles with his letter – the proceeds of winning a court appeal. Anna Akimovna disliked and feared such words as 'appeal', 'winning' and 'court'. She knew that justice had to be administered, but for some reason, whenever Nazarych, her works manager, or her forest manager – two inveterate litigants – won a case for her, she always felt bad about it and rather ashamed. And now too she felt apprehensive and embarrassed, and she wanted to put those fifteen hundred roubles away somewhere, out of sight.

She thought regretfully about women of her own age (she was twenty-five) who were busy in the house, who slept soundly because they were tired, and who would wake up tomorrow in truly festive mood. Many of them were long since married and had children. Somehow she alone was obliged to bury herself in these letters like an old woman, making notes on them, penning answers and then doing nothing the entire evening, right up to midnight, except wait until she felt sleepy. All next day people would be wishing her merry Christmas and asking for favours, and the day after that there was bound to be some trouble at the works – someone would be beaten up or someone would die from vodka and she would feel somehow conscience-stricken. After the holidays Nazarych would dismiss about twenty workers for absenteeism and all twenty would huddle together bare-headed at her front door. She would feel too ashamed to go out to them and they would be driven away like dogs. And everyone she knew would talk about it behind her back and send her anonymous letters, saying that she was a millionairess, an exploiter, that she was ruining people's lives and squeezing the last drop out of them.

Over there was a pile of letters that had been read and put to one side. They were appeals for money. The people here were hungry, drunken, burdened with large families, ill, humiliated, unrecognized. Anna Akimovna had already specified on each letter that one man was to get three roubles, another five. These letters would be taken to the office today, where the dispensation of charity – 'feeding-time at the zoo' as the clerks called it – would take place.

They would also distribute, in fiddling amounts, four hundred and seventy roubles – this was the interest on the capital that the late Akim Ivanych had left to the poor and needy. There would be nasty pushing and shoving. A queue, a long file of peculiar-looking people with animal-like faces, ragged, frozen stiff, hungry and already drunk, would stretch from the factory gates right down to the office. Hoarsely they would call out the name of their 'mother', their benefactress, Anna Akimovna and her parents. Those at the rear would jostle the ones in front, those in front would swear at them. The clerk would grow tired of the noise, swearing and general wailing, leap out of his office and cuff someone's ear – much to everyone's enjoyment. But her own people – workers who had been paid their wages without any holiday bonus and had already spent the lot, down to the last copeck – would be standing in the middle of the yard looking and laughing, some enviously, others sarcastically.

'Industrialists, especially women, feel more for beggars than their own workers,' Anna Akimovna thought. 'That's always the case.'

Her glance fell on the wad of money. It would be nice to hand out this unnecessary filthy lucre to the workers tomorrow, but one couldn't give them something for nothing, otherwise they would ask for more the next time. And what did those fifteen hundred roubles in fact amount to, since there were more than eighteen hundred workers at the factory, not counting wives and children? Perhaps she could pick out someone who had written a pleading letter, some miserable wretch who had long lost any hope of a better life, and give *him* the fifteen hundred roubles. The poor devil would be stunned by the money, as if he'd been struck by a thunderbolt, and perhaps would consider himself happy for the first time in his life. This thought appeared original, amusing and entertaining. She picked one letter at random from the pile and read it. Some clerk by the name of Chalikov, long jobless and ill, was living in Gushchin's house. His wife was consumptive and there were five young daughters. Anna Akimovna was very familiar with that four-storey building belonging to Gushchin where Chalikov lived – and what an evil, rotten, unhealthy place it was!

'I'll give this Chalikov something,' she decided. 'But I'd better take it myself rather than send it, to avoid any unnecessary dramas.'

'Yes,' she reasoned, hiding the fifteen hundred roubles in her pocket, 'I'll go and have a look and perhaps fix the little girls up with something too.'

Cheered at this thought, she rang the bell and ordered the horses to be brought round.

It was after six in the evening when she got into her sledge. The windows in every factory block were brightly lit and this made the enormous yard seem very dark. Electric lamps glowed by the gates, in the remote part of the yard, near the storehouses and workers' huts.

Anna Akimovna disliked and feared those dark, gloomy blocks, storehouses and workers' huts. Since her father died she had only once visited the main block. Those high ceilings with iron girders, dozens of huge, rapidly turning wheels, drive-belts and levers, the piercing hiss, the screech of steel, clattering trolleys, the harsh breath of steam; faces that were pale, crimson, or black with coal dust, shirts wet with sweat; the glitter of steel, copper and fire; the smell of coal and oil; the wind that was scorching and cold in turn – all this made the place seem like hell to her. She thought that the wheels, levers and hot, hissing cylinders were trying to break loose from their couplings and destroy people, while anxious-looking men ran around without hearing each other, fussing with the machinery in an attempt to bring its terrible movements to a halt. They showed

Anna Akimovna some object which they respectfully explained. She remembered a piece of white-hot iron being drawn out of the furnace in the forge shop; how an old man with a strap round his head and another – younger, in a dark-blue blouse with a chain on his chest, angry-faced and probably a foreman – struck a piece of iron with hammers, making golden sparks fly in all directions; and how, a little later, they had rolled an enormous piece of sheet iron in front of her with a sound like thunder. The old man stood to attention and smiled, while the younger one wiped his wet face on his sleeve and explained something to her. And she could still remember a one-eyed old man in another section scattering filings as he sawed the piece of iron, and a red-haired workman in dark glasses and with holes in his shirt working away at the lathe making something from a piece of steel. The lathe roared and screeched and whistled, and all this noise made Anna feel sick and as if something were boring into her ears. She looked and listened without understanding, smiled graciously and felt ashamed. To earn one's living and receive thousands of roubles from a business one didn't understand and which one couldn't bring oneself to like – how strange this was!

Not once had she visited the workers' blocks, where there was said to be damp, bed-bugs, debauchery, lawlessness. Amazingly, thousands were spent every year on their upkeep, but if the anonymous letters were to be believed, the workers' lot deteriorated with every year that passed.

'Things were better organized when Father was alive,' Anna Akimovna thought as she drove out of the yard, 'because he was a factory worker himself and he knew what had to be done. But I know nothing and only do stupid things.'

Again she felt bored and no longer pleased at having made the journey. The thought of that lucky man, suddenly to be showered with fifteen hundred roubles like manna from heaven, did not seem original or amusing any more. Going to see this Chalikov while a million-rouble business at home gradually declined and fell apart, while the workers lived worse than convicts in their blocks – that was a stupid act and it meant she was trying to cheat her conscience. Workers from the neighbouring cotton and paper mills were crowding along the high road and across the nearby fields on their way to the lights in town. Laughter and cheerful conversation rang out in the frosty air. As she looked at the women and young ones, Anna Akimovna suddenly yearned for simplicity, roughness, overcrowding. She vividly pictured those far-off times when she was a little girl called Annie, sharing her mother's blanket, while their lodger – a laundress – worked away in the next room. From the adjoining flats she could hear laughter, swearing, children crying, an accordion, the buzzing of lathes and sewing-machines which penetrated the thin walls, while Akim Ivanych, her father and jack-of-all-trades, did some soldering at the stove or drew plans, or worked with his plane oblivious of the cramped conditions and the noise. And now she had a strong urge to wash and iron, to run back and forwards to shop and pub as she had done every day when she lived with her mother. Rather be a worker than a factory owner! Her large house with its chandeliers and paintings, her footman Misha with his coat and tails, and small, velvety moustache, the grand Barbara, the toadying Agafya, the young people of both sexes who came almost every day to beg for money and with whom she always felt somewhat guilty, those civil servants, doctors, ladies dispensing charity on her behalf, flattering her and at the same time despising her humble origin – how boring and alien all this was!

She came to the level crossing and barrier. Houses alternated with vegetable gardens. Here at last was the broad street where Gushchin's celebrated house stood. The normally quiet street was very busy, as it was Christmas Eve. A great deal of noise came from the pubs and bars. If some stranger to the district, someone from the middle of the town, had driven down the street, then he would have seen only filthy, drunken, foul-mouthed people. But Anna Akimovna, who had lived in the district from childhood, imagined she could see her late father, then her mother, then her uncle in the crowd. Her father had been a gentle, vague soul, something of a dreamer, carefree and light-headed. He had no liking for money, position or power. He often used to say that working men had no time to think of holidays or going to church. But for his wife, he might never have observed the fasts and would have eaten meat during Lent. In contrast, her

Uncle Ivan Ivanych had been a man of steel. In everything that was connected with religion, politics or morals he had been strict and unbending, and made sure that not only he himself practised what he preached, but the servants and his acquaintances too. Heaven help anyone coming into his room without making the sign of the cross. He kept the luxurious apartment where Anna Akimovna now lived under lock and key, opening it only on special holidays, for important guests, while he himself lived in that poky little icon-filled room which was his office. He believed in the Old Creed,[1] always entertaining bishops and priests who believed as he did, although he had been christened and married and had buried his wife according to the rites of the Orthodox Church. He did not like his brother Akim – his sole heir – for his frivolous attitude, calling it simple-minded and stupid, and for his indifference to religion. He had treated him badly, just like a workman, paying him sixteen roubles a month. Akim would speak to his brother most respectfully, and at Shrovetide went with his whole family to prostrate himself before him. But three years before he died Ivan relented, forgave him and told him to engage a governess for Anna.

The gates to Gushchin's house were dark, deep, and had a terrible stench about them. Men could be heard coughing near the walls. Leaving her sledge in the street, Anna Akimovna entered the yard, where she asked the way to flat No. 46, where Chalikov the clerk lived. She was directed to the last door on the right, on the second floor. In the yard, and near the last door, even on the staircase, there was the same terrible smell as at the gates. In her childhood, when her father was a simple workman, Anna Akimovna had lived in similar houses. Then, when her circumstances changed, she often visited them as a charity worker. The filthy narrow stone staircase with a landing on each floor, the greasy lamp in the stair-well, the stench, the slop-basins, pots, rags outside doors on the landings – all this she was long familiar with. One door was open and she could see Jewish tailors, wearing caps, sitting on top of tables and sewing. She met people on the stairs, but she did not think for one moment that they could do her any harm. She feared workmen and peasants, whether drunk or sober, as little as she did her own cultivated friends.

Flat No. 46 had no hall and opened straight into the kitchen. Factory workers' and craftsmen's flats usually smell of varnish, tar, leather or smoke, depending on the occupant's trade. But flats belonging to impoverished gentlefolk and clerks can be recognized by their dank, rather acrid smell. Hardly had Anna Akimovna crossed the threshold than she was enveloped in this revolting stench. A man in a frock-coat was sitting at a table in one corner, his back to the door – most probably Chalikov himself. With him were five little girls. The eldest, broad-faced and thin, with a comb in her hair, looked about fifteen, while the youngest was a plump little girl with hair like a hedgehog and not more than three. All six were eating. Near the stove, with an oven-fork in her hands, stood a small, very thin, sallow-faced woman in a skirt and white blouse. She was pregnant.

'I didn't expect such disobedience from you, Liza,' the man said reproachfully. 'It's a disgrace! Would you like Daddy to give you a good hiding? Yes?'

When she saw a strange lady on the threshold, the thin woman shuddered and put down her oven-fork.

'Vasily Nikitich!' she called out in a hollow voice, after a moment's hesitation – as though she could not believe her eyes.

The man looked round and jumped up. He was a bony, narrow-shouldered person with sunken temples and a flat chest. His eyes were small, deep-set, with dark rings round them; his nose was long, bird-like and slightly twisted to the right; his mouth was wide and his forked beard and clean-shaven upper lip made him look more like a footman than a clerk.

'Does Mr Chalikov live here?' Anna Akimovna asked.

'That's right, lady,' Chalikov replied gruffly, but then he recognized Anna Akimovna and cried out 'Miss Glagolev! Anna Akimovna!', and suddenly he gasped for breath and threw his arms up as if scared out of his wits. 'Our saviour!'

Groaning and mumbling like a paralytic as he ran over to her (there was cabbage on his beard and he smelt of vodka), he laid his forehead on her muff and seemed to lose consciousness.

'Your hand, your divine hand!' he gasped. 'It's a dream, a beautiful dream! Children, wake me up!'

He turned towards the table and waved his fists.

'Providence has heard our prayers!' he sobbed. 'Our rescuer, our angel has come! We're saved! Children, on your knees! On your knees!'

For some reason Mrs Chalikov and the girls – with the exception of the youngest – began hurriedly clearing the table.

'You wrote that your wife was very ill,' Anna Akimovna said, and she felt ashamed and annoyed. 'I won't give him that fifteen hundred,' she thought.

'That's her, that's my wife!' Chalikov said in a shrill, woman's voice, and he seemed about to burst into tears. 'There she is, the poor woman, with one foot in the grave! But we're not complaining, ma'am. Death is better than a life like that. Die, you miserable woman!'

'Why is he putting on such an act?' Anna Akimovna wondered indignantly. 'I can see right away that he's used to dealing with rich people.'

'Please talk to me properly, I don't like play-acting,' she said.

'Yes, ma'am. Five orphans round their mother's coffin, with the funeral candles burning! You call *that* play-acting! Oh, God!' Chalikov said bitterly and turned away.

'Shut up!' his wife whispered, tugging him by the sleeve. 'It's a terrible mess here, ma'am,' she said to Anna Akimovna. 'Please forgive us. Please understand . . . it's a family matter. It's so overcrowded, but we mean no offence.'

'I won't give them the fifteen hundred,' Anna Akimovna thought again.

To make a quick escape from these people and that acrid smell, she took out her purse and decided to leave them twenty-five roubles – and no more. But suddenly she felt ashamed of having travelled so far and having troubled these people for nothing.

'If you'd like to give me some paper and ink I'll write straight away to a doctor, a very good friend of mine, and tell him to call,' she said, blushing. 'He's a very good doctor. And I'll leave you some money for medicine.'

Mrs Chalikov hurriedly began wiping the table down.

'It's filthy in here! What are you doing?' Chalikov hissed, giving her a vicious look. 'Take her to the lodger's room. Please, ma'am, go into the lodger's room, if you don't mind,' he said, turning to Anna Akimovna. 'It's clean there.'

'Osip Ilich says no one's to go into his room!' one of the little girls said sternly.

But Anna Akimovna had already been led out of the kitchen, through a narrow, intercommunicating room, between two beds. From the position of these beds she could tell that two people slept lengthways on one of them and three crossways on the other. The next room, where the lodger lived, really was clean. There was a tidy bed with a red woollen cover, a pillow in a white case, even a special little holder for a watch. There was a table covered with a linen cloth, and on this stood a milky-white ink-pot, pens, paper, framed photographs – all neatly arranged. And there was another table, which was black, with watchmaker's instruments and dismantled watches neatly laid out on it. On the walls hung little hammers, pincers, gimlets, chisels, pliers and so on. And there were three wall clocks, all ticking away. One of them was quite huge, with the kind of fat pendulum weights you see in taverns.

As she started on the letter, Anna Akimovna saw a portrait of her father, and one of herself, on the table in front of her, which surprised her.

'Who lives here?' she asked.

'The lodger, ma'am. Pimenov works at your factory.'

'Really? I thought a watchmaker must be living here.'

'He repairs watches privately, in his spare time. It's his hobby, ma'am.'

After a brief silence, during which only the ticking of the clocks and the scraping of pen on paper could be heard, Chalikov sighed and said in a disgruntled, sarcastic voice, 'There's no getting away from it, you can't make much money from being a gentleman or office clerk. You can wear decorations on your chest, you can have a title, but you'll still starve. If you ask me, if some ordinary man from the lower classes helps the poor, he's much more of a gentleman than some Chalikov who's bogged down in poverty and vice.'

To flatter Anna Akimovna he produced a few more sentences that were derogatory to his own social position, and he was obviously trying to lower himself, since he considered he was her superior. Meanwhile she had finished the letter and sealed it. The letter would be thrown away, the money would not be spent on medicine – all this she knew and yet she still put twenty-five roubles on the table, adding two ten-rouble notes after further reflection. Mrs Chalikov's gaunt yellow hand flashed before her like a hen's claw, crumpling the money.

'You've been kind enough to give us money for medicine,' Chalikov said in a trembling voice. 'But please lend me a helping hand – and my children as well,' he added, sobbing. 'My poor, poor children! I don't fear for myself, but for my daughters. I fear the Hydra of corruption!'

As she tried to open her purse with its jammed lock, Anna Akimovna grew flushed with embarrassment. She felt ashamed that people were standing there before her, looking at her hands, waiting, and most probably silently laughing at her. Just then someone entered the kitchen and stamped his feet to shake the snow off.

'The lodger's back,' Mrs Chalikov said.

Anna Akimovna grew even more embarrassed. She did not want any of the factory workers to find her in that ridiculous situation. And then, at the worst possible moment, the lodger came into his room – just as she had finally managed to break the lock open and was handing Chalikov some banknotes, while that same Chalikov bellowed like a paralytic and moved his lips as if looking for somewhere to kiss her. She recognized the lodger as that workman who had once made an iron sheet clatter in front of her in the foundry and had explained things to her. Clearly, he had come straight from the works, as his face was smudged with soot. His hands were completely black and his unbelted shirt gleamed with greasy dirt. He was a broad-shouldered man, about thirty, of medium height, with black hair and he was obviously very strong. Anna Akimovna immediately recognized that foreman whose wages were not less than thirty-five roubles a month. He was a harsh, loud-mouthed man who knocked workmen's teeth out – that was plain from the way he stood, from the pose he suddenly, instinctively, assumed when he saw a lady in his room, but chiefly from his habit of wearing his trousers outside his boots, from the pockets on the front of his shirt, from his sharp, beautifully trimmed beard. Although her late father Akim Ivanych had been the owner's brother, he had been scared of foremen like this lodger and tried to keep in their good books.

'Excuse me, we seem to have set up house here while you were out,' Anna Akimovna said.

The workman gave her a surprised look, smiled awkwardly, but did not say a word.

'Please speak a bit louder, ma'am,' Chalikov said softly. 'When he comes home of an evening Mr Pimenov's a bit hard of hearing.'

But Anna Akimovna, pleased now that there was nothing more to do there, nodded and left quickly. Pimenov saw her out.

'Have you been working for us long?' she asked in a loud voice, without looking at him.

'Since I was nine. I got my job in your uncle's time.'

'That was ages ago! My uncle and father knew all the workers, but I know hardly any of them. I've seen you before, but I didn't know that your name is Pimenov.'

Anna Akimovna felt that she should defend herself by pretending she hadn't been serious just before, when she gave the money away – that it was only a joke.

'Oh, this poverty!' she sighed. 'We do good deeds every single day, but it makes no sense. I think it's pointless trying to help people like Chalikov.'

'How right you are,' Pimenov agreed. 'Everything you give him will go on drink. And now that husband and wife will spend the whole night squabbling and trying to take the money away from each other,' he added, laughing.

'Yes, our acts of charity are useless, tiresome and ludicrous, I must admit. However, one can't just give up the struggle; something has to be done. Now, what can be done about those Chalikovs?'

She turned to Pimenov and stopped, waiting for his answer. He stopped too and slowly shrugged his shoulders without saying a word. Evidently he knew what should be done about the Chalikovs, but this was so crude and inhuman that he could not bring himself to mention it. For him, the Chalikovs were so boring and mediocre that a moment later he had forgotten all about them. As he looked into Anna Akimovna's eyes he smiled with pleasure, like someone having a wonderful dream. Only now as she stood close to him could Anna Akimovna tell from his face, particularly his eyes, how exhausted and sleepy he was.

'I should give *him* the fifteen hundred!' she thought, but the idea struck her as rather absurd, and insulting to Pimenov.

'You must be aching all over from that work, but it doesn't stop you seeing me out,' she said, going downstairs. 'Please go back.'

But he did not hear. When they came out into the street he ran on ahead, unbuttoned the sledge cover and said 'Happy Christmas!' to Anna Akimovna as he helped her into her seat.

II

MORNING

'The bells stopped ringing *ages* ago! There'll be no one left in church by the time you get there! Heaven help us! Please get up!'

'Two horses running, running . . .' Anna Akimovna said as she woke up. Masha, her red-haired maid, was standing before her with a candle. 'What's the matter? What do you want?'

'The service is over already!' Masha said despairingly. 'It's the third time I've tried to wake you! I don't care if you sleep till evening, but you yourself asked me to wake you.'

Anna Akimovna raised herself on her elbow and looked out of the window. Outside it was still quite dark, apart from the lower edge of the window frame that was white with snow. The rich, deep ringing of bells could be heard, but it came from a parish church some distance away. The clock on the small table showed three minutes past six.

'All right, Masha . . . Just two minutes,' Anna Akimovna pleaded, covering her head with the blanket.

She pictured the snow by the porch, the sledge, the dark sky, the crowded church and the smell of juniper, but despite the misgivings this filled her with she decided to get up right away and go to early service. The whole time she lay there in her warm bed, struggling against sleep – sleep is so sweet when one *has* to get up – and conjuring up visions of a huge garden on a hill, Gushchin's house, there was the nagging thought that she should get up immediately and go to church.

But when she did get up it was quite light and the clock showed half past nine. During the night a great deal of fresh snow had piled up, the trees were clothed in white and the air was unusually bright, clear and serene, so that when Anna Akimovna looked through the window she wanted first to take a very deep breath. But as she was washing herself, a vestige of the joy she had felt as a child on Christmas Day stirred within her – and then she felt easier, free and pure at heart, as if her soul itself had been cleansed or dipped in white snow. In came Masha, in her best clothes and tightly corseted, and wished her happy Christmas, after which she spent a long time combing her hair and helping her to dress. The smell and feel of that beautiful, magnificent new dress, with its rustle, and the smell of fresh perfume all excited Anna Akimovna.

'So, it's Christmas,' she gaily told Masha. 'Now let's do some fortune-telling.'

'Last year it came out that I would marry an old man. Three times it came out like that, it did.'

'Don't worry, God is merciful.'

'I'm not so sure, ma'am. As I see it, I'd be better off married to an old man than running around getting nowhere,' Masha sighed sadly. 'I'm past twenty now and that's no joke.'

Everyone in the house knew that red-haired Masha was in love with Misha the butler and that this deep but hopeless passion had lasted for three years now.

'Don't talk such nonsense,' Anna Akimovna said consolingly. 'I'll soon be thirty, but I still intend marrying someone young.'

While the mistress of the house was dressing, Misha – in his new tailcoat and lacquered boots – paced the ballroom waiting for her to come out so that he could wish her happy Christmas.

He had his own peculiar manner of walking, and treading softly and delicately. If you watched his legs, arms and the angle of his head you might have thought that he wasn't just walking, but practising the first figure of the quadrille. Despite his fine, velvety moustache and his handsome, even rather roguish exterior, he was as staid, sober-minded and pious as an old man. He always prostrated himself when praying and he loved burning incense in his room. He respected and revered the rich and influential, but he despised the poor and any kind of humble petitioner with the whole might of his 'holier-than-thou' flunkey's soul. Under his starched shirt was a flannel vest which he wore winter and summer – he attached great importance to his health. His ears were stuffed with cottonwool.

When Anna Akimovna and Masha came across the ballroom, he leant his head downwards, slightly to one side, and said in a pleasant, sugary voice, 'I have the honour, ma'am, to offer my compliments on the solemn occasion of Jesus Christ's nativity.'

Anna Akimovna gave him five roubles and poor Masha was stunned. His festive appearance, his pose, his voice and what he said astounded her with their elegance and beauty. As she followed her mistress she had no thoughts, saw nothing, smiling first blissfully and then bitterly.

The upper storey was called 'the best rooms' or 'the apartment', whereas the lower floor, where Aunt Tatyana Ivanovna held sway, was called the 'tradesmen's', 'old people's' or simply the 'women's quarters'. In the best rooms they usually received upper-class, educated people, and in the downstairs section ordinary people and Auntie's personal friends. Beautiful, buxom, healthy, still young and fresh, and highly conscious of her magnificent dress, which, she felt, was radiating light in all directions, Anna Akimovna went down to the lower floor.

There she was greeted with reproaches: an educated person like her had forgotten God, had missed morning service by oversleeping and had not come down to break her fast. All clasped their hands and assured her most sincerely that she was exceptionally pretty. She took them at their word and laughed, kissed them and gave them one, three or five roubles each, depending on the person. She liked it downstairs. Wherever she looked there were icon-cases, icons, icon-lamps, portraits of church dignitaries. It smelt of monks. Knives clattered in the kitchen and a rich, very savoury smell spread everywhere. The yellow stained floors shone and narrow rugs with bright blue stripes stretched like little paths from the doors to the corners where the icons were. The sun blazed through the windows.

Some old women – strangers – were sitting in the dining-room. In Barbara's room there were old women as well, together with a deaf and dumb girl who appeared very shy and who kept making a mumbling sound. Two skinny little girls who had been asked over from the orphanage for the holidays came up to kiss Anna Akimovna's hand but stopped, dumbfounded by the richness of her dress. She noticed that one of the girls was a little cross-eyed, and although she was in a relaxed, holiday mood, her heart suddenly sank at the thought that the girl would be ignored by the young men and would never marry. Five huge peasants in new shirts – not factory workers but relatives of the kitchen servants – were sitting over the samovar in Agafya the cook's room. As soon as they saw Anna Akimovna the peasants jumped up and stopped chewing, out of politeness, although all had a full mouth. Stefan her chef, in white hat and knife in hand, came out from the kitchen to wish them merry Christmas. House porters in felt boots arrived and offered their good wishes too. A water-carrier with icicles on his beard showed his face but dared not enter.

Anna Akimovna walked through all the rooms, the whole assembly following her: Auntie, Barbara, Nikandrovna, Martha the seamstress, and 'downstairs Masha'. Slim and slender, taller than anyone else in the house, dressed all in black and smelling of cypress wood and coffee, Barbara crossed herself and bowed before the icon in every room. Each time you looked at her you were somehow reminded that she had prepared her own shroud for the day she died, and that in the same trunk where she kept this shroud she had hidden her lottery tickets.

'Come on, Anna dear, show some Christmas spirit!' she said, opening the kitchen door. 'Forgive that miserable wretch! What a crowd!'

Panteley the coachman, who had been dismissed for drunkenness in November, was on his knees in the middle of the kitchen. A kind man, he was liable to become violent when drunk. Then he just couldn't sleep and he marched round the factory blocks shouting menacingly 'I know everything!' From his bloated lips, puffy face and bloodshot eyes it was plain that he had been on the bottle non-stop since November.

'Please forgive me, Anna Akimovna!' he said hoarsely, banging his forehead on the floor and revealing a neck like a bull's.

'It was my aunt who dismissed you, so go and ask *her*.'

'Did you say "aunt"?' asked Auntie as she came puffing and panting into the kitchen. She was so fat one could have put a samovar and tray of cups on her chest. 'What's all this about your aunt? You're mistress here, so you see to it. I'd rather these ruffians cleared out of here altogether. Come on, get up, you great pig!' she shouted, losing patience. 'Out of my sight! I'll forgive you this one last time, but if it happens again don't expect any mercy.'

They went into the dining-room for coffee. People could be heard blowing their noses and there was a low, deep coughing and a sound of footsteps as if newly shod horses were being led into the anteroom near the ballroom. All was quiet for about half a minute, then suddenly the carol singers shrieked so loud that everyone jumped. While they sang, the almshouse priest arrived with the deacon and lay reader. As he put on his stole the priest slowly declared that 'it had snowed during the night when the bells were ringing for early morning service', that 'it hadn't been cold but towards morning the frost began to harden, confound it, and it was twenty below, in all likelihood'.

'Many people, however, maintain that winter is healthier than summer,' the deacon said, but he immediately assumed a serious expression and followed the priest in singing 'Thy Nativity, Oh, Christ Our Lord'.[2]

Shortly after, the priest from the factory sickbay arrived, then nurses from the community hospital and children from the orphanage. The singing went on almost non-stop. They sang, they ate, they left.

About twenty of the works staff came to offer their compliments of the season. They were all senior men – engineers, their assistants, pattern-makers, the accountant and so on. All looked eminently respectable in their new black frock-coats and they were all fine men, the select few, and each knew his worth. If any one of them were to lose his job that day, another factory would be only too pleased to take him on tomorrow. They seemed to take a great liking to Anna Akimovna's aunt, since they were relaxed with her and even smoked, while the accountant put his arm around her ample waist as they all crowded over to the food. Perhaps they felt so free and easy because Barbara, who had wielded great power in the old man's day and had been custodian of the servants' morals, now had no authority at all in the house. Perhaps another reason was that many of them still remembered the time when Aunt Tatyana, who was kept on a tight rein by her brothers, had dressed like a simple peasant, in the same style as Agafya, and when even Miss Anna had run round the yard near the factory blocks and everyone had called her Annie.

The factory staff ate their food, talked and glanced at Anna Akimovna in bewilderment. How she had grown up, how pretty she had become! But this elegant girl, brought up by governesses and tutors, was a stranger to them, a mystery, and they could not help staying close to the aunt, who spoke to them as though they were on her level, constantly urged them to eat and drink and clinked glasses with them, having already drunk two glasses of rowanberry vodka. Anna Akimovna had always feared that they might think she was vain, an upstart, a crow in peacock's feathers. And now, as the staff crowded around the food, she stayed in the dining-room, where she took part in the conversation. She asked Pimenov, whom she had met the day before, 'Why are there so many clocks in your room?'

'I repair them,' he replied. 'It's something I do in my spare time, during holidays, or when I can't sleep.'

'So, if my watch goes wrong I can ask you to repair it?' Anna Akimovna asked, laughing.

'Of course, that would give me great pleasure,' Pimenov said, and he seemed deeply touched when, without knowing why, she unhooked her magnificent watch from her corsage and handed it to him. Silently he inspected it. 'Why, yes, with pleasure,' he repeated. 'I don't usually repair pocket watches nowadays. My eyes are bad and the doctor advised me not to do any close work. But for you I'll make an exception.'

'Doctors are liars,' the accountant said. Everyone burst out laughing. 'Don't you believe what they say,' he continued, flattered by the laughter. 'Last year, during Lent, a cog-wheel flew out of a drum and hit old Kalmykov right on the head; you could see his brains. The doctor said he would die, but he's still alive and working, only he talks with a stutter after what happened.'

'Doctors *can* talk rubbish, I do agree, but not that much,' Auntie sighed. 'Pyotr Andreyevich, God rest his soul, lost his sight. Like you, he worked all day in the factory near a hot furnace and he went blind. Heat damages the eyes. Well, what's the use of talking?' She gave a start. 'Let's have a drink! Merry Christmas, my dears! I don't usually drink, but I'll have one with you. God forgive me! Cheers!'

After what had happened yesterday, Anna Akimovna felt that Pimenov despised her as a 'do-gooder', but that, as a woman, she enchanted him. She glanced at him and it seemed he was behaving very nicely and was properly dressed for the occasion. True, his coat sleeves were rather short, the waist was too high and the trousers not broad, according to the latest style. On the other hand his tie was knotted with tasteful neglect and it wasn't as loud as the others'. And he clearly was a good-natured man, for he obediently ate everything that Auntie put on his plate. She remembered how black he had looked the day before, how much he had wanted to sleep, and for some reason the memory of it moved her.

When the staff were ready to leave, Anna Akimovna offered Pimenov her hand and wanted to ask him to visit her some time, but her tongue would not obey her and she could not produce one word. In case his workmates thought she had taken a fancy to Pimenov, she offered them her hand as well.

Then the boys arrived from the school of which she was a governor. All of them had short hair and all were dressed in identical grey smocks. Their master, a tall young man, without a moustache and his face covered in red blotches, obviously felt nervous and made his pupils stand in rows. The boys began to sing in harmony, but their voices were harsh and unpleasant. Nazarych, the works manager, a bald, eagle-eyed believer in the Old Creed, had never got on with the schoolmasters, but he really hated and despised this teacher, who was fussily giving directions with his arm. Why this was so, he himself couldn't say. He treated him arrogantly and rudely, withheld his wages, interfered with the teaching. In an effort to get rid of him for good, he had appointed a distant relative of his own wife as school caretaker – a drunken peasant who disobeyed the schoolmaster in front of the boys.

Anna Akimovna knew all about this, but she was unable to help, as she herself was scared of Nazarych. Now she wanted at least to be kind to the schoolmaster and tell him that she was very satisfied with him. But when the singing was over and he embarked on a highly embarrassed apology for something, and after Auntie had spoken to him like a little boy and unceremoniously bundled him over to the table, she felt bored and awkward. After leaving instructions for the children to receive their presents she went upstairs to her own part of the house.

'There's really a great deal of cruelty about these festivities,' she said aloud to herself a little later as she looked through the window at the crowd of boys on their way from the house to the gates, shrinking from the cold and putting their furs and coats on as they went. 'On holidays all one wants is some rest, to be at home with the family, but those poor boys, that schoolmaster, the staff – for some reason they're obliged to go out into the freezing cold to wish you merry Christmas and convey their respects. They feel awkward . . .'

Misha, who was standing just by the ballroom doors, heard this. 'We didn't start it,' he said, 'and it won't finish with us. Of course, I'm not an educated man, Anna Akimovna, but as I see it the poor always have to pay their respects to those what's rich. They say God puts his mark on rogues. You'll only find poor folk in prisons, doss-houses, pubs, but respectable folk are always the rich ones, you see. Money comes to money, that's what they say about the rich.'

'Misha, you always talk such boring stuff that it's impossible to understand you,' Anna Akimovna said and went to the far end of the ballroom.

It was only just twelve o'clock. The silence of those huge rooms, broken only now and then by the sound of singing that drifted up from the ground floor, made one feel like yawning. The bronzes, the albums, the paintings on the walls depicting an ocean scene with small ships, a meadow with cows, views of the Rhine, were really so dull, one's eyes swiftly glided over them without seeing a thing. The holiday mood had already begun to pall. Anna Akimovna still considered herself as beautiful, kind and exceptional as before, but she felt these virtues were useless to anyone. It seemed that there had been no point at all in wearing that expensive dress. Whom did she want to please? And as usually happened on every holiday, she began to tire of the loneliness and was unsettled by the nagging thought that her beauty, health and wealth were nothing but an illusion, since she was a superfluous sort of person, unwanted, unloved by anyone. She walked through all her rooms, humming and looking through the windows. Stopping in the hall she could not help starting a conversation with Misha.

'I really don't know, Misha, who you think you are,' she sighed. 'God will surely punish you for this.'

'What do you mean, ma'am?'

'You know very well. Forgive me for interfering with your personal affairs, but I have the impression you're ruining your life out of sheer obstinacy. Don't you agree it's the right time for you to marry now, she's such a beautiful, deserving girl? You won't find a better. She's beautiful, clever, gentle, devoted . . . And as for her looks! If she were one of our circle, or in high society, everyone would love her for her wonderful red hair alone. Just look how her hair suits her complexion! God, you understand nothing and don't know yourself what you want,' Anna Akimovna said bitterly, the tears welling up in her eyes. 'That poor girl. I feel so sorry for her! I know you're looking for someone with money, but I've already told you that I'll give Masha a dowry.'

Misha imagined that his future wife could only be someone tall, buxom, well-shaped and religious, with a walk like a peacock's and never without a long shawl on her shoulders. But Masha was thin, delicate, tightly corseted and with an unpretentious walk. Most important, she was too seductive and at times Misha did feel strongly attracted to her. However, according to him, that kind of thing was only conducive to loose behaviour, not marriage. He had hesitated a little when Anna Akimovna promised a dowry. But then some poor student with a brown coat over his tunic[3] had arrived with a letter for Anna Akimovna and had been so enraptured with Masha that he couldn't control himself and had embraced her near the coat hooks downstairs. She had given a faint cry. Misha saw what happened from the staircase above and ever since had felt aversion for her. A poor student! Who knows, things might have turned out quite differently if some rich student or officer had embraced her instead . . .

'Why don't you marry her?' Anna Akimovna asked. 'What more do you want?'

Misha did not answer and stood quite still staring at an armchair, eyebrows raised.

'Do you love someone else?'

Silence. In came red-haired Masha with some letters and visiting cards on a tray. She guessed that they were talking about her and blushed until the tears came.

'The postmen are here,' she muttered. 'And there's a clerk called Chalikov, he's waiting downstairs. Says you told him to come here today for something.'

'What impertinence!' Anna Akimovna said furiously. 'I told him nothing of the sort! Tell him to clear off, I'm not at home!'

The doorbell rang: the priests from her own parish had arrived. They were always received in the best part of the house – and that was upstairs. They were followed by Nazarych the works manager and the factory doctor. Then Misha announced the inspector of secondary schools. The reception had begun.

Whenever she had a free moment, Anna Akimovna would sit deep in an armchair in the drawing-room, close her eyes and conclude that her loneliness was something quite natural, since she had not married and never would. But this wasn't her fault. Fate itself had taken her from an ordinary working-class background (where, if her memory was to be trusted, she felt so comfortable and at home) and thrown her into these vast rooms where she never knew what to do with herself. Nor could she understand why so many people were dashing in and out. The present events struck her as of no consequence, fruitless, since they had never brought her a moment's happiness and they never could.

'If only I could fall in love,' she thought, stretching herself, and this thought alone warmed her heart. 'And if I could get rid of that factory,' she brooded, imagining all those ponderous blocks, those barracks, that school, being eased from her conscience. Then she remembered her father and thought that had he lived longer he would surely have married her to some ordinary man, like Pimenov, and that would have been that. It would have been a good thing, as the factory would have fallen into the right hands.

She pictured his curly hair, the bold profile, those fine, mocking lips, the strength – the terrible strength – of his shoulders, arms and chest, and how moved he had been when he inspected her watch earlier in the day. 'Why not?' she said. 'I can't see anything against it. Yes, I'd marry him.'

'Anna Akimovna!' Misha called as he noiselessly entered the drawing-room.

'What a fright you gave me!' she said, trembling all over. 'What do you want?'

'Anna Akimovna,' he repeated, putting his hand to his heart and raising his eyebrows. 'You are the lady of the house, my benefactress, and you alone can tell me whom to marry, as you're like a mother to me. But please tell them to stop teasing me, laughing at me downstairs. They don't give me a moment's peace!'

'And how do they tease you?'

'They keep calling me Masha's Misha!'

'Ugh, what rubbish!' Anna Akimovna said, getting angry. 'What a stupid lot you all are! You included, Misha. I'm sick and tired of you and I don't want to see you!'

III

DINNER

Like the previous year, the last guests to come were actual state councillor[4] Krylin and Lysevich, the well-known lawyer. When they arrived it was quite dark already. Krylin, in his sixties, had a wide mouth, grey mutton-chop whiskers and the face of a lynx. He was in uniform and white trousers, and wore the ribbon of St Anne.[5]

He held Anna Akimovna's hand for a long time in both of his, staring into her face and moving his lips. Finally he said in a slow, deliberate voice pitched on one note, 'I respected your uncle . . . and your father, and they were well-disposed towards me. Now, as you can see, I consider it my pleasant duty to convey seasonal greetings to their respected heiress, despite my being ill and having to travel so far. And I'm delighted to see you looking so well.'

Lysevich the barrister, a tall, handsome fair-haired man, with slightly greying temples and beard, was celebrated for his exceptionally refined manners. He would dance into the room, execute an apparently reluctant bow, twitch his shoulders as he spoke, all this being executed with the lazy grace of a spoilt horse grown idle from standing about. He was well-fed, extremely healthy and rich. Once he won as much as forty thousand roubles, but didn't breathe a word about it to his friends. He loved eating well, especially cheese, truffles, grated radish with hempseed oil, and he maintained he had eaten fried, uncleaned giblets in Paris. He spoke articulately, smoothly, never hesitating, and only rarely allowed himself a simpering pause or click of the fingers, as if indicating he was at a loss for the *mot juste*. He had long stopped believing anything he was called upon to say in court: perhaps he did believe what he said, but attached no importance to it: it was all such old hat, so trivial. He believed only in the esoteric, the unusual. Copy-book ethics, expressed in an original form, reduced him to tears. His two notebooks were crammed with unusual sayings culled from various authors, and whenever he felt in need of some expression, he would nervously rummage in both books, usually failing to find what he wanted. Once old Akim Ivanych, in a moment of euphoria and wanting to go one better than his competitors, had engaged him as lawyer at the works, at a fixed salary of twelve thousand. But the only legal matters that cropped up there were a few minor cases that Lysevich delegated to his assistants.

Anna Akimovna knew that there was no work for him at the factory, but could not bring herself to dismiss him – she did not have the courage, and, what was more, had grown used to him. He termed himself her 'legal adviser', calling his salary – which he sent for every first day of the month, on the dot – that 'mundane affair'. Anna Akimovna knew that after her father died and the forest was sold for timber to make railway sleepers, Lysevich had made more than fifteen thousand from the sale and split it with Nazarych. When she found out about the swindle she wept bitterly but then accepted the fact.

After wishing her happy Christmas and kissing both her hands, Lysevich looked her up and down and frowned.

'There's no need for it,' he said with genuine distress. 'I said, my dear, that there's no need for it!'

'What are you talking about, Viktor Nikolaich?'

'What I said was, you shouldn't put on weight. Your whole family has this unfortunate tendency. There's no need for it,' he pleaded again and kissed her hand. 'You're such a good person! You're so wonderful!' He turned to Krylin and said, 'My dear sir, I can recommend the only woman in this world I ever loved seriously.'

'That doesn't surprise me. At your age, to know Anna Akimovna and not to love her is impossible.'

'I adore her!' the lawyer continued with complete sincerity, but with his usual lazy gracefulness. 'I love her – not because I'm a man and she's a woman. When I'm with her I feel as if she is some third kind of sex, and myself a fourth, and we seem to be whirling away into the realm of the most delicate hues, where we blend into one spectrum. Leconte de Lisle[6] is best at defining such relationships. He has a wonderful passage, somewhere, it's really amazing.'

Lysevich rummaged first in one book, then the other. Not managing to find the passage, he grew quiet. They began discussing the weather, the opera, Duse's[7] imminent arrival. Anna Akimovna remembered that Lysevich and (so she thought) Krylin had dined with her the previous Christmas. Now, as they prepared to leave, she urged them in the most genuinely pleading voice to stay for dinner, arguing that they had no more visits to make. After a moment's hesitation they agreed.

Besides the usual dinner, consisting of cabbage soup, roast sucking-pig, goose with apples and so on, a French or 'chef's special' dinner was prepared in the kitchen on major holidays, in case any of the upstairs guests felt like indulging themselves. When the clatter of crockery came from the dining-room, Lysevich began to show visible excitement. He rubbed his hands, twitched his shoulders, screwed up his eyes and talked with great feeling about the dinners the old men used to give and the superb turbot *matelote*[8] the present chef could produce – more a divine revelation than a *matelote*! He was so looking forward to the dinner, mentally relishing and savouring it in advance. When Anna Akimovna took his arm and led him into the dining-room and he had drunk his glass of vodka and popped a tiny slice of salmon into his mouth, he even purred with pleasure. He chewed noisily and disgustingly, making curious sounds through his nose, while his eyes became oily and greedy.

It was a sumptuous *hors-d'œuvre*. Among other things there were fresh white mushrooms in sour cream and *sauce provençale* made with fried oysters and crayfish tails well flavoured with sour pickles. The main meal consisted of delicately refined dishes with a festive flavour, and the wines were excellent. Misha served like someone in a trance. Whenever he placed a fresh dish on the table and removed the lid from a glittering tureen, or poured out wine, he performed it with the solemnity of a professor of black magic. From his expression and the way he walked, he seemed to be executing the first figure of a quadrille, and the lawyer thought to himself several times 'What an idiot!'

After the third course Lysevich turned to Anna Akimovna.

'A *fin de siècle* woman – I mean young and rich, of course – must be independent, clever, refined, intelligent, bold and rather corrupt.

I say *rather* corrupt, just a little bit, since, as you'll agree, anything in excess becomes exhausting. And you, my dear, you must not vegetate, you must not live like all the others, but must relish life, and moderate dissipation is the spice of life. Bury yourself deep in flowers of overpowering fragrance, choke on musk, eat hashish, but above all, you must love, love . . . The first thing I would do, if I were in your place, would be to have seven men, one for each day of the week. One would be called Monday, the next Tuesday, the third Wednesday and so on, each would know his allotted day.'

What he said disturbed Anna Akimovna. She did not eat a thing and drank only one glass of wine.

'Let me have my say!' she exclaimed. 'Personally, I don't recognize love without the family. I'm lonely, lonely as the moon in the sky above – a waning moon, what's more, and for all you say I'm convinced, I feel intuitively, that this waning can only be reversed by love in its usual meaning. This kind of love defines my responsibilities, my work, it illumines my view of life. I require spiritual peace and calm from love. I want to escape as far as possible from musk, your occultism and *fin de siècle* hocus-pocus. Briefly,' she added, growing embarrassed, 'I want a husband and children.'

'You want to get married? All right, that's also possible,' Lysevich agreed. 'You must try everything – marriage, jealousy, the sweetness of the first infidelity, children even . . . But do hurry up and *live*, my dear. Hurry! Time's passing, it won't wait.'

'Then I *shall* marry!' she said angrily, glancing at his smooth, self-satisfied face. 'I shall marry in the most ordinary, the most vulgar way and I'll be radiant with happiness. And I'll marry some simple working man, a mechanic or a draughtsman, if you can imagine that.'

'That wouldn't be a bad idea either. A princess falls for a swineherd – being a princess she can do that. And you too will be allowed to do the same, as you're no ordinary person. If you want to love a Negro or Arab, my dear, don't be shy, go and order a Negro. Don't deny yourself a thing. You should be as bold as your own desires, don't lag behind them.'

'Why do you find me so hard to understand?' Anna Akimovna said in amazement, her eyes glistening with tears. 'Please try and understand. I have an enormous business on my hands, I'm responsible for two thousand workers before God. People who work for me go blind and deaf. Life terrifies me, just terrifies me! While I'm suffering like this you can be so heartless as to talk about some Negro or other and smile!' Anna Akimovna thumped her fist on the table. 'To continue living as I do now, to marry someone as idle, feckless as myself would be criminal. I can't go on living like this,' she said furiously, 'I just can't!'

'How pretty she is!' Lysevich said, enraptured. 'Good God, how pretty! But why are you so angry, my dear? I admit I could be wrong, but do you think it will make things any better for the workers if, for the sake of ideals, which I happen to respect deeply, you're miserable all the time and renounce all joy in life? Not one little bit. There *has* to be depravity, dissipation!' he said determinedly. 'You *must* be corrupt, it's your duty! Have a good think about that, my dear.'

Anna Akimovna was glad that she had spoken her mind and she cheered up. She was pleased to have spoken so eloquently and now she was convinced that if Pimenov, for example, were to fall in love with her she would be delighted to marry him.

Misha poured some champagne.

'You irritate me, Viktor Nikolaich,' she said, clinking glasses with the lawyer. 'It annoys me that you can offer advice when you have no knowledge of life at all. You seem to think that mechanics or draughtsmen are ignorant peasants. But they're terribly clever, they're really remarkable!'

'I knew your father and uncle . . . and I respected them,' Krylin said with slow deliberation. He was sitting as rigid as a statue and had been eating non-stop the whole time. 'They were people of the highest intellect and . . . the loftiest moral qualities.'

'All right, we know all about those qualities,' the lawyer muttered and asked permission to smoke.

When dinner was over, Krylin was led off to sleep. Lysevich finished his cigar and followed Anna Akimovna into her study, walking unsteadily after all the food he had eaten. He had no love for cosy nooks with photographs, fans on the walls, the inevitable pink or light-blue lamp in the middle of the ceiling, considering them the expression of a dull, unoriginal kind of personality. Furthermore, memories of certain previous affairs, of which he was now ashamed, were bound up with that type of lamp. But he did like Anna Akimovna's study with its bare walls and tasteless furniture. It was soft and comfortable sitting there on the sofa, looking at Anna Akimovna, who usually sat on the carpet in front of the hearth, her knees clasped in her hands as she pensively stared into the fire. At that moment he felt that her peasant, Old Believer's blood[9] was throbbing in her veins now.

After dinner, when coffee and liqueurs were served, he would always liven up and tell her various bits of literary news. He used the florid, inspired style of someone carried away by his own oratory as she listened and – as always – concluded that she would pay him not twenty thousand but three times as much for the entertainment. And she would forgive him for everything she found unlikeable in him. At times he told her the plots of short stories, even novels, and on those occasions two or three hours would pass like minutes without them noticing. Now he began in a somewhat listless, feeble voice, his eyes closed.

'It's a long time since I read anything, my dear,' he said when she asked him to tell her some story. 'However, I sometimes read Jules Verne.'[10]

'And I thought you had something new to tell me.'

'Hm . . . new,' Lysevich murmured sleepily and sank even further into the corner of the sofa. 'None of modern literature is for you or me, dear lady. Of course, it is what it is and can't be anything else. Not to accept it would be the same as rejecting the natural order of things, and I do accept it, but . . .'

Lysevich seemed to have fallen asleep, but soon his voice was heard again: 'The whole of modern literature is like the autumn wind in the chimney, moaning and groaning: "Oh, you're so unhappy! Oh, your life is a prison. Oh, how dark and damp for you there! Oh, you are doomed, there's no escape!" That's all very nice, but I would prefer a literature that teaches you how to escape from prison. The only contemporary writer I read now and then is Maupassant.'[11]

Lysevich opened his eyes. 'A good writer, an excellent writer!' Lysevich slid forward a little on the sofa. 'A remarkable artist! A terrifying, monstrous, supernatural artist!' Lysevich got up from the sofa and raised his right arm. 'Maupassant!' he exclaimed rapturously. 'Read Maupassant, my dear! One page of his will give you more than all the world's riches. Every line is a new horizon! The most subtle, tender movements of the soul alternate with violent, tempestuous sensations, as if a forty-thousand-fold atmospheric pressure had been brought to bear on it, turning it into an insignificant particle of some indeterminate pinkish matter which might taste sharp and sensuous if you could put it on the tongue. Such frenzied transitions, motifs, melodies! You are resting on a bed of lilies and roses when suddenly a terrifying, beautiful, irresistible thought descends on you out of the blue, like a locomotive enveloping you in hot steam and deafening you with its whistle. Read, read Maupassant! My dear, I insist!'

Lysevich waved his arms and walked up and down in great agitation. 'No, it's not possible,' he said, as if in desperation. 'His last work exhausted, intoxicated me![12] But I'm afraid you'll be indifferent to it. In order to be carried away you have to savour it, slowly squeeze the juice from each line, drink. Yes, you must drink it!'

After a long preamble full of many phrases like 'demoniac sensuality', 'network of the most delicate nerves', 'simoom',[13] 'crystal' and so on, he finally began to tell her the novel's plot. He no longer indulged in flowery language and he went into great detail, quoting entire descriptive passages and conversations. He was enchanted by the characters and assumed different poses as he described them, altering his voice or facial expression, like a true actor. In his delight he would laugh out loud, first in a low-pitched voice, then very shrilly, clasping his hands or clutching his head as if he expected it to burst any minute. Although she had read the book, she listened enchanted, finding the lawyer's rendering far more beautiful and complex than the novel itself. He directed her attention to various fine points and emphasized exquisitely turned expressions and profound thoughts. But she could only see real life itself there, and herself, as if she were one of the characters in the book. She cheered up, laughed out loud and clasped her hands like him, thinking it was impossible to go on with the life she had been leading, that there was no need to lead a wretched existence when one could live beautifully. She remembered what she had said and thought during dinner and she was proud of it. When the figure of Pimenov suddenly loomed large in her mind, she felt gay and wanted him to love her.

When he had finished his exposition, Lysevich sank back exhausted on the sofa.

'What a wonderful, beautiful person you are!' he began a little later, in a feeble, ailing voice. 'I'm happy when I'm near you, my dear. But why am I forty-two and not thirty? Your tastes and mine don't coincide. You should be dissipated, but I've long outlived that phase and I desire the most refined kind of love, as insubstantial as a sunbeam. I mean to say, I'm no damned good to a woman of your age.'

He said that he liked Turgenev, the bard of virginal love, youth and the melancholy Russian countryside. But his fondness for this 'virginal love' was not something directly experienced, but only something he had heard speak of, abstract, beyond the bounds of reality. Now he was trying to convince himself that his love for Anna Akimovna was platonic, idealistic, although he didn't know the meaning of the words. He felt comfortable, warm and at ease, though, and Anna Akimovna seemed enchanting in her eccentricity. He thought that this pleasant feeling of wellbeing generated by his surroundings was identical with that so-called 'platonic love'.

He pressed his cheek to her hand and asked in the kind of voice usually resorted to in order to win over young children, 'Why have I been punished, my dear?'

'How? When?'

'I didn't receive my Christmas bonus.'

Anna Akimovna had never heard of lawyers receiving Christmas bonuses and now she felt awkward, not knowing how much to give him. But give she must, as he was expecting it, even as he looked at her with loving eyes.

'Nazarych must have forgotten,' she said. 'But it's not too late to rectify matters.'

Suddenly she remembered yesterday's fifteen hundred roubles that were lying on her bedroom dressing-table. When she brought down that loathsome money and handed it to the lawyer, who stuffed it into a side pocket, with effortless grace, it was all so charming and natural. That unexpected reminder of the bonus, the fifteen hundred roubles – all this seemed so right for Lysevich.

'*Merci*,' he said, kissing her finger.

Krylin entered with a blissful, sleepy look, and without his ribbons. He and Lysevich sat for a little longer, drank a glass of tea each and prepared to leave. Anna Akimovna was in something of a quandary: she had completely forgotten where Krylin worked and she wondered if she should give him money as well. If so, should she give it him there and then, or send it in an envelope?

'Where does he work?' she whispered to Lysevich.

'Damned if I know,' the lawyer muttered, yawning.

Anna Akimovna concluded that if Krylin had visited her uncle and father to pay his respects, it would not have been for nothing. Obviously he had acted for them in performing good deeds, having been employed by some charitable institution. As she said goodbye, she thrust three hundred roubles into his hand. He seemed amazed at this and stood looking at her for a short while in silence, with lustreless eyes. But then he seemed to cotton on.

'But, my dear Anna Akimovna, I can't give you a receipt before the New Year.'

Lysevich had grown quite limp and he staggered as Misha helped him into his fur coat. As he went downstairs he looked completely enervated and it was plain that he would fall asleep the moment he was in his sledge.

'My dear sir,' he asked Krylin languidly, stopping halfway down, 'have you ever had the feeling that some invisible power was stretching you out, making you longer and longer until you finally turned into the finest wire? Subjectively speaking it's a special, voluptuous sensation that you can't compare with anything else.'

Anna Akimovna could see them both hand Misha a banknote.

'Now don't forget me! Goodbye!' she shouted after them and ran into her bedroom.

Quickly she threw off that dress which she was now tired of, put on her house-coat. Like a child she made her feet clatter as she ran downstairs. She desperately wanted some fun and games.

IV

EVENING

Auntie, in a loose cotton-print dress, Barbara and two old women were having supper in the dining-room. On the table in front of them was a large chunk of salt-beef, a ham, and various other salted delicacies. Steam rose to the ceiling from the very fat, tasty-looking salt-beef. Downstairs they did not drink wine, but there was a large assortment of spirits and fruit liqueurs. Agafya the cook, a plump, fair-haired, well-fed woman, was standing at the door with her arms crossed, talking to the old women, while 'downstairs Masha' – a brunette with a crimson ribbon in her hair – took the dishes round and served. The old women had been gorging themselves since morning, and an hour before supper had eaten a sweet, rich pie with their tea, so that now they were forcing themselves to eat, as if it were their duty.

'Oh, dear me!' Auntie sighed when Anna Akimovna suddenly dashed into the dining-room and sat on the chair next to her. 'You nearly frightened the life out of me!'

The whole household was pleased when Anna Akimovna was in good spirits and started playing the fool, which never failed to remind them that the old men were dead, that the old women no longer held power in that house and that they could all do as they liked without fear of being mercilessly made to answer for it. Only the two old women whom Anna Akimovna didn't know squinted at her in amazement: she was singing – and singing at table was a sin.

'Our mistress is as pretty as a picture,' Agafya droned in a sugary voice. 'Our precious jewel! So many came to see our princess today, Lord be praised! Generals, and officers, and gentlemen . . . I kept looking through the window, trying to count them all I was, but I couldn't keep up, so I stopped.'

'I'd rather those rogues had stayed at home,' Auntie said. She gazed sadly at her niece and added, 'All they've done is waste the poor girl's time.'

Anna Akimovna was starving, having eaten nothing since the morning. They poured her a very bitter-tasting fruit cordial, which she drank; and she ate some salt-beef with mustard and found it exceptionally tasty. Then 'downstairs Masha' served turkey, soused apples and gooseberries. This she liked too. What was unpleasant was the heat pouring out of the tiled stove in waves, which made the room stuffy, and everyone's cheeks were burning. After supper they took the cloth away and put dishes of mint cakes, nuts and raisins on the table.

'Come on, sit down with us!' Auntie told the cook.

Agafya sighed and sat down at the table. Masha stood a cordial glass in front of her too and Anna Akimovna had the impression that as much heat was coming from Agafya's white neck as from the stove. Everyone said how difficult it was to marry these days, and that at one time men had at least been tempted by money; now it was hard to tell what they wanted. At one time only hunchbacks and cripples had been left on the shelf; nowadays even the rich and beautiful were ignored. Auntie began by saying that this immoral situation arose from people not fearing God, but then she suddenly remembered that her brother Ivan and Barbara had both led devout lives and both believed in God. For all that they had had children from illicit unions and packed them off to a home. Then she suddenly pulled herself up and changed the subject to someone who had once courted her, a factory worker, and how she had loved him. But her brothers had forced her to marry a widowed icon-painter, who died two years later, thank God. 'Downstairs Masha' also took a seat at the table and told them, with a very mysterious look, that a black-moustached stranger in a black coat with a lambskin collar had started appearing in their yard every morning for the past week. He would come into the yard, look at the windows of the big house, and then go on to the factory blocks. He was a fine figure of a man, quite handsome, in fact . . .

All this talk gave Anna Akimovna a sudden urge to get married – so strong it was quite painful. She felt that she would give half her life and all her wealth just to know that there was a man upstairs closer to her than anyone in the world, who loved her deeply and who yearned for her. The thought of such an enchanting intimacy, so impossible to put into words, excited her. And the healthy instincts of a young woman flattered her with the false message that the true poetry of life had not yet arrived, but lay ahead, and she believed it. She leant back in her chair so that her hair hung loose and she started laughing, which made the others follow suit. For a long time the dining-room was filled with inconsequential laughter.

Someone then announced that 'Beetle' had come to spend the night. With Pasha or Spiridonovna as her real names, this small, pious lady of about fifty, in her black dress and white shawl, was sharp-eyed, sharp-nosed and sharp-chinned. She had cunning, spiteful eyes and seemed to look right through people. Her lips were pursed. Because she was so spiteful and hateful she was known as 'Beetle' in merchants' houses.

After she came into the dining-room she went straight over to the icons without so much as a glance at anyone and sang in an alto voice 'Thy Nativity', then 'Virgin this Day' and 'Christ Is Born', after which she turned around and gave everyone a piercing look.

'Happy Christmas!' she said, kissing Anna Akimovna on the shoulder. 'It was an awful job, really awful, getting here, my ladies of charity.' She kissed Auntie on the shoulder. 'I set off this morning, but on my way I stopped at some kind people's house for a little rest. "Please stay," they said. It was evening before I noticed it.'

As she didn't eat meat she was served caviare and salmon. She scowled at everyone as she ate, and she drank three glasses of vodka. When she had finished she said a little prayer and bowed low to Anna Akimovna. They started playing Kings, as they had done the previous year and the year before that. Every single servant from the two floors crowded at the door to watch the game. Anna Akimovna thought that she twice glimpsed Misha, with that condescending smile of his, in the crowd of common peasant men and women. First to be king was 'Beetle'. Anna Akimovna, a soldier, had to pay her a forfeit. Then Auntie became king and Anna Akimovna was a peasant or 'yokel', which delighted everyone, while Agafya became a prince and was embarrassed at feeling so pleased. Another card game started at the far end of the table: both Mashas, Barbara and Martha the seamstress (whom they specially woke up to play Kings and who looked sleepy and irritable).

During the game the conversation turned to men, to how difficult it was to find a good man nowadays, whether a spinster was better off than a widow.

'You're a pretty, healthy, strong lass,' Beetle told Anna Akimovna. 'Only I just don't understand who you're saving yourself for, my girl.'

'What can I do if no one will have me?'

'Perhaps you made a vow never to marry,' Beetle continued as if she had not heard. 'All right, that's fine, don't marry . . .' she repeated, eyeing her cards attentively, viciously. 'Stay as you are . . . yes . . . But spinsters, bless their hearts, come in all shapes and sizes,' she sighed, dealing a king. 'Oh, all shapes and sizes, my dear! There's some what live like nuns, pure as angels they are. But if one of them happens to sin, the poor girl goes through such torments you just couldn't bring yourself to tell her off. And there's others as wear black and make their own shrouds, while they love rich old men on the sly. Yes, my little songbirds, there's witches who'll put spells on an old man and keep him under their thumbs. Oh, yes, my dears, they'll call the tune, do what they like with him and as soon as they've pinched his money and lottery tickets they'll bewitch him, so he dies.'

All Barbara did was sigh in reply to these remarks and look at the icon. Her face was filled with Christian humility.

'There's a girl I know, my fierce enemy,' Beetle went on, surveying everyone triumphantly. 'She's always sighing away and looking at the icons, the she-devil. When she had an old man under her thumb and you went to see her, she'd give you a little something to eat and order you to bow down to the ground while she read out loud "A Virgin brought forth". On holidays she'd give you a morsel to eat, but on ordinary days she'd tell you off. So, now I'm off to have a good laugh at her, my little pets!'

Barbara looked at the icons again and crossed herself.

'No one will have me, Spiridonovna,' Anna Akimovna said, to change the subject. 'What can I do?'

'It's your own fault, dear. The only thing is to wait for a gentleman, someone educated. You should marry your own kind, a businessman.'

'We don't want a businessman, God help us,' Auntie said in alarm. 'A gentleman'll squander all your money, but he won't be too hard on you, you silly woman! But a businessman'll be so strict with you that you'll never feel at home in your own house. You'll be wanting to snuggle up close to him, but he'll be after your money. If you sit down at table with him, the oaf'll blame you for eating all *his* food – and in your own house! Go and marry a gentleman!'

Everyone spoke at once, noisily interrupting each other, while Auntie banged the nutcrackers on the table.

'You don't need a businessman,' she said, angry and red-faced. 'If you bring one into this house I'll go into a workhouse!'

'Shush! Be quiet!' Beetle shouted. When everyone was silent she screwed up one eye and said 'Do you know what, Anna, my precious? There's no point in your marrying like ordinary folk do. You're rich, free, your own mistress. But I don't think it's right for you to stay an old maid, my child. I'll go and find you some useless fool whom you'll marry for show – and then off on the town! Oh, you'll shove five or ten thousand under your husband's nose and let him go back where he belongs and then you'll be mistress in your own house. And then you'll be able to love who you like and no one can say a word about it. You'll be able to love your educated gentlemen all right then. Oh, you'll be living in clover!' Beetle clicked her fingers and whistled. 'Go and have a good time, dear!'

'But that would be sinning!' Auntie said.

'So, it's a sin then,' Beetle said grinning. 'She's educated, she understands. Of course it's a sin cutting someone's throat or bewitching an old man, but loving your boyfriend is no sin. What is it, after all? No sin in it at all! All that was thought up by pious old women to hoodwink simple folk. I'm always saying that a sin is a sin, but I don't know why.'

Beetle drank some fruit liqueur and cleared her throat. 'Go and have a good time,' she said, evidently talking to herself this time. 'For thirty years I've been thinking about sin and was always scared of it, but now I seem to have missed out. I've let my chance slip. Oh, what a fool I am!' she sighed. 'A woman's life is short and she should treasure every day. You're beautiful, Anna, and very rich into the bargain, but when your thirty-fifth or fortieth birthday comes along, that'll be the end of you. Now don't listen to what people say, dear, go and enjoy yourself until you're forty – there'll be plenty of time for praying, for making amends and sewing shrouds. Let your hair down! Well, what do you say? Do you want to give pleasure to some man?'

'I do,' Anna Akimovna laughed. 'But I couldn't care less now, I'd marry an ordinary working man.'

'Yes, and that would be a good thing too. Oh, then you could take your pick!' Beetle frowned and shook her head. 'By heaven you could!'

'That's what I keep telling her,' Auntie said. 'If you can't wait for a gentleman, then don't go and marry a businessman, but someone more ordinary. At least we'd have a man in the house. And there's no shortage of good men, is there? Just take some of our own factory workers, all sober and respectable.'

'And how!' Beetle agreed. 'All wonderful lads. What if I arranged a match for Anna with Vasily Lebedinsky, Auntie?'

'Well, Vasily's got long legs,' Auntie said seriously. 'He's very dull, nothing much to look at.'

The crowd at the door laughed.

'Well, Pimenov then. Would you like to marry Pimenov?'

'Yes, marry me to Pimenov.'

'Do you mean it?'

'Yes, go ahead and arrange it,' Anna Akimovna said determinedly and thumped the table. 'I'll marry him, word of honour!'

'You really will?'

Anna Akimovna suddenly felt ashamed that her cheeks were burning and that everyone was looking at her. She mixed up the cards on the table and tore out of the room. After she had dashed upstairs, reached the upper floor and sat by the grand piano in the drawing-room, she heard a rumbling from down below, like the roar of the sea. They must be talking about her and Pimenov, and perhaps Beetle was taking advantage of her absence to insult Barbara – and of course she wouldn't be too particular about her language.

Only one lamp was lit on the whole upper floor – in the ballroom – and its dim light found its way through the doorway into the dark drawing-room. It was about ten, no later. Anna Akimovna played a waltz, then a second, then a third, without stopping. She peered into the dark corner behind the piano, smiled, imagined she was calling out to someone, and then she had an idea: why not go at once to town and visit just anyone – Lysevich, for example – and tell him what was going on in her heart? She wanted to talk non-stop, to laugh, play the fool, but that dark corner behind the piano was gloomily silent; and all around her, in every room on that floor, it was quiet and deserted.

She loved sentimental songs, but as her voice was rough and untrained, she could only play accompaniments and she sang barely audibly, in gentle breaths. She sang one song after the other in a whisper, and all of them were mainly about love, parting, lost hope. She imagined herself stretching out her hands: 'Pimenov, take this burden from me!' she would tearfully plead. And then, as if her sins had been forgiven, she would feel joyful and relieved. A free and perhaps happy life would follow. In an agony of expectation she bent over the keys and longed for the change in her life to come right away, that very minute. She was terrified to think that her present way of life would continue for some time to come. Then she began to play again and she sang barely audibly, while all around it was quiet. No longer could she hear the roar from downstairs; they must all have gone to bed. It had struck ten ages ago. A long, lonely, tedious night was approaching.

Anna Akimovna paced through all the rooms, lay down on the study sofa and read some letters delivered that evening. There were twelve wishing her happy Christmas and three anonymous ones, unsigned. In one of these an ordinary workman complained, in dreadful, barely decipherable handwriting, that, in the factory shop, workers were sold only rancid vegetable oil that smelt of kerosene.

In another, someone politely denounced Nazarych for accepting a thousand-rouble bribe when buying iron at an auction. In another she was abused for her inhumanity.

The mood of festive excitement was fading now and in an attempt to maintain it Anna Akimovna sat at the piano and quietly played a new waltz. Then she remembered how cleverly and frankly she had reasoned and expressed her thoughts over dinner. She looked round at the dark windows, at the paintings on the walls, at the weak light coming from the ballroom and suddenly, quite unexpectedly, she burst into tears. She was upset because she was so alone, because she had no one to talk to and to whom she could turn for advice. She tried to cheer herself up by picturing Pimenov in her mind, but she was unsuccessful.

The clock struck twelve. In came Misha, wearing a jacket now and no longer in tailcoat; silently he lit two candles. Then he left and a minute later returned with a cup of tea on a tray.

'What's funny?' she asked, seeing the smile on his face.

'I was downstairs and heard you joking about Pimenov,' he said, covering his laughing face with one hand. 'You should have invited him to dinner along with Viktor Nikolayevich and the general, he would have died of fright.' Misha's shoulders shook with laughter. 'He probably doesn't even know how to hold a fork.'

The servant's laughter, what he said, his jacket and his little whiskers, all left Anna Akimovna with an impression of dirtiness. She closed her eyes so as not to have to look at him, and she could not help imagining Pimenov dining with Lysevich and Krylin. And then Pimenov's subservient, stupid appearance struck her as pathetic, helpless, and filled her with revulsion. Only now did she understand clearly – and for the first time that day – that all she had thought and said about Pimenov, about marrying an ordinary workman, was senseless, absurd and opinionated. In an effort to convince herself that the opposite was the case, and to overcome her disgust, she wanted to remember exactly what she had said during dinner, but was unable to. The feeling of shame at her own thoughts and behaviour, the fear that she might have said something stupid, revulsion at her own lack of nerve – all these things troubled her deeply. She took a candle and dashed downstairs as if someone were chasing her; she woke Spiridonovna and assured her that she had been joking. Then she went to her bedroom. Red-headed Masha, who had been drowsing in an armchair near the bed, jumped up to arrange the pillows. Her face was weary and sleepy, and her magnificent hair had fallen to one side.

'That clerk Chalikov was here again this evening,' she said, yawning. 'But I didn't dare tell you. He was dead drunk. Says he'll come back tomorrow.'

'What does he want from me?' Anna Akimovna said angrily, flinging her comb on the floor. 'I don't want to see him, I don't!'

She concluded that there was nothing in her life besides this Chalikov now. He would never stop hounding her – a daily reminder of how boring and absurd her life was.

Without undressing, she lay down and burst out sobbing from shame and boredom. Most annoying and ridiculous of all, she thought, was the fact that earlier in the day her thoughts about Pimenov had been decent, noble, honourable. But at the same time she felt that Lysevich and even Krylin were closer to her than Pimenov and all the factory workers put together. Now she thought that if it were only possible to reproduce that long day she had just gone through in a painting, then everything that was nasty and cheap – the dinner, for example, what the lawyer had said, the game of Kings – would have been the truth, whereas her dreams and the conversation about Pimenov would have stood out as something false and artificial.

And she thought that now it was too late to dream of happiness, that it was impossible to return to that kind of life where she had slept in her mother's bed, to devise some new, special lifestyle.

Red-headed Masha was kneeling in front of the bed looking at her sadly and in astonishment. Then she too burst into tears and pressed her face to her hand. There was no need for words to express why she felt so distressed.

'We're a pair of fools, you and I,' Anna Akimovna said, both crying and laughing. 'We're fools! Oh, what fools!'

The Two Volodyas

'Let me go, *I* want to drive. I'm going to sit next to the driver,' Sophia Lvovna shouted. 'Driver, wait. I'm coming up on to the box to sit next to you.'

She stood on the sledge while her husband Vladimir Nikitych and her childhood friend Vladimir Mikhaylych held her by the arm in case she fell. Away sped the troika.

'I said you shouldn't have given her brandy,' Vladimir Nikitych whispered irritably to his companion. 'You're a fine one!'

From past experience the Colonel knew that when women like his wife Sophia Lvovna had been in riotous, rather inebriated high spirits he could normally expect fits of hysterical laughter and tears to follow. He was afraid that once they got home he would have to run around with the cold compresses and medicine instead of being able to go to bed.

'Whoa!' Sophia Lvovna shouted. 'I want to drive.'

She was really very gay and in an exultant mood. For two months after her wedding she had been tormented by the thought that she had married Colonel Yagich for his money or, as they say, *par dépit*. That same evening, in the out-of-town restaurant, she finally became convinced that she loved him passionately. In spite of his fifty-four years, he was so trim, sprightly and athletic, and he told puns and joined in the gypsy girls' songs with such charm. It is true that nowadays old men are a thousand times more interesting than young ones, as though age and youth had changed places. The Colonel was two years older than her father, but was that important if, to be quite honest, he was infinitely stronger, more energetic and livelier than she was, even though she was only twenty-three?

'Oh, my darling!' she thought. 'My wonderful man!'

In the restaurant she had come to the conclusion too that not a spark remained of her old feelings. To her childhood friend Vladimir Mikhaylych, whom only yesterday she had loved to distraction, she now felt completely indifferent. The whole evening he had struck her as a lifeless, sleepy, boring nobody and the habitual coolness with which he avoided paying restaurant bills exasperated her so much this time that she very nearly told him, 'You should have stayed at home if you're so poor.' The Colonel footed the bill.

Perhaps it was the trees, telegraph poles and snowdrifts all flashing past that aroused the most varied thoughts. She reflected that the meal had cost one hundred and twenty roubles – with a hundred for the gypsies – and that the next day, if she so wished, she could throw a thousand roubles away, whereas two months ago, before the wedding, she did not have three roubles to call her own and she had to turn to her father for every little thing. How her life had changed!

Her thoughts were in a muddle and she remembered how, when she was about ten, Colonel Yagich, her husband now, had made advances to her aunt and how everyone in the house had said that he had ruined her. In fact, her aunt often came down to dinner with tear-stained eyes and was always going away somewhere; people said the poor woman was suffering terribly. In those days he was very handsome and had extraordinary success with women; the whole town knew him and he was said to visit his admirers every day, like a doctor doing his rounds. Even now, despite his grey hair, wrinkles and spectacles, his thin face looked handsome, especially in profile.

Sophia Lvovna's father was an army doctor and had once served in Yagich's regiment. Volodya senior's father had also been an army doctor and had once served in the same regiment as her own father and Yagich. Despite some highly involved and frantic amorous adventures Volodya junior had been an excellent student. He graduated with honours from university, had decided to specialize in foreign literature and was said to be writing his thesis. He lived in the barracks with his doctor father and he had no money of his own, although he was now thirty. When they were children, Sophia

Lvovna and he had lived in different flats, but in the same building, and he often came to play with her; together they had dancing and French lessons. But when he grew up into a well-built, exceedingly good-looking young man, she began to be shy of him. Then she fell madly in love with him and was still in love until shortly before she married Yagich. He too had extraordinary success with women, from the age of fourteen almost, and the ladies who deceived their husbands with him exonerated themselves by saying Volodya was 'so little'. Not long before, he was said to be living in digs close to the university and every time you knocked, his footsteps could be heard on the other side of the door and then the whispered apology: *'Pardon, je ne suis pas seul.'* Yagich was delighted with him, gave him his blessing for the future as Derzhavin had blessed Pushkin,[1] and was evidently very fond of him. For hours on end they would silently play billiards or piquet, and if Yagich went off somewhere in a troika, he would take Volodya with him; only Yagich shared the secret of his thesis. In earlier days, when the Colonel was younger, they were often rivals, but were never jealous of one another. When they were in company, which they frequented together, Yagich was called 'Big Volodya' and his friend 'Little Volodya'.

Besides Big Volodya and Little Volodya, and Sophia Lvovna, there was someone else in the sledge, Margarita Aleksandrovna – or Rita as everyone called her – Mrs Yagich's cousin. She was a spinster, in her thirties, very pale, with black eyebrows, pince-nez, who chain-smoked even when it was freezing; there was always ash on her lap and chest. She spoke through her nose and drawled; she was cold and unemotional, could drink any quantity of liqueur or brandy without getting drunk and told stories abounding in *doubles entendres* in a dull, tasteless way. At home she read the learned reviews all day long, scattering ash all over them; or she would eat crystallized apples.

'Sophia, don't play the fool,' she drawled; 'it's really so stupid.'

When the town gates came into view the troika slowed down; they caught glimpses of people and houses, and Sophia quietened down, snuggled against her husband and gave herself up to her thoughts. And now gloomy thoughts began to mingle with her happy, carefree fantasies. The man opposite knew that she had loved him (so she thought), and of course he believed the reports that she had married the Colonel *par dépit*. Not once had she confessed her love and she did not want him to know. She had concealed her feelings, but his expression clearly showed that he understood her perfectly, and so her pride suffered. But most humiliating of all about her situation was the fact that Little Volodya had suddenly started paying attention to her after her marriage, which had never happened before. He would sit with her for hours on end, in silence, or telling her some nonsense; and now in the sledge he was gently touching her leg or squeezing her hand, without saying a word. Evidently, all he wanted was for her to get married. No less obviously, he did not think much of her and she interested him only in a certain way, as an immoral, disreputable woman. And this mingling of triumphant love for her husband and injured pride was the reason for her behaving so irresponsibly, prompting her to sit on the box and shout and whistle . . .

Just as they were passing the convent the great twenty-ton bell started clanging away. Rita crossed herself.

'Our Olga is in that convent,' Sophia Lvovna said, crossing herself and shuddering.

'Why did she become a nun?' the Colonel asked.

'*Par dépit*,' Rita answered angrily, obviously hinting at Sophia Lvovna's marriage to Yagich. 'This *par dépit* is all the rage now. It's a challenge to the whole of society. She was a proper good-time girl, a terrible flirt, all she liked was dances and dancing partners. And then suddenly we have all this! She took us all by surprise!'

'That's not true,' Little Volodya said, lowering the collar of his fur coat and revealing his handsome face. 'This wasn't a case of *par dépit*, but something really terrible. Her brother Dmitry was sentenced to hard labour in Siberia and no one knows where he is now. The mother died of grief.' He raised his collar again. 'And Olga did the right thing,' he added dully. 'Living as a ward, and with a treasure like our Sophia Lvovna, what's more – that's enough food for thought!'

Sophia Lvovna noted the contempt in his voice and wanted to say something very nasty in reply, but she said nothing. Once more euphoria gripped her. She stood up and shouted tearfully, 'I want to go to morning service. Driver, turn back! I want to see Olga!'

They turned back. The convent bell had a dull peal and Sophia Lvovna felt there was something in it reminding her of Olga and her life. Bells rang out from other churches. When the driver had brought the troika to a halt, Sophia leapt from the sledge and rushed unescorted to the gates.

'Please don't be long!' her husband shouted. 'It's late.'

She went through the dark gates, then along the path leading to the main church; the light snow crunched under her feet and the tolling of the bells sounded right over her head now and seemed to penetrate her whole being. First she came to the church door, the three steps down, then the porch, with paintings of the saints on both sides; there was a smell of juniper and incense. Then came another door, which a dark figure opened, bowing very low . . . In the church the service had not yet begun. One of the nuns was in front of the icon-screen lighting candles in their holders, another was lighting a chandelier. Here and there, close to the columns and side-chapels, were motionless, black figures. 'They'll be standing in exactly the same places till morning,' Sophia Lvovna thought and the whole place struck her as dark, cold, depressing – more depressing than a graveyard. Feeling bored, she glanced at the motionless, frozen figures and suddenly her heart sank. Somehow she recognized one of the nuns – short, with thin shoulders and a black shawl on her head – as Olga, although when she had entered the convent she had been plump and taller, she thought. Deeply disturbed for some reason, Sophia Lvovna hesitantly walked over to the lay sister, looked over her shoulder into her face and saw it *was* Olga.

'Olga!' she said, clasping her hands and too excited to say anything else. 'Olga!'

The nun recognized her immediately, raised her eyebrows in astonishment and her pale, freshly washed face (even, it seemed, her white kerchief visible under her shawl) glowed with joy.

'God has performed a miracle,' she said and also clasped her thin, pale little hands.

Sophia Lvovna firmly embraced her and kissed her, frightened as she did so that her breath might smell of drink.

'We were just passing and we thought of you,' she said breathlessly, as though she had just completed a fast walk. 'Heavens, how pale you are! I'm . . . I'm very pleased to see you. Well, how are you? Bored?' Sophia Lvovna looked round at the other nuns and now she lowered her voice: 'So much has happened . . . you know I married Volodya Yagich. You must remember him . . . I'm very happy.'

'Well, thank the Lord for that! And is your father well?'

'Yes, he often remembers you. But you must come and see us during the holidays, Olga. Will you do that?'

'Yes, I'll come,' Olga said smiling. 'I'll come the day after tomorrow.'

Without even knowing why, Sophia burst into tears and cried in silence for a whole minute. Then she dried her eyes and said, 'Rita will be very sorry she didn't see you. She's with us too. And Little Volodya. They're at the gate. How pleased they would be to see you! Come out and see them, the service hasn't started yet.'

'All right,' Olga agreed. She crossed herself three times and walked out with Sophia Lvovna.

'So, you said you're happy, Sophia,' she said after they were past the gates.

'Very.'

'Well, thank God.'

When Big Volodya and Little Volodya saw the nun they got off the sledge and greeted her respectfully. They were visibly moved by her pale face and her nun's black habit, and they were both pleased that she remembered them and had come to greet them. Sophia Lvovna wrapped her in a rug and covered her with one flap of her fur coat to protect her from the cold. Her recent tears had lightened and cleansed her soul and she was glad that the noisy, riotous and essentially immoral night had unexpectedly come to such a pure and quiet conclusion. Then to keep Olga by her side longer, she suggested, 'Let's take her for a ride! Olga, get in. Just a little one.'

The men expected the nun to refuse – religious people don't go around in troikas – but to their amazement she agreed and got in.

When the troika hurtled off towards the town gates, no one said a word; their only concern was to make her warm and comfortable. Each one of them thought about the difference in her from before. Her face was impassive, somewhat expressionless, cold, pale, transparent, as though water flowed in her veins instead of blood. Two or three years ago she had been buxom and rosy-cheeked, had talked about eligible bachelors and laughed loud at the least thing.

The troika turned round at the town gates. Ten minutes later they were back at the convent and Olga climbed out. The bells were ringing a series of chimes.

'God be with you,' Olga said, giving a low, nun-like bow.

'So you will come then, Olga?'

'Of course I will.'

She quickly left and soon disappeared through the dark gateway. After the troika had moved on everyone somehow felt very sad. No one said a word. Sophia Lvovna felt weak all over and her heart sank. Making a nun get into a sledge and go for a ride with that drunken crowd struck her now as stupid, tactless and almost sacrilegious. The desire for self-deception vanished with her tipsiness and now she clearly realized that she did not and could not love her husband, it was all nothing but silly nonsense. She had married for money because, as her ex-schoolgirl friends put it, he was 'madly rich', because she was terrified of becoming an old maid, like Rita, because her doctor father got on her nerves and because she wanted to annoy Little Volodya. Had she guessed when she was contemplating marriage that it would turn out to be so nasty, painful and ugly, she would never have agreed to it, not for anything in the world. But the damage was done now, she had to accept things.

They arrived home. As she lay in her warm, soft bed and covered herself with a blanket, Sophia Lvovna recalled the dark porch, the smell of incense, the figures by the columns, and she was distressed at the thought that these figures would still be standing there, quite motionless, all the time she was sleeping. Early morning service would be interminably long, and after that there would be the hours, then Mass, then more prayers . . .

'But surely God exists? He certainly exists and I must certainly die. Therefore, sooner or later, I must think of my soul, eternal life, like Olga does. Olga is saved now, she has solved all her problems for herself . . . But what if there is *no* God? Then her life has been wasted. But how has it been wasted? Why?'

A minute later another thought entered her head. 'God exists, death will certainly come. I should be thinking of my soul. If Olga could see her death this very minute she would not be afraid. She's ready. But the most important thing is, she's solved the riddle of existence for herself. God exists . . . yes. But isn't there another way out apart from becoming a nun? *That* means renouncing life, destroying it . . .' Sophia Lvovna became rather scared and hid her head under the pillow. 'I mustn't think about it,' she whispered, 'I mustn't.'

Yagich was walking up and down in the next room, his spurs softly jingling; he was deep in thought. Sophia Lvovna thought that this man was near and dear to her only in one thing – he was called Volodya too. She sat on her bed and tenderly called, 'Volodya!'

'What do you want?' her husband replied.

'Nothing.'

She lay down again. There were bells tolling – from that same convent, perhaps – and once again she recalled the porch and the dark figures. Thoughts of God and inescapable death wandered through her mind; she pulled the blanket over her head to drown the sound of the bells. She expected, before old age and death came, that her life would drag on for such a terribly long time, and from one day to the next she would have to cope with the nearness of someone she did not love, and who had come into the room just at that moment and was getting into bed; and she would have to suppress that hopeless love for another – someone who was so young, so charming and apparently so unusual. She looked at her husband and wanted to say good night, but she suddenly burst into tears instead. She felt annoyed with herself.

'Well, we're off again,' Yagich said.

She did calm down, but not until later, towards ten in the morning. She had stopped crying and shaking all over; she developed a severe headache, however. Yagich was hurrying, getting ready for late Mass and in the next room he was grumbling at the batman helping him dress. He came into the bedroom once, his spurs softly jingling, took something, and when he came in a second time he was wearing epaulettes and decorations; he limped slightly from rheumatism. He gave Sophia Lvovna the impression he was a beast of prey, prowling and looking round.

Then she heard him on the telephone. 'Please put me through to the Vasilyevsky Barracks,' he said. A minute later he went on, 'Is that Vasilyevsky Barracks? Please ask Dr Salimovich to come to the phone.' Then, a minute later, 'Who am I speaking to? Volodya? Fine. My dear chap, please ask your father to come over right away, my wife is terribly off colour after what happened yesterday. What's that? He's out? Hm . . . thanks . . . Yes, I'd be much obliged. *Merci.*'

Yagich came into the bedroom for the third time, bent over his wife, made the sign of the cross over her, let her kiss his hand (women who loved him would kiss his hand, he was used to this), and said he would be back for dinner. And he left.

Towards noon the maid announced Little Volodya. Swaying from weariness and her headache, Sophia Lvovna quickly put on her stunning new lilac, fur-trimmed negligee and hurriedly tidied her hair. In her heart she felt inexpressibly tender and trembled for joy – and for fear he might leave. She wanted just one look at him.

Little Volodya was paying her a visit in formal dress – tailcoat and white tie. When Sophia Lvovna came into the drawing-room he kissed her hand, said how deeply sorry he was to see her so unwell. When they had sat down he praised her negligee.

'Seeing Olga last night has upset me,' she said. 'At first it was painful for me, but now I envy her. She is like an immovable rock, it's impossible to budge her. But was there really no other way out for her, Volodya? Can burying oneself alive really solve life's problems? You'd call that death, not life, wouldn't you?' At the mention of Olga, Little Volodya's face showed deep emotion. 'Now look, Volodya, you're a clever man,' Sophia Lvovna said. 'Teach me to be like her. Of course, I'm a non-believer and I couldn't become a nun. But couldn't I do something that would be just as good? I find life hard enough.' After a brief silence she continued, 'Teach me . . . tell me something that will convince me. Just one word.'

'One word? Okay. Ta-ra-ra-boomdeay.'[2]

'Volodya, why do you despise me?' she asked excitedly. 'You speak to me in some special – if you'll forgive the expression – fancy language that one doesn't use with friends and respectable women. You're a successful scholar, you love your studies, but why do you never tell me about them? Why? Aren't I good enough?'

Little Volodya frowned irritably and said, 'Why this sudden passion for scholarship? Perhaps you want us to have a constitution? Or perhaps sturgeon with horseradish?'[3]

'Oh, have it your way then. I'm a mediocre, worthless, unprincipled, stupid woman . . . I've made thousands, thousands of mistakes. I'm not right in the head, a loose woman, and for that I deserve contempt. But you're ten years older than me, Volodya, aren't you? And my husband is thirty years older. You watched me grow up and if you'd wanted to, you could have made me anything you wanted, an angel even. But you . . .' (here her voice shook) 'treat me dreadfully. Yagich was an old man when he married me, and you . . .'

'Well, enough of that. Enough,' Volodya said, drawing closer to her and kissing both her hands. 'We'll leave the Schopenhauers[4] to philosophize and argue about anything they like, but now we're going to kiss these sweet little hands.'

'You despise me and if only you knew the suffering it causes me,' she said hesitantly, knowing beforehand that he would not believe her. 'If you only knew how I want to improve myself, to start a new life! It fills me with joy just thinking about it,' she murmured and actually shed a few joyous tears. 'To be a good, honest, decent person, not to lie, to have a purpose in life.'

'Stop it please! You don't have to put on an act for me, I don't like it,' Volodya said, looking peevish. 'Heavens, you'd think we were at the theatre! Let's behave like normal human beings!'

To prevent him from leaving in a temper she began to make excuses, forced herself to smile – to please him – mentioned Olga again and that she wanted to solve the riddle of her existence, to become a real human being.

'Ta-ra-ra-boomdeay,' he chanted softly. 'Ta-ra-ra-boomdeay!'

And then quite suddenly he clasped her waist. Barely conscious of what she was doing she put her hands on his shoulders and for a whole minute looked rapturously at his clever, sarcastic face, his forehead, eyes, handsome beard . . .

'You've known for a long time that I love you,' she confessed with an agonized blush and she felt that even her lips had twisted in a paroxysm of shame. 'I love you. So why do you torment me?'

She closed her eyes and kissed him firmly on the lips. For a long time – a whole minute perhaps – she just could not bring herself to end this kiss, although she knew very well that she was behaving badly, that he might tell her off, or that a servant might come in . . .

Half an hour later, when he had got what he wanted, he sat in the dining-room eating a snack while she knelt before him, staring hungrily into his face. He told her she was like a small dog waiting for someone to toss it a piece of ham. Then he sat her on one knee, rocked her like a child and sang, 'Ta-ra-ra-boomdeay . . . Ta-ra-ra-boomdeay!'

When he was about to leave she asked him passionately, 'When? Later on? Where?' And she held out both hands to his mouth, as if wanting to catch his reply in them.

'It's not really convenient today,' he said after a moment's thought. 'Perhaps tomorrow, though.'

And they parted. Before lunch Sophia Lvovna went off to the convent to see Olga, but was told that she was reading the Psalter for someone who had died. From the convent she went to her father's and drove aimlessly up and down the main streets and side-streets until evening. While she was riding, for some reason she kept remembering that aunt with the tear-stained eyes, who was fretting her life away.

That night they all went riding on troikas again and heard the gypsies in that out-of-town restaurant. And when they were once again passing the convent Sophia Lvovna thought of Olga and became terrified at the thought that there was no escape for girls and women in her circle, except perpetual troika-rides or entering a convent to mortify the flesh . . .

The following day she had a lovers' rendezvous once again. She went for solitary cab-rides around town and thought of her aunt.

A week later Little Volodya dropped her. Then life reverted to normal and was just as boring, dreary – and sometimes just as excruciating as it had ever been. The Colonel and Little Volodya had long billiards and piquet sessions, Rita told her tasteless anecdotes in the same lifeless fashion, Sophia Lvovna kept driving in cabs and asking her husband to take her for troika-rides.

Almost every day she called at the convent, boring Olga with her complaints of intolerable suffering; she cried and felt that she had brought something impure, pathetic and shabby into the cell. Olga, however, as if repeating a well-learnt lesson parrot-fashion, told her that there was nothing to worry about, that it would all pass and that God would forgive her.

Three Years

I

It was dark, but in some houses lights had already been lit, and at the end of the street, behind the barracks, a pale moon was rising. Laptev was sitting on a bench by the gate waiting for evening service to finish at St Peter and St Paul's. He reckoned that Julia Sergeyevna would pass him on her way home from church, and then he could talk to her and perhaps spend the rest of the evening with her.

He had been sitting there an hour and a half, picturing in his mind his Moscow flat, his Moscow friends, Pyotr his valet, his writing-desk. He looked in bewilderment at the dark, motionless trees and thought it peculiar that he wasn't living in his villa at Sokolniki[1] any more, but in a provincial town, in a house past which a large herd of cattle was driven every morning and evening, raising dreadful clouds of dust – to the accompaniment of blowing horns. He remembered those long conversations in Moscow in which he had taken part not so very long ago, about the possibility of life without love, about passionate love being a psychosis and, finally, about love not existing at all, being only physical attraction, and so on. As he recalled all this he sadly reflected that if someone had asked him now what love really was, he would have been at a loss for an answer.

The service was over now and the congregation appeared. Laptev looked intently at the dark figures. The Bishop had driven past in his carriage, the bells had stopped ringing, the red and green lights on the belfry had been put out, one after the other – these were the illuminations in celebration of the patronal festival – and people were in no hurry, stopping to talk under the windows. But at last Laptev heard familiar voices, his heart started pounding and he was gripped by despair, since Julia Sergeyevna wasn't alone, but with two other ladies.

'That's terrible, really terrible!' he whispered jealously. 'That's terrible!'

At the corner of a small side-street she stopped to say goodbye to the ladies, and then she glanced at Laptev.

'I'm going to your place,' he said. 'To talk to your father. Is he at home?'

'Probably,' she replied. 'It's too early for the club.'

The side-street had an abundance of gardens. Lime trees grew by the fences, casting broad shadows in the moonlight, so that the fences and gates on one side were completely enveloped in darkness, from which came the sound of women, restrained laughter and someone quietly playing the balalaika. It smelt of lime trees and hay. The whispers of those invisible women and the smell excited Laptev. Suddenly he felt a strong urge to embrace his companion, to shower her face, arms and shoulders with kisses, to fall at her feet and tell her how long he had been waiting for her. There was a faint, barely perceptible smell of incense about her, which reminded him of the time when he too had believed in God, had gone to evening service, had dreamed a great deal about pure, poetic love. Because this girl did not love him he felt that any possibility of the kind of love he had dreamt of then had faded for ever.

She sounded very concerned about his sister Nina Fyodorovna's health – two months ago she had had an operation for cancer and everyone was expecting a relapse now.

'I was with her this morning,' Julia Sergeyevna said, 'and it struck me that she hasn't only grown thinner this past week, she's simply lost all her colour.'

'Yes, yes,' Laptev agreed. 'There hasn't actually been a relapse, but I can see that she's growing weaker every day – she seems to be wasting away before my eyes. I can't understand what the trouble is.'

'Heavens, how healthy, buxom and rosy-cheeked she used to be!' Julia Sergeyevna said after a brief silence. 'Everyone here used to call her "The Moscow Girl". The way she used to laugh! On holidays she'd wear simple peasant costume and it really suited her.'

Dr Sergey Borisych was at home. A stout, red-faced man, with a long frock-coat that stretched below his knees and made him appear short-legged, he was pacing the study, hands in pockets, humming softly and pensively. His grey side-whiskers were dishevelled and his hair wasn't combed, as if he'd just got out of bed. And his study, with those cushions on the couches, piles of old papers in the corners and an unhealthy looking, dirty poodle under the table, produced the same scruffy, slovenly impression as the master.

'Monsieur Laptev would like to see you,' his daughter said, entering the study.

He hummed louder, offered Laptev his hand as he came into the drawing-room and asked, 'Well, what's new?'

It was dark in the drawing-room. Laptev did not sit down. Still holding his hat he started apologizing for disturbing him. He asked what could be done to help his sister to sleep at night and why she was growing so terribly thin. He felt embarrassed, as he thought that he had already asked the identical questions when he had called that morning.

'Tell me,' he asked, 'shouldn't we call in some specialist in internal diseases from Moscow? What do you think?'

The doctor sighed, shrugged his shoulders and made some vague gesture with both hands.

He was clearly offended. This doctor was an exceptionally touchy, suspicious person, permanently convinced that no one trusted him, recognized him or respected him enough, that he was being generally exploited and that his colleagues were all hostile towards him. He was always ridiculing himself, maintaining that idiots like himself had been created only for everyone else to trample on.

Julia Sergeyevna lit a lamp. Her pale, languid face and sluggish walk showed how tired she was after the church service. She felt like resting and sat on the couch, put her hands on her lap and became lost in thought. Laptev knew that he wasn't handsome and now he was physically conscious of his own ugliness. He was short and thin, with flushed cheeks, and his hair had thinned out so much his head felt cold. His expression had none of that natural grace which makes even coarse, ugly faces likeable. In women's company he was awkward, over-talkative and affected – now he was almost despising himself for this. To stop Julia Sergeyevna from being bored he had to talk about something. But about what? About his sister's illness again?

He produced some platitudes about medicine, praising hygiene. He said that it had long been his wish to establish a hostel for the poor in Moscow and that he already had estimates for the work. According to this scheme of his, workmen coming to the hostel in the evenings would get (for five or six copecks) a portion of hot cabbage soup, bread, a warm dry bed with blankets and a place to dry their clothes and footwear.

Julia Sergeyevna usually kept silent in his presence and, in some strange way – perhaps it was a man in love's intuition – he was able to guess her thoughts and intentions. Now he concluded that as she hadn't gone to her room to change and have tea after the service she must be going out to visit someone that evening.

'But I'm in no rush with the hostel,' he continued and he felt annoyed and irritated as he turned towards the doctor, who was giving him vague, bewildered looks, evidently unable to see why he needed to talk about hygiene and medicine. 'It will probably be some time before I put it all into motion. I'm frightened the hostel might fall into the hands of those prigs and lady do-gooders in Moscow who wreck any new undertaking.'

Julia Sergeyevna stood up and offered Laptev her hand. 'Do excuse me,' she said, 'but I must be going. Remember me to your sister.'

The doctor started humming pensively again.

Julia Sergeyevna left and not long afterwards Laptev said goodbye to the doctor and went home. When one feels unhappy and disgruntled, how vulgar lime trees, shadows and clouds seem – all these smug, indifferent beauties of nature! The moon was high, clouds scurried beneath it. 'What a stupid provincial moon!' Laptev thought. 'What pathetic, scraggy clouds!'

He was ashamed of having mentioned medicine and working men's hostels and was horrified at the thought that he wouldn't be able to resist trying to see her and talk to her tomorrow: once again he would learn that he was like a complete stranger to her. It would be exactly the same the day after tomorrow. What was the point of it all? When and how would it all finish?

When he was home he went to see his sister. Nina Fyodorovna still looked strong and appeared to be a well-built, powerful woman. But that pronounced pallor made her look like a corpse, especially now as she lay on her back with her eyes closed. Her ten-year-old elder daughter Sasha was sitting reading to her from a school book.

'Aleksey is here,' the sick woman said softly to herself.

A tacit agreement had long been in effect between Sasha and her uncle and they had organized a rota. Sasha now closed her reader and left the room quietly, without a word. Laptev took a historical novel from the chest of drawers, found the page and started reading to her.

Nina Fyodorovna was from Moscow. She and her two brothers had spent their childhood and youth in the family house (they were merchants) on Pyatnitsky Street,[2] and what a long, boring childhood it had been. Their father was a strict man and had birched her on three occasions. Her mother had died after a long illness. The servants had been dirty, coarse and hypocritical. Priests and monks often called at the house and they too were coarse and hypocritical. They drank, ate their fill and crudely flattered her father, whom they did not like. The boys were lucky enough to go to high school, but Nina had no formal education, had written in a scrawly hand all her life and had read nothing but historical novels. Seventeen years ago, when she was twenty-two, she had met her present husband Panaurov – he came from a landowning family – at a villa in Khimki,[3] had fallen in love and was married in secret, against her father's wishes. Panaurov, a handsome and rather arrogant person, who liked lighting cigarettes from icon-lamps and who was a habitual whistler, struck her father as a complete and utter nobody. Later on, when the son-in-law started demanding a dowry in his letters, the old man had written to tell his daughter that he was sending some fur coats to her place in the country, some silver and odds and ends left by her mother, together with thirty thousand roubles in cash, but without his paternal blessing. Afterwards he had sent a further twenty thousand. The money and dowry were all squandered and Panaurov and family moved to town, where he had taken a job in local government. In town he started another family, which caused many tongues to wag since this illegitimate family didn't bother to conceal itself at all.

Nina Fyodorovna adored her husband. As she listened to the historical novel she thought about how much she had gone through and suffered all this time and what a pathetic narrative her life would make. Since the tumour was in the breast, she was convinced that the cause of her illness was love and family life, and that jealousy and tears had made her bedridden.

Shutting the book, Aleksey Fyodorych said, 'That's the end, thank God. We'll start another tomorrow.'

Nina Fyodorovna laughed. She had always been easily amused, but Laptev had begun to notice that sometimes her judgement was affected by her illness and she would laugh at the slightest nonsense, for no reason.

'Julia called just before dinner, while you were out,' she said. 'I can see that she doesn't trust her father very much. "All right, let my father treat you," she says, "yet you still write, without anyone knowing, to an elderly monk and ask him to pray for you." It's some wise old man they know who lives locally.' After a brief pause she continued, 'Julia left her umbrella behind. Send it over tomorrow ... No, if this is the end neither doctors nor holy sages will be any use.'

'Nina, why don't you sleep at night?' Laptev asked, to change the subject.

'Oh, I just can't, that's all. I lie thinking.'

'What about, my dear?'

'The children ... you ... my own life. After all, I've been through a lot, haven't I? When you start remembering ... when you ... Good heavens!' She burst out laughing. 'It's no joke having five children and burying three. I'd be about to have a baby and my Grigory Nikolaich would be with another woman and there'd be nobody I could send to fetch the midwife, or someone. If you went into the hall or kitchen for the servants you'd find only Jews, tradesmen and money-lenders waiting for him to come home. It quite made my head go round. He didn't love me, although he never said so. Now I'm reconciled to it, though, and I feel as if a weight has been lifted from me. But it did hurt me when I was younger, it hurt me terribly! Once – we were still living in the country – I caught him in the garden with some woman and I walked away, not caring where I was going, until I found myself in the church porch. There I fell on my knees and repeated "Holy Mother". It was night, the moon was shining . . .'

Exhausted, she started gasping for breath. After a little rest she caught hold of her brother's arm and continued in a faint, almost inaudible voice, 'How kind you are, Aleksey! You're so clever . . . What a fine man you've become!'

At midnight Laptev wished her goodnight and on his way out took the umbrella that Julia Sergeyevna had forgotten. Despite the late hour, the servants, male and female, were drinking tea in the dining-room. What chaos! The children hadn't gone to bed – they were in the dining-room too. Everyone there was softly talking, whispering, and no one noticed that the lamp was growing dim and would soon go out. All these people, large and small, were worried by a whole series of unfavourable omens and they felt very miserable. The mirror in the hall had been broken, the samovar hummed every day and was humming away now as if to annoy them. A mouse had jumped out of Mrs Panaurov's shoe while she was dressing, so they said. The dreadful significance of these portents was already known to the children. The elder daughter, Sasha, a thin little girl with dark hair, was sitting still at the table with a frightened, mournful look, while seven-year-old Lida, the younger girl, plump and fair-haired, stood by her sister, scowling at the light.

Laptev went down to his low-ceilinged, stuffy rooms on the ground floor – they always smelt of geraniums. Panaurov, Nina Fyodorovna's husband, was sitting reading the newspaper in his dining-room. Laptev nodded and sat opposite. Neither said a word. They often spent entire evenings like this, unembarrassed by the mutual silence.

The girls came down to say goodnight. Silently, without hurrying, Panaurov made the sign of the cross over both of them several times and let them kiss his hand. This kissing and curtseying ceremony took place every evening.

When the girls had left, Panaurov laid his paper to one side and said, 'This blessed town is so boring!' Sighing, he went on, 'I must confess, my dear man, I'm delighted you've at last found some entertainment.'

'What do you mean?' Laptev said.

'Just now I saw you leaving Dr Belavin's house. I hope you didn't go there on Papa's account.'

'Of course I did,' Laptev replied, blushing.

'Well, *of course*. By the way, you'd have a job finding another old mule like that Papa in a month of Sundays. What a filthy, inept, clumsy oaf he is. Words fail me! You Muscovites have only a kind of poetic interest in provincial landscapes, in the wretched existence of yokels whom our writers wax lyrical about.[4] But you can take it from me, old man, there's nothing lyrical about this place. There's only savagery, meanness and vileness – that's all. Just look at our local high priests of learning, the intelligentsia, so to speak. Can you imagine, we have twenty-eight doctors here, they've all become very rich, they've bought themselves houses, while the rest of the inhabitants are in the same hopeless situation as they've always been. For example, Nina needed an operation, really a very minor one, but we had to send to Moscow for a surgeon because no one here would do it. You can't imagine what it's like. They know nothing, understand nothing and are interested in nothing. Just ask them what cancer is, for example, what causes it.'

Panaurov started explaining cancer. He was a specialist in every branch of learning and had a scientific explanation for anything you could think of. His way of solving problems was something quite unique to himself. He had his own special theory of the circulation of the blood, his own chemistry and astronomy. He spoke slowly, softly, convincingly, pronouncing the words 'you just have no idea about it' as if he were pleading with you. He screwed his eyes up, sighed languidly and smiled graciously like an emperor: he was evidently highly satisfied with himself and quite untroubled at being fifty years old.

'I could do with a bite to eat,' Laptev said. 'Something nice and spicy.'

'That's no problem. I can fix you up right away.'

Shortly afterwards, Laptev was upstairs in the dining-room, having supper with his brother-in-law. Laptev drank a glass of vodka and then changed to wine. Panaurov drank nothing. He never drank, never played cards, but in spite of this had managed to run through his own and his wife's property and accumulate a whole pile of debts. To fritter so much money away in so short a time, something besides sexual craving was needed – some special talent. Panaurov loved tasty food, fine table appointments, music with dinner, bowing waiters to whom he could casually toss ten- or even twenty-rouble tips. He took part in all subscription schemes and lotteries, sent bouquets to ladies he knew on their name-days, bought cups, glass-holders, cufflinks, ties, canes, perfume, cigarette-holders, pipes, dogs, parrots, Japanese goods and antiques. He wore silk nightshirts, his bed was of ebony, inlaid with mother-of-pearl, he had a genuine Bokhara dressing-gown, and so on. Every day he spent 'heaps of money', as he put it, on these things.

During supper he kept sighing and shaking his head. 'Yes, everything in this world comes to an end,' he said softly, screwing up his dark eyes. 'You'll fall in love, fall out of love. You'll be deceived, because faithful women don't exist. You'll become desperate and do some deceiving yourself. But the time will come when all this will be only a memory and you'll coolly reflect that it was all absolutely trivial.'

Laptev was tired and slightly drunk. As he looked at the other man's fine head, his trimmed beard, he felt that he could understand why women loved that spoilt, self-assured, physically attractive man.

After supper Panaurov didn't stay at home but went off to his other flat. Laptev accompanied him. Panaurov was the only man in the entire town who wore a top hat, and against a background of grey fences, pathetic three-windowed little houses and nettle clumps his elegant, smart figure, top hat and orange gloves never failed to produce a strange, sad impression.

After saying goodnight, Laptev started off home, without

hurrying. The moon shone brightly, making every scrap of straw on the ground visible, and Laptev felt that the moonlight was caressing his uncovered head – it was just as though someone were running feathers over his hair.

'I'm in love!' he said out loud and he had a sudden urge to run after Panaurov and embrace him, forgive him and present him with a lot of money – and then dash off into the fields or a copse, forever running, without looking back.

Back home, on a chair, he saw the umbrella that Julia Sergeyevna had forgotten. He seized it and hungrily kissed it. It was made of silk, was not new and had a piece of old elastic tied round it. The handle was of cheap bone. Laptev opened it over his head and it seemed that the sweet scent of happiness was all around.

He settled himself more comfortably in his chair and started writing a letter to one of his Moscow friends, still holding the umbrella.

My dearest Kostya,

Here's some news for you: I'm in love again. I say 'again', because six years ago I was in love with a Moscow actress whom I never even met and over the past eighteen months I've been living with a 'personage' who is familiar to you, a woman who is neither young nor beautiful. My dear friend, how unlucky I've been in love! I've never had any success with women and if I say 'again', it's only because it's so sad, it hurts me so much to have to acknowledge that my youth has passed by without any love at all, and that I'm only really in love now for the first time, at the age of thirty-four. So, may I write that I'm in love 'again'?

If you only knew the kind of girl she is. One wouldn't call her a beauty – she has a broad face, she's terribly thin. But what a wonderfully kind expression, what a smile! Her voice is so resonant, she seems to be singing when she speaks. She never starts a conversation when she's with me, I don't really know her, but when I'm close to her I sense she is a rare, unusual person, imbued with intelligence and lofty ideals. She's religious and you just can't imagine how deeply this moves me, how much it raises her in my estimation. I'm ready to argue with you endlessly on this point. You're right, you can think what you like, but I still love her going to church. She's from the provinces, but she went to school in Moscow – she loves our Moscow – and she dresses in true Muscovite style. For that I love her, love her, love her.

I can see you frowning and getting up to read me a long lecture about the nature of love, whom one may or may not love, and so on. But before I fell in love I too knew exactly what love is, my dear Kostya!

My sister thanks you for your good wishes. She often remembers once taking Kostya Kochevoy to preparatory class. She still calls you 'poor', since she still remembers you as the little orphan. So, my poor orphan, I'm in love. It's a secret for the time being – don't say anything *there* to the familiar 'personage'. That will all come right in the end – or as the servant says in Tolstoy, 'everything will sort itself out . . .'[5]

Having finished the letter, Laptev went to bed. He was so tired, his eyes closed of their own accord, but for some reason he couldn't sleep – the street noises seemed to be disturbing him. The herd of cattle was driven past and the horn blown, and soon after that the bells rang for early mass. A cart would creak past, then he would hear the voice of a woman going to market. And the sparrows never stopped chirping.

II

It was a cheerful, festive morning. At about ten o'clock Nina Fyodorovna, in a brown dress, hair combed, was led into the drawing-room and there she walked up and down. Then she stood by the open window with a broad innocent smile on her face. Looking at her, you were reminded of a local artist, a drunkard, who had called her face a 'countenance' and had wanted to include her in a painting of a Russian Shrovetide. Everyone, the children, servants and even her brother Aleksey Fyodorych, even she herself, was suddenly convinced that she was bound to recover. The little girls screamed with laughter as they pursued their uncle and tried to catch him, and the house grew noisy.

People from outside came to inquire about her health. They brought communion bread and said that prayers were being offered for her today in almost every church. She had done a great deal of good in that town and the people loved her. She dispensed charity with the same lack of fuss as her brother, who gave away money very readily, without stopping to consider whether he should or not. Nina Fyodorovna paid poor schoolboys' fees, took tea, sugar and jam to old ladies, gave indigent brides dresses, and if she happened to see a newspaper she would first look for appeals or stories about anyone in dire straits.

Now she was holding a bundle of chits with which various impecunious petitioners had obtained goods at the grocer's. This grocer had sent these to her yesterday, requesting eighty-two roubles.

'Heavens, they've been taking so much, they really have no shame!' she said, barely recognizing her own ugly handwriting. 'That's no joke, eighty-two roubles! I don't feel like paying!'

'I'll pay it today,' Laptev said.

'But what on earth for?' Nina Fyodorovna said anxiously. 'It's really enough for me, those two hundred and fifty roubles I get every month from you and our brother. God bless you,' she added in a soft voice, so that the servants wouldn't hear.

'Well, I spend two thousand five hundred a month,' he said. 'Let me tell you again, my dear, you're just as entitled to spend money as Fyodor and myself. Never forget that. Father has three children, so one in every three copecks belongs to you.'

But Nina Fyodorovna didn't understand and she looked as if she was trying to do a very complicated piece of mental arithmetic. This obtuseness in financial matters always worried and embarrassed Laptev. Moreover, he suspected that she had some personal debts which she was too ashamed to tell him about and which were distressing her.

They heard footsteps and heavy breathing. It was the doctor coming upstairs, as scruffy and unkempt as ever. He was humming away as usual.

To avoid meeting him, Laptev went into the dining-room, then down to his own rooms. It was quite clear to him that getting on more intimate terms with the doctor and calling informally was impossible. Any encounter with that 'old mule', as Panaurov called him, was unpleasant. This was why he saw Julia Sergeyevna so seldom. He reckoned that if he took the umbrella back now, when her father was out, he would catch her alone in the house, and his heart leapt with joy. He must hurry, hurry!

Greatly excited, he took the umbrella and flew off on the wings of love. It was hot in the street. At the doctor's house, in the huge courtyard overgrown with tall weeds and nettles, about twenty boys were playing ball. They were all children of the tenants – working people who lived in the three old, unsightly outbuildings which the doctor was meaning to repair every year, but was always putting off. Healthy voices rang out. Far to one side, near her front porch, stood Julia Sergeyevna, her arms behind her back as she watched the game.

'Good morning!' Laptev called out.

She turned round. Usually she looked cool and indifferent when he saw her, or tired, as yesterday. But now she seemed as lively and playful as those boys at their game. 'Just look at them,' she said, going over to him. 'They don't enjoy themselves like that in Moscow. But they don't have such large yards there, so there's no room for running about. Father's just gone over to your place,' she added.

'I know, but it's you I've come to see, not him,' Laptev said, admiring her youthfulness, which he hadn't noticed before, apparently seeing it only for the first time today. And he felt that he was looking at her delicate white neck, with its little golden chain, for the very first time.

'I've come to see *you*,' he repeated. 'My sister's sent this umbrella you forgot yesterday.'

She stretched out her hand to take it, but he pressed the umbrella to his chest and said in a passionate, uncontrolled voice, as he surrendered once again to the exquisite delight experienced the previous night beneath the umbrella, 'I beg you, give it to me. I shall keep it in memory of you, of our friendship. It's a really wonderful umbrella!'

'Keep it,' she said, blushing. 'I don't think it's so wonderful.'

He looked at her in speechless ecstasy.

'Why am I making you stand in this heat?' she said after a short silence, laughing. 'Let's go inside.'

'I hope I'm not disturbing you.'

They entered the hall. Julia Sergeyevna ran upstairs, rustling her white dress with its blue flower pattern.

'You can't disturb *me*,' she replied, stopping on the stairs. 'After all, I never do a thing. Every day's a holiday for me, from morning to night.'

'That's something I can't understand,' he said, going up to her. 'I grew up in surroundings where everyone without exception – men and women – had to slave away, every single day.'

'But supposing there's nothing to do?' she asked.

'Then you must organize your life so that you just can't avoid working. Without work life can never be honest and happy.'

He pressed the umbrella to his chest again and said in a soft voice that didn't sound like his, 'If you would agree to be my wife I would give anything. Just *anything*. There's no price I wouldn't pay, no sacrifice I wouldn't make.'

She shuddered and looked at him in surprise and fear.

'What are you saying!' she exclaimed, turning pale. 'It's out of the question, I do assure you. I'm sorry.'

Still rustling her dress as before, she dashed upstairs and vanished through a door.

Laptev understood what this meant and his mood changed abruptly, as if the light had suddenly gone out in his soul. Suffering the shame and humiliation of someone who had been rejected, who wasn't loved, who was thought unattractive, repulsive and perhaps even hateful, and whom everyone avoided, he walked out of the house. 'I'd give *anything*,' he said, mimicking himself as he walked home in the heat and recalled the details of his declaration. '"Give *anything*" – why, that's how shopkeepers talk! A fat lot of good your *anything* is!'

All the things he had said just now struck him as sickeningly stupid. Why had he lied to her about growing up in surroundings where everyone worked 'without exception'? Why had he adopted that didactic tone about the 'honest, happy life'? It was silly, boring, hypocritical – typical Moscow pomposity. But gradually he lapsed into the indifference felt by criminals after a harsh sentence. Now, thank God, it was all over, he thought, no longer was there that dreadful uncertainty, no longer would he have to wait day after day, suffer, forever thinking about the same thing. Everything was clear now. He must abandon all hope of personal happiness and live without desire or hope; he must never have yearnings or expectations any more. If he wanted to dispel the boredom that he was so sick and tired of, he could start caring about what other people did, about their happiness. Old age would then creep up on him unnoticed, his life would come to an end – and that was the long and short of it. Now he didn't care about a thing, he wanted nothing and he could reflect coolly. But he felt a certain heaviness in his face, especially under the eyes. His forehead was as taut as stretched elastic and it seemed that tears would spurt at any moment. Feeling weak all over, he climbed into bed and in five minutes he was fast asleep.

III

Julia Sergeyevna was plunged into despair by Laptev's proposal, which had been so unexpected.

She didn't know him very well and they had met by chance. He was rich, a director of the well-known Moscow firm of Fyodor Laptev & Sons. He was always very serious, obviously highly intelligent and preoccupied with his sister's health. She had thought that he had been completely ignoring her, and on her part she had treated him with the utmost indifference. But suddenly there was that declaration on the stairs, that pathetic, enraptured face . . .

His proposal had disturbed her by its very suddenness, and she was upset at his using the word 'wife' and that she had had to refuse him. She had forgotten what she actually told Laptev, but vestiges of that impetuous, unpleasant feeling she had experienced when refusing him still lingered. She did not like him. He looked like a shop assistant, he was boring, and the only possible reply was *no*.

All the same, she felt awkward, as if she had behaved badly. 'My God, not even in the flat. Right there, on the stairs,' she said despairingly, turning towards the small icon above the bed-head. 'And he never paid me any attention before. It's all rather unusual, strange . . .'

In her loneliness she felt more uneasy by the hour, unable to cope unaided with those oppressive feelings. She needed someone to listen to her and tell her that she had behaved correctly. But there was no one to talk to. Her mother had died long ago, and she looked on her father as some kind of eccentric with whom she couldn't have a serious conversation. He embarrassed her with his whims, his excessive touchiness and vague gestures. The moment you started a discussion with him he would start talking about himself. Even in her prayers she hadn't been completely frank, since she wasn't sure exactly what she should ask of God.

The samovar was brought in. Very pale and tired, with a helpless-looking face, Julia Sergeyevna entered the dining-room, made the tea – this was her responsibility – and poured her father a glass. In that long frock-coat that reached below the knees, with his red face, uncombed hair, hands in pockets, the doctor paced the dining-room – not from corner to corner, but haphazardly, like a beast in a cage. He would stop by the table, drink with relish from his glass and then pensively pace the room again.

'Laptev proposed to me today,' Julia Sergeyevna said, blushing.

The doctor looked at her and didn't seem to understand. 'Laptev?' he asked. 'Nina Panaurov's brother?'

He loved his daughter. She would most probably marry sooner or later and leave him, but he tried not to think about it. He was scared at the prospect of loneliness and (for some reason) he felt he might have a stroke if he were left alone in that large house, but he didn't like to say it outright.

'I'm really very pleased,' he said, shrugging his shoulders. 'My heartiest congratulations! Now you have an excellent chance of abandoning me and *that* must give you great pleasure. I understand you very well. Living with a senile, sick, half-demented father must be rotten for someone of your age. I understand you perfectly. If only I were to peg out soon, if only the devil would cart me off, everyone would be so delighted. I congratulate you most heartily.'

'I turned him down.'

The doctor felt relieved, but now he couldn't stop talking and he continued, 'I'm amazed. I've been asking myself this for a long time now, why haven't they put me in a lunatic asylum? Why am I wearing this frock-coat, instead of a straitjacket? I still believe in truth, goodness, I'm a stupid old idealist – surely that's madness in this day and age? And what do I get for my love of truth, for being honest with people? I'm almost stoned in the streets, everyone rides roughshod over me. Even my nearest and dearest walk all over me. So to hell with me, stupid old fool!'

'It's impossible to have a proper talk with you!' Julia said. Abruptly, she stood up from the table and furiously went to her room. She well remembered how often her father had been unfair to her. But after a little while she began to feel sorry for him, and when he left for his club she went downstairs with him and shut the door after him. The weather was bad, very blustery. The door shook from the force of the wind and in the hall there were draughts everywhere which nearly blew the candle out. Julia went all through her rooms upstairs and made the sign of the cross over all windows and doors. The wind howled and someone seemed to be walking about on the roof. Never had she felt so low, never had she felt so lonely.

She wondered if she had behaved badly in refusing a man just because she didn't care for his looks. She didn't love him – that was true – and marrying him would have meant saying farewell to her dreams and ideas of a happy married life. But would she ever meet the man of her dreams and fall in love? She was already twenty-one. There were no eligible bachelors in town. She thought of all the men she knew – civil servants, teachers, officers. Some of them were already married and their family life was staggeringly empty and boring. Others were dull, colourless, stupid and immoral. Whatever you said about Laptev, he was a Muscovite, he'd been to university, he spoke French. He lived in Moscow, the capital, where there were so many clever, idealistic, remarkable people, where everything was so lively, with magnificent theatres, musical evenings, first-class dressmakers and patisseries. The Bible says that a wife must love her husband and love is of prime importance in novels. But wasn't all that going too far? Surely family life *without* love was somehow possible? Wasn't it said that love soon passes, that it becomes a mere habit and that the purpose of family life isn't love and happiness, but responsibility – bringing up children, looking after the house and so on. Perhaps what the Bible meant was loving one's husband in the same way as one's neighbour, having respect, making allowances . . .

That night Julia Sergeyevna attentively read her evening prayers, then she knelt down, clasped her hands to her breast and looked at the icon-lamp. 'Teach me to understand, Holy Mother. Teach me, O Lord!' she said, with deep feeling.

In the course of her life she had met poor, pathetic old maids who bitterly regretted having turned down their suitors at some time. Wouldn't the same thing happen to her? Shouldn't she enter a convent or become a nurse?

She undressed and got into bed, crossing herself and the air around. Suddenly a bell rang sharply, plaintively, in the corridor. 'Good God!' she said, feeling intense irritation all over her body at this sound. She lay there thinking about provincial life, so uneventful and monotonous, yet so disturbing at times: you were always being forced to shudder, to feel angry and guilty and in the end your nerves became so shattered you were too frightened to look out from under the blankets.

Half an hour later the bell rang again, just as sharply. The servants were most probably asleep and didn't hear it. Annoyed with them and shivering, Julia Sergeyevna lit a candle and started dressing. When she had finished and gone out into the corridor the maid was bolting the downstairs door. 'I thought it was the master, but it was somebody one of the patients sent over,' she said.

Julia Sergeyevna returned to her room. She took a pack of cards from her chest of drawers and decided that if, after shuffling them well and cutting them, the bottom card turned out red, that would mean *yes*, that is, she had to accept Laptev. If it was black she must say *no*. The card was the ten of spades.

This had a calming effect and she fell asleep. But in the morning it was neither 'yes' nor 'no' again. She realized that she could change her whole life now if she so wanted. These thoughts wearied her – she felt exhausted and ill. However, just after eleven o'clock, she dressed and went to visit Nina Fyodorovna. She wanted to see Laptev – he might strike her as more attractive now and perhaps she had been making a mistake.

Fighting one's way against that wind was hard work. She hardly made any progress, and she held her hat with both hands, seeing nothing for dust.

IV

When he entered his sister's room and unexpectedly saw Julia Sergeyevna there, Laptev again felt the humiliation of someone who has been snubbed. He concluded that if, after yesterday, she had no qualms about visiting his sister and meeting him, then either he didn't exist as far as she was concerned, or he was considered a complete nonentity. But when he greeted her and she looked at him sadly and guiltily with a pale face and dust under her eyes, he could see that she too was suffering.

She was not feeling well. After sitting there for a very short time – about ten minutes – she made her farewell. 'Please take me home, Aleksey Fyodorych,' she said on her way out. They walked in silence down the street, holding on to their hats; he kept behind her, trying to shield her from the wind. It was calmer in a side-street and here they walked side by side.

'Please forgive me if I was unkind yesterday,' she began and her voice shook, as if she were about to cry. 'It's sheer torture! I haven't slept all night.'

'I had an excellent night,' Laptev replied without looking at her, 'but that doesn't mean I feel all right. My life is in shreds, I'm deeply unhappy after your turning me down yesterday, I feel as if I've taken poison. The most painful things were said yesterday, but today I don't feel at all inhibited and can speak quite frankly. I love you more than my sister, more than my late mother. I could – and I did – live without my sister and mother, but life without you makes no sense. I just can't . . .'

As usual, he had guessed her intentions. He saw that she wanted to continue yesterday's conversation: it was only for this that she had asked him to accompany her and now she was taking him to her house. But what could she add to her refusal? Was there any more to say? Her glance, her smile, even the way she held her head and shoulders as she walked with him – everything indicated that she still did not love him, that he was a stranger to her. So what else was there for her to say?

Dr Sergey Borisych was at home. 'Welcome! Delighted to see you, Fyodor Alekseich,' he said, getting the name wrong. 'Delighted, absolutely delighted.'

He had never been so friendly before and Laptev concluded that the doctor already knew about the proposal – and he found this unpleasant to think about. He was sitting in the drawing-room now: it produced a strange impression, with its cheap, vulgar furniture and poor pictures. Although there were armchairs and a huge lamp with a shade, it looked unlived-in, rather like a spacious barn. Obviously, only someone like the doctor could feel at home in such a room. Another room, almost twice as big, was called 'The Ballroom' – here there were only chairs, as at a dancing-class. And something suspicious began to worry Laptev as he sat in the drawing-room talking to the doctor about his sister. Had Julia Sergeyevna been to see his sister Nina and then brought him here to announce that she had accepted his proposal? This was bad enough, but even worse was having a nature that was prey to such suspicions. He imagined father and daughter having lengthy deliberations yesterday evening and night, long arguments perhaps, and then agreeing that Julia Sergeyevna had behaved recklessly in refusing a rich man. Even the words spoken by parents on such occasions – 'It's true, you don't love him, but on the other hand think of the good deeds you'll be able to perform!' – rang in his ears.

The doctor prepared to leave on his rounds. Laptev wanted to go with him but Julia Sergeyevna said, 'Please stay, I beg you.'

She had been suffering from dreadful depression and now she was trying to reassure herself that to refuse a respectable, kind man who loved her just because he didn't attract her, especially when this marriage provided the opportunity of changing her life, so cheerless, monotonous and idle, when her youth was passing and the future held no hope of anything brighter – to refuse him in these circumstances was insane, irresponsible and perverse, and God might even punish her for it.

Her father left the house. When his footsteps had died away she suddenly stopped in front of Laptev.

'I spent a long time thinking it over yesterday, Aleksey Fyodorych, and I accept your proposal,' she said decisively, turning pale.

He bent down and kissed her hand. Awkwardly, she kissed his head with cold lips. He felt that the essential thing, her love, was absent from this amorous declaration, which none the less stated what was superfluous. He felt like shouting, running away, setting off for Moscow immediately. But she was standing close to him and she seemed so beautiful that he was suddenly gripped with desire. He saw that it was too late now for further discussion, embraced her passionately, pressed her to his chest, muttered something, addressed her intimately, kissed her neck, cheek and head . . .

She retreated to the window, frightened by these caresses. Now they both regretted their declarations. 'Why did this happen?' they asked themselves in their embarrassment.

'If only you knew how unhappy I feel!' she said, wringing her hands.

'What's wrong?' he asked, going up to her and wringing his hands too. 'My dear, tell me what's wrong, for God's sake! But only the truth. I beg you, only the truth!'

'Don't take any notice,' she said, forcing a smile. 'I promise to be a faithful, devoted wife. Come over this evening.'

Later, as he sat reading the historical novel to his sister, he remembered all this and felt insulted that his admirable, pure and generous feelings had elicited such a trivial response. He was *not* loved, but his proposal had been accepted, probably only because he was rich. In other words, they valued that part of him he valued least. The pure, devout Julia had never given any thought to money – he granted her that – but she didn't love him, did she? No, she did not, and obviously there had been some sort of calculation here – even though it was somewhat vague and not wholly intentional perhaps, it was calculation none the less. The doctor's house, with its vulgar décor, repelled him and the doctor himself resembled some fat, pathetic miser, rather like the buffoon Gaspard in *The Bells of Corneville*.[6] The very name Julia sounded common. He imagined Julia and himself during the wedding, essentially complete strangers and without a scrap of feeling on her part, as if it were an arranged marriage. And now his only consolation (as banal as the marriage itself) was that he wasn't the first and wouldn't be the last and that thousands of men had made similar marriages and that, in time, when she knew him better, Julia might perhaps come to love him.

'Romeo and Julia!' he said, closing the book and laughing. 'I'm Romeo, Nina. You may congratulate me. I proposed to Julia Belavin today.'

Nina Fyodorovna first thought that he was joking, then she believed him and burst into tears. The news didn't please her. 'All right, congratulations,' she said. 'But why so sudden?'

'It's not, it's been going on since March, only you never notice a thing. I've been in love since March, when I first met her here in your room.'

'But I thought you'd marry someone we know, from Moscow,' Nina Fyodorovna said after a brief silence. 'The girls from our little circle are not so complicated. But the main thing, Aleksey, is for you to be happy, that's what's important. My Grigory Nikolaich never loved me, and you can see how we live – it's an open secret. Of course, any woman would love you for your kindness and intellect. But Julia went to a boarding-school, she's out of the top drawer. Intellect and kindness don't mean much to her. She's young. As for you, Aleksey, you're neither young nor handsome.'

To soften these last words she stroked his cheek and said, 'You're not handsome, but you're a wonderful person.'

She was so excited her cheeks flushed slightly and she talked enthusiastically about whether it would be correct to bless Aleksey with an icon. All said and done, she was his elder sister and was like a mother to him. And she kept trying to convince her despondent brother that the wedding should be celebrated correctly, cheerfully and with great ceremony, so that people didn't start criticizing.

Then the husband-to-be started calling on the Belavins three or four times a day and he was no longer able to take Sasha's place reading the historical novel. Julia received him in her own two rooms, away from the drawing-room and her father's study, and he liked them very much. There were dark walls and a full icon-case in one corner; and there was a smell of fine perfume and lamp oil. She lived in the remotest rooms, her bed and dressing-table were surrounded by screens and her book-case doors were curtained inside with a green material. She had carpets, so that she couldn't be heard walking about, and all this led him to believe that hers was a secretive nature, that she loved a quiet, peaceful, enclosed life. Legally, she was only a minor in that house. She had no money of her own: during their walks she was sometimes embarrassed at not having a single copeck on her. Her father gave her a little money for dresses and books, not more than a hundred roubles a year. And the doctor himself had hardly any money, despite his first-class practice: every evening he played cards at the club and always lost. Besides that, he bought houses on mortgage through a mutual credit society and rented them out. His tenants were always behind with their payments, but he was confident that the property deals were highly profitable. He had mortgaged his own house, where he lived with his daughter, and had bought a plot of waste ground with the money. He was already building a large, two-storey house there, with the intention of mortgaging it.

Laptev now seemed to be living in some kind of haze, as if replaced by his double, and he was doing many things he would never have attempted before. Three times he accompanied the doctor to the club, had supper with him and volunteered money for the house-building. He even visited Panaurov in his other flat. One day Panaurov invited him to dinner and, without thinking, Laptev accepted. He was greeted by a lady of about thirty-five, tall and thin, slightly greying and with black eyebrows. She was obviously not

Russian. She had white powder blotches on her face and a sickly smile, and she shook his hand brusquely, making the bracelets jingle on her white arm. Laptev thought that she smiled that way to hide the fact she was unhappy from others and from herself. He saw two little girls there too, five and three years old, who looked like Sasha. For dinner they had milk soup, cold veal and carrots, and then chocolate. It was all sickly-sweet and not very tasty, but on the table were gleaming gold forks, bottles of soya sauce and cayenne pepper, an exceptionally ornate sauceboat and a golden pepper pot.

Only after he had finished his soup did Laptev realize the mistake he had made in coming here for dinner. The lady was embarrassed and kept smiling and showing him her teeth the whole time. Panaurov offered a scientific explanation of falling in love and its origins.

'Here we are dealing with an electrical phenomenon,' he said in French, addressing the lady. 'Everyone's skin has microscopic glands with currents running through them. If you meet someone whose currents are parallel to yours – there's love for you!'

Back home, when his sister asked where he had been, Laptev felt awkward and didn't answer.

Right up to the wedding he had felt in a false position. With every day his love for Julia grew – she seemed ethereal, sublime. All the same, she didn't return this love: basically, he was buying her, she was selling herself. Sometimes, after much reflection, he simply grew desperate and wondered whether he should run away from it all. Night after night he didn't sleep, all he did was think of meeting that lady in Moscow after the wedding – that lady he had called a 'personage' in letters to friends. And he wondered how his father and brother, both difficult characters, would react to his marriage and to Julia. He was afraid his father might say something rude to Julia at the first meeting. And his brother Fyodor had been acting very strangely lately. In his lengthy letters he wrote about the importance of health, about the influence of illness on one's state of mind, about the nature of religion, but not one word about Moscow and business. These letters irritated Laptev and he thought that his brother's character had taken a turn for the worse.

The wedding was in September. The actual ceremony was held

after morning service at the Church of St Peter and St Paul and that same day the couple left for Moscow. When Laptev and his wife (she wore a black dress and train and now resembled a grown woman instead of a girl) were saying goodbye to Nina Fyodorovna, the invalid's whole face twisted, but not one tear flowed from her dry eyes.

'If I should die, God forbid,' she said, 'take care of my little girls.'

'Oh, I promise!' Julia Sergeyevna replied, her lips and eyelids twitching nervously too.

'I'll come and see you in October,' Laptev said, deeply moved. 'Get better now, my dearest.'

They had a railway compartment to themselves. Both felt sad and embarrassed. She sat in one corner without taking her hat off, pretending to be dozing, while he lay on the couchette opposite, troubled by various thoughts: about his father, about the 'personage', about whether Julia would like his Moscow flat. As he glanced at his wife who didn't love him he gloomily asked himself 'How did all this happen?'

V

In Moscow the Laptevs ran a wholesale haberdashery business, selling fringes, ribbons, braid, knitting items, buttons and so on. The gross receipts amounted to two million roubles a year. What the net profit was no one knew except the old man. The sons and assistants put it at about three hundred thousand and said that it could have been a hundred thousand more if the old man hadn't 'frittered profits away' by giving credit indiscriminately. Over the past ten years they had accumulated nearly a million worthless bills of exchange alone, and when the matter was discussed the senior assistant would produce a crafty wink and use language that many couldn't understand: 'It's the psychological aftermath of the age.'

The main business was carried on in the city's commercial quarter, in a building called the warehouse. This was entered from a perpetually gloomy yard that smelt of matting, where hoofs of drayhorses clattered over asphalt. A very modest looking, iron-bound door led from this yard into a room whose walls, brown from the damp, were covered in charcoal scribbles. This room was lit by a narrow, iron-grilled window. To the left was another room, a little larger and cleaner, with a cast-iron stove and two tables, but with a prison-like window too. This was the office and from it a narrow stone staircase led up to the first floor, where the main business was carried on. This was a fairly large room but, because of the perpetual twilight, low ceiling and lack of space caused by crates, packages and people rushing about, it struck newcomers as just as unprepossessing as the two rooms down below. Up on this floor, and on the office shelves too, goods lay in stacks, bales and cardboard boxes. They were all displayed any old how, with no attempt at order or creating a nice show. If it hadn't been for the crimson threads, tassels and pieces of fringe sticking out of paper-wrapped parcels here and there, no one could have guessed, at first glance, what kind of business was being carried on here. Looking at those crumpled paper parcels and boxes it was hard to believe that millions of roubles were spent on these trifles and that fifty men – excluding buyers – were busy in that warehouse every day.

When Laptev appeared at the warehouse at noon, the day after arriving in Moscow, men were packing goods and making such a racket with the crates no one in the first room or office heard him come in. A postman he knew was going downstairs with a bundle of letters in his hand – he was frowning at the noise and didn't notice him either. The first person to welcome him upstairs was his brother Fyodor, who was so like him people thought that they were twins. This similarity kept reminding Laptev of his appearance and now, seeing before him a short man with flushed cheeks, thinning on top, with lean thighs of poor pedigree, so dull and unbusinesslike, he asked himself: 'Surely *I* don't look like that?'

'I'm so glad to see you!' Fyodor exclaimed, exchanging kisses with his brother and firmly shaking his hand. 'I've been waiting impatiently every day, my dear brother. When you wrote that you were getting married I was racked with curiosity. I've really missed you, old man. Just think, we haven't seen each other for about six months. Well now, what's new? How's Nina? Is she *very* bad?'

'Yes.'

'It's God's will,' Fyodor sighed. 'Well, how's the wife? I dare say she's a beauty. I love her already. After all, she's the same as a little sister to me. We'll spoil her, the two of us.'

Just then Laptev spotted the long familiar, broad, bent back of his father, Fyodor Stepanych. The old man was sitting on a stool by the counter, talking to a customer.

'Papa, God has sent us joy today!' Fyodor cried. 'My brother's arrived!'

Fyodor Stepanych senior was tall and so very powerfully built that despite his wrinkles and eighty years he still looked like a strong, healthy man. He spoke in a deep, heavy, booming voice that came thunder ing from his broad chest as if from a barrel. He shaved his beard, sported an army-style trimmed moustache and smoked cigars. Since he was always feeling warm, he wore a loose-fitting canvas jacket in the warehouse and at home, at all seasons. Recently he'd had a cataract removed, his sight was poor and he no longer took an active part in the business, merely chatting to people and drinking tea with jam.

Laptev bent down and kissed his hand, then his lips.

'It's been such a long time since we saw each other, my dear sir,' the old man said. 'Yes, such a long time. Well, I suppose I must congratulate you on your marriage? All right. Congratulations.'

He offered his lips to receive a kiss. Laptev bent down and kissed them.

'Well now, have you brought the young lady with you?' the old man asked and without waiting for an answer turned to the customer and said, '"I hereby inform you, dear Papa, that I'm marrying Miss So-and-So." Yes. But asking for Papa's blessing and advice isn't in the rules. They just do what they like now. I was over forty when I married and I fell down at my father's feet and asked his advice. They don't do that sort of thing these days.'

The old man was delighted to see his son, but thought it improper to display any affection or show that he was pleased. His voice, his manner of speaking and that 'young lady' expression put Laptev in the bad mood which invariably came over him in that warehouse. Every little detail here reminded him of the past, when he had been whipped and given plain, lenten food. He knew that boys were still whipped and punched on the nose until it bled, and that when these boys grew up they would do the punching. Only five minutes in that warehouse, so it seemed, was enough for him to expect abuse or a punch on the nose at any moment.

Fyodor slapped the customer on the shoulder and said to his brother, 'Aleksey, let me introduce Grigory Timofeich, the firm's right arm in Tambov.[7] He's a shining example to the youth of today. He's in his sixth decade, yet he has children still at their mother's breast.'

The clerks laughed – and so did the customer, a skinny, pale-faced old man.

'It's contrary to the course of nature,' observed the senior clerk, who was also standing behind the counter. 'Whatever goes in must come out the same.'

This senior clerk, a tall man of about fifty, with a dark beard, spectacles and a pencil behind the ear, usually expressed his thoughts ambiguously, in far-fetched allusions, and it was plain from his cunning smile that he attached some special, subtle meaning to his words. He loved obscuring what he said with bookish expressions that he interpreted in his own peculiar way, often giving common words – 'furthermore', for example – a different meaning from their original one. Whenever he said something categorically and didn't want to be contradicted, he would stretch out his right arm and say 'Furthermore!'

Most surprising of all, the other clerks and the customers understood him perfectly. His name was Ivan Vasilich Pochatkin and he came from Kashira.[8] Congratulating Laptev, he expressed himself as follows: 'It is a valiant service on your part, for a woman's heart is bold and warlike!'

Another person of consequence in the warehouse was the clerk Makeichev, a stout, fair-haired pillar of the community, with a bald patch on top and side-whiskers. He went over to Laptev and congratulated him respectfully, in a low voice: 'I have the honour, sir . . . The Lord has listened to your good father's prayers, sir. The Lord be praised, sir.'

Then the others came over to congratulate him on his marriage. They were all smartly dressed and all seemed impeccably honest, educated men. They spoke with provincial accents and as they said 'sir' after every other word their rapidly delivered congratulations – 'I wish you, sir, all the best, sir' – sounded like whiplashes in the air.

Laptev soon grew bored with all this and wanted to go home. But leaving was awkward. For propriety's sake, he must spend at least two hours in the warehouse. He walked away from the counter and asked Makeichev if they had had a good summer and if there was any news. Makeichev replied politely, without looking him in the eye. A boy with close-cropped hair, in a grey blouse, handed Laptev a glass of tea without a saucer. Soon afterwards another boy stumbled on a crate as he went past and nearly fell over. The stolid Makeichev suddenly pulled a terrifying, vicious, monster-like face and shouted at him, 'Look where you're going!'

The clerks were glad that the young master was married now and had finally returned. They gave him inquisitive, welcoming looks, each considering it his duty to make some pleasant, polite remark as he went past. But Laptev was certain that all this was insincere and that the flattery came from fear. He just couldn't forget how, fifteen years before, a mentally ill clerk had run into the street in his underclothes, barefoot, had waved his fist menacingly at the windows in the boss's office and shouted that they were tormenting the life out of him. People kept laughing at the poor devil for a long time after he had been cured, reminding him how he had called the bosses 'explanters' instead of 'exploiters'. On the whole, life was very hard for the Laptev employees and this had long been the main topic for discussion in the whole commercial quarter. Worst of all was the oriental deviousness with which old Laptev treated them. Because of this, no one knew what salary his favourites Pochatkin and Makeichev received – actually they got no more than three thousand a year, including bonuses, but he pretended he was paying them seven. The bonuses were paid every year to all the clerks, but in secret, so that those who didn't get much were forced by pride to say they'd received a lot. Not one of the junior boys knew when he would be promoted to clerk, and none of the staff ever knew whether the boss was satisfied with him or not. Nothing was categorically forbidden the clerks, so they didn't know what was allowed and what wasn't. They were not in fact forbidden to marry, but they didn't marry for fear of displeasing the boss and losing their job. They were allowed to have friends and to pay visits, but the gates were locked at nine in the evening and every morning the boss would eye his staff suspiciously and test them to see if they smelt of vodka: 'You there, let's smell your breath!'

Every church holiday the staff had to go to early service and stand in church so the boss could see them all. The fasts were strictly observed. On special occasions – the boss's or his family's name-days, for example – the clerks had to club together and buy a cake from Fley's,[9] or an album. They lived on the ground floor of the house on Pyatnitsky Street, as well as in the outbuilding, three or four to a room, and they ate from a common bowl, although each had his own plate in front of him. If any of the boss's family came in during a meal they would all stand up.

Laptev realized that only those ruined by receiving their education through the old man could seriously consider him their benefactor – the remainder saw him as an enemy and 'explanter'. Now, after a six-month absence, he saw that nothing had improved and that a change had taken place which didn't augur well. His brother Fyodor, who used to be quiet, thoughtful and exceptionally sensitive, was rushing around the place now, looking extremely efficient and businesslike, pencil behind ear, slapping buyers on the shoulder and calling the clerks 'My friends!' Evidently he was acting a part, one in which Aleksey didn't recognize him at all.

The old man's voice droned on non-stop. As he had nothing else to do, Laptev senior was instructing a clerk in decent living and the best way to conduct his affairs, setting himself as a good example the whole time.

Laptev had heard that boasting, authoritarian, crushing tone of voice ten, fifteen, twenty years ago. The old man adored himself. What he said invariably gave the impression that he had made his late wife and her family happy, had encouraged his children with rewards, had been a benefactor to his clerks and the rest of the staff, and had made the whole street and all who knew him eternally grateful. Whatever he did was absolutely perfect, and if other men's business went badly this was only because they hadn't followed his advice, without which *no* business enterprise could ever hope to succeed. In church he always stood right in front of the congregation and even rebuked the priests when, according to him, they made mistakes in the ritual. This would please God, he thought, since God loved him.

By two o'clock everyone in the warehouse was busy, except the old man, who was still going on in that thunderous voice. To give himself something to do, Laptev took some braid from a female worker and then sent her away. Then he listened to a buyer – a Vologda[10] merchant – and instructed a clerk to look after him.

The prices and serial numbers of goods were denoted by letters and cries of T-V-A and R-I-T rang out from all sides.

When he left Laptev said goodbye only to his brother.

'I'm coming to Pyatnitsky Street with the wife tomorrow,' he said. 'But I'm warning you, if Father says one rude word to her I won't stay one minute.'

'Just the same as ever!' Fyodor sighed. 'Marriage hasn't changed you. You must be kind to the old man, dear chap. All right then, see you there tomorrow at eleven. We look forward to it – come straight after church.'

'I don't go to church.'

'Well, it doesn't matter. The main thing is, don't be later than eleven – we have to pray to the Lord before we have lunch. Regards to my little sister-in-law, please kiss her hand for me. I have the feeling I'm going to like her very much,' Fyodor added in complete sincerity. 'I envy you, my dear brother!' he shouted as Aleksey was on his way downstairs.

'Why all that cringing, that shyness, as if he felt naked?' Laptev wondered as he walked down Nikolsky Street[11] trying to fathom the reason for the change in Fyodor. 'And this new way of speaking – "dear brother", "old chap", "God's mercy", "Let's pray to the Lord" – what sanctimonious nonsense!'[12]

VI

At eleven the next day – a Sunday – Laptev drove down Pyatnitsky Street with his wife in a one-horse carriage. He was afraid his father might have tantrums and he felt anxious even before arriving. After two nights in her father's house, Julia Sergeyevna considered her marriage a mistake, a disaster even. If she'd gone to live anywhere but Moscow with her husband she would not have survived such horrors, she thought. But Moscow did have its diversions. She loved the streets, houses and churches: had it been possible to drive around Moscow in this magnificent sledge with expensive horses, drive all day, from morning till night, at high speed, breathing in the cool, autumn air, she might perhaps have felt a little happier.

The coachman halted the horse near a white, newly plastered two-storey house, then turned right. Here everyone was waiting. A house porter stood at the gate in his new tunic, high boots and galoshes, together with two police constables. The whole area, from the middle of the street to the gate and then across the yard to the porch, was strewn with fresh sand. The house porter doffed his cap, the constables saluted. His brother Fyodor greeted them at the porch with a grave expression.

'Delighted to meet you, my dear sister-in-law,' he said, kissing Julia's hand. 'Welcome.'

He led her upstairs by the arm, then along a corridor, through a crowd of men and women. The vestibule was packed with people too, and there was a smell of incense.

'I'm going to introduce you to Father now,' Fyodor whispered amid that solemn, funereal silence. 'A venerable old man, a true paterfamilias.'

In the large hall, near a table prepared for divine service, stood Fyodor Stepanych, a priest with his high hat, and a deacon, all evidently expecting them. The old man offered Julia his hand without a word. Everyone was quiet. Julia felt awkward.

The priest and deacon began robing themselves. A censer, scattering sparks and smelling of incense and charcoal, was brought in.

Candles were lit. Clerks entered the hall on tiptoe and stood by the wall, in two rows. It was quiet – no one even coughed.

'Bless us, oh Lord,' the deacon began.

The service was performed solemnly, with nothing omitted, and two special prayers, 'Sweetest Jesus' and 'Holy Mother', were chanted. Laptev noticed how embarrassed his wife had just been. While the prayers were being chanted and the choristers sang a triple 'God have mercy', in varying harmonies, he felt dreadfully tense, expecting the old man to look round any minute and rebuke him with something like 'You don't know how to make the sign of the cross properly.' And he felt annoyed: what was the point of all that crowd, ceremony, priests, choir? It reeked too much of the old merchant style. But when she joined the old man in allowing the Gospel to be held over her head and then genuflected several times, he understood that it was all to her liking and he felt relieved. At the end of the service, during the prayers for long life, the priest gave the old man and Aleksey the cross to kiss, but when Julia Sergeyevna came up to him he covered it with one hand and apparently wanted to say a few words to her. They waved to the choristers to keep quiet.

'The Prophet Samuel[13] came to Bethlehem at the Lord's command,' the priest began, 'and the elders of that town besought him, trembling: "Comest thou peaceably, O prophet?" And the Prophet said, "Peaceably, I am come to make sacrifice unto the Lord! Sanctify yourselves and rejoice this day with me." Shall we question thee, Julia, servant of the Lord, if thou comest peaceably to this house?'

Julia was deeply moved and she blushed. After he had finished, the priest handed her the cross to kiss and then continued in a completely different tone of voice, 'The young Mr Laptev should get married, it's high time.'

The choir began to sing again, the congregation moved about and it became noisy. The old man was deeply touched and his eyes were full of tears as he kissed Julia three times and made the sign of the cross before her face. 'This is your house,' he said. 'I'm an old man, I don't need anything.'

The clerks offered their congratulations and added a few words, but the choir sang so loud it was impossible to hear anything. Then they had lunch and drank champagne. Julia sat next to the old man, who told her that living apart was not good, that one should live together, in the same house, and that divisions and disagreements led to ruin.

'I made my fortune, all my children can do is spend it,' he said. 'Now you must live in the same house as me and make money. I'm an old man, time I had a rest.'

Julia kept glimpsing Fyodor, who was very much like her husband, but more fidgety and more reserved. He fussed around nearby, repeatedly kissing her hand.

'My dear sister-in-law!' he exclaimed, 'we're just ordinary people,' and as he spoke red blotches broke out all over his face. 'We lead simple Russian, Christian lives, dear sister.'

On the way home Laptev felt very pleased everything had gone so well and that, contrary to what he had been expecting, nothing disastrous had happened.

'You seem surprised,' he told his wife, 'that such a strong, broad-shouldered father should have such undersized, weak-chested children like myself and Fyodor. That's easy to explain! Father married Mother when he was forty-five and she was only seventeen. She used to turn pale and tremble in his presence. Nina was first to be born and Mother was comparatively healthy at the time, so she turned out stronger, better than us. But Fyodor and myself were conceived and born when Mother was worn out from being in a perpetual state of terror. I remember Father started giving me lessons – putting it bluntly, he started beating me – before I was five even. He birched me, boxed my ears, hit me on the head. The first thing I did when I woke up every morning was wonder whether I'd be beaten that day. Fyodor and I were forbidden to play games or have any fun. We had to go to matins and early service, kiss the priests' and monks' hands, read special prayers at home. Now, you're religious and you like that kind of thing, but I'm scared of religion and when I pass a church I remember my childhood and I'm frightened. When I was eight they made me start work at the warehouse. I was just a simple factory hand and this was rotten, as I was beaten almost every day. Then, after I'd started high school, I'd sit and do my homework before dinner and from then until very late I'd have to stay in that same warehouse. This went on until I was twenty-two and met Yartsev at university. He persuaded me to leave my father's house. This Yartsev has done me a lot of good. Do you know what?' Laptev said, cheerfully laughing. 'Let's go and see Yartsev right now. He's a terribly decent person, he'll be so touched!'

VII

One Saturday in November, Anton Rubinstein[14] was conducting at the Conservatoire.[15] The concert hall was extremely crowded and hot. Laptev stood behind some pillars, while his wife and Kostya Kochevoy sat far off, in the front, in the third or fourth row. Right at the beginning of the interval the 'personage', Polina Nikolayevna Rassudina, came by, quite out of the blue. Since the wedding he had often worried at the thought of meeting her. As she looked at him, openly and frankly, he remembered that he had so far made no attempt to patch things up or write a couple of friendly lines – it was just as if he were hiding from her. He felt ashamed and he blushed. She shook his hand firmly and impulsively, and asked, 'Have you seen Yartsev?'

Without waiting for a reply she moved swiftly on, with long strides, as if someone were pushing her from behind.

She was extremely thin and ugly, with a long nose, and she looked constantly tired and worn out: apparently she was always having great difficulty in keeping her eyes open and not falling over. She had beautiful, dark eyes and a clever, kind, sincere expression, but her movements were jerky and brusque. She wasn't easy to talk to since she was incapable of listening or speaking calmly. Loving her had been a difficult proposition. When she stayed with Laptev she used to have long, loud fits of laughter, covering her face with her hands and maintaining that her life didn't revolve around love. She was as coy as a seventeen-year-old and all the candles had to be extinguished before someone kissed her. She was thirty and had married a teacher, but had long lived apart from her husband. She earned her living from music lessons and playing in quartets.

During the Ninth Symphony she once again went past, as if by accident, but a large group of men standing behind some pillars barred her way and she stopped. Laptev noticed that she was wearing the same velvet blouse she had worn for last year's concerts, and the year before that. Her gloves were new – and so was her fan, but cheap. She wanted to be smartly dressed, but she had no flair for it and grudged spending money. As a result, she was so badly and scruffily turned out that she could easily be mistaken for a young monk as she strode hurriedly down the street on her way to a lesson.

The audience applauded and demanded an encore.

'You're spending this evening with me,' Polina Nikolayevna said, going up to Laptev and eyeing him severely. 'We'll go and have tea together when the concert's finished. Do you hear? I insist on it. You owe me a lot and you have no moral right to refuse me this little trifle.'

'All right, let's go then,' Laptev agreed.

After the symphony there were endless encores. The audience rose and left extremely slowly. But Laptev couldn't leave without telling his wife, so he had to stand at the door and wait.

'I'm just dying for a cup of tea,' Rassudina complained. 'I'm simply burning inside.'

'We can get some tea here,' Laptev said. 'Let's go to the bar.'

'No, I don't have the money to throw away on barmen. *I'm* not a businessman's wife!'

He offered her his arm, but she refused, producing that long, tedious sentence he had heard from her so often before, to the effect that she didn't consider herself one of the weaker or fair sex and could dispense with the services of gentlemen.

As she talked to him she kept looking at the audience and greeting friends – fellow-students from Guerrier's courses[16] and the Conservatoire, and her male and female pupils too. She shook their hands firmly, impulsively, with a jerky movement. But then she started twitching her shoulders and trembling as if she were feverish. Finally she looked at Laptev in horror and said softly, 'Who's *this* you've married? Where were your eyes, you madman? What did you see in that stupid, insignificant little cow? Didn't I love you for your mind, for what's deep down inside you? All that china doll wants is your money!'

'That's enough, Polina,' he pleaded. 'Everything you might say about my marriage I've already told myself dozens of times. Don't cause me any unnecessary pain.'

Julia Sergeyevna appeared in a black dress with a large diamond brooch that her father-in-law had sent her after the prayer service. She was followed by her retinue: Kochevoy, two doctor friends, an officer and a stout young man in student uniform by the name of Kish.

'You go with Kostya,' Laptev told his wife. 'I'll join you later.'

Julia nodded and moved on. Trembling all over and twitching nervously, Polina Nikolayevna followed her with a look of revulsion, hatred and anguish.

Laptev was scared of going to her room as he anticipated some nasty showdown, harsh words and tears, so he suggested having tea in a restaurant. But she said, 'No, no, come to my place. Don't you dare mention restaurants to me!'

She didn't like restaurants, because the air in them seemed poisoned by tobacco and men's breath. She was peculiarly prejudiced towards strange men, considering them all libertines, capable of pouncing on her at any moment. Besides, the music in restaurants irritated her and gave her headaches.

After leaving the Gentry Club they took a cab to Savelovsky Street, off Ostozhenka Street,[17] where Rassudina lived. Laptev thought about her the whole way. In actual fact, he did owe her a great deal. He had met her at his friend Yartsev's, whom she was teaching theory. She had fallen deeply in love with him, without ulterior motives, and after becoming his mistress she continued giving lessons and working until she dropped. Thanks to her he began to understand and love music, to which he had been almost completely indifferent.

'Half my kingdom for a glass of tea!' she said in a hollowish voice, covering her mouth with her muff to avoid catching cold. 'I've given five lessons today, damn it. My pupils are such clots and blockheads I nearly died of anger. I just don't know when this hard labour will end. I'm absolutely flaked. The moment I've saved three hundred roubles I shall give everything up and go to the Crimea. I shall lie on the beach and gulp oxygen. How I love the sea, how I love it!'

'You won't go anywhere,' Laptev said. 'Firstly, you won't save a thing and secondly, you're mean. Forgive me, but I must say it again: your amassing three hundred roubles, a few copecks at a time, from those idlers who only take lessons from you because they have nothing to do – is that any less degrading than borrowing it from your friends?'

'I have no friends,' she said, irritably. 'And I would ask you not to talk such rubbish. The working class, to which I belong, has one privilege – consciousness of its own incorruptibility, plus the right to despise shopkeepers and not be beholden to them. No, you can't buy *me*, I'm not a Julia!'

Laptev didn't pay the cab-driver, knowing that this would provoke that all too familiar torrent of words. She paid herself.

She was renting a small furnished room with board, in a flat that belonged to a single lady. Her Becker grand piano was kept at Yartsev's place in Great Nikitsky Street[18] for the time being and she went there every day to play. In her room were armchairs with covers, a bed with a white summer quilt, and flowers put there by the landlady. On the walls were oleographs, and there was nothing to suggest that a university woman was living in that room. There was no dressing-table, no books, not even a desk. It was obvious that she went to bed immediately she came home and left the house the moment she got up in the morning.

The cook brought in the samovar and Polina Nikolayevna made tea. Still trembling – it was cold in her room – she started criticizing the choir which had sung in the Ninth Symphony. Her eyes closed from weariness and she drank one glass of tea, then another, then a third.

'So, you're married,' she said. 'Don't worry, though, I shan't start moping. I'll manage to tear you out of my heart. But I'm annoyed.

It hurts me to discover you're a lousy rotter like everyone else, that it's not a woman's mind and intellect you need, but her body, her beauty, her youth . . . Youth, youth!' she said through her nose as if mimicking someone, and she laughed. 'You need purity, *Reinheit*!'[19] she added amid loud peals of laughter, leaning back in her chair. '*Reinheit!*'

When she had finished laughing her eyes were full of tears. 'Are you happy at least?' she asked.

'No.'

'Does she love you?'

'No.'

Upset and miserable, Laptev got up and paced the room. 'No,' he repeated. 'If you really want to know, Polina, I'm very unhappy. But what can I do? That was a silly thing I did and I can't repair the damage now. I must be philosophical about it. She didn't marry for love. It was stupid of her, perhaps. She married me for my money, but without thinking. Now she clearly realizes how wrong she was and she's suffering for it. That's painfully obvious. At night we sleep together, but during the day she's scared of staying alone with me for five minutes. She's looking for entertainment, some social life. She's ashamed and scared when she's with me.'

'But she takes your money all the same, doesn't she?'

'Don't be silly, Polina,' Laptev shouted. 'She takes money because she couldn't care less whether she has any or not. She's an honest, high-principled person. She married me simply to get away from her father, that's all.'

'But are you sure that she would have married you if you hadn't been rich?' Rassudina asked.

'I'm not sure about anything,' Laptev replied wearily. 'I don't understand a thing. For God's sake, Polina, let's not talk about it.'

'Do you love her?'

'Madly.'

Silence followed. She drank a fourth glass, while he kept pacing the room, thinking that his wife was probably, at that moment, having supper at the Doctors' Club.

'But is it possible to love not knowing why?' Polina asked,

shrugging her shoulders. 'No, it's the animal passion in you. You're intoxicated, you're poisoned by that beautiful body, by that *Reinheit*! Leave me, you're filthy! Go to her!'

She waved him away, picked up his hat and threw it at him. Silently, he put on his fur coat and left, but she ran into the hall, feverishly grabbed hold of the upper part of his arm and burst into sobs.

'Stop it, Polina, that's enough!' he said, unable to unclench her fingers. 'Please calm down!'

She closed her eyes and turned pale; her long nose took on the nasty waxen colour of a corpse. And still Laptev couldn't unclench her fingers. She had fainted. Carefully, he lifted her, laid her on the bed and sat by her side for about ten minutes until she came round. Her hands were cold, her pulse weak and irregular.

'Go home,' she said, opening her eyes. 'Go home, or I'll start howling again. I must take a grip on myself.'

After leaving her he did not go to the Doctors' Club, where they were expecting him, but straight home. All the way he kept reproaching himself with the question: why had he settled down with another woman instead of this one, who loved him so much, who was his real wife and true friend? She was the only person at all attached to him. And besides, wouldn't it have been a rewarding, worthy undertaking to bring happiness and quiet sanctuary to this clever, proud, overworked woman? That longing for beauty, youth and impossible happiness which seemed to be punishing or mocking him by keeping him in a dreadful state of depression for three months – was that in character? The honeymoon was long over and he still didn't know what kind of person his wife really was, which was quite ludicrous. She penned long letters, on five sheets of paper, to her old boarding-school friends and her father, so there was plenty to write about, in fact. But all she could find to talk to him about was the weather, that it was time for lunch or supper. When she took a long time over her prayers before going to bed and then kissed her nasty little crosses and icons, he would look at her with loathing and think: 'There she is praying, but what, what is she praying about?' He was insulting the two of them by telling himself – when he went to bed with her and took her in his arms – that he was only getting what he was paying for. That was a shocking thought. If she'd been a healthy, uninhibited, loose woman it wouldn't have mattered. But here was youth, religious devotion, gentleness, those pure, innocent eyes. When they had become engaged he had been touched by her religious faith, but now the conventional, definitive nature of her views and convictions was a barrier between him and the truth. His whole domestic life was sheer hell now. When his wife sighed or laughed heartily as she sat by him in the theatre, he was embittered by her enjoying herself on her own, by her reluctance to share her pleasure with him. Remarkably, she had got on well with all his friends. All of them knew the kind of person she was, whereas he did not. All he could do was mope and feel jealous without saying anything about it.

When he arrived home Laptev put on his dressing-gown and slippers and sat down in his study to read a novel. His wife was out, but barely half an hour passed before he heard the bell ring in the hall, and then the hollow patter of Pyotr's footsteps as he ran to open the door. It was Julia. She entered the study in her fur coat and her cheeks were red from the frost.

'There's a big fire at Presnya,'[20] she said, gasping for breath. 'The glow is really enormous. I'm going there with Kostya Kochevoy.'

'Good luck, then.'

Her fresh, healthy look and the childlike fear in her eyes calmed Laptev. He read for another half hour and then went to bed.

Next day Polina Nikolayevna sent two books she had once borrowed from him to the warehouse, and all his letters and photographs, together with a note consisting of one word: *basta*.[21]

VIII

At the end of October, Nina Fyodorovna had a pronounced relapse. She was rapidly losing weight and her face was changing. Despite the severe pain she imagined that she was recovering and every morning she dressed herself as if she was well and then lay in bed the whole day in her clothes. Towards the end she had become very talkative. She would lie on her back and after a great effort managed to talk quietly, gasping the whole time.

She died suddenly, in the following circumstances.

It was a bright, moonlit night. Out in the street people were riding in sleighs over the fresh snow, and the noises from outside drifted into the room. Nina Fyodorovna was lying in bed, on her back, while Sasha, who had no one to take her place, was sitting nearby dozing.

'I can't remember his second name,' Nina Fyodorovna said softly, 'but his Christian name was Ivan and his surname Kochevoy. He was a poor clerk, a terrible drunkard, God rest his soul. He used to call on us and every month we'd give him a pound of sugar and a few ounces of tea. Of course, we gave him money too. Yes . . . Well now, this is what happened after that. Kochevoy hit the bottle really hard and he popped off – it was vodka that finished him. He left a son, a little seven-year-old. That poor little orphan! We took him in and hid him in the clerks' place and he managed to get by a whole year without Father finding out. But the moment Father saw him he dismissed him with a wave of the arm and said nothing. When Kostya, this poor little orphan, was eight – I was engaged then – I tried to get him into high school. I took him here, there and everywhere, but they just wouldn't accept him. He wouldn't stop crying. "You silly little boy, why are you crying?" I asked. I took him to the Second High School on Razgulyay Square[22] and there, God bless them, they accepted him. Every day the little lad would walk from Pyatnitsky Street to Razgulyay Square and back. Aleksey paid his fees. Thank God, the boy was good at his work, very quick to learn, so everything turned out all right in the end. Now he's a lawyer in Moscow and a friend of Aleksey's. They're both of them very bright. We didn't turn our noses up at him, we took him in, and now he's surely mentioning us in his prayers. Oh, yes . . .'

Nina Fyodorovna began to speak more and more softly, with long pauses. Then, after one brief silence, she suddenly lifted herself up in bed. 'Mm . . . I don't feel so good,' she said. 'Oh God, I just can't breathe!'

Sasha knew that her mother was soon going to die. When she saw how her face had sunk she guessed that this was the end and she panicked.

'Mama, please don't!' she sobbed. 'Please don't!'

'Run into the kitchen and tell them to send for your father. I feel really shocking.'

Sasha tore through every room in the house calling out, but not one of the servants was in. Only Lida was there, and she was sleeping in her clothes, without any pillow, on a chest in the dining-room. Just as she was, without galoshes, Sasha ran into the yard, then out into the street. Her nanny was sitting on a bench outside the gate watching the sleighs drive past. From the river, where there was a skating-rink, came the sound of a military band.

'Nanny, Mama's dying!' sobbed Sasha. 'We must fetch Papa.' Nanny went upstairs to the bedroom, took one look at the sick woman and thrust a lighted wax candle into her hand. Sasha was horrified and rushed around begging someone – anyone – to go and fetch Father. Then she put on her coat and scarf and ran into the street. The servants had told her that her father had another wife and two little children with whom he was living in Market Street. At the gate she ran to the left, weeping and terrified of the strange people. Soon she was sinking into the snow and shivering with cold.

An empty cab came along but she didn't take it. Perhaps the driver would take her right out of town, rob her and throw her into the cemetery – the servants had spoken of such things over tea. She walked on and on, exhausted, gasping for breath and sobbing. When she came out on to Market Street she asked where Mr Panaurov lived. Some woman she didn't know gave her lengthy directions, but seeing that she didn't understand a thing took her by the hand and led her to a one-storey house with a porch. The door wasn't locked. Sasha ran through the hall, across a corridor, until finally she found herself in a bright warm room where her father was sitting by a samovar with a lady and two little girls. But by now she was unable to produce one word and all she did was sob. Panaurov understood.

'Mother's ill, isn't she?' he asked. 'Tell me, Mother's not well then?'

He grew alarmed and sent for a cab.

When they reached the house Nina Fyodorovna was sitting surrounded by pillows, candle in hand. Her face had grown dark, her eyes were closed. Nanny, cook, the chambermaid, the peasant Prokofy and some other ordinary working folk she didn't know crowded at the door. Nanny was whispering some orders which no one understood. Looking pale and sleepy, Lida was standing at the other end of the room by the window, grimly eyeing her mother.

Panaurov took the candle from Nina's hands, frowned disgustedly and flung it behind the chest of drawers.

'This is dreadful!' he said, his shoulders trembling. 'Nina, you must lie down,' he said tenderly. 'Please lie down, dear.'

She looked at him without recognizing him. They laid her back on the bed. When the priest and Dr Sergey Borisych arrived, the servants were devoutly crossing themselves and saying prayers for the dead.

'A fine thing!' the doctor remarked thoughtfully as he came out into the drawing-room. 'She was so young, not yet forty.'

The loud sobbing of the little girls was heard. Pale-faced, with moist eyes, Panaurov went up to the doctor and said in a weak, lifeless voice, 'My dear man, please do me a favour and send a telegram to Moscow. I'm just not up to it at the moment.'

The doctor obtained some ink and wrote the following telegram to his daughter: NINA PANAUROV DIED 8 PM TELL HUSBAND HOUSE ON DVORYANSKY STREET FOR SALE WITH TRANSFERABLE MORTGAGE STOP BALANCE NINE THOUSAND TO PAY AUCTION ON TWELFTH ADVISE NOT TO MISS OPPORTUNITY.

IX

Laptev lived on one of the side-streets off Little Dmitrovka Street,[23] not far from Old St Pimen's Church.[24] Besides that large house facing the street, he rented a two-storey lodge in the courtyard for his friend Kochevoy, a junior barrister called simply Kostya by the Laptevs, as they had all seen him grow up. Opposite the lodge was another, also with two storeys, where a French family lived – husband, wife and five daughters.

It was twenty degrees below freezing and the windows were frosted over. When he woke up in the mornings, Kostya would drink fifteen drops of medicine with an anxious look, then he would take two dumb-bells from a book-case and do his exercises. He was tall and very thin, with a large reddish moustache, but the most striking thing about him was the exceptional length of his legs.

Pyotr, a middle-aged handyman, in a jacket and with cotton trousers tucked into his high boots, brought in the samovar and made the tea.

'Very fine weather it is we're 'aving, Konstantin Ivanych,' he said.

'Yes, very fine it is, only it's a pity you and I aren't coping too well, old chap.'

Pyotr sighed out of politeness.

'What are the girls doing?' Kochevoy asked.

'The priest 'asn't come. Aleksey Fyodorych's teaching them 'imself.'

Kostya found a part of the window free of ice and looked through his binoculars, directing them at the French family's windows.

'Can't see them,' he said.

Just then Aleksey Fyodorych was giving Sasha and Lida a scripture lesson downstairs. They had been living in Moscow for about six weeks with their governess, on the ground floor of the lodge, and three times a week a priest and a teacher from a municipal school came to give them lessons. Sasha was studying the New Testament, while Lida had recently started the Old. At the last lesson Lida had been asked to revise everything up to Abraham.

'So, Adam and Eve had two sons,' Laptev said. 'Good, but what were their names? Please try and remember.'

Grim-faced as ever, Lida gazed silently at the table and just moved her lips. But her elder sister Sasha peered into her face and suffered torments.

'You know it very well, only you mustn't be so nervous,' Laptev said. 'Well now, what were Adam's sons called?'

'Abel and Cabel,' Lida whispered.

'Cain and Abel,' Laptev corrected.

A large tear trickled down Lida's cheek and dropped on to the book. Sasha looked down and blushed, on the verge of tears too. Laptev didn't have the heart to say anything and he gulped back the tears. He got up from the table and lit a cigarette. Just then Kochevoy came down with a newspaper. The little girls stood up and curtsied without looking at him.

'For heaven's sake, Kostya, *you* try and teach them,' Laptev said. 'I'm afraid I'll burst out crying as well and I must call at the warehouse before lunch.'

'All right.'

Aleksey Fyodorych left. Frowning, with a very serious expression, Kostya sat at the table and drew the Bible over to him. 'Well,' he asked, 'what are you doing now?'

'She knows all about the Flood,' Sasha said.

'The Flood? Good, we'll give that a good bash then. Let's do the Flood.'

Kostya ran through the brief account of the Flood in the Bible and said, 'I must point out that no flood like this ever took place. And there wasn't any Noah. Several thousand years before Christ was born there was an extraordinary inundation of the earth which is mentioned not only in the Hebrew Bible, but also in the books of other ancient peoples such as the Greeks, Chaldees and Hindus. No matter what kind of inundation this may have been, it couldn't have flooded the whole earth. Okay, the plains were flooded, but the mountains remained, you can be sure of that. Carry on reading your little book if you like, but don't put too much faith in it.'

Lida's tears flowed again. She turned away and suddenly started sobbing so loudly that Kostya shuddered and rose from his chair in great confusion.

'I want to go home,' she said. 'To Papa and Nanny.'

Sasha cried too. Kostya went up to his room and telephoned Julia Sergeyevna. 'The girls are crying again, my dear. It's quite impossible!'

Julia Sergeyevna came running across from the main house, just in her dress and with a knitted scarf. Half-frozen, she comforted the girls.

'Believe me, you must believe me,' she pleaded, pressing first one, then the other to her. 'Your Papa *is* coming today, he's sent a telegram. You're sad about your Mama. So am I. My heart is breaking. But what can one do? You can't go against what God has willed!'

When they had stopped crying, she wrapped them up and took them for a cab ride. First they drove down Little Dmitrovka Street, then past Strastnoy Boulevard[25] to the Tver Road. They stopped at the Iverian Chapel[26] and each of them placed a candle there and knelt in prayer. On the way back they called at Filippov's[27] and bought some lenten poppy-seed rolls.

The Laptevs usually had lunch between two and three, with Pyotr serving at table. During the day this same Pyotr would run errands to the post office, then to the warehouse, or the local court for Kostya, and helped out with lots of jobs. In the evening he packed cigarettes, at night he would run back and forwards to open the door, and after four o'clock in the morning would see to the stoves: no one knew when he actually slept. He loved opening bottles of soda water, which he did easily, noiselessly, without spilling a drop.

'Cheers!' Kostya said, drinking a glass of vodka before his soup.

Julia Sergeyevna had at first taken a dislike to Kostya, his deep voice, the crude expressions he would come out with, such as 'clear off', 'sock on the jaw', 'dregs of humanity', 'ginger up the samovar', as well as his habit of waxing sentimental after vodka. All of it seemed so trite. But after she knew him better she began to feel much more at ease with him. He was quite open with her, loved a quiet talk in the evenings, and even let her borrow novels that he had written himself and which up to now had been kept a complete secret – even from friends like Laptev and Yartsev. She would read and praise them in order not to upset him, which pleased him, since he had aspirations of becoming a famous writer – sooner or later. He wrote only about the countryside and manor houses, although he saw the country very seldom, when he was visiting friends in their holiday villas. Only once in his life had he stayed on a country estate, when he had gone to Volokolamsk[28] on some legal business. Avoiding any love interest, as if ashamed of it, he filled his novels with nature descriptions and showed a great partiality for expressions such as 'the hills' intricate outlines', 'quaint shapes of clouds' and 'chord of mysterious harmonies'. No one published his novels, for which he blamed the censorship.

He liked being a barrister, but he considered novels, not legal work, his true vocation in life. He felt that he possessed a subtle, artistic make-up and constantly felt drawn to the fine arts. He didn't sing, nor did he play an instrument, and he had no ear at all for music. However, he went to all the symphony and philharmonic concerts, organized charity performances and kept company with singers.

During lunch they talked. 'It's really amazing,' Laptev said. 'My brother Fyodor's completely stumped me again! He says we must find out when our firm's going to celebrate its centenary, so that we can apply to become gentlefolk. He's really serious! What's happening to him? To be honest, it worries me.'

They discussed Fyodor and the current fashion for self-dramatization. Fyodor, for example, was trying to act the simple merchant, although he wasn't one any more, and when the teacher came from the school (where old Laptev was a governor) for his salary, he would even alter his walk and speech, behaving as if he were the teacher's superior officer.

After lunch there was nothing to do, so they went into the study. They discussed the Decadent Movement and the *Maid of Orleans*.[29] Kostya delivered a whole monologue and felt that he gave a very good imitation of Marya Yermolov.[30] Then they sat down to cards. The little girls didn't return to the lodge. Instead, they sat there, pale-faced and sad, in the same armchair, listening to the street noises and trying to hear if their father was coming. They felt miserable in the dark evenings, when candles were alight. The conversation over cards, Pyotr's footsteps, the crackle in the fireplace – all this irritated them and they didn't want to look at the fire. In the evenings they didn't even feel like crying, and were uneasy and heavy at heart. They couldn't understand how people could talk and laugh when Mother had died.

'What did you see today through your binoculars?' Julia Sergeyevna asked Kostya.

'Nothing. But yesterday the old Frenchman himself took a bath.'

At seven o'clock Julia Sergeyevna and Kostya went off to the Maly Theatre. Laptev stayed behind with the girls.

'It's time your father was here,' he said, glancing at his watch. 'The train must be late.'

The girls sat silently in the chair, snuggling close to each other like tiny animals feeling the cold, while Laptev kept pacing the rooms, looking impatiently at his watch. The house was quiet, but just before nine someone rang the bell. Pyotr went to open the door.

When they heard that familiar voice the girls shrieked, burst out sobbing and ran into the hall. Panaurov was wearing a splendid fur coat and his beard and moustache were white with frost.

'Just a moment, just a moment,' he muttered while Sasha and Lida, sobbing and laughing, kissed his cold hands, his cap, his fur coat.

A handsome, languid sort of man who had been spoilt by love, he unhurriedly caressed the girls and went into the study. Rubbing his hands he said, 'It's only a brief visit, my dear friends. Tomorrow I'm off to St Petersburg. I've been promised a transfer to another city.'

He was staying at the Dresden Hotel.[31]

X

Ivan Gavrilych Yartsev was a frequent visitor at the Laptevs'. He was a sturdy, strongly-built, black-haired man with a clever, pleasant face. People thought him handsome, but recently he'd put on weight, which spoilt his face and figure, as did the way he had his hair cut very short, almost to the scalp. At one time his fellow-students at university called him 'Muscle Man', on account of his strength and powerful build.

He had graduated from the arts faculty together with the Laptev brothers and had then changed to science; he had a master's degree in chemistry. Without any aspirations to a professorship, he had never been a laboratory assistant even, but taught physics and zoology at a boys' secondary school and at two high schools for girls. Thrilled with his students – especially the girls – he used to say that a remarkable generation was growing up. Besides chemistry, he also studied sociology and Russian history at home and his short papers were sometimes published in newspapers and learned journals under the signature 'Ya'. Whenever he talked about botany or zoology, he resembled a historian; when he was trying to settle some historical problem, he looked like a scientist.

Kish, who was nicknamed the 'eternal student', was also a close friend of the Laptevs. He had studied medicine for three years, then had changed to mathematics, taking two years for each year of the course. His father, a provincial pharmacist, sent him forty roubles a month, and his mother (unbeknown to the father) sent him ten. This money sufficed for everyday expenses and was even enough for luxuries such as an overcoat with Polish beaver trimmings, gloves, scent and photography – he often had his portrait done and sent copies around to his friends. Neat, slightly balding, with golden whiskers around the ears, he was a modest man, who always seemed ready to oblige. He was forever helping others, running round collecting subscriptions, freezing at dawn outside a theatre box-office to buy a ticket for a lady friend. Or he would go and order a wreath or bouquet at someone's command. All one heard about him was: 'Kish will fetch it', or 'Kish will do it', or 'Kish will buy it'. He usually made a mess of the errands, for which he was showered with reproaches. People often forgot to pay him for purchases. But he never said a word, and in particularly ticklish situations all he would do was sigh. He was never very pleased, never annoyed and he was always telling long, boring stories: his jokes invariably made people laugh, but only because they weren't at all funny. Once, for example, trying to be witty, he told Pyotr, 'You are not a sturgeon.'[32] Everyone burst out laughing and he himself couldn't stop laughing, so pleased he was with his highly successful joke. At professors' funerals he liked walking in front, with the torch-bearers.

Yartsev and Kish usually came over for tea in the afternoon. If the master and mistress weren't going out to the theatre or a concert the tea would drag on until supper-time. One evening in February the following conversation took place in the dining-room:

'Works of art are only significant and useful when they are concerned with some serious social problem,' Kostya said, angrily looking at Yartsev. 'If there's some protest against serfdom in a book, or if the author takes up arms against high society and all its vulgarity, then that work is significant and useful. But novels and short stories which contain nothing but moaning and groaning, about her falling in love with him, or him falling out of love with her – I maintain those types of work are worthless and to hell with them.'

'I agree with you, Konstantin Ivanych,' Julia Sergeyevna said. 'One writer will describe a lover's assignation, another a betrayal, another a meeting after separation. Surely there are other things to write about, aren't there? There's lots of sick, unhappy, wretchedly poor people who must feel revolted when they read all that stuff.'

Laptev didn't like it when his wife, a young woman, not yet twenty-two, argued so seriously, so coolly, about love. But he guessed the reason for it.

'If poetry doesn't solve problems that strike you as important,' Yartsev said, 'then you'd better turn to technical books, to criminal and financial law. You should read scientific papers. There's no point at all in *Romeo and Juliet* containing discussions about freedom of education or disinfecting prisons if you can find it all in specialized articles or reference books.'

'But that's going too far, old chap,' Kostya interrupted. 'We're not discussing giants like Shakespeare or Goethe, we're talking about a hundred or so talented or less talented writers who'd be a lot more use if they steered clear of love and concentrated on bringing knowledge and humane ideals to the masses.'

Talking slightly through his nose and burring his r's, Kish began to relate the plot of a story he had recently read. He gave a detailed account and took his time. Three minutes passed, then five, then ten, but he rambled on and on, and no one had the faintest idea what he was talking about. His face became more and more apathetic, his eyes grew dim.

Julia Sergeyevna could stand it no longer and said, 'Come on, Kish, make it short! It's sheer torment!'

'Pack it in, Kish,' Kostya shouted.

Everyone laughed – including Kish.

In came Fyodor. He had red blotches on his face. Hurriedly, he greeted them all and led his brother into the study. Recently he had been avoiding large gatherings, preferring the company of just one person.

'Let those young people laugh, you and I must have a heart-to-heart,' he said, settling into a deep armchair away from the lamp. 'When were you last in the warehouse? I should think it must be a week now.'

'Yes, there's nothing for me to do and I must confess I'm sick and tired of the old man.'

'Of course, they can cope without you and me in the warehouse, but you must have some sort of occupation. "In the sweat of thy face[33] shalt thou eat bread" as it is said. God likes hard-working people.'

Pyotr brought in a glass of tea on a tray. Fyodor drank it without sugar and asked for some more. He liked to drink a lot of tea and could polish off ten glasses in an evening.

'Do you know what, old man?' he said, getting up and going over to his brother. 'Why don't you just stand as candidate for the city council? We'll gradually get you on to the board and after that you'll be deputy mayor. The further you go, the bigger you'll be. You're an intelligent, educated man. They'll take notice of you, they'll invite you to St Petersburg. Local and municipal officials are in fashion there now. Before you know it you'll be a privy councillor with a ribbon over your shoulder – before you're fifty.'

Laptev didn't reply. He realized that Fyodor himself had set his heart on promotion to privy councillor, on wearing a ribbon, and he was at a loss for an answer.

The brothers sat in silence. Fyodor opened his watch and scrutinized it for an interminably long time, as if he wanted to check that the hands were moving correctly. His expression struck Laptev as peculiar.

They were called in to supper. Laptev entered the dining-room, while Fyodor remained in the study. The argument had finished and Yartsev was speaking like a professor delivering a lecture.

'Because of differences of climate, energy, tastes and age, equality among people is a physical impossibility. But civilized man can render this inequality harmless, just as he has done with swamps and bears. One scientist has succeeded in getting a cat, a mouse, a falcon and a sparrow to eat from the same bowl. So we can only hope that education can achieve the same with human beings. Life is forever marching on, we are witnesses to the great progress that culture is making, and obviously the time will come when the present condition of factory workers, for example, will strike us as just as absurd as serfdom – when girls were exchanged for dogs – does now.'

'That won't be soon, all that's a long way off,' Kostya laughed. 'It'll be a long time before Rothschild will think that his vaults with all their gold are absurd and until then the worker will have to bend his back and starve till his belly swells. No, old man, we mustn't stand doing nothing, we must fight. If a cat eats from the same saucer as a mouse would you say it does it from a sense of community? Never. Because it was *forced* to.'

'Fyodor and I are rich, our father's a capitalist, a millionaire, so it's *us* you have to fight!' Laptev said, wiping his forehead with his palm. 'A battle against myself – that's what I find so hard to accept! I'm rich, but what has money given me up to now? What has this power brought me? In what way am I happier than you? My childhood was sheer purgatory and money never saved me from birching. Money didn't help Nina when she fell ill and was dying. If I'm not loved I can't force anyone to love me, even if I were to spend a hundred million.'

'On the other hand you can do a lot of good,' Kish said.

'What do you mean by *good*? Yesterday you asked me to help some musician looking for work. Believe me, I can do as little for him as you can. I can give him money, but that's not what he's after, is it? Once I asked a well-known musician to find a position for an impecunious violinist and all he said was, "You only turned to *me* for help because you're not a musician yourself." So I'm offering you the same answer: you feel so confident when you ask me for help precisely because you've never known what it's like to be rich yourself.'

'But why this comparison with a famous musician?' Julia said, blushing. 'What's a famous musician got to do with it?'

Her face quivered with rage and she lowered her eyes to hide her feelings. However, her expression was understood not only by her husband, but by everyone sitting at the table.

'What's a famous musician got to do with it?' she repeated softly. 'There's nothing easier than helping the poor.'

Silence followed. Pyotr served hazel-grouse. No one ate any, however – they just had some salad. Now Laptev couldn't remember what he'd said, but he saw quite clearly that it wasn't his words that made her hate him, but the mere fact that he had joined in the conversation.

After supper he went to his study. His heart pounded as he listened – very tensely – to what was happening in the drawing-room, and he anticipated fresh humiliations. Another argument started. Then Yartsev sat at the piano and sang a sentimental song. He was jack-of-all-trades – he could sing, play and even do conjuring tricks.

'Please yourself what you do, gentlemen, but I don't want to stay at home,' Julia said. 'Let's go for a drive.'

They decided to drive out of town and sent Kish to the Merchants' Club[34] for a troika. Laptev wasn't invited, as he hardly ever went on such trips and because he had his brother with him. But he took it that they found him boring and that he was completely out of place among that cheerful, young crowd. He was so annoyed and bitter he almost wept. He even felt pleased that they were being so nasty to him, that he was despised, that he was looked upon as a stupid, boring husband, as an old moneybags. He would have been even more pleased, he felt, if his wife were to betray him that night with his best friend and admit it with loathing in her eyes . . . He was jealous of the students, actors and singers she knew, of Yartsev – even of chance acquaintances – and he dearly longed for her to be unfaithful now. He wanted to surprise her with someone, then poison himself to rid himself of the nightmare for good.

Fyodor gulped his tea noisily and then he too started leaving.

'There's something wrong with the old man,' he said, putting on his fur coat. 'His eyesight's very poor.'

Laptev put on his coat too and left. After seeing his brother as far as Strastnoy Boulevard he took a cab to Yar's[35] restaurant.

'And they call this domestic bliss!' he said, laughing at himself. 'This is supposed to be love.'

His teeth were chattering – whether from jealousy or something else he didn't know. At Yar's he walked up and down by the tables and listened to a ballad singer in the ballroom. He didn't have one sentence ready in case he should meet his wife or friends and was convinced in advance that if she did happen to turn up he would only smile pathetically and stupidly – then everyone would understand what kind of feeling had compelled him to come here. The electric lights, the loud music, the smell of powder, those staring women – all this made his head go round. He stopped by the doors, trying to spy and overhear what was going on in the private rooms: he felt that he was acting in concert with that singer and those women, playing some vile, despicable role. Then he went on to the Strelna,[36] but met none of his friends there either. Only when he was on his way home and approaching Yar's restaurant again did a troika noisily overtake him – the drunken coachman was shouting and he could hear Yartsev's loud guffaws.

Laptev returned home after three in the morning. Julia Sergeyevna was in bed, but when he saw that she wasn't sleeping he went over and snapped, 'I can understand your revulsion, your hatred. But you might have spared me before strangers, you might have tried to hide your feelings.'

She sat up in bed, her legs dangling. In the lamplight her eyes were large and black.

'Please forgive me,' she said.

He couldn't say one word for agitation and trembling, and he stood silently in front of her. She too was trembling and she sat there like a criminal waiting to be charged.

'This is sheer torture!' he said at last, clutching his head. 'I seem to be in hell. I feel I've gone mad!'

'And do you think it's easy for *me*?' she asked, her voice shaking. 'God only knows how *I* feel.'

'You've been my wife for six months, but there's no spark of love in your heart, no hope of any – not even a glimmer! Why did you marry me?' Laptev continued despairingly. 'Why? What demon drove you into my arms? What were you hoping for? What did you want?'

She looked at him in horror, as if frightened he might kill her.

'Did you ever like me? Did you ever love me?' he gasped. 'No! Then what was it? Tell me, *what*?' he shouted. 'Yes, it was that damned money!'

'I swear to God it wasn't!' she cried and crossed herself. The insult made her wince and for the first time he heard her cry. 'I swear to God it wasn't!' she repeated. 'I wasn't thinking about money, I don't need any. I simply thought that it would be nasty of me to refuse you. I was afraid of spoiling your life and mine. And now I'm suffering for my mistake, suffering unbearably!'

She sobbed bitterly. Not knowing what to say and realizing how painful everything was for her, he sank before her on the carpet.

'Please don't. Please don't!' he muttered. 'I insulted you because I love you madly.' Suddenly he kissed her foot and passionately embraced her. 'All I want is just one spark of love!' he said. 'Well, tell me lies! Don't say it was a mistake!'

But she went on crying and he felt that she was only putting up with his caresses because they were the unavoidable consequence of her mistake. Like a bird she drew in beneath her that foot he had kissed. He felt sorry for her.

She lay down and covered herself with the blanket. He undressed and lay down as well. In the morning they both felt awkward – neither knew what to talk about. He even had the impression that she was treading unsteadily with the foot he had kissed.

Before lunch Panaurov dropped in to say goodbye. Julia had an irresistible urge to go back home to her native town. It would be nice to leave, she thought, to have a rest from married life, from all this embarrassment, from the ever-present awareness of having behaved badly. Over lunch they decided that she should leave with Panaurov and stay with her father for two or three weeks, until she got bored.

XI

Panaurov and Julia travelled in a private railway compartment. He was wearing a rather odd lambskin cap.

'Yes, St Petersburg was a letdown,' he sighed, speaking slowly and deliberately. 'They promise you a lot, but nothing definite. Yes, my dear, I've been Justice of the Peace, a Permanent Secretary, President of the Court of Appeal and finally adviser to the district council. I think I've served my country and have a right to some attention. But would you believe it, there's just no way I can get a transfer to another town.'

Panaurov closed his eyes and shook his head. 'They won't recognize me,' he continued and he seemed to be dozing off. 'Of course, I'm no administrative genius, but on the other hand I'm a respectable, honest man and even that's quite rare these days. I must admit I've deceived women just a little, but I've always been a perfect gentleman in my relations with the Russian government. But enough of that,' he added, opening his eyes. 'Let's talk about you. What made you suddenly want to go and visit your dear papa?'

'I'm not getting on very well with my husband,' Julia said, glancing at his cap.

'Yes, he's a queer fish. All the Laptevs are weird. Your husband's not so bad really, he'll pass. But that brother of his, Fyodor, is a real idiot.'

Panaurov sighed and asked seriously, 'And do you have a lover?'

Julia looked at him in astonishment and laughed. 'Good God, what a thing to ask!'

After ten, at some large station, they both got out and had supper. When the train moved off Panaurov took off his coat and cap and sat next to Julia.

'You're very nice, I must say,' he began. 'Pardon the pub simile, but you put me in mind of a freshly salted gherkin. It still has the smell of the hothouse, so to speak, but it's already a bit salty and smells of dill. You're gradually developing into a wonderful woman, so marvellous and refined. If this journey had taken place about five years ago,' he sighed, 'then I'd have considered it my pleasant duty to join the ranks of your admirers. But now, alas, I'm just an old pensioner.'

He gave her a smile that was at once sad and kind, and he put his arm around her waist.

'You're out of your mind!' she said, blushing. She was so frightened that her hands and feet went cold. 'Stop it, Grigory Nikolaich!'

'Why are you so scared, my dear?' he asked softly. 'What's so dreadful about it? You're just not used to this sort of thing.'

If a woman happened to protest, then for him that only meant that he had made a good impression and that she liked him. Holding Julia around the waist, he kissed her firmly on the cheek, then the lips, quite certain he was giving her great pleasure. Then Julia recovered from her fright and embarrassment and started laughing. He kissed her again and as he donned his comical cap he said, 'That's all an old campaigner can give you. There was a Turkish Pasha, a kind old man, who was once presented with – possibly as an inheritance – a whole harem. When his beautiful young wives paraded before him, he inspected them, saying as he kissed each one, "That's all I'm able to give you now." That's what I'm saying too.'

She thought all this stupid but unusual, and it cheered her up. Feeling rather playful, she stood on the seat humming, took a box of sweets from the luggage rack and shouted, 'Catch' as she threw him one.

He caught it. Laughing out loud, she threw him another, then a third, and he caught them all, popping them in his mouth and looking at her with imploring eyes.

She felt that there was much that was feminine and childlike about his face, features and expression. When she sat down, out of breath, and kept looking at him and laughing, he touched her cheek with two fingers and said in mock annoyance:

'You naughty little girl!'

'Take it,' she said, handing him the box. 'I don't like sweets.'

He ate the whole lot and then locked the empty box in his trunk – he loved boxes with pictures on them.

'Enough of this larking about,' he said. 'Time for bye-byes, for the old campaigner!'

He took his Bokhara dressing-gown and a cushion from a holdall, lay down and covered himself with the dressing-gown.

'Goodnight, my sweet!' he said softly, sighing as if his whole body were aching.

The sound of his snoring soon followed. Without feeling in the least inhibited she lay down too and was soon fast asleep.

Next morning, as she was driving home from the station in her native town, the streets seemed deserted and empty, the snow grey and the houses small, with a squashed look about them. She met a funeral procession – the body was in an open coffin, with banners.

'They say a funeral brings good luck,' she thought.

The windows of the house where Nina Fyodorovna had once lived had white posters stuck all over them.

Her heart sank as she drove into the yard and rang the doorbell. A strange, sleepy-looking maid in a warm quilted jacket opened the door. As she went upstairs Julia remembered that Laptev had declared his love there. But now the stairs were unwashed, with footmarks all over them. In the cold corridor on the first floor patients in fur coats were waiting. For some reason her heart pounded and she could barely walk for agitation.

The doctor – stouter than ever, red as a brick, his hair dishevelled – was drinking tea. He was delighted to see his daughter and even shed a few tears. She was his only joy, she thought. Deeply moved, she firmly embraced him and told him she would be staying for a long time, until Easter. After she had changed in her room she went into the dining-room to have tea with him. He kept pacing up and down, hands in pockets, humming away – this meant he was annoyed about something.

'You're having quite a gay time in Moscow,' he remarked. 'I'm so pleased for you, but an old man like me doesn't need anything. I'll soon peg out and free the lot of you. Aren't you amazed that I've such a tough skin, that I'm still in the land of the living! It's really amazing!'

He said that he was a robust old beast of burden, whom everyone liked to ride. He had been lumbered with Nina Fyodorovna's treatment, with looking after her children and taking care of the funeral: that dandified Panaurov just didn't want to know and had even borrowed a hundred roubles from him which, up to now, he hadn't returned.

'Take me to Moscow and put me in a lunatic asylum,' the doctor said. 'You must think I'm mad, a simple child, believing as I do in truth and justice!'

Then he reproached her husband with lack of foresight – he had failed to buy houses that were being offered at very favourable prices. And now Julia realized that she was no longer the old man's only joy. While he was receiving patients or on his rounds she roamed through the house, not knowing what to do or think. She had become a stranger in her home town, in her own house. She felt no urge to go out into the street, to call on old friends, and when she remembered her former girl friends and her life as a young girl she did not feel sad, nor did she regret the past.

In the evening she put on a smart dress and went to late service. But there was no one of importance in the church and her magnificent fur coat and hat were wasted there. She thought that both she and the church had undergone a transformation. In the past she had been fond of hearing the canon read out at vespers, when the choirboys sang hymns such as 'I Shall Open My Lips'. Once she had loved slowly moving with the congregation towards the priest who stood in the middle of the church and then feeling the holy oil on her forehead. But now she couldn't wait for the service to finish. As she left the church she felt frightened that beggars might approach her for money – rummaging through her pockets would have been a nuisance. In any case, she had no small change, only roubles.

She went early to bed but fell asleep very late, constantly dreaming of certain portraits and the funeral procession she had seen that morning. The open coffin with the corpse was borne into the yard, the bearers stopped at a door, rocked the coffin on some sheets for some time and then swung it against the door as hard as they could. Julia woke and jumped up in terror. Someone was in fact knocking on the downstairs door and the bell-wire was rustling along the wall, although she hadn't heard anyone ring.

The doctor coughed. After this she heard the maid going downstairs and coming back.

'Madam!' she exclaimed, knocking at the door.

'What is it?' Julia asked.

'It's a telegram!'

Julia went out with a candle. Behind the maid stood the doctor, his coat over his underclothes. He was also holding a candle.

'The bell's broken,' he yawned, half-asleep. 'It should have been repaired ages ago.'

Julia opened the telegram and read it.

WE DRINK YOUR HEALTH. YARTSEV, KOCHEVOY

'Oh, the idiots!' she said, laughing out loud.

She began to feel relaxed and cheerful.

Back in her room she quietly washed and dressed, and then spent a long time packing – right until dawn broke. At noon she set off for Moscow.

XII

During Easter week the Laptevs went to a painting exhibition at the School of Art.[37] The whole household went – in Moscow style – and both little girls, the governess and Kostya were taken along.

Laptev knew the names of all the famous artists and never missed an exhibition. During the summers at his country villa he sometimes painted landscapes himself, believing that he had superb taste and that he would have made an excellent painter had he studied. When abroad he sometimes dropped into antique shops, inspected their contents and expressed his opinion with the air of an expert. He would buy some object and the dealer would charge him as much as he liked. Subsequently, the piece would be stuffed into a box and lie in the coach-house until it disappeared no one knew where. Or he would call at a print shop, spend a long time carefully inspecting the prints and bronzes, make various remarks and then suddenly buy some cheap frame or box of worthless paper. All the pictures at home were of ample dimensions, but poorly painted. Those that were any good were badly hung. More than once he had paid dearly for what afterwards turned out to be crude forgeries. Strangely enough, although a timid person on the whole, he was particularly bumptious and outspoken at exhibitions. Why?

Julia Sergeyevna looked at the paintings in the same way as her husband, through parted fingers or opera glasses, and she was amazed that the people in them seemed so alive, the trees so real. But she didn't understand them and thought that many paintings at the exhibition were really identical and that the whole aim of art was making people and objects appear real when viewed through the fingers.

'This wood is a Shishkin,'[38] her husband explained. 'He always paints the same old thing . . . Just look, you'll never find snow as violet as that. And that boy's left arm is shorter than his right.'

When everyone was exhausted and Laptev had gone to look for Kostya, so that they could all go home, Julia stopped by a small landscape and looked at it rather indifferently. In the foreground was a small stream with a wooden bridge across it and a path disappearing into dark grass on the far bank. There were fields and a strip of wood on the right with a bonfire near it – horses were probably being pastured for the night over there. In the distance the sunset glow was dying . . .

Julia imagined herself crossing the bridge, then walking further and further down the path. It was quiet all around, sleepy landrails cried and a distant fire flickered. Suddenly she had the feeling that many times, long ago, she had seen those clouds stretching across the red sky, that wood, those fields. She felt lonely and wanted to go on and on, down that path. And there, near the sunset glow, lay the reflection of something unearthly and eternal.

'How well painted!' she exclaimed, amazed that she suddenly understood the picture. 'Look, Aleksey! See how calm it is!'

She tried to explain why she liked that landscape so much, but neither her husband nor Kostya understood. She continued looking at the painting, sadly smiling: she was upset at the others seeing nothing special in it. Then she went through the rooms again and looked at the paintings. She wanted to understand them. There no longer seemed to be so many identical pictures at the exhibition. When she was home she turned her attention (for the first time ever) to the large picture above the grand piano in the hall. It made her feel hostile.

'How can anybody want that sort of picture!' she said.

On top of that, the golden cornices, the Venetian mirrors with flowers, paintings like the one over the piano – all this, plus her husband's and Kostya's arguments about art, made her feel bored, irritable and sometimes even full of loathing.

Life ran its normal course, from day to day, and promised nothing special. The theatre season was over and warm days had arrived – the weather was always fine now. One morning the Laptevs went off to the local assizes to hear Kostya, who had been appointed by the court, defend someone. They had taken their time before leaving and arrived when the cross-examination of witnesses had already started. A soldier from the reserves was accused of burglary. Many of the witnesses were laundresses, who testified that the accused often visited their employer, the laundry proprietress. Late on the eve of the Exaltation of the Cross[39] this soldier had come to ask for money to buy himself a drink for the 'morning after', but no one gave him any. Then he had left, but returned an hour later with some beer and peppermint cakes for the girls. They drank and sang almost till dawn, but in the morning they noticed that the lock to the loft entrance had been broken and some linen was missing – three men's nightshirts, a skirt and two sheets. Kostya sarcastically asked each witness if she had drunk any of the beer that the accused had brought that night. He was obviously trying to make it look as if the laundresses had robbed their own laundry. He delivered his speech coolly, angrily eyeing the jury.

He explained burglary and petty larceny. He spoke in great detail and with conviction, displaying an outstanding talent for expatiating long and solemnly about what was common knowledge to everyone.

And it was difficult to make out what precisely he *was* getting at. The jurors were able to draw only the following conclusion from his lengthy speech: either there had been a burglary, but no petty larceny, since the money from the sale of the linen was spent by the laundresses on drink; or that there had been larceny, but no burglary. But Kostya was evidently on the right tack, since his speech deeply moved the jury and public and pleased everyone. Julia nodded to Kostya when an acquittal was brought and afterwards shook him firmly by the hand.

In May the Laptevs went to their villa at Sokolniki, as Julia was pregnant.

XIII

More than a year passed. At Sokolniki, not far from the main Yaroslavl[40] railway line, Julia and Yartsev were sitting on the grass. Kochevoy was lying nearby, his hands under his head, gazing up at the sky. All three had had enough of walking and were waiting for the six o'clock suburban train so that they could go home for tea.

'Mothers always think their children are exceptional, Nature's arranged it that way,' Julia said. 'A mother will stand by the cot for hours on end looking rapturously at her baby's tiny ears, eyes and nose. If some stranger kisses her baby the poor woman thinks this gives him the utmost pleasure. And mothers can talk of nothing but babies. I know that mothers tend to have this weakness and I'm guarding against it myself. But my Olga really *is* exceptional, honestly! The way she looks at me when she's feeding, the way she laughs! She's only eight months old, but I swear to you I've never seen such clever eyes, even in a three-year-old.'

'Incidentally, whom do you love more?' asked Yartsev. 'Your husband or your baby?'

Julia shrugged her shoulders. 'I don't know,' she said. 'I never felt deep affection for my husband and Olga's really my first love. You know I didn't marry Aleksey for love. I used to be stupid, I went through absolute hell and I couldn't stop thinking that I had ruined his life and mine. But I realize now that one doesn't need love, it's a lot of nonsense.'

'So, if it isn't love, then what kind of feeling attaches you to your husband? Why do you stay with him?'

'I don't know . . . Must be force of habit, I think. I respect him, I miss him when he's away for a long time, but that's not love. He's a clever, honest man and that's enough to make me happy. He's very kind and unpretentious . . .'

'Aleksey's clever, Aleksey's kind,' Kostya said, lazily raising his head. 'But you need to know him for ages before you ever find out that he's intelligent, kind and fascinating, my dear. And what's the use of his kindness or his brains? He'll stump up as much money as you want – he's capable of *that*. But when it comes to showing strength of character, seeing off some cheeky devil or smart aleck, then he fights shy and loses heart. Men like your dear Aleksey may be fine people, but they're absolutely useless in battle. Yes, they're actually fit for absolutely nothing.'

At last the train came into sight. Bright pink steam poured from its funnel and rose over the small patch of forest. Two windows in the last carriage suddenly flashed so brilliantly in the sun it hurt one's eyes.

'Teatime!' Julia Sergeyevna said, standing up.

She had recently put on weight and now she walked rather lazily, like a middle-aged lady.

'All the same, it's not much of a life without love,' Yartsev said, following her. 'We're always talking and reading about love, but we don't put it into practice – and that's a bad thing, I must say.'

'That's not important, Ivan,' Julia said. 'You won't find happiness there.'

They drank tea in the little garden, where mignonette, stocks and tobacco plants were in flower and early gladioli were opening out. From the expression on Julia Sergeyevna's face, Yartsev and Kochevoy could tell that this was a happy time of spiritual calm and equilibrium for her and that she needed nothing besides what she already possessed; they too began to feel relaxed, tranquil at heart.

Whatever one might think, things were turning out very well – just right, in fact. The pines were beautiful, the smell of resin was more wonderful than ever, the cream was delicious. Sasha was a clever, fine girl.

After tea Yartsev sang some sentimental songs, accompanying himself on the piano, while Julia and Kochevoy listened in silence – only Julia got up now and then and quietly left the room to have a look at the baby, and at Lida, who had had a temperature for two days and wasn't eating.

'"My dear, tender love",'[41] Yartsev sang. Then he shook his head and said, 'By the life of me I can't understand what you have against love. If I weren't busy fifteen hours a day I'd fall in love myself – no question about it.'

Supper was laid on the terrace. It was warm and quiet, but Julia wrapped herself in her shawl and complained of the damp. When it was dark she grew rather restless, kept shivering and asked her guests to stay on. She regaled them with wine and after supper had them served with brandy to stop them leaving. She didn't want to be on her own with the children and servants.

'We lady villa-dwellers are organizing a show for the children,' she said. 'We already have everything – theatre, actors. All that's missing is a play. We've been sent a score of different ones, but none is any good.' Turning to Yartsev she said, 'Now, you love the theatre and you're a history expert. Why don't you write a historical play for us?'

'All right.'

The guests finished all the brandy and prepared to leave. It was past ten, which was late for people in holiday villas.

'It's so dark, it's pitch-black,' Julia said, seeing them through the gate. 'I don't know how you'll find the way back, my friends. It's really *very* cold!'

She wrapped herself more tightly and went back to the porch.

'My Aleksey must be playing cards somewhere!' she exclaimed. 'Goodnight!'

After the bright lights in the house they couldn't see a thing. Yartsev and Kostya groped along like blind men until they reached the railway line, which they crossed.

'Can't see a damned thing!' Kostya said in a deep voice, stopping to gaze at the sky. 'Look at those stars – like new fifteen copeck pieces! Yartsev!!'

'What?' came back Yartsev's voice.

'I said I can't see a thing. Where are you?'

Whistling, Yartsev went up to him and took his arm.

'Hey, all you holiday-makers!' Kostya suddenly shouted at the top of his voice. 'We've caught a socialist!'

Whenever he'd had a few drinks he was boisterous, shouting and picking quarrels with policemen and cabbies, singing and laughing furiously.

'To hell with Nature!' he shouted.

'Now now,' Yartsev said, trying to calm him down. 'That's enough. *Please!*'

The friends soon grew used to the dark and began to make out the silhouettes of lofty pines and telegraph poles. Now and then whistles could be heard from railway stations in Moscow, and telegraph wires hummed mournfully. But no sound came from that patch of forest and there was something proud, strong and mysterious about the silence. And now, at night, the tops of the pines seemed almost to touch the sky. The friends found the correct cutting and went down it. Here it was pitch-black and only the long strip of star-strewn sky and the well-trodden earth beneath their feet told them that they were on the path. Silently they walked, side by side, both imagining that people were coming towards them. Yartsev had the idea that souls of Muscovite tsars, boyars and patriarchs might be wandering around the forest. He wanted to tell Kostya, but stopped himself.

When they reached the city gate dawn was just glimmering. Still without a word, Yartsev and Kochevoy walked down a road past cheap holiday villas, pubs and timber yards. Under the branch-line railway bridge they suddenly experienced a pleasant dampness, smelling of lime trees. Then a long, broad street opened up without a soul or light on it. When they reached Krasny Prud,[42] dawn was breaking.

'Moscow's a city that will have to go through a lot more suffering in the future!' Yartsev said, looking at the Alekseyev Monastery.

'What makes you think that?'

'I just do. I love Moscow.'

Both Yartsev and Kostya were born in Moscow and they adored it – for some reason they felt hostile towards other cities. They were convinced that Moscow was a remarkable city, and Russia a remarkable country. Away in the Crimea or the Caucasus, or abroad, they felt bored, uncomfortable, out of place, and their beloved Moscow's dreary grey weather was the most pleasant and healthy of all, they thought. Days when the cold rain beats on windows and dusk comes on early, when walls of houses and churches take on a sombre, brownish colour, when you don't know what to wear when you go out into the street – days like these pleasantly stimulated them. In the end they took a cab near the station.

'Actually, I'd like to write a historical play,' Yartsev said, 'but without all those Lyapunovs and Godunovs. I'd write about the times of Yaroslav or Monomakh. I hate all Russian historical plays, except for Pimen's soliloquy.[43] When you're dealing with some historical source or reading text books on Russian history, everything Russian appears so incredibly talented, competent and interesting. But when I see a historical play at the theatre, Russian life strikes me as inept, morbid and uninspiring.'

The friends parted at Dmitrovka Street and Yartsev drove on to his rooms in Nikitsky Street. He rocked to and fro, dozing, his whole mind on that play. Suddenly he imagined a terrible noise, clanging, shouts in some incomprehensible language – Kalmuck, most likely. There was a village engulfed in flames, and the nearby woods, covered in hoar frost and faint pink in the conflagration, could be so clearly seen for miles around that every little fir tree was distinguishable. Some wild savages, on horse and on foot, tore through the village: both they and their steeds were as crimson as the glow in the sky.

'They're Polovtsians,'[44] thought Yartsev.

One of them – old, bloody-faced and covered all over with burns – was tying a young, white-faced Russian girl to his saddle. The old man was ranting and raving, while the girl looked on with sad, intelligent eyes.

Yartsev shook his head and woke up.

'"My dear, tender love",' he chanted.

He paid the cab-driver and went up to his rooms, but he just couldn't return to reality and saw the flames spreading to the trees. The forest crackled and began to smoke. An enormous wild boar, maddened with fear, charged through the village. And the girl who was tied to the saddle was still watching.

It was light when Yartsev entered his rooms. Two candles were burning low on the piano, near some open music books. In a dark dress with a sash, a newspaper in her hands, Polina lay fast asleep on the couch. She must have been playing for some time waiting for Yartsev and fallen asleep.

'God, she looks worn out!' he thought.

Carefully removing the paper from her hands, he covered her with a rug, snuffed the candles and went to his bedroom. As he lay down he thought of that historical play and couldn't get that line – 'My dear, tender love' – out of his head.

Two days later Laptev dropped in for a moment to say that Lida had diphtheria and that Julia Sergeyevna and the baby had caught it from her. Five days later came the news that Lida and Julia were recovering, but that the baby had died and the Laptevs had dashed back to town from the villa at Sokolniki.

XIV

Laptev didn't like spending much time at home now. His wife often went over to the lodge, saying that she had to see to the girls' lessons. However, she didn't go there for that, but to cry at Kostya's. The ninth, twentieth, fortieth day passed and still he had to go to the St Alexis Cemetery[45] for requiem mass, after which he had a hellish twenty-four hours thinking only of that unfortunate baby and uttering various platitudes to console his wife. He seldom went to the warehouse now and busied himself solely with charitable work, inventing sundry little jobs or worries for himself, and he was delighted when he had to ride around the whole day on some trivial matter.

Recently he had been intending to go abroad to learn about organization of hostels for the poor and now this idea provided some diversion.

It was one day in autumn. Julia had just gone to the lodge to cry, while Laptev was lying on his study couch wondering where to go. Then Pyotr announced that Polina had arrived. Absolutely delighted, Laptev leapt up and went to greet his unexpected visitor, that former friend he had almost forgotten now. Since that evening when he had seen her last she hadn't changed at all.

'Polina!' he said, stretching out both hands. 'It's been so long! You just can't imagine how glad I am to see you. Welcome!'

Rassudina greeted him by tugging at his hand, entered the study and sat down without taking off her coat or hat.

'I've only dropped in for a minute, I've no time for chit-chat. Please sit down and listen. I couldn't care less whether you're pleased or not to see me, as I don't give a damn for the gracious attentions of members of the male sex. The reason I'm here now is that I've already called at five places today and was refused in every one of them. It's an urgent matter. Now, listen,' she added, looking him in the eye. 'Five students I know, all with limited brain-power, but indubitably poor, haven't paid their fees and have been expelled. Your wealth makes it incumbent on you to go to the university immediately and pay their fees for them.'

'With pleasure, Polina.'

'Here are their names,' Rassudina said, handing Laptev a note. 'You must go this minute, you can wallow in domestic bliss later.'

Just then came a vague rustling sound from behind the door into the drawing-room – it was most probably the dog scratching itself. Rassudina blushed and leapt to her feet. 'Your little Dulcinea's trying to eavesdrop,' she said. 'That's a rotten trick!'

Laptev felt insulted on Julia's behalf.

'She's not here, she's at the lodge,' he said. 'And don't talk about her like that. We've lost our baby and she's terribly depressed.'

'You can set her mind at rest,' Rassudina laughed, sitting down again. 'She'll have another dozen of them. You don't need brains to have babies!'[46]

Laptev remembered hearing this, or something similar, many times before, long ago, and he recaptured that idyllic past, his free bachelor life when he had felt young and capable of anything, when love for a wife and memories of a child just didn't exist for him.

'Let's go together,' he said, stretching himself.

When they reached the university Rassudina waited at the gates, while Laptev went to the bursar's office. After a short time he returned and handed Rassudina five receipts.

'Where are you off to now?' he asked.

'To see Yartsev.'

'I'm coming with you.'

'But you'll interrupt him in his work.'

'I won't, I assure you!' he replied, looking at her imploringly.

She was wearing a black mourning hat with crêpe trimmings, and a very short, shabby coat with bulging pockets. Her nose seemed longer than ever and her face had no colour, in spite of the cold. Laptev liked following and obeying her, and listening to her grumbling. On the way he reflected on the inner strength she must have if, despite her ugliness, clumsiness and restlessness, despite her lack of dress sense, despite her hair always being dishevelled and despite her rather ungainly figure, she was still a woman of great charm.

They made their way into Yartsev's rooms by the back door – through the kitchen, where they were welcomed by the cook, a neat old woman with grey curls. Deeply embarrassed, she smiled sweetly at them and this made her small face look like a piece of puff pastry.

'Please come in,' she said.

Yartsev was out. Rassudina sat at the piano and started some boring, difficult exercises, having instructed Laptev not to interrupt. He didn't distract her with conversation, but sat to one side leafing through the *European Herald*.[47] After practising for two hours – that was her daily stint – she ate something in the kitchen and went off to give some lessons. Laptev read an instalment of some novel, then sat there for some time, neither reading nor feeling bored, but pleased that he was already late for dinner at home.

'Ha, ha, ha!' he heard Yartsev laugh – and then the man himself came in. He was healthy, hearty, red-cheeked, and wore a new tailcoat with shiny buttons. 'Ha, ha, ha!'

The friends dined together. Then Laptev lay on the couch, while Yartsev sat near him and lit a cigar. Twilight fell.

'I must be getting old,' Laptev said. 'Since my sister Nina died I've taken to thinking about death, for some reason.'

They talked of death and immortality, about how lovely it would be if they were resurrected and then flew off to Mars or somewhere to enjoy eternal idleness and happiness – and, most of all, if they could think in some special, non-terrestrial way.

'But I don't want to die,' Yartsev said softly. 'No philosophy can reconcile me to death and I look upon it simply as destruction. I want to live.'

'Do you love life, old man?'

'Yes, I love life.'

'Well, in that respect I just can't make myself out. Gloomy moods alternate with apathetic ones. I'm timid, I've no self-confidence, I'm cowardly in matters of conscience, I cannot adapt to life at all or become master of it. Other people talk rubbish or behave like rogues – and with such gusto! As for me, sometimes I consciously perform good deeds, but in the event I experience only anxiety or complete indifference. My explanation for all this is that I'm a slave – a serf's grandson. Many of us rank and file will fall in battle before we find the right path.'

'That's all very well, dear man,' Yartsev sighed. 'It only goes to show yet again how rich and varied Russian life is. Yes, very rich! Do you know, every day I'm more convinced that we're on the threshold of some fantastic triumph. I'd like to survive till then and take part in it myself. Believe it or not, in my opinion a remarkable generation is growing up now. It's a pleasure teaching children, especially girls. Wonderful children!'

Yartsev went over to the piano and struck a chord.

'I'm a chemist,' he continued. 'I think like a chemist and I'll die a chemist. But I'm greedy, I'm afraid I'll die without having gorged myself. Chemistry alone isn't enough for me. I clutch at Russian history, at the history of art, at educational theory, music. Your wife told me this summer to write a historical play and now I want to write, write, write. I feel I could sit down and write for three days and nights, without ever getting up. Images have exhausted me, my head is crammed with them, I feel a pulse beating in my brain. I don't want to make anything special out of myself or achieve something really great. All I want is to live, dream, hope, to be everywhere at the same time. Life, my dear man, is short and we must live it as best we can.'

After this friendly chat, which finished only at midnight, Laptev began calling at Yartsev's almost every day. He felt drawn to the place. He usually arrived just before evening, lay down and waited impatiently for Yartsev to arrive, not feeling bored in the least. When he had returned from the office and eaten, Yartsev would sit down to work. But Laptev would ask him something, a conversation would start, work would be forgotten and the friends would part at midnight feeling very pleased with each other.

But this didn't last long. Once, after arriving at Yartsev's, Laptev found only Rassudina there, sitting practising at the piano. She gave him a cold, almost hostile look. Without shaking hands she asked, 'Please tell me when all this will end?'

'All *what*?'

'You come here every day and stop Yartsev working. Yartsev's no lousy little shopkeeper, he's a scholar – every minute of his life is precious. Try and understand that, show some consideration at least!'

'If you think I'm interfering,' Laptev replied curtly, somewhat embarrassed, 'then I'll put a stop to these visits.'

'That's all right by me. Leave now or he might come and find you here.'

The tone in which Rassudina said this, her apathetic look, was the finishing touch to his embarrassment. She had no feeling at all for him, all she wanted was for him to leave as soon as possible – what a difference from their former love! He left without shaking hands, thinking she might call him back. But he heard the scales again and as he slowly made his way downstairs he realized that he was a stranger to her now.

Three days later Yartsev came over to spend the evening with him.

'I've news for you,' he laughed. 'Polina Nikolayevna has moved in with me.' He became rather embarrassed and added in a low voice, 'Well now, we're not in love of course but . . . hm . . . that doesn't matter. I'm glad I can offer her a quiet sanctuary and the chance to stop working if she becomes ill. Well, she thinks there'll be a lot more order in my life now that she's living with me and that I'll become a great scholar under her influence. If that's what she thinks, then let her. There's a saying down south: Idle thoughts give wings to fools. Ha, ha, ha!'

Laptev said nothing. Yartsev paced the study, glanced at the paintings he had seen many times before and heaved a sigh as he said, 'Yes, my friend. I'm three years older than you and it's too late for me to start thinking about true love. Really, a woman like Polina is a godsend and I'll live happily with her until old age, of course. But to hell with it, I have regrets and I'm always hankering after something and imagining that I'm lying in a valley in Daghestan,[48] dreaming I'm at a ball. In short, one's never satisfied with what one has.'

He went into the drawing-room and sang some songs, as if he had no worries at all, while Laptev stayed in the study, eyes closed, trying to fathom why Rassudina had moved in with Yartsev. Then he kept mourning the fact that there was no such thing as a firm, lasting attachment. He was annoyed about Rassudina having an affair with Yartsev and he was annoyed with himself for feeling quite differently towards his wife now.

XV

Laptev was sitting in his armchair, rocking himself as he read. Julia was also in the study reading. Apparently there was nothing to discuss and neither had said a word since morning. Now and then he looked at her over his book and wondered if it made any difference if one married from passionate love or without any love at all. That time of jealousy, great agitation and suffering seemed remote now. He had already managed a trip abroad and was now recovering from the journey, hoping to return to England, which he had liked very much, at the beginning of spring.

Julia Sergeyevna had grown inured to her grief and no longer went to the lodge to cry. That winter she didn't visit the shops, or go to the theatre or concerts, but stayed at home. She didn't like large rooms and was always either in her husband's study or in her own room, where she had some icon-cases that were part of her dowry and where the landscape painting she had admired so much at the exhibition hung on the wall. She spent no money on herself and got through as little as in her father's house.

Winter passed cheerlessly. All over Moscow people were playing cards, but whenever some other entertainment was devised – singing, reciting, sketching, for example – this made life even more boring. Because there were so few talented people in Moscow and because the same old singers and reciters were to be found at every soirée, enjoyment of the arts gradually palled and for many was transformed into a boring, monotonous duty.

Besides this, not one day passed at the Laptevs without some upset. Old Fyodor Stepanych's eyesight was very poor, he no longer went to the warehouse and the eye surgeons said he would soon go blind. For some reason Fyodor stopped going there too, staying at home the whole time to write. Panaurov had obtained his transfer – he had been promoted to Councillor of State – and he was living at the Dresden Hotel now. Almost every day he called on Laptev to borrow money. Kish had finally left university and while he was waiting for the Laptevs to find him a job would hang around for days on end, regaling them with long, boring stories. All this was very irritating and wearisome, and made everyday life most unpleasant.

Pyotr entered the study to announce the arrival of a lady they didn't know: the name on her visiting card was 'Josephine Milan'. Julia Sergeyevna lazily stood up and went out, limping slightly from pins and needles in one leg. A thin, very pale lady with dark eyebrows, dressed completely in black, appeared at the door. She clasped her breast and said pleadingly, 'Monsieur Laptev, please save my children!'

Laptev was familiar with the clink of those bracelets and that powder-blotched face. He recognized her as the lady at whose house he had been so stupid as to dine just before the wedding. She was Panaurov's second wife.

'Save my children!' she repeated and her face trembled and suddenly looked old and pathetic. Her eyes reddened. 'Only you can save us and I've spent my last rouble to come and see you in Moscow. My children will starve!'

She made as if to go down on her knees. This scared Laptev and he gripped her arms above the elbows.

'Please sit down, I beg you,' he muttered as he gave her a chair.

'We have no money for food now,' she said. 'Grigory Nikolaich is leaving to take up his new position but he doesn't want to take me or the children, and that money you were so generous to send us he only spends on himself. What on earth can we do? I'm asking you. Those poor, unfortunate children!'

'Please calm yourself! I'll tell the people at the office to send the money direct to *you*.'

She burst out sobbing, then calmed down, and he noticed that the tears had made little channels on her powdered cheeks and that she had a little moustache.

'You're *infinitely* generous, Monsieur Laptev. But please be our guardian angel, our good fairy. Persuade Grigory Nikolaich not to leave me, to take me with him. I do love him, I'm mad about him. He's the light of my life.'

Laptev gave her a hundred roubles and promised he would have a talk with Panaurov. As he saw her into the hall he became frightened she might start sobbing again or fall on her knees.

Kish was next to arrive. Then in came Kostya, with a camera. Recently he'd become keen on photography and would take snaps of everyone in the house several times a day. This new hobby was causing him a great deal of distress and he'd even lost weight.

Fyodor arrived before afternoon tea. He sat down in a corner of the study, opened a book and stared at the same page for ages, obviously not reading. Then he lingered over his tea; his face was red. Laptev felt depressed in his presence and even found his silence unpleasant.

'You can congratulate Russia on her new pamphleteer,' Fyodor remarked. 'Joking aside, old man, it's to put my pen to the test, so to speak, and I've come here to show you it. Please read it, dear chap, and tell me what you think. Only please be quite frank.'

He took an exercise book from his pocket and handed it to his brother. The article was called 'The Russian Soul' and it was written in that dull flat style usually employed by untalented people who are secretly conceited. Its main idea was as follows: intellectuals have the right not to believe in the supernatural, but they are obliged to conceal their lack of belief so as not to lead others astray or shake them in their faith. Without faith there is no idealism, and idealism is destined to save Europe and show humanity the true path.

'But you don't say from *what* Europe must be saved,' Laptev commented.

'That's self-evident.'

'No it's not,' Laptev said, walking up and down excitedly. 'It's not at all clear why you wrote it. However, that's your affair.'

'I want to have it published as a pamphlet.'

'That's your affair.'

For a minute they didn't speak, then Fyodor sighed and said, 'I deeply, infinitely regret that we see things differently. Oh, Aleksey, my dear brother Aleksey! We're both Russians, we belong to the Orthodox Church, we have breadth of vision. Those rotten German and Jewish ideas – do they really suit us? We're not a pair of blackguards, are we? We're representatives of a distinguished family.'

'Distinguished my foot!' Laptev exclaimed, trying to keep back his irritation. 'Distinguished family! Our grandfather was knocked around by rich landowners, the most miserable little clerk used to hit him in the face. Grandfather beat Father, Father beat you and me. What ever did this "distinguished family" of yours give you or me? What kind of nerves and blood did we inherit? For close on three years you've been blethering away like some wretched parish priest, spouting no end of drivel. And now this thing you've penned – why, it's the ravings of a lackey! And what about *me*? Just take a look. I'm quite unadaptable, I've no spirit or moral fibre.

'For every step I take I'm scared of being flogged. I cringe before nonentities, idiots, swine who are immeasurably inferior to me both intellectually and morally. I'm afraid of house porters, janitors, city police. I'm scared of everyone because I was born of a persecuted mother – from childhood I've been beaten and bullied. We'd both do well not to have children. Let's hope, God willing, that this distinguished merchant house comes to an end with us!'

Julia Sergeyevna entered the study and sat by the desk.

'Were you having an argument?' she asked. 'I'm not interrupting, am I?'

'No, my dear sister-in-law,' Fyodor replied. 'We're discussing questions of principle. So, you were saying,' he went on, turning to his brother, 'that our family is this and that. But this family built up a million-rouble business. That's something!'

'Blast your million-rouble business! A man without any special intelligence or ability becomes a merchant by accident, makes his fortune and does his business day in day out without any method or purpose – without even any craving for wealth. He carries on like a machine and the money just pours in, without him lifting a finger. His whole life is business and he likes it only because he can lord it over his clerks and make fun of customers. He's a churchwarden only because he can bully the choir and keep them under his thumb. He's a school governor because he likes to see the schoolmaster as his subordinate and can order him around. It's not business you merchants care for, it's being the boss. That warehouse of yours is no business premises, it's a torture-chamber! Yes, for your sort of business you need clerks with no personality, deprived of any material share in it, and you train them to be that way. From childhood you force them to prostrate themselves before you for every crust of bread, from childhood you bring them up to believe that you are their benefactors. I could never imagine you having university men in your warehouse – no question about that!'

'Graduates are no good in our kind of business.'

'That's not true!' Laptev shouted. 'That's a lie!'

'I'm sorry, but you seem to be fouling your own water,' Fyodor said, getting up. 'You find our business hateful, yet you still enjoy the profits!'

'Aha, so now we've come to the point!' Laptev laughed and gave his brother an angry look. 'Yes, if I didn't belong to your distinguished family, if I had one iota of willpower and courage, I'd have chucked away all these profits of yours years ago and gone out to earn my own living. But you in your warehouse have been stripping me of all individuality since I was a child. I'm yours now!'

Fyodor glanced at his watch and hurriedly made his farewell. He kissed Julia's hand and left the room. But instead of going into the hall he went into the drawing-room, then into a bedroom.

'I've forgotten which rooms are which here,' he said, deeply embarrassed. 'It's a strange house, don't you think? Most peculiar.'

While he was putting on his fur coat he seemed stunned by something and his face was full of pain. Laptev no longer felt angry: he was afraid and at the same time he felt sorry for Fyodor. That fine, heartfelt love for his brother that had seemingly died within him during those past three years awoke now and he felt a strong urge to express it.

'Fyodor, come and have lunch tomorrow,' he said, stroking his brother's shoulder. 'Will you come?'

'Oh, all right. But please fetch me some water.'

Laptev dashed into the dining-room himself, picked up the first thing he found on the sideboard – a tall beer jug – poured some water and took it to his brother. Fyodor started drinking thirstily, but suddenly he bit on the jug and then the gnashing of teeth could be heard, followed by sobbing. The water spilt onto his fur coat and frock-coat. Laptev, who had never seen a man weep before, stood there embarrassed and frightened, at a loss what to do. In his bewilderment he watched Julia and the maid remove Fyodor's fur coat and take him back into the house. He followed them, feeling that he was to blame.

Julia helped Fyodor lie down and sank to her knees before him.

'It's nothing, it's only nerves,' she said comfortingly.

'My dear, I feel so low,' he said. 'I'm so unhappy, but I've been trying to keep it a secret the whole time.'

He put his arms round her neck and whispered in her ear, 'Every night I dream of my sister Nina. She comes and sits in the armchair by my bed.'

An hour later, when he was putting on his fur coat again in the hall, he was smiling and he felt ashamed because of the maid. Laptev drove with him to Pyatnitsky Street.

'Please come and have lunch tomorrow,' he said on the way, holding his arm, 'and let's go abroad together at Easter. You must get some fresh air – you've really let yourself go.'

'Yes, of course I'll come. And we'll take sister-in-law Julia with us.'

Back home Laptev found his wife terribly overwrought. That incident with Fyodor had shocked her and she just wouldn't calm down. She wasn't crying, but she looked very pale, tossing and turning in bed and clutching at the quilt, pillow and her husband's hands with cold fingers. Her eyes were dilated with fear.

'Don't leave me, please don't leave me,' she said to her husband. 'Tell me, Aleksey, why have I stopped saying my prayers? Where is my faith? Oh, why did you have to talk about religion in my presence? You and those friends of yours have muddled me. I don't pray any more.'

He put compresses on her forehead, warmed her hands and made her drink tea, while she clung to him in terror . . .

By morning she was exhausted and fell asleep with Laptev sitting by her holding her hand. So *he* didn't get any sleep. All next day he felt shattered and listless, his mind a blank as he sluggishly wandered round the house.

XVI

The doctors said that Fyodor was mentally ill. Laptev didn't know what was happening at Pyatnitsky Street, but that dark warehouse, where neither the old man nor Fyodor appeared any more, reminded him of a crypt. Whenever his wife told him that he should visit the warehouse and Pyatnitsky Street every day, he either said nothing or talked irritably about his childhood, about his inability to forgive his father the past, about his hatred for Pyatnitsky Street and the warehouse, and so on.

One Sunday morning Julia went to Pyatnitsky Street herself. She found old Fyodor Stepanych in the same room where the service to celebrate her arrival had once been held. Without any tie, in canvas jacket and slippers, he was sitting motionless in an armchair, blinking his blind eyes.

'It's me, your daughter-in-law,' she said, going over to him. 'I've come to see how you are.'

He was breathing heavily from excitement. Touched by his unhappiness and loneliness, she kissed his hand, while he felt her face and head. Then, as if having convinced himself that it really was her, he made the sign of the cross over her.

'Thank you so much,' he said. 'I've lost my sight, I can hardly see a thing. I can just make out the window and the light too, but not people and things. Yes, I'm going blind and Fyodor's ill. It's really bad without the boss's eye on them – if there's trouble and no one to take charge they'll just run wild. And what's wrong with Fyodor? Got a cold, has he? As for me, I've never been ill, never been to the doctor's. No, can't say I've had anything to do with doctors.'

As usual, the old man started boasting. Meanwhile the servants hurriedly began laying the table in that large room, placing savouries and bottles of wine on it. They brought in about a dozen bottles, one of which was the same shape as the Eiffel Tower. Then they brought a whole plateful of hot pies that smelt of boiled rice and fish.

'Please have something, my dear,' the old man said.

She took his arm, led him to the table and poured him some

vodka. 'I'll come again tomorrow,' she said, 'and I'll bring your granddaughters Sasha and Lida. They'll pamper and comfort you.'

'Oh, no, don't go bringing them here, they're not legitimate.'

'What? Not legitimate? Surely their father and mother were married?'

'Yes, but without my permission. I never blessed them and I don't want anything to do with them, blast them.'

'What a strange way to speak, Father,' Julia sighed.

'According to the Gospels children must honour and fear their parents.'

'Nothing of the sort. The Gospels say that we must forgive even our enemies.'

'In our kind of business you can't forgive anyone. If you started forgiving everyone you'd go bust within three years.'

'But forgiving, saying a kind, friendly word to someone – even if he's done wrong – that's better than business and wealth!'

Julia wanted to mollify the old man, to inspire him with compassion and make him feel repentant, but he listened to what she had to say condescendingly, like a parent listening to a child.

'Father, you're an old man,' Julia said decisively. 'God will soon be calling you to him. He won't ask what kind of business you had, or if you made a profit. He'll ask whether you've been kind to others. Haven't you been hard on those weaker than yourself – your servants or clerks, for example?'

'I've always been generous to my staff. They should always mention me in their prayers,' the old man said with great conviction. However, he was touched by Julia's sincere tone of voice and, to please her, he added, 'Good, bring my little granddaughters tomorrow. I'll see they get some presents.'

The old man was untidily dressed and there was cigar ash on his chest and lap. Evidently no one cleaned his shoes or clothes. The rice in the pies was undercooked, the tablecloth smelt of soap, the servants trod noisily. The old man, the whole house on Pyatnitsky Street, had a neglected look. Sensing this, Julia felt ashamed on her own and her husband's account.

'I'll come and see you tomorrow, without fail,' she said.

She walked through the house and ordered the servants to tidy up the old man's bedroom and light his icon-lamp. Fyodor was sitting in his room looking at an open book without reading. Julia spoke to him and ordered his room to be tidied too. Then she went down to the clerks' quarters. In the middle of the room where they ate stood an unpainted wooden column, which propped up the ceiling. The ceilings here were low and the walls cheaply papered, and there was a smell of fumes from the stove and cooking. As it was Sunday, all the clerks were at home, sitting on their beds waiting for their meal. When Julia came in they jumped up, timidly answered her questions, lowering at her like convicts.

'Heavens, what a dreadful place you live in!' she exclaimed, clasping her hands. 'Don't you feel cramped here?'

'Yes, it's cramped all right,' Makeichev said, 'but it don't do us no harm. We're very thankful to you and we lift up our prayers to all-merciful God.'

'Corresponding to the plenitude of the personality,' Pochatkin said.

Noticing that Julia hadn't understood Pochatkin, Makeichev hastened to explain, 'We're humble folk and must live according to our station in life.'

She inspected the boys' quarters and the kitchen, met the housekeeper and was highly dissatisfied.

At home she told her husband, 'We must move to Pyatnitsky Street as soon as possible. And you'll go to the warehouse every day.'

Afterwards they sat next to each other in the study without speaking. Laptev felt miserable and didn't want to go to Pyatnitsky Street or the warehouse. But he guessed what his wife was thinking and didn't have the strength to offer any opposition.

'I feel as if our life's over and that some dull half-life is just beginning. When I heard that my brother Fyodor is hopelessly ill, I just wept. We spent our childhood and youth together. I once loved him deeply. Now this catastrophe comes along and I feel that losing him is the final break with the past. When you spoke just now about moving to Pyatnitsky Street, to that prison, I began to think that I've no future either.'

He stood up and went over to the window.

'Whatever happens, I can say goodbye to any hope of happiness,' he said, looking into the street. 'It doesn't exist. I've never experienced happiness, so there probably isn't such a thing. However, I *was* happy once in my life, when I sat under your umbrella that night. Do you remember leaving your umbrella at my sister Nina's?' he asked, turning towards his wife. 'I was in love with you then and I remember sitting up the whole night under that umbrella in a state of bliss.'

In the study, by the bookcases, stood a mahogany chest of drawers, with bronze handles, where Laptev kept various things that weren't needed, including the umbrella. He took it out and handed it to his wife.

'There you are.'

Julia looked at the umbrella for about a minute and recognized it with a sad smile. 'I remember,' she said. 'You were holding it when you said you loved me.'

When she saw that he was preparing to leave she added, 'Please come home early if you can. I miss you.'

Then she went to her room and stared at the umbrella for a long time.

XVII

Despite the complexity of the business and the enormous turnover, there was no accountant at the warehouse and it was impossible to make any sense of the ledger clerk's books. Every day commission agents – German and English, with whom the clerks discussed politics and religion – called at the warehouse. An alcoholic nobleman (a sick, pathetic man) would come to translate the office's foreign correspondence. The clerks called him 'Midget' and gave him tea with salt in it. On the whole, the business struck Laptev as one vast operation in eccentricity.

Every day he called at the warehouse and tried to introduce a new system. He forbade them to whip the boys or make fun of customers, and he lost his temper whenever the clerks laughed as they cheerfully despatched useless old stock to the provinces, trying to pass it off as new and fashionable. Now he was in charge at the warehouse, but he still had no idea how much he was worth, whether the business was prospering or what salary his chief clerks received. Pochatkin and Makeichev thought him young and inexperienced, concealed many things from him, and had mysterious whispering sessions with the blind old man every evening.

One day in early June, Laptev and Pochatkin went to Bubnov's inn for a business lunch. Pochatkin had been with the Laptevs for ages, having joined the firm when he was eight. He was really part of the place and was trusted implicitly: when he took all the money from the cash-box on his way out and stuffed his pockets this didn't arouse the least suspicion. He was boss at the warehouse, at home and in church too, where he stood in as warden for the old man. Because of his cruel treatment of his inferiors he had been nicknamed Ivan the Terrible[49] by the clerks and boys.

When they arrived at the inn he nodded to the waiter and said, 'Look here, old chap, bring us half a prodigy and twenty vexations.'

After a short while, the waiter brought them half a bottle of vodka on a tray and various plates of savouries.

'Now look here, old fellow-me-lad,' Pochatkin said, 'bring us a portion of the leading expert in slander and scandal with some mashed potatoes.'

The waiter didn't understand, grew embarrassed and looked as if he wanted to say something. But Pochatkin eyed him sternly and said, 'Furthermore!'

The waiter racked his brains and then went off to consult his colleagues. Finally he guessed correctly and brought a portion of tongue. When they had each drunk two glasses and eaten, Laptev asked, 'Tell me, Pochatkin, is it true our business has been in decline over the past few years?'

'Not at all.'

'Now, be quite straight with me, don't equivocate. Tell me how much profit we used to make, how much we're making now, and how much capital we have. We can't go around like blind men, can we? The warehouse accounts were done not so long ago, but I'm very sceptical, I'm sorry to say. You feel you must hide something from me and you only tell my father the truth. You've been mixed up in shady dealings since you were young and now you can't do without them. But what's the use? Now, I'm asking you. Please be open with me. What's the state of the business?'

'That depends on oscillation of credit,' Pochatkin replied after pausing for thought.

'What do you mean, "oscillation of credit"?'

Pochatkin began explaining, but Laptev understood nothing and sent for Makeichev. He came at once, said a short prayer, ate some savouries and, in his rich, pompous baritone expatiated chiefly on the clerks' duty to pray night and day for their benefactors.

'Fine, but please don't include me among your benefactors,' Laptev said.

'Every man must remember what he is and be conscious of his station in life. By the grace of God you are our father and benefactor and we are your slaves.'

'I'm just about sick and tired of all this!' Laptev fumed. 'Now, *you* be my benefactor for a change and tell me how the business stands. Please stop treating me like a child or I'll close down the warehouse tomorrow. My father's gone blind, my brother's in a mad-house, my nieces are still very young. I hate the business and I'd love to get out of it. But there's no one to replace me, you know that too well. So, enough of your fiddling, for God's sake!'

They went into the warehouse to check the accounts and that evening they were still working on them in the house – the old man himself helped them. As he initiated his son into his business secrets he gave the impression he had been practising black magic, not commerce. It turned out that the profits were increasing yearly by about ten per cent and that the Laptevs' wealth, in cash and securities alone, amounted to six million roubles.

It was about one o'clock in the morning when Laptev went out into the fresh air after doing the accounts, and he felt hypnotized by those figures. It was a calm, moonlit, fragrant night. The white walls of the houses in Moscow's suburbs south of the river, the sight of heavy, locked gates, the silence and those black shadows created the general impression of a fortress – only a sentry with rifle was missing. Laptev went into the little garden and sat on a bench near the fence separating it from next door's garden. The bird-cherry was in bloom. Laptev remembered that this cherry had been just as gnarled and exactly the same height when he was a child – it hadn't changed at all since then. Every corner of the garden and yard reminded him of the remote past. In his childhood, just as now, the whole yard, flooded in moonlight, had been visible through the sparse trees, with shadows that were as mysterious and menacing as before. And just as then, a black dog lay in the middle of the yard and the clerks' windows were all wide open. But all these were sombre memories.

Beyond the fence, the sound of footsteps came from next door.

'My dearest, my darling,' a man's voice whispered – so close to the fence that Laptev could hear breathing.

Then there was a kiss. Laptev was sure that all those millions of roubles, that business he disliked so much, would ruin his life and turn him into a slave in the end. He imagined gradually settling down in his new position, gradually assuming the role of head of a business house, growing dull and old, and finally dying the way mediocrities usually do – shabbily, miserably, depressing all his associates. But what was stopping him abandoning all those millions and the business, and leaving that garden and yard he had hated since he was a boy?

The whispering and kissing on the other side of the fence disturbed him. He went into the middle of the yard, unbuttoned his shirt and looked at the moon: he felt that he wanted to order the gate to be unlocked immediately so that he could leave and never return. His heart thrilled at the prospect of freedom and he laughed with joy as he imagined how wonderful, idyllic and perhaps even saintly that life might be.

But he did not make a move and asked himself, 'What in heaven's name is keeping me here?' He felt annoyed with himself and with that black dog which lay sprawled over the stones instead of running off into fields and forest where it would be free and happy. Obviously, the same thing was preventing both him and the dog from leaving that yard – the habit of bondage, slavery.

Next day, at noon, he went to his wife's and invited Yartsev to come along too, in case he got bored. Julia Sergeyevna was living in a villa at Butovo and he hadn't been there for five days. When they arrived at the station the friends entered a carriage and Yartsev waxed lyrical about the wonderful weather the whole way. The villa was in a park, not far from the station. Julia Sergeyevna was sitting under a poplar waiting for her guests right at the beginning of the main avenue, about twenty yards from the gate. She was wearing a light, elegant, cream-coloured, lace-trimmed dress and was holding that familiar umbrella. Yartsev greeted her and went towards the villa, from which he could make out Sasha and Lida's voices, while Laptev sat beside her to talk business.

'Why have you been so long?' she asked. 'I've been waiting here for days on end. I really miss you!'

She got up, ran her hand through his hair and looked quizzically at his face, shoulders, hat.

'You know, I do love you,' she said, blushing. 'You're very dear to me. You're here, I can see you now and I'm too happy for words! Well, let's talk. Tell me something.'

As she declared her love he felt as though he had already been married for ten years; and he wanted his lunch. She put her arms round his neck, tickling his cheek with her silk dress. He carefully removed her hand, stood up and went off towards the villa without a word. The girls came running to meet him.

'How they've grown!' he thought. 'There's been so many changes over these three years. But perhaps I've another thirteen, thirty years left. What does the future hold in store? Time will tell.'

He embraced Sasha and Lida, who clung to his neck.

'Grandfather sends his regards,' he said. 'Uncle Fyodor is going to die soon. Uncle Kostya has sent us a letter from America and sends his regards. He's bored with the Exhibition[50] and he'll be back soon. And Uncle Aleksey is hungry.'

Afterwards he sat on the terrace and saw his wife strolling down the path towards the villa. She seemed deep in thought and wore an enchantingly sad expression. Tears glistened in her eyes. She wasn't the delicate, fragile, pale-faced girl of before, but a mature, beautiful, strong woman. Laptev noticed how rapturously Yartsev was looking at her and how her fresh, beautiful expression was reflected on his face, which displayed a similar sad enchantment. As they had lunch on the terrace Yartsev smiled a somewhat timid, happy smile and he couldn't take his eyes off Julia and her beautiful neck. Laptev felt compelled to watch him closely as he thought of the thirteen or thirty years he might have left. And what would he have to go through during that time? What does the future hold for us? And he thought, 'Time will tell.'

The Student

At first the weather was fine and calm. Thrushes sang and in the marshes close by some living creature hummed plaintively, as if blowing into an empty bottle. A woodcock flew over and a shot rang out, echoing cheerfully in the spring air. But when darkness fell on the forest, an unwelcome, bitingly cold wind blew up from the east and everything became quiet. Ice needles formed on puddles and the forest became uninviting, bleak and empty. It smelt of winter.

Ivan Velikopolsky, a theology student and parish priest's son, was returning home along the path across the water meadows after a shooting expedition. His fingers were numb and his face burned in the wind. It seemed that this sudden onset of cold had destroyed order and harmony in all things, putting Nature herself in fear and making the evening shadows thicken faster than was necessary. All was deserted and somehow particularly gloomy. Only in the widows' vegetable plots by the river did a light gleam. Far around, though, where the village stood about three miles away, everything was completely submerged in the chill evening mists. The student remembered that when he left home his mother had been sitting barefoot on the floor of the hall, cleaning the samovar, while his father lay coughing on the stove. As it was Good Friday no cooking was done at home and he felt starving. Shrinking from the cold, the student thought of similar winds blowing in the time of Ryurik, Ivan the Terrible and Peter the Great[1] – during their reigns there had been the same grinding poverty and hunger. There had been the same thatched roofs with holes in them, the same ignorance and suffering, the same wilderness all around, the same gloom and feeling of oppression. All these horrors had been, existed now and would continue to do so. The passing of another thousand years would bring no improvement. He didn't feel like going home.

The vegetable plots were called 'widows' because they were kept by two widows, mother and daughter. A bonfire was burning fiercely, crackling and lighting up the ploughed land far around. Widow Vasilisa, a tall, plump old woman in a man's sheepskin coat, was standing gazing pensively at the fire. Her short, pock-marked, stupid-faced daughter Lukerya was sitting on the ground washing a copper pot and some spoons. Clearly they had just finished supper. Men's voices could be heard – some local farm-workers were watering their horses at the river.

'So, winter's here again,' the student said as he approached the bonfire. 'Good evening.'

Vasilisa shuddered, but then she recognized the student and gave him a welcoming smile.

'Heavens, I didn't know it was you,' she said. 'That means you'll be a rich man one day.'

They started talking. Vasilisa, a woman of the world, once a wet-nurse to some gentry and then a nanny, had a delicate way of speaking and she always smiled gently, demurely. But her daughter Lukerya, a peasant woman who had been beaten by her husband, only screwed up her eyes at the student and said nothing. She had a strange expression, as if she were a deaf-mute.

'It was on a cold night like this that the Apostle Peter warmed himself by a fire,' the student said, stretching his hands towards the flames. 'That is to say, it was cold then as well. Oh, what a terrible night that was, Grandma! A dreadfully sad, never-ending night!'

He peered into the surrounding darkness, violently jerked his head and asked, 'I suppose you were at the Twelve Readings from the Gospels yesterday?'

'Yes,' Vasilisa replied.

'You'll remember, during the Last Supper, Peter said to Jesus, "I am ready to go with Thee, both into prison and to death." And the Lord replied, "I tell thee, Peter, the cock shall not crow this day, before that thou shalt thrice deny that thou knowest me."[2] After the Supper, Jesus prayed in the garden, in mortal agony, while poor

Peter was downhearted and his eyes grew heavy. He couldn't fight off sleep, and he slept. Then, as you know, Judas kissed Jesus on that night and betrayed him to the torturers. They led him bound to the High Priest and they beat him, while Peter, exhausted and sorely troubled by anguish and fear – he didn't have enough sleep, you understand – and in expectation of something dreadful taking place on earth at any moment, followed them. He loved Jesus passionately, to distraction, and now, from afar, he could see them beating him.'

Lukerya put the spoons down and stared intently at the student.

'They went to the High Priest,' he continued, 'they started questioning Jesus and meanwhile the workmen,[3] as it was so cold, had made a fire in the middle of the hall and were warming themselves. Peter stood with them by the fire, warming himself as well, as I am now. One woman who saw him said, "This man was also with Jesus."[4] So she really meant that this man too had to be led away for questioning. And all the workmen around the fire must have looked at him suspiciously and sternly, as he was taken aback and said, "I know him not."[5] Soon afterwards someone recognized him as one of Jesus's disciples and said, "Thou also wast with Him." But again he denied it and for the third time someone turned to him and asked, "Did I not see you in the garden with Him this day?"[6] He denied him for the third time. And straight after that a cock crowed and as he looked on Jesus from afar Peter remembered the words he had spoken to him at supper. He remembered, his eyes were opened, he left the hall and wept bitterly.[7] As it is said in the Gospels, "And he went out, and wept bitterly." I can imagine that quiet, terribly dark garden, those dull sobs, barely audible in the silence . . .'

The student sighed and became deeply pensive. Still smiling, Vasilisa suddenly broke into sobs and large, copious tears streamed down her cheeks. She shielded her face from the fire with her sleeve as if ashamed of her tears, while Lukerya stared at the student and blushed. Her face became anguished and tense, like someone stifling a dreadful pain.

The workmen were returning from the river and one of them, on horseback, was quite near and the light from the bonfire flickered on him. The student wished the widows goodnight and moved on.

Again darkness descended and his hands began to freeze. A cruel wind was blowing – winter had really returned with a vengeance and it did not seem as if Easter Sunday was only the day after tomorrow.

Now the student thought of Vasilisa: she had wept, so everything that had happened to Peter on that terrible night must have had some special significance for her.

He glanced back. The solitary fire calmly flickered in the darkness and no one was visible near it. Once again the student reflected that, since Vasilisa had wept and her daughter had been deeply touched, then obviously what he had just been telling them about events centuries ago had some significance for the present, for both women, for this village, for himself and for all people. That old woman had wept, but not at his moving narrative: it was because Peter was close to her and because she was concerned, from the bottom of her heart, with his most intimate feelings.

His heart suddenly thrilled with joy and he even stopped for a moment to catch his breath. 'The past,' he thought, 'is linked to the present by an unbroken chain of events, each flowing from the other.' He felt that he had just witnessed both ends of this chain. When he touched one end, the other started shaking.

After crossing the river by ferry and climbing the hill, he looked at his native village and towards the west, where a narrow strip of cold crimson sunset was glimmering. And he reflected how truth and beauty, which had guided human life there in the garden and the High Priest's palace and had continued unbroken to the present, were the most important parts of the life of man, and of the whole of terrestrial life. A feeling of youthfulness, health, strength – he was only twenty-two – and an inexpressibly sweet anticipation of happiness, of a mysterious unfamiliar happiness, gradually took possession of him. And life seemed entrancing, wonderful and endowed with sublime meaning.

PUBLISHING HISTORY AND NOTES

The Grasshopper

First published in the journal *North* in 1892, then in *Tales and Stories* of 1894. For some reason Chekhov had difficulty in finding a suitable title. He wrote to V. A. Tikhonov, the editor, when sending the story: 'I'm sending you a small sensitive novel for family reading. This is *The Philistines*, but after writing this story I've given it, as you can see, another name' (letter of 30 November 1891). (This was *A Great Man*.) Neither of these satisfied Chekhov (he had also suggested simply *A Story*) and he finally settled on 'The Grasshopper'. Ivan Bunin, who greatly admired the story, considered the title 'awful'.

This story served to create a long rift between Chekhov and the painter Isaak Levitan (1861–1900), who saw the story as an attack on his affair with a certain lady called S. P. Kuvshinnikova, a doctor's wife, whose Moscow salon was attended by many artists, painters, actors and writers, some of whom may well have served as prototypes for Olga's guests in 'The Grasshopper': in a letter of 29 April 1892 to Lidiya Avilova, Chekhov wrote that 'the whole of Moscow is accusing me of libel'.

1. *Kineshma*: Small town on the Volga, about 200 miles north-east of Moscow.
2. *Masini*: Angelo Masini (1844–1926), Italian tenor. Toured Italy, Spain, sang in St Petersburg. Sang tenor role in Verdi's *Requiem* in London and Vienna.
3. *Show me that abode . . .* : From the poem *Reflections at a Main Entrance* by the civic poet N. A. Nekrasov (1821–78). This poem was very popular amongst the young intelligentsia of the 1860s; later, it was often sung by young doctors at Chikino hospital, where Chekhov worked in 1883.
4. *Polenov*: V. D. Polenov (1844–1927), leading Russian landscape painter, influenced by Barbizon plein air school. Taught at Moscow School of

Painting; among his pupils was Isaak Levitan, satirized in the person of Ryabovsky in this story.

5. *Barnay*: Ludwig Barnay (1842–1924), German actor. Toured Russia with the Meiningen Troupe in 1890 and met with a rapturous reception.

6. *Gogol's Osip*: Khlestakov's comic servant in N. V. Gogol's *The Inspector General*. In Russian the play upon words is *Osip khrip, a Arkhip osip*, lit. 'Osip wheezed, but Arkhip went hoarse.'

Ward No. 6

'Ward No. 6' was first published in *Russian Thought*, 1892, and then in a collection entitled *Ward No. 6* (1893). Originally the story was offered to the journal *Russian Review*, but long delays in payment of fees compelled Chekhov to take the story back and in June 1892 Chekhov was invited to become a contributor to V. M. Lavrov's[21] *Russian Thought*.

First details of work on the story appear in a letter to A. S. Suvorin (1834–1912) of 31 March 1892, where Chekhov states: 'I'm writing a story. Before having it printed I wanted to send it to you regarding the censorship as your opinion is like gold for me, but I must hurry, as I don't have any money . . . There is much argumentation in the story, but no love element . . .' And to Lidiya Avilova: 'I'm completing a story which is very boring, as there's a complete absence of women and any love interest. I can't stand such stories and I wrote it rather at random, flippantly' (29 April 1892). P. A. Arkhangelsky, whom Chekhov had assisted in his rural hospital at Chikino, recalled that in the late eighties and early nineties Chekhov had shown great interest in his *Account of an Inspection of Russian Psychiatric Institutions* (1887), of which Chekhov had seen proofs at Babkino. In this book there was mention of the use of fists to discipline inmates of lunatic asylums that resembled prisons, where doctors only occasionally visited the inmates – who were at the 'full disposal' of the warder.

The description of conditions in the hospital in 'Ward No. 6' is very close to that of the prison sickbays in chapter 23 of *The Island of Sakhalin* (1893–5), where Chekhov paints a dreadful picture of the insane being kept in the same wards as syphilitics and of the appallingly unhygienic conditions. One commentator remarks: 'One can speak of "Ward No. 6" as being *dictated* by Sakhalin . . . the warder Nikita, the people behind bars and much else that Chekhov first saw on Sakhalin' (A. Roskin: *A. P. Chekhov: Articles and Sketches*, Moscow, 1959). In a letter to Lavrov of 25 November 1892 Chekhov stresses his own distaste for the story which 'reeks of the hospital and morgue'.

At the time of writing Chekhov was extremely interested in the Stoic philosophers, especially Marcus Aurelius, whose name is mentioned in 'A Dreary Story' and three times in letters of this period. His copy of the *Meditations*, in Prince L. Urusov's translation (Tula, 1882) was very heavily annotated.

1. *Order of St Stanislas*: Awarded for merit in peace or war, first introduced by Peter the Great.
2. *Pushkin*: Aleksandr Pushkin (1799–1837) suffered for two days after being fatally wounded in the stomach, in a duel with Georges D'Anthès.
3. *Heine*: Heinrich Heine (1797–1856) suffered for the last eight years of his life from a crippling spinal disease.
4. *white tie*: Normally worn by doctors at this time (cf. also 'A Dreary Story').
5. *Svyatogorsk Monastery*: Near Pskov. Burial place of Pushkin.
6. *The Physician*: At the back of this medical magazine (published from 1880) was a chronicle of events, small news items, obituaries, etc.
7. *isn't it time for your beer?*: According to the short story writer A. I. Kuprin, the mistress of the bibulous poet and friend of Chekhov's, L. I. Palmin, would use this phrase. Chekhov was apparently annoyed when Kuprin tactlessly remarked that this was the origin of the phrase in 'Ward No. 6'.
8. *Pirogov*: N. I. Pirogov (1810–81), famous surgeon, Professor at St Petersburg Medico-Surgical Academy (cf. 'A Dreary Story').
9. *Pasteur*: Louis Pasteur (1822–95), French chemist and biologist. Discovered role of microorganisms in human and animal disease.
10. *Koch*: Robert Koch (1843–1910), German bacteriologist, established bacterial origin of anthrax, tuberculosis and cholera.
11. *psychiatry with its current classification* . . . : In Chekhov's library was *A Course in Psychiatry* (1893) by S. S. Korsakov. In this book Korsakov advocated the latest diagnostic methods and the establishment of psychiatric clinics. Korsakov strongly opposed straitjackets.
12. *Someone in Voltaire or Dostoyevsky* . . . : Voltaire's famous phrase is quoted in Dostoyevsky's *The Brothers Karamazov* (1879–80), book 5, chapter 3. The original phrase occurs in Voltaire's *Epîtres*, xcvi: *A l'Auteur du Livre des Trois Imposteurs*: 'Si Dieu n'existait pas, il faudrait l'inventer.'
13. *Diogenes*: Diogenes (born c. 412 BC), celebrated Cynic philosopher, frequently mentioned by Chekhov. He was distinguished for his asceticism and austerity of life. He was said to have rolled in hot sand in summer, to have embraced snow-covered statues in winter, to have lived on the simplest food and to have finally taken up residence in a tub. In an amusing letter to A. S. Suvorin of September 1891, Chekhov accuses the great philosophers,

convinced of their own impunity, of being 'as despotic as generals'. In this respect he calls Tolstoy a 'latter-day Diogenes'.

14. *Marcus Aurelius*: Marcus Aurelius (AD 121–180), Roman emperor and Stoic philosopher who gave his view of life in his famous *Meditations*. Chekhov frequently quotes Aurelius (especially in 'A Dreary Story') and had a much-used Russian translation in his library (and see 'The Black Monk', note 14, p. 325).

15. . . . *but prayed in the Garden of Gethsemane* . . . : The biblical reference is: 'O my Father, if this cup may not pass away from me, except I drink it, thy will be done', Matthew 26:42.

16. *Pripet marshes*: In southern Belorus. The River Pripet is a tributary of the Dnieper, flowing through an extensive area of forest and marsh.

17. *Iverian Madonna*: Situated in the Iverian Chapel, near Red Square. Most celebrated icon in Moscow.

18. *Tsar-Cannon and the Tsar-Bell*: Both in Moscow Kremlin. The Tsar-Cannon, one of the largest cannon ever made. Cast in 1586, it has never been fired. The Tsar-Bell, weighing 200 tons, is the largest in the world.

19. *St Saviour's Temple and the Rumyantsev Museum*: St Saviour's Temple, a memorial to the Napoleonic Wars (1812–14: Napoleon had invaded Russia in 1812); Rumyantsev Museum, a famous museum and art gallery, founded through the beneficence of Count N. Rumyantsev in 1787.

20. *Testov's*: A well-known restaurant.

21. V. M. Lavrov (1852–1912), editor of radical journal *Russian Thought*. Chekhov met him in the mid eighties.

Ariadna

'Ariadna' was first published in *Russian Thought*, 1895. In revising this story for his collected works Chekhov made significant cuts of what he considered superfluous detail that interfered with the development of the main story. It was originally written for the journal *The Artist*, but when the editor of *Russian Thought*, Lavrov, informed Chekhov that *The Artist* had 'crashed' Chekhov asked for the story to be printed in *Russian Thought*. Although Chekhov did not think this story was suitable for *Russian Thought* and had strong reservations, Lavrov was very pleased with it and 'Ariadna' was printed in his journal in December of that year.

1. *Sevastopol*: Port and naval base in Crimea. The scene of the famous siege of 1854–5.

2. *Volochisk*: Frontier station in north-west Ukraine, on the border with Austria.

3. *Max Nordau*: Hungarian philosopher and publicist (1849–1923). In a letter to Suvorin (27 March 1894) Chekhov writes: 'I'm sick and tired of arguments and I read such idle loud-mouths as Nordau with revulsion.' Chekhov had possibly read in the early nineties some of Nordau's works in Russian translation: *Degeneration* (1893) and *The Disease of the Age* (1893).

4. *Veltman*: A. F. Veltman (or Weltman) (1800–70), minor author of historical novels of great length. Chekhov here refers to the story 'Salome' (1848), from the first volume of a five-volume epic, *Adventures Drawn from the Sea of Life*, which took twenty-five years to write.

5. *Novodevichy Convent*: In southern Moscow.

6. *Slav Fair Hotel*: Large hotel in central Moscow, where Chekhov often stayed. It is mentioned in 'Peasants' as the hotel where Chikildeyev worked as a waiter.

7. *Hermitage*: Well-known restaurant in Trubny Square, Moscow.

8. *Tiflis*: Tbilisi, capital of Georgia, a favourite watering-place famous for its warm sulphur springs and with many literary associations.

9. *Abbazia*: Opatiya, seaside resort on Bay of Fiume; now in Croatia, it belonged to Austria before 1914. In letters of 3 and 4 October 1894 to the architect F. O. Shekhtel, Chekhov first calls Abbazia 'splendid' and then 'boring', infinitely preferring the French Riviera.

10. *Fiume*: Rijeka, chief port of Croatia. Austro-Hungarian before First World War, it was seized by Italy and then passed to Yugoslavia.

11. *Merano*: Alpine spa town in northern Italy. Very popular with nineteenth-century aristocracy.

12. *Boleslav Markevich*: Minor reactionary novelist (1822–84) and, as it happened, an inveterate enemy of Turgenev. Had been guest of the Kiselevs at Babkino, where Chekhov met him, considering him pompous and a third-rate writer.

13. *non habeo*: 'I don't have any.'

14. *Addio, bella Napoli*: 'Farewell, beautiful Naples.'

15. *Yalta*: Seaside resort on Crimean coast, home of Chekhov for many years.

16. *. . . don't go telling them . . .* : In K. A. Skalkovsky's compilation *Of Women* (1886–95), well known to Chekhov, there had appeared a chapter headed: 'Of female intellect and erudition.' Skalkovsky had tried to show, with allusions to Schopenhauer and Nicolas Chamfort, that women were inferior to men because their skulls and brains were smaller. Chekhov had earlier ridiculed this book in 1886 in his humorous piece: 'Oh, women!'

The Black Monk

'The Black Monk' was first published in the struggling journal *The Artist*, 1894, and then in the collection of that year, *Tales and Stories*. Chekhov turned down Suvorin's offer to print it in the newspaper *New Times* as he did not always want his stories to be printed with the words: 'to be continued'. The editor of the *The Artist*, F. A. Kumanin, had pleaded with Chekhov to support his journal. When asked by Chekhov's friend, the playwright L. L. Leontyev-Shcheglov (1855–1911), if he had given him something for *The Artist* Kumanin replied: 'Yes, he gave me a little story, but not very good, I must confess. Even a bit wishy-washy and unnatural' (22 September 1893). But Kumanin was led more by Chekhov's reputation and what it would do for his journal than its literary merit. After Kumanin's death his widow asked Chekhov permission to reprint 'The Black Monk' in the journal *The Reader*, but Chekhov refused.

This story directly reflects life at Melikhovo, where it was written. Chekhov was a keen gardener and his brother Mikhail records: 'From very early morning he went out into the garden and spent a long time inspecting every fruit tree, every shrub, pruned them or squatted for some time by the trunk, observing something' (M. P. Chekhov, *Around Chekhov*, Moscow/ Leningrad, 1933). Mikhail also records several concrete events reflected further in the story: for example, when Lika Mizinova sat at the piano and played the then popular *Wallachian Legend* of Braga (see note 3, p. 325). Chekhov's brother also records conversations about mirages, refraction of the sun's rays through the air. Chekhov was in very low spirits when he wrote 'The Black Monk', but in answer to Suvorin's statement that he had portrayed himself in Kovrin, Chekhov replied: 'I seem to be mentally healthy. True, I don't have any particular desire to live, but as yet this isn't an illness in the true sense of the word, but something transient and normal in life. At any rate, if an author portrays someone who is mentally ill that doesn't mean that he himself is. I wrote "The Black Monk" without any melancholy thoughts, in cold reflection. I simply had the urge to depict megalomania. I dreamt of the monk who floats over the field and when I woke up I wrote about him to Misha' (Chekhov's brother Mikhail) (letter of 25 January 1894). According to Mikhail, Chekhov was in a highly-strung state at Melikhovo and had a terrible nightmare about a black monk. At the time of writing this story Chekhov was particularly interested in psychiatry and had conversations with the famous psychiatrist V. I. Yakovenko at Melikhovo.

1. *Oporto*: A variety of eating-apple, very large and juicy and known for its long-lasting qualities.
2. *Onegin, I will not hide it . . .* : Gremin's aria from Tchaikovsky's opera, *Eugene Onegin* (1878, libretto by Tchaikovsky and K. S. Shilovsky).
3. *Braga's famous Serenade*: Gaetano Braga (1829–1907), Italian composer. The *Serenade* is otherwise known as *Wallachian Legend.* Chekhov's brother Mikhail records Chekhov saying that he found 'something mystical, full of beautiful romanticism in this romance' (M. P. Chekhov, *Around Chekhov*, Moscow/Leningrad, 1933).
4. *Gaucher's article*: Nikolaus Gaucher (1846–1911), celebrated French horticulturalist, widely read in Russia. Chekhov, a keen and accomplished gardener, was familiar with his books; among them were *Guide to Grafting of Trees and Shrubs* and *Guide to Fruit Growing for the Practical Gardener.*
5. *Pesotsky is monarch of all he surveys*: Lit. 'Kochubey is rich and famous', a line from Pushkin's narrative poem *Poltava* (1829).
6. *audiatur altera pars*: 'Let the other side be heard.'
7. *sapienti sat*: 'Enough for a wise man.'
8. *'In my Father's house . . .'*: John 14:2.
9. *mens sana in corpore sano*: 'A sound mind in a sound body', Juvenal (AD 60–130), *Satires*, x.
10. *The Fast of the Assumption*: (or Feast) 15 August.
11. *Polycrates*: Tyrant of Samos. Built up a large navy. Lured to the Greek mainland by Oroetes, Satrap of Sardis, he was crucified in 522 BC.
12. *Socrates*: Celebrated Athenian philosopher (c. 470–399 BC) who held that virtue is understanding. Sentenced to death for corrupting the youth of Athens.
13. *Diogenes*: See 'Ward No. 6', note 13, p. 321. Features prominently in the discussion between Ragin and Gromov in this story.
14. *Marcus Aurelius*: See 'Ward No. 6', note 14, p. 322. In his argument with Ragin in 'Ward No. 6', Gromov supports his idea that sufficient hardship or torture will break down any man's fortitude.
15. *'Rejoice evermore'*: St Paul's First Epistle to the Thessalonians 5:16.
16. *the eve of Elijah's Day*: Evening of 20 July.
17. *jalap*: Mexican climbing plant (*Exogonium purga*).

Murder

'Murder' was first published in *Russian Thought*, 1895, originally with the subtitle 'A Story'. To intensify the emotional impact Chekhov significantly shortened this story for the collected edition of his works, cutting out lengthy descriptions and extended reflections on the part of the main characters. 'Murder' had been fermenting for some time in Chekhov's mind, as is shown by copious notes in his *Note Books* for 1892–5. It was written shortly after the death of N. S. Leskov (1831–95), who had given the most powerful and intimately knowledgeable portraits of sectarianism and fanaticism in Russian literature.

There are very strong echoes of Chekhov's Sakhalin experiences in the story and the character of Yakov Ivanych is possibly based on an actual convict. There are also many passages reflecting conditions on Sakhalin – the descriptions of the convicts' labours, the unloading of the ships, the description of the gulf and coast, the appalling weather.

1. *'Song of Archangels'*: Solemn canticle for Festival of the Annunciation. In a letter of 1892 Chekhov describes how he sang it in church with his brothers as a child.
2. *St Andrew's Vigil and the Te Deum*: This canon was sung during first week of Lent.
3. *already reading the Acts and the Epistles*: The reading of these during Mass was entrusted to the particularly devout.
4. *Mount Athos*: Athos – a Greek peninsula in Chalcidice (Macedonia), with numerous monasteries and churches, the object of pilgrimages since the eleventh century.
5. *Molokans*: Religious sect formed in the eighteenth century. A clean-living, industrious people, their name derived from their drinking of milk on fast days, contrary to Orthodox practice. In the hope that the Kingdom of Christ would be revealed in the Trans-Caucasian regions, they flocked there from the 1830s onwards.
6. *Forgiveness Day*: Last Sunday before Lent.
7. *'voice of one crying in the wilderness'*: Matthew 3:3. Chekhov often used this phrase in letters and stories.
8. *dormeuses*: Carriages adapted for sleeping.
9. *Flagellant meetings . . . went around in a white kerchief*: The Flagellants, in existence since the church schism of the seventeenth century, led a particularly austere life. Renowned for their neat dress and purity. As a

symbol of this clean living, the women members went around in snow-white kerchiefs.

10. Matthew 5:24.

11. *Dué Roads*: The convict settlement at Dué is described in Chekhov's *The Island of Sakhalin* (serialized 1893–5); trans. B. Reeves (Cambridge: Ian Faulkner, 1993).

12. *Voyevoda prison*: Chekhov gives a chilling account of this grimmest of prisons in chapter 8 of *The Island of Sakhalin*. Prisoners were chained to wheelbarrows and the whole place was swarming with bugs. (The prison at Dué is described in the same chapter.)

A Woman's Kingdom

First published in *Russian Thought*, 1894, then in the collection *Tales and Stories*, 1894. Much material for this story possibly came from Chekhov's experience at a cotton factory in Voskresensk, whose owner was A. S. Tsurikova, an educated woman who loved to be philanthropic and who was a trustee of the school where Chekhov's brother Ivan was a teacher. In a letter to A. S. Suvorin of 18 December 1893 Chekhov had announced that the story – a 'description of a certain spinster' – would be appearing in the January issue of *Russian Thought*. Originally, the story was planned on a much larger scale.

1. *Old Creed*: The supporters of the Old Creed (Old Believers or Nonconformists) broke away from the Russian Orthodox Church in the seventeenth century, refusing to recognize the reforms in ritual and correction of prayer books introduced by Patriarch Nikon.

2. *'Thy Nativity . . .'*: Troparion (hymn) for Christmas.

3. *brown coat over his tunic*: Students at schools and universities wore uniform at that time.

4. *actual state councillor*: An actual state councillor was fourth highest in the Table of Ranks instituted by Peter the Great in 1722.

5. *ribbon of St Anne*: Decoration for civic and military distinction, worn around the neck.

6. *Leconte de Lisle*: Charles Marie René, Leconte de Lisle (1818–94), French poet, leader of the Parnassian school.

7. *Duse's*: Eleonora Duse (1859–1924), Italian actress who toured Russia in 1891–2. Famous for roles in Ibsen and D'Annunzio.

8. *turbot matelote*: Turbot cooked in a wine sauce.

9. *Old Believer's blood*: Cf. note 1 above.
10. *Jules Verne*: French writer (1828–1905) of adventure stories. Chekhov had parodied him in his early *Flying Islands* (1883).
11. *Maupassant*: Guy de Maupassant (1850–93), French writer, greatly admired by Chekhov and a strong influence.
12. *His last work exhausted, intoxicated me!*: Possibly a reference to Maupassant's *Bel-Ami* (1885).
13. *simoom*: A dry, suffocating, dust-laden wind blowing in African and Asiatic (Arabian) deserts in spring and summer.

The Two Volodyas

This story was first published in *Russian Gazette*, 1893, then in the collection *Tales and Stories*, 1894. At the time of printing Chekhov was furious with the editors of the magazine for cutting out apparently risqué passages, writing in December 1893 to V. A. Goltsev, co-editor of *Russian Thought*: 'Oh, my story in *Russian Gazette* has been shorn so severely that they've cut off the head with the hair. Such puerile chastity and amazing cowardice! If they'd only thrown out a few lines that wouldn't have been so bad, but they've brushed aside the middle, gnawed off the end and so drained my story of colour that it makes me sick.'

In preparing the story for the collected edition of his works, Chekhov made a number of stylistic corrections and changes. In particular, a passage containing severe criticism by the heroine of her husband and father who were to blame for her failure, was cut out.

1. *as Derzhavin had blessed Pushkin*: The aged poet Gavrila Romanovich Derzhavin (1743–1816) had blessed Pushkin as a schoolboy when he recited his celebratory poem before him at Tsarskoye Selo.
2. *Ta-ra-ra-boomdeay*: Lit. *Tararabumbiya*, a Russian version of refrain to famous French song of Parisian demi-monde at end of nineteenth century, *Tha ma ra boum die* (cf. A. Langux, *Amours*, 1900; 1961). This expression is also used by Chebutykin at the close of *Three Sisters*.
3. *Why this sudden passion . . . horseradish?*: Chekhov here almost literally quotes a passage from 'Cultured People' (1876), an article by the satirical novelist and publicist M. E. Saltykov-Shchedrin (1826–89). He quotes the same passage in a letter to Suvorin (2 May 1897), when he writes: 'I really don't know what to do with myself and what's beneficial for my health: a constitution or sturgeon with horseradish.' In his article Saltykov-Shchedrin

had ridiculed liberals, whose dreams of a constitution easily changed into dreams of sturgeon with horseradish.
4. *Schopenhauers*: Arthur Schopenhauer (1788–1860), German pessimistic philosopher. There are echoes of Schopenhauer in many of Chekhov's stories, e.g., 'A Dreary Story'.

Three Years

The most 'novelistic' in scope and length of Chekhov's stories, 'Three Years' was first published in *Russian Thought*, 1895. For the collected edition the story underwent heavy revision, especially in the characterization of Laptev and his friends, and his relationship with Julia.

In a letter of September 1894 Chekhov wrote to his sister that he was writing 'a novel based on Moscow life', describing the work as most laborious. In December of that year he wrote to a female friend, E. M. Shavrova: 'The intention was one thing, but something rather different resulted – rather limp, not silk as I wanted, but cambric . . . I'm bored with the same thing over and over again. I want to write about devils, about terrifying, volcanic women, about sorcerers – but alas! People demand well-intentioned stories and tales from the lives of so many Ivan Gavriloviches and their wives.'

Chekhov had first considered offering the story to the magazine *Niva* (*The Cornfield*), but he could not promise to complete this long work in time for the editor's deadline. Original titles suggested by Chekhov were 'Scenes from Family Life,' 'From Family Life', and simply 'A Story'. In January 1895 he wrote furiously to Suvorin, complaining that the censors had 'thrown out the lines referring to religion' – adding that as a result, when writing, he always felt he had 'a bone stuck in my throat'.

1. *Sokolniki*: District in north-east Moscow, with a large pleasure park, highly popular for summer outings. Named after the royal falconers (*sokolniki*) who lived there in the seventeenth century.
2. *Pyatnitsky Street*: Long thoroughfare in the merchant quarter, south of the Moscow River.
3. *Khimki*: River port to north-west of Moscow.
4. *wretched existence of yokels . . .* : Lit. 'from the point of view of landscape and Anton Goremyka'. Anton Goremyka (Anton the Wretched), eponymous hero of sentimental, humanitarian novel (1847) of that name by D. V. Grigorovich (1822–99), where peasants were depicted against a background of idyllic nature.

5. *as the servant says in Tolstoy, 'everything will sort itself out . . .': Anna Karenina*, part I, chapter 2.
6. *The Bells of Corneville*: Comic operetta (1877) by French composer Robert Planquette (1848–1903).
7. *Tambov*: Large town about 300 miles south-east of Moscow, founded in 1636 as a stronghold in the Muscovite southern defence line against the Crimean Tatars.
8. *Kashira*: Town about seventy miles south of Moscow.
9. *Fley's*: Well-known patisserie in central Moscow.
10. *Vologda*: Ancient town about 300 miles north of Moscow. Once an important trading point.
11. *Nikolsky Street*: A main thoroughfare leading from Red Square.
12. *what sanctimonious nonsense!*: Lit: 'just like Saltykov's Iudushka'. Reference to M. E. Saltykov-Shchedrin's novel *The Golovlyov Family*, in which Iudushka is the archetypal canting hypocrite.
13. *The Prophet Samuel . . .* : 1 Samuel 16:4–5.
14. *Anton Rubinstein*: Anton Grigoryevich Rubinstein (1830–94), pianist and prolific composer.
15. *Conservatoire*: Founded in 1864 by Anton Rubinstein's brother Nikolay.
16. *Guerrier's courses*: V. I. Guerrier (1837–1919) was Professor of History at Moscow University.
17. *Ostozhenka Street*: In south-west Moscow. Savelovsky Street leads off it.
18. *Great Nikitsky Street*: In western Moscow.
19. *Reinheit*: 'Purity' (Germ.). Apparently this was one of the virtues Chekhov demanded in his female friends.
20. *Presnya*: District in western Moscow.
21. *basta*: 'Enough' (Ital.).
22. *Razgulyay Square*: In north-west Moscow.
23. *Little Dmitrovka Street*: In north-west Moscow. Chekhov liked this street so much that he lived in three different houses there. During the Soviet period it was named after him.
24. *Old St Pimen's Church*: About 400 metres west of Little Dmitrovka Street.
25. *Strastnoy Boulevard*: In northern Moscow. The Tver Road was the point of departure for the St Petersburg stagecoach and Moscow's main thoroughfare.
26. *Iverian Chapel*: Site of miracle-working Iverian Madonna icon, near Red Square. Built in 1669 it was one of the most highly revered places of worship in Russia. See also 'Ward No. 6', note 17, p. 322.
27. *Filippov's*: Before the Revolution Moscow's most fashionable coffee-house. Ornately decorated, it was founded by the court baker.

28. *Volokolamsk*: Small town about sixty miles north-west of Moscow.
29. *Maid of Orleans*: Opera (1881) by Tchaikovsky, after the play by Schiller.
30. *Marya Yermolov*: Famous actress (1853–1928) of the time who spent five decades at the Maly Theatre.
31. *Dresden Hotel*: Near the Tver Road, in central Moscow.
32. *... he told Pyotr, 'You are not a sturgeon.'*: The Russian for sturgeon is *osyotr*, thereby rhyming with Pyotr. In fact, a very weak joke, but funny as it is so very bad.
33. *'In the sweat of thy face ...'*: Genesis 3:19.
34. *Merchants' Club*: In Little Dmitrovka Street.
35. *Yar's*: Highly popular out-of-town restaurant in Petrovsky Park, to north-west of Moscow.
36. *Strelna*: Like Yar's, situated in Petrovsky Park. Baedeker describes both these restaurants as: 'much frequented in the evening (not cheap)'.
37. *School of Art*: In north-west Moscow.
38. *Shishkin*: I. I. Shishkin (1832–98), landscape painter. In a letter of November 1892 to Suvorin, Chekhov wrote disparagingly of two leading Russian painters: 'Do the paintings of Repin and Shishkin turn your head? ... They're charming, talented, you admire them. But at the same time you're dying for a smoke.'
39. *Exaltation of the Cross*: Celebrated on 14 September.
40. *Yaroslavl*: Large town about 200 miles north-east of Moscow.
41. *'My dear, tender love'*: Words from Pushkin's poem *Night* (1827), set to music by Anton Rubinstein.
42. *Krasny Prud*: 'Red Pond' – in north-west Moscow, about three miles from Red Square.
43. *Lyapunovs and Godunovs ... Yaroslav or Monomakh ... Pimen's soliloquy*: P. P. Lyapunov (d. 1611), national hero against invading Poles in early seventeenth century; Boris Godunov (1552–1605) was first Regent and then Tsar of Russia from 1598 until his death; Yaroslav I, 'The Wise', Prince of Kiev from 1019 to 1054; Vladimir Monomakh, Prince of Kiev from 1113 to 1125; a famous speech from Pushkin's historical drama *Boris Godunov* (1831).
44. *Polovtsians*: Cumans – Turkic-speaking people who battled against Kievan Russia.
45. *St Alexis Cemetery*: To north of Moscow.
46. *You don't need brains to have babies!*: Inaccurate quotation from A. S. Griboyedov's (1797–1829) famous comedy *Woe from Wit* (1823–4).
47. *European Herald*: Liberal monthly published 1860–1918 in St Petersburg. Devoted equally to history, politics and literature.

48. . . . *lying in a valley in Daghestan* . . . : Reference to M. Lermontov's poem *The Dream* (1841).
49. *Ivan the Terrible*: Lit. Malyuta Skuratov, most depraved of the *oprichniki*, Ivan the Terrible's elite militia, who had total licence to torture, kill, burn and loot.
50. *the Exhibition*: The World's Columbian Exposition, held in Chicago in 1893.

The Student

Originally entitled 'In the Evening', 'The Student' was first published in the *Russian Gazette*, 1894, and then in the collection *Tales and Stories* of the same year. Evidently written in Yalta, this story was Chekhov's favourite. When preparing this story for the 1894 *Tales and Stories* Chekhov introduced three significant additions: he intensified Velikopolsky's reaction to his surroundings with the phrase 'He peered into the surrounding darkness, violently jerked his head and asked . . .'; gave a clearer explanation why Vasilisa was crying; and at the end of the story strengthened the affirmation of eternity and the continuity of truth and beauty in the world.

This story is saturated with biblical allusions and quotations, of which the principal ones are given here. Commenting on the religious background to Chekhov's difficult childhood, Ivan Bunin remarked: '. . . its only justification is that had there been no church choir and choral practice, no intimate knowledge of church services and simple believers, there would have been no "Easter Night", no "Student", no "Bishop" and perhaps no "Murder" . . .' (I. A. Bunin, *Sobranie Sochinenii*, vol. 9, Moscow, 1965–7).

1. *Ryurik, Ivan the Terrible and Peter the Great*: Ryurik (d. 879), first Varangian (Viking) prince of Russia. He established control of Novgorod and his descendants ruled Russia until 1598; Ivan the Terrible (1530–84), Tsar of Russia from 1547; Peter the Great (1672–1725), Tsar of Russia, 1682–1725. Westernized Russian institutions and founded St Petersburg.
2. '*I am ready to go with Thee* . . .': Luke 22:33–4.
3. '*and meanwhile the workmen* . . .': A distinct echo of: 'And the servants and officers stood there, who had made a fire of coals; for it was cold: and they warmed themselves: and Peter stood with them, and warmed himself' John 18:18.
4. '*This man was also with Jesus*': Cf. 'This fellow was also with Jesus of Nazareth', Matthew 26:71.

5. *'I know him not'*: Luke 22:57.
6. *'Did I not see you in the garden with Him this day?'*: Cf. 'Did not I see thee in the garden with him?', John 18:26.
7. *. . . he left the hall and wept bitterly'*: 'And he went out, and wept bitterly', Matthew 26:75.

THE STORY OF PENGUIN CLASSICS

Before 1946 ...'Classics' are mainly the domain of academics and students, without readable editions for everyone else. This all changes when a little-known classicist, E. V. Rieu, presents Penguin founder Allen Lane with the translation of Homer's *Odyssey* that he has been working on and reading to his wife Nelly in his spare time.

1946 *The Odyssey* becomes the first Penguin Classic published, and promptly sells three million copies. Suddenly, classic books are no longer for the privileged few.

1950s Rieu, now series editor, turns to professional writers for the best modern, readable translations, including Dorothy L. Sayers's *Inferno* and Robert Graves's *The Twelve Caesars*, which revives the salacious original.

1960s The Classics are given the distinctive black jackets that have remained a constant throughout the series's various looks. Rieu retires in 1964, hailing the Penguin Classics list as 'the greatest educative force of the 20th century'.

1970s A new generation of translators arrives to swell the Penguin Classics ranks, and the list grows to encompass more philosophy, religion, science, history and politics.

1980s The Penguin American Library joins the Classics stable, with titles such as *The Last of the Mohicans* safeguarded. Penguin Classics now offers the most comprehensive library of world literature available.

1990s The launch of Penguin Audiobooks brings the classics to a listening audience for the first time, and in 1999 the launch of the Penguin Classics website takes them online to a larger global readership than ever before.

The 21st Century Penguin Classics are rejacketed for the first time in nearly twenty years. This world famous series now consists of more than 1300 titles, making the widest range of the best books ever written available to millions – and constantly redefining the meaning of what makes a 'classic'.

The Odyssey continues ...